Susan Meier is the author of over fifty books for Mills & Boon. *The Tycoon's Secret Daughter* was a Romance Writers of America RITA® Award finalist, and *Nanny for the Millionaire's Twins* won the Book Buyers' Best award and was a finalist in the National Readers' Choice awards. She is married and has three children. One of eleven children herself, she loves to write about the complexity of families and totally believes in the power of love.

Brenda Harlen is a former attorney who once had the privilege of appearing before the Supreme Court of Canada. The practice of law taught her a lot about the world and reinforced her determination to become a writer—because in fiction, she could promise a happy ending! Now she is an award-winning, RITA® Award-nominated nationally bestselling author of more than thirty titles for Mills & Boon. You can keep up-to-date with Brenda on Facebook and Twitter, or through her website, brendaharlen.com

Also by Susan Meier

The Missing Manhattan Heirs
Cinderella's Billion-Dollar Christmas
The Bodyguard and the Heiress
Hired by the Unexpected Billionaire

Also by Brenda Harlen

Match Made in Haven
The Sheriff's Nine-Month Surprise
Her Seven-Day Fiancé
Six Weeks to Catch a Cowboy
Claiming the Cowboy's Heart
Double Duty for the Cowboy
One Night with the Cowboy
Meet Me Under the Mistletoe
Maverick Christmas Surprise
Bring Me a Maverick for Christmas!

Discover more at millsandboon.co.uk

STOLEN KISS WITH HER BILLIONAIRE BOSS

SUSAN MEIER

A COWBOY'S CHRISTMAS CAROL

BRENDA HARLEN

MILLS & BOON

First Published in Great Britain 2020
by Mills & Boon, an imprint of HarperCollinsPublishers,
1 London Bridge Street, London, SE1 9GF

Stolen Kiss with Her Billionaire Boss © 2020 Harlequin Books S.A.
A Cowboy's Christmas Carol © 2020 Harlequin Books S.A.

Special thanks and acknowledgement are given to Susan Meier for her contribution to the *Christmas at the Harrington Park Hotel* collection.

Special thanks and acknowledgement are given to Brenda Harlen for her contribution to the *Montana Mavericks: What Happened to Beatrix?* series.

ISBN: 978-0-263-27906-1

1220

MIX
Paper from
responsible sources
FSC™ C007454

This book is produced from independently certified FSC™ paper to ensure responsible forest management.

For more information visit: www.harpercollins.co.uk/green

Printed and bound in Spain
by CPI, Barcelona

STOLEN KISS WITH HER BILLIONAIRE BOSS

SUSAN MEIER

To my dad, who loved Christmas Eve. He's the model I used to create Hugo, James and Sally's dad, who always made Christmas Eve special.

With abundant thanks to Liz Fielding and Kandy Shepherd… So fun to work with you ladies on these wonderful stories!

PROLOGUE

Late November

AT ITS HEART, betrayal was always personal. It plowed deep ruts in a man's soul and weakened him until he almost couldn't breathe.

Though only seventeen when his betrayal hit, Hugo Harrington had fought the emotions threatening to suffocate him. He'd been framed for the embezzling done by his stepfather, and his mother had taken the side of her new husband, who had ordered Hugo to leave their home.

He hadn't been given time to say goodbye to his younger brother and sister, twins. He'd been told to pack and go. Every year, he'd sent a Christmas card to his siblings. Every year, he'd had no response. It was as if he'd been erased. Forgotten.

Still, he'd refused to let his losses or the wounds from being cast aside destroy him. Recognizing that if he let himself wallow he'd live the rest of his life alone, in the muck and mire of grief—taking the blame for something he hadn't done—his brain had sharpened. Not to save himself, but because some losses were unacceptable. Some wrongs had to be avenged. Some wounds wouldn't heal without justice.

He'd waited seventeen years for the chance to take possession of London's Harrington Park Hotel, and with it the opportunity to extend an olive branch to his brother and sister, but it had finally arrived.

"Mr. Harrington…" The voice of his personal assistant entered his private office via the speaker of his phone.

He turned from the wall of glass that displayed a jaw-dropping view of the Manhattan skyline with buildings appearing to be so close he could reach out and touch them. The sense that he was standing on top of the world filled him. That bolstered him too. It hadn't been easy getting here. But just like his opportunity, *he* had also arrived.

"Yes, Victoria."

"Your ten o'clock appointment is here."

"Send her in."

He walked from the window to his desk but didn't sit. The door opened and Erin Hunter entered. Her straight red hair fell to her shoulders in a blunt cut that always reminded Hugo of her no-nonsense attitude about work. Her efficient navy-blue wool suit appealed to the buttoned-up businessman in him. He currently resided in Manhattan, but he was a Londoner, born and raised. Precise and driven, he'd surrounded himself with only the best.

Erin Hunter was the best.

"Good morning, Erin." He motioned to the chairs across from his desk. "Please have a seat."

She sat, primly angling her legs toward the back of the chair and crossing her ankles.

"I have a new project. Probably the most important project of my life."

Her eyebrows rose. But a prudent subcontractor of his hotel development firm, she didn't pounce at his first words. She waited.

"The property in question is old and in need of so many repairs that work will be nonstop. It's in London. Formerly family-owned—" He nearly choked on those words. He wouldn't explain that it was *his* family who had owned it. The horrible truth would come out in good time. Maybe in London, after they'd been at the hotel a few days, when the sting of it wouldn't be so sharp, so cutting. "It passed to the hands of an incompetent and fell into bankruptcy. I scooped it up for a song."

She smiled. She loved a good business deal as much as he did.

"I want the grand opening to occur on Christmas Eve."

At that her mouth dipped. He was telling her they had weeks, not months, as they usually had. Still, she'd always risen to every challenge.

"Christmas Eve? Four weeks from now?"

"Yes."

She might have risen to every other challenge, but today she pushed herself up off the chair. "I'm sorry, Mr. Harrington. I'm booked."

"Booked?" He stood too. It wasn't that he didn't realize she had other clients. He simply assumed the high fee he paid her always propelled him to the top of her job list.

"You're talking about me spending the next weeks in London." She shook her head, causing her curtain of shiny red hair to sway. "*Christmas* in London. It's not possible." To soften the blow, she smiled at him, a quick, professional, no-hard-feelings lift of her lips.

For the first time since he'd known her, he reacted to the fact that she was beautiful. He'd *noticed* before. But something about the spark in her eyes at refusing him shifted her from beautiful to stunning and caused an unexpected scramble of his pulse.

Ridiculous!

He took a quiet breath to clear his head. Hugo Harrington didn't mix business with pleasure, and the crackle of heat that raced through his blood definitely signaled pleasure.

Had to be an aberration.

"What do you mean, not possible?"

She raised her hands. "I have things scheduled. It is the holiday season. Plus, you typically give me more lead time."

"There's a reason I didn't." A master at winning arguments and swaying decisions, he motioned for her to sit again. "The property became available suddenly. I put in a bid they couldn't refuse, paid cash, and voilà, it was mine. I didn't have lead time."

"Maybe a later grand opening date?"

He gaped at her. "No! In its heyday, the hotel was renowned for its elaborate Christmas Eve celebrations. That's the prime time for the grand opening. The best way to demonstrate that the hotel everyone remembers is back!"

And the perfect way to remind his brother and sister of their shared past. A way to soften everyone enough that they could have the kind of conversation needed to clear the air.

Her brow furrowed. "Maybe next Christmas Eve?"

The weird heat crackled through his blood again. It was almost as if he enjoyed her arguing with him.

Couldn't be. He loved haggling and bartering. But he never argued with subcontractors. *He paid them.* They did what he wanted.

He spoke logically and concisely, as he motioned for her to sit again because she hadn't taken the last cue. "This hotel is very important to me."

Once again, she didn't sit.

His nerves jangled with annoyance this time. "You could even say it's personal."

"I'm sorry." Regret filled her eyes. "But being away

from New York at Christmastime doesn't work for me."
She extended her hand to shake his. Baffled, he took it.
"Thank you, though, for thinking of me for this oppor-
tunity."

With that she was out the door. He stood behind his
desk, in front of the magnificent view of the Manhattan
skyline, the proof that he was at the top of his game. Not
someone to be refused.

He heard the elevator doors open, then close, and his
flummoxed thoughts cleared. She'd regretted turning him
down, but she had turned him down. What the hell could
be so important that she'd refuse him?

He grabbed his overcoat from his private closet and
strode past his assistant's desk. "Have my car downstairs
when I reach the street."

"Yes, sir."

He pressed the elevator button and one of three sets of
doors opened. He hoped to catch Erin in the lobby. If he
didn't, he had his coat and could follow her wherever she
walked on this cold late November day. If she walked too
fast, he would have a car.

That's the kind of guy he was. His plans had plans and
those plans had contingency plans.

He didn't lose. Especially not someone as important as
Erin. She was the preeminent party planner in Manhattan, but he'd used her all over the United States. If anyone
could bring to life his memories of Christmas Eve at the
Harrington Park Hotel, it would be Erin.

He caught up to her at the curb. When she saw him suddenly beside her, her blue eyes widened.

"We never talked money."

She frowned. "There's no reason to. I'm booked."

"For a bunch of office Christmas parties?" He made a

pfft noise. "What if I agree to pay three times your normal rate?"

A taxi pulled up. She walked over and opened the back door. "I'm sorry, Mr. Harrington. The timing doesn't work for me."

She got into the taxi and the blasted thing drove away. Hugo jumped into his limo. Though it sounded like something out of a bad movie, he said, "Follow that cab."

He expected Erin's car to stop in the business district. Maybe at one of the high-rises housing the offices of one of the clients for whom she'd be working in December. Instead, it kept going. It seemed as if they turned every few blocks, and after forty long minutes, including driving through a tunnel under the Hudson, Hugo found himself in Jersey City.

Jersey City?

The taxi stopped at a modest four-story building. Hugo instructed his driver to hang back until Erin made a move.

After enough time passed for her to pay for the ride, she exited the vehicle, ran up the front steps and disappeared inside. He jumped out of his car and raced after her. He didn't reach her in time, but saw the elevator stop on the third floor.

When it returned, he followed her up. The doors opened and he stepped out cautiously, glancing around like Dorothy in Oz. He didn't expect Munchkins to pop out at him. He'd simply never seen an office building like this with white doors with two-digit identifiers. These couldn't be businesses. The doors had to lead to…*apartments?*

He knocked on the first one. An elderly woman in a housecoat answered, confirming his suspicions. He winced. "Sorry, wrong flat."

She laughed. "Flat?"

Baffled that he'd forgotten to shift his British slang to

Americanisms, he apologized again and moved to the next door. No one answered. He knocked on the third door and a little boy opened it. The kid couldn't have been more than three.

Hugo froze for a few seconds, then said, "Sorry. Wrong…apartment."

"Noah! What are you doing answering the door?" Erin stepped out of a kitchen area, drying her hands on a towel. When she saw him, her mouth dropped open.

Well, she could join the club. Now he didn't feel like Dorothy in Oz. He felt like a man who'd inadvertently overstepped some boundaries.

The little boy had Erin's coloring—red hair and blue eyes—but a totally different face and eye shape. The flat behind them was simple, including an old-fashioned floral sofa that sat in front of a big window with plain beige drapes, and a kitchen without modern cabinets or shiny granite countertops. The cupboards were stained oak from another era. God only knew the material of the countertops.

Confusion and disbelief battled. From her familiarity with the home, he assumed she lived here. But why? He paid her a small fortune.

And the child who had her coloring—

It couldn't be—

Could his top-performing, always-there-for-him, executive-level event planner be…a mum?

"Can I come in?"

She hesitated. Hugo couldn't tell if it was from embarrassment or annoyance with him. But he hated this feeling of not being in the know. He always investigated everyone in his employ thoroughly. But as a subcontractor, Erin wasn't really in his employ—

Still, he needed to know.

He raised his hands imploringly. "I feel like we didn't sufficiently discuss my project."

She walked to the little boy—Noah—and put her hands on his shoulders to shift him away from the door. "Sure. Come in. Would you like some coffee?"

"Yes. That would be great."

Hugo Harrington stepped inside Erin's apartment, shrugging out of his cashmere overcoat. Their dealings had always been so crisp and professional, she hadn't for even a minute thought he wouldn't accept her refusal of his latest project.

But here he was. In her little condo. Her gorgeous, sexy as sin, biggest client, who always looked better in a suit than anyone had a right to, was in her apartment.

Tall and broad-shouldered, with dark chestnut hair that gleamed in the light from her overly bright kitchen, and brooding gray eyes, he'd been the object of her fantasies for the two and a half years they'd worked together. She'd never said a word, never made a move, always kept things strictly professional between them because she wasn't ready for another man in her life, but it didn't hurt to look.

And, oh, he was fun to look at.

She stopped the shimmer of attraction that lit her nerve endings. Nothing would come of her being attracted to him. Because that was how she wanted it.

As she popped a one-cup pod into her coffee maker, her short, auburn-haired mom called up the hall that led to the bedrooms. "Erin? If you're home for the day, I'm going out to get in my walk."

Seeing Hugo, she stopped dead in her tracks. "Oh, hello."

"That's Hugo Harrington, Mom. Mr. Harrington, that's my mom, Marge Winters."

He faced her mom with his always proper smile. "It's a pleasure to meet you."

She almost rolled her eyes. She might be super attracted to him, but she'd seen the way he'd looked at her apartment, the disdain that became confusion as he took in her out-of-date furniture and the cramped quarters. The attraction hadn't ever been mutual, but now that he'd seen how she lived she wasn't even sure he'd keep her as a friend.

Though come to think of it, they weren't really friends either. Her other clients invited her to parties and dinners to discuss their projects. Hugo Harrington only did business in his office.

Which might be for the best considering how attractive she found him.

"Can Noah go on your walk, too?"

"Sure," her mom said, overly cheerful, because she knew Hugo Harrington didn't merely pay for their apartment; he was the biggest contributor to the money she'd been saving to expand her business, employ more people and hopefully make enough to buy a condo in Manhattan, closer to her work, something with sufficient space that all three of them could be comfortable.

In the thirty seconds it took to brew Hugo Harrington's coffee, Erin's mom slid Noah into a coat and pulled a knit cap over his red curls. Erin bent down, placed a smacking kiss on her son's cheek and watched them leave the apartment.

Then she faced Hugo Harrington. He might be gorgeous and the object of her fantasies, but as a businessman he was single-minded. She'd told him no. He would try to talk her out of it.

Walking into her living room area of the open–floor plan space, she handed him his cup of coffee and motioned for him to sit. "I'm not sure what part of my decision you felt left room for discussion. But there is no room."

He looked around at her meager home. "I offered you three times your rate."

And assumed she should have been eager for it.

"There's more to a life than money." That's why her expansion was basically a dream right now. Noah was the only part of her deceased husband she still had. He was her world. Not her career and certainly not money.

Hugo Harrington blinked as if the concept of there being more to life than money was completely foreign to him.

She stifled a sigh. "December is Christmas, discussions about Santa, buying gifts, teaching my son to be generous and kind…" She lowered herself to the sofa across from the armchair he'd chosen. "I can usually work around your schedule and still have time for my son…but not if I'm in London."

Hugo's confused expression shifted as comprehension dawned. The fact that she had to explain the excitement of Christmas to him reinforced all her beliefs about the real Hugo Harrington. He wasn't the romantic, sensual man who inhabited her daydreams. He was a hard-nosed businessman, a guy who didn't have time for family, who didn't understand the meaning of the word *family*, a man who lived to work.

Well, she didn't live to work. She *couldn't*. Her mom may have been able to move in with her to help care for Noah when Josh died, but it wasn't the same for her little boy as having a dad. Erin knew that she had to be both mother and father and she refused to abdicate that responsibility… the way Josh had.

She closed her eyes briefly, hating that she felt that way.

After all, her late husband hadn't asked for the heart attack that had taken him.

Thoughts of Josh rippled through her, her despair over his death, the sense of betrayal that came when she learned he'd been sick for months and hadn't told her—but he *had* confided in a woman he'd worked with. She'd told Erin that Josh had believed he was saving her the heartache of knowing her husband was dying while she was pregnant.

But good as his intentions might have seemed, not only had he confided in another woman, proving she and Josh didn't have the deep, wonderful bond Erin had always believed, but also they rang hollow as she'd stood at his graveside, ready to have his baby, without the opportunity to say goodbye.

She could have cried with him. They could have absorbed the first waves of loss together. Made videos of him laughing for their son. Made videos of him teaching Noah the kind of things a father longs to share with his child—

"You don't have any other clients, do you?"

She forced herself back to the present, to her discussion with Hugo Harrington. Sexy man with a heart of stone. Maybe that's what had reminded her of Josh?

"It looks to me like you can't afford to lose me."

Not about to give up Christmas with Noah, she sat taller. "I have other clients. Especially in December."

"But not clients who pay you as much as I do. Scattered Christmas parties. Grand openings. Not clients who pay a fee over the norm."

She took a breath. Part of her wanted to bluff her way through. The other part didn't like lying or even hedging. Josh hadn't out-and-out lied, but he'd kept a secret that had leveled her. She would never, ever again lie, distort the facts or omit anything.

She would face the truth. Always.

"You *are* my biggest client."

"Then let me suggest a compromise."

She brightened with hope. "I could supervise the project from New York?"

He chuckled. "No. But I could fly your son and your mum to London with you."

Her breath stalled in her chest. The casual way he'd called her mom "mum" hit her oddly. He did not sound like always proper Hugo Harrington. For a few seconds, he was the man in her fantasies. Not a businessman. Not a keen negotiator. But just a guy.

A handsome guy with chestnut hair and intriguing gray eyes—

"You may not be able to take your son to see Macy's Santa, but we have Santa in London. And wonderful shops." He caught her gaze. "Think of it as an opportunity to show Noah a more diverse Christmas."

She blinked, trying to see the real Hugo Harrington— the businessman, not the guy who suddenly seemed family friendly—as his idea of her mom and Noah going with her to London tickled her brain and began to take hold.

"I won't put you up in a hotel. I'll find you a flat. A place you can decorate with a tree and garland. And I'll make sure you leave work in time to tuck your son into bed every night."

She stared at him. She knew she did a good job for him. So it wasn't outlandish that he'd want her for a project with a looming deadline. And showing her son more of the world than one little corner in New Jersey appealed to her on so many levels. Noah would see one of the most beautiful cities on the planet, experience new traditions. She could teach him to think wider, beyond himself—

It was a generous offer from a guy who normally wasn't this kind.

Skepticism rose. "I'd still get three times my usual fee?" He frowned.

She smiled shrewdly. "You can't take back something you've already offered."

He rose. "Sure I can. This is a negotiation."

And the real Hugo Harrington was back.

"Yeah, well. The way I see it, I have to pay staff extra to compensate for the fact that I won't be around to supervise my bread-and-butter projects in Manhattan."

He caught her gaze. "And the way I see it, you're already getting paid for those projects. The money will simply shift from your profits to the employees who assume your tasks."

"Which just took away my incentive to go to London." His frown returned.

"Do the deal," she said, confident that if he really wanted her, he'd pay.

He sighed. "You don't have me over a barrel."

"Wouldn't think of even considering that. I'm simply someone who knows how to hold her ground." Her smile grew. "Whether you want to admit it or not, you like this side of me because I negotiate some very good prices for food and decorations and fancy pastries for your parties. You simply don't appreciate that I've turned that skill on you."

He rolled his eyes. Took a breath. And suddenly the ordinary guy was back. In all the years she'd done business with Hugo Harrington, he'd never been as normal, as human, as he had been today. He certainly wasn't the romantic man in her dreams, but she could swear he had a beating heart.

He sighed and said, "All right. Three times your usual rate. Lodging in London for three."

"And airfare."

"And airfare."

She extended her hand to shake his. "We have a deal."

CHAPTER ONE

"I DON'T SEE why you can't just flirt a little bit."

Two weeks before Christmas Eve, Erin Hunter stuffed the reports she'd worked on the night before into her brief-case. Holding Erin's son, Noah, her mom stood behind her in the open-plan apartment Harrington Enterprises had rented for them.

"I mean, look at this place," Erin's mom continued, glancing around at the gray walls that were trimmed with shiny white wood that matched the white cabinets in the kitchen. Black-and-white geometric-print tiles separated the cooking space from the huge living room/dining room area, which had hardwood floors accented by bright blue-and-white-print rugs.

"Only someone who really likes you would go to the trouble of getting us such a lovely apartment." She shook her head. "And I saw the way you looked at him when he came to beg—and I'm accenting the word *beg* here—you to come to London. I swear you all but swooned. You can't tell me you aren't interested."

Erin had been ignoring comments like these from her mom since she'd heard they would be spending Christmas in London. But that last one? That about stopped her heart. All this time she'd believed she was hiding the stupid crush she had on Hugo Harrington. But what if she wasn't?

"I didn't swoon. If you remember correctly, he'd shocked me."

"Which was probably why your true feelings came out."

She shoved more papers into her briefcase. She almost said there were no true feelings. Because what she felt for Hugo Harrington was one-sided and wrong. But she'd made that vow never to lie. "It's all totally irrelevant."

"Why is it irrelevant? You've been alone over three years," her mom said, following Erin as she walked to get her coat. "It's time. Even if nothing comes of it, you should flirt with him, if only to get your mojo back."

"Mojo?" She gaped at her mom. "I never had mojo. I fell in love in college before I knew mojo was a thing. And Josh had been the sweetest, kindest man I'd ever met, yet look what he did to me."

Her mom's expression saddened. "Erin, you have to let that go."

"Let what go, Mom? The fact that he never told me he had cancer or the fact that he *had* confided in another woman?"

"A *coworker*. He confided in a coworker. And you should be glad he did. She knew he'd been having experimental treatments for his cancer. So when he had his heart attack, she knew what to tell the ambulance people. It was awful that he died, but at least she gave him a fighting chance."

"And in the end, it didn't matter. The treatments he'd agreed to had pushed his body too far and he died long before he should have. He didn't even get to meet his own child. If he'd talked to me, I wouldn't have let him try something so risky."

"Faced with mortality, people do all kinds of weird things. Besides, your Hugo probably isn't anything like Josh at all."

She slid into her coat. "He's not my Hugo." But that was the problem, and the reason her mom's comments were so troubling. If her mom had noticed her looking at Hugo Harrington oddly, she wasn't hiding her crush as well as she'd thought.

And she knew why. She was losing her grip on the bottom-line reason she shouldn't like him. Damn that stupid conversation where he'd shown her his nice side!

"I think he could be your Hugo," her mom singsonged, hoisting Noah higher on her hip.

Ignoring that, she asked, "Will you and Noah be okay today?"

"He loves it here. I told you about our walks."

"Yes. It's good to get him outside."

"Give me another two days and we'll totally know the neighborhood." Her mom gave her a quick once-over. "Are you sure you want to wear jeans and a T-shirt? Maybe you should go put on that expensive blue sweater I bought you for your birthday?"

"Wear my *only* nice sweater to a hotel that's a construction zone?" She laughed. "I need clothes I can throw in the washer when I get home at night."

Her mother sighed, clearly disappointed Erin wouldn't dress up for Hugo Harrington. "Okay, if you think that's best."

"I do." Just as she thought flirting with Hugo would be a disaster.

Mojo.

For the love of God. She did not need mojo. She needed to stop thinking about Hugo Harrington, as if he were a nice guy. He was a businessman. He'd brought her to London because he liked her work.

That was it.

She kissed Noah's cheek, then smiled at her mom. "I'll be back a little after seven tonight."

Noah said, "Bye."

Her mom said, "Bye."

And Erin stepped out into the hall, squeezing her eyes shut as the apartment door closed behind her. She wished her feelings about Hugo hadn't changed. The crush she'd had on a fantasy version of him had been fun. Now everything felt real. She could barely take notes in meetings with him because the sound of his voice gave her goose bumps.

Damn it!

All because he'd shown her an inkling of a nice guy.

It was stupid…weird…*wrong.*

On the bus ride to Regent's Park, she told herself the whole mess had to be an extension of jet lag or exhaustion after the hectic week of getting herself, her child and her mother settled across an ocean, followed by a week of nonstop work with Hugo, setting out his plans for the grand opening.

Entering the hotel, she walked past scaffolding set up on concrete floors. Every room, hall and office waited for new carpet, hardwood or tile. Because *everything* was so old and had been neglected for so long, it all needed replacing.

As much as it was none of her business and potentially trouble, she couldn't stop her mind from tiptoeing over into the question that had plagued her since she'd arrived in London and her feelings toward Hugo had—softened.

Why the hell does he care so much about this hotel?

Sure, it was fabulous with high ceilings, chandeliers and decorative carved column caps throughout the lobby, corridors and event rooms, but there were easier projects than this shabby hotel. Even the marquis with the name had rotted and fallen off. The place was a disaster.

After taking her briefcase to her office and removing her coat, she dodged ladders and workers on her way to see Hugo Harrington, her heart adding an extra beat or two of excitement. Not because she entertained as much as an inkling of a thought of acting on her growing attraction to him. And not even to ask him why he cared so much about this old hotel. She'd never be that forward, especially when the British in him seemed to be more pronounced in his own country.

No. She was searching for Hugo for something entirely mundane: a check.

After striding through what would eventually be a workstation for the general manager's assistant, she opened the door to the manager's office—where Hugo set up shop when he was at the hotel. *His* assistant worked across town in a huge office inhabited by the New York staff in charge of renovations, so protocol was to simply walk in.

The enormous room had probably been a showstopper in its day. Dusty velvet drapes covered huge windows that looked out over the back of the property. Cleaning and painting this room had been scheduled for last because it wasn't a space that guests would use or even see. That was why the old filing cabinets along the left wall had been brought here when their original office space came up in rotation for painting.

Unfortunately, the chair behind the big mahogany desk was empty.

She should have turned and left, but she'd given Hugo a voucher to sign the day before and she needed the resultant check. If she had to pull the signed voucher from his out-box and walk it to the office across town, that's what she'd do. Though it was freezing out, she had to have that check.

She headed toward the desk. Rifling through the out-box, she didn't find it. With a wince, she rounded the area to the chair and sat, intending to only look through the small mountain of paperwork that had accrued, but an open drawer caught her eye.

A newspaper sat faceup. The front page picture was of the hotel—*the hotel*, the very one she sat in—in all its glory.

Her month fell open. The place was gorgeous. She could understand why Hugo wanted to restore it to its former artistry—

She stopped dead as the headline glared at her.

> *Harrington Park Hotel…*
> *Is even more failure on the horizon?*

Harrington Park Hotel?
Harrington?
As in Hugo Harrington?

Her gaze jumped to the top of the paper. Dated two days before her arrival in London, the newspaper had been off the stands by the time she'd come to the hotel. And she hadn't interacted with any of the contractors working on repairs—

She'd been too busy settling her son and mother into the apartment Hugo had rented for her and getting instructions from him about the party.

She read the first few paragraphs, interested in the hotel's history, but also confused as to why Hugo *Harrington* had bought this hotel. A hotel bearing his name? Maybe once belonging to his family?

> The full details of Hugo Harrington's disappearance from the family had never been made public.

Oh, damn. It had belonged to his family.

The rumor was that Hugo had rebelled when his mother signed Harrington Park over to his stepfather, expecting to inherit the hotel himself. At a time when the hotel needed him the most, he'd packed his bags and left his family to fend for themselves.

Not the caliber of businessman Rupert Harrington, Nick Wolfe had tried to maintain the hotel, especially its Christmas Eve traditions, but without the help of the oldest son, Nick's efforts had failed. Too busy building his empire, Hugo hadn't even returned when his mother died. But he hadn't been too busy to keep watch over the hotel and snap it up when the last owner fell into bankruptcy.

"What are you doing?"

Erin's heart about burst in her chest and her gaze flew up as Hugo entered his office.

She sprang from his desk chair. "Looking for the voucher I gave you yesterday."

She just barely managed to keep her voice from shaking. He'd scared her, but the newspaper article had done more damage. Her stupid crush had been snuffed out. Totally. Brutally. She should have known someone so work-focused wouldn't give a damn about anybody but himself—wouldn't give a damn about his *family*.

But his not returning for his mother's funeral? Because he wouldn't inherit his family's sole possession? That was hard-core petty.

She tried to stop the comparison between Hugo and Josh, but it rose in a tidal wave of anger. Both thought only of themselves. Neither cared about the feelings of those around him.

Those *closest* to him.

To have made the decision he had, Josh clearly hadn't known her at all. And now it appeared, after two and a half years of working together, she didn't know her boss at all.

"I need the check today."

"I'm sure it will be coming when my office sends their courier with the mail."

And that was another thing—

Why did he have her *here*, in a makeshift office, among the construction and noise? Why wasn't she in the space rented for his New York staff?

Was it because he didn't want her to know his family had owned the hotel he'd scooped up for a song?

Scooped up for a song!

If his family had retained any part of the hotel at all, their share of the sale would be next to nothing. Was that what he'd been so proud of? That he'd shortchanged his family?

The man was scum.

As she scrambled around his desk, to the front of it where an employee belonged, he glanced down into the open desk drawer and frowned.

Then looked up at her.

Their gazes met and held.

He knew she'd seen the newspaper.

She swallowed but didn't shift her eyes away. Let him yell at her. She now knew the truth.

Her unspoken revulsion washed over Hugo as he slowly took his seat. He'd expected the story of the hotel would be printed in the business section of legitimate press. He hadn't expected the tabloids to pick it up…or that their accusations would skim along his skin like lightning before a bad storm.

"Satisfy your curiosity?"

Her chin rose. "Enough to know you're pretty heartless."

Anyone in London could say that to him and he'd shrug and go on with his life. But Erin Hunter had been like a right-hand person to him. She'd played a major part in his recent successes. He'd believed she respected him. No. She *had* respected him.

And one unsanctioned tabloid story seemed to have totally changed her mind.

Anger bubbled again.

"You didn't even come back for your mother's funeral?"

He hadn't been told his mother had died. No one spared the thirty seconds of internet searching it would have taken to find him.

"I wasn't told about my mother's death, let alone her funeral." He slammed his hand on the desk. He had absolutely no idea why Erin's disgust hit him in the chest like a stab of betrayal, but it did.

He wanted to scream, *Get out.* Instead, he drew a slow, calming breath, one that quelled the rising anger, not just with Erin but with his brother and sister who seemed so cautious about him. He'd wanted a happy reunion. What he got were two supercareful siblings. Though Jay seemed to be coming around, his only hope of repairing his relationship with Sally was the Christmas Eve grand opening party.

And for that, he needed Erin.

"I'll phone my office and track down the check."

She primly said, "Thank you," turned on her heel and raced out of the room.

He cursed, squeezed his eyes shut, then went back to work. Or tried. Her blatant hatred haunted him. They'd worked together amicably for the past week, got so many details nailed down—

So what?

People he *loved* hated him and he had survived.

He always survived.

To hell with her. His goal was repairing his family.

He worked until his brain forgot Erin Hunter and completely focused on his plan to bring his family's hotel back to life. At a little after six that night, the sounds of hammers and saws still filling the high-ceiling spaces of the first floor, he left the hotel. Tired, he ambled out to his waiting limo in time to see Erin heading up the long sidewalk around the driveway to the street.

Confusion overcame his automatic burst of anger with her. "Where's she going?"

The driver holding the limo door for him snapped to attention. "Ms. Hunter?"

"Yes."

"Probably to a bus stop."

Hugo gaped at him. "How far away is the apartment my staff rented for her?"

His driver opened the door a little wider, a hint for him to get inside and get them both out of the cold. "I'm afraid I don't know, sir."

"Well, it looks like we're going to find out. Stop when we reach her."

The limo took the circular drive around the hotel to the entry to the main road, then stopped. Hugo lowered his window.

She might despise him, and his feelings for her might also be in the toilet, but he wouldn't let her walk when he'd promised her a nice stay in London. "It's too cold to walk."

She tugged the sides of her coat collar closer together. "I'm fine."

And there was her pride again. Misplaced for sure, but he'd never allow her close enough that she'd see just how wrong she was.

Still… He wouldn't let a single mum, trying to get home to her family, take the bus when he had a limo.

"Let me give you a ride."

Miss Pride looked about ready to refuse, but she sucked in a breath. "For the record, I'm sure Manhattan is much colder right now."

He laughed as he opened the car door and got out, offering her entry to the warm back seat.

She slid in. He slid in beside her. "And for the record, I'm not in any way, shape or form showing you a nice side of myself, so you won't hate me after what you read in that paper."

She sniffed.

"I don't care if you hate me. I don't care if anyone hates me."

She snorted. "No kidding."

"And if you think I'm trying to repair our relationship, we don't have one. Except professional."

She glanced at him.

He held her gaze. "To ruin that, you'd have to screw up the Christmas Eve grand opening. You're too good to do that. Otherwise, I wouldn't have wasted the money bringing you here."

She said nothing, just stared at him, and he felt immeasurably better. He'd rather she hated him for being an unfeeling businessman than for things he hadn't done.

He gestured to the driver. "Give Ronnie your address."

She did and then settled back on the seat with a long sigh.

"Rough day?"

"My boss is a taskmaster."

He chuckled, not sure why her disrespectful side amused him, except that it felt good to have their argument from the morning out of the way. Or maybe he liked that she was always honest with him?

"He may be a taskmaster. But his hotels are some of the best in the world."

With another sigh, Erin realized she had to give him that one. "True."

"And you're a big part of that."

The sincerity in his voice warmed her more than the limo's heaters. She didn't want to like him or hate him and was glad that he seemed to be taking them back to their original impersonal work relationship. "Thanks."

"You're welcome. I don't ever say it, but I always hope the fee I pay you shows you that I appreciate you."

Grateful to be back on neutral ground, she glanced at him. When their gazes met, something trickled down her spine. She immediately blamed her stupid attraction, but her brain wouldn't accept that because her crush was gone. It had been snuffed out when she'd read that newspaper article. This felt more like a connection of some sort.

She hauled in a long breath, telling herself that was ridiculous. Guys like Hugo Harrington didn't connect. He'd proved that with how he treated his family.

He looked away and they drove a few blocks in total silence before he said, "Are your son and mum settling in?"

She peered over at him. A personal question after that weird connection? Her brain tried to make the leap that maybe *he'd* noticed her crush on him and he was making a move, but her crush on him was dead. Frankly, she'd like to keep it that way.

Deciding he was only making conversation, she said,

"Yes. Noah is thrilled. I've taken him a few places, but we haven't officially been sightseeing yet. We're saving that for the weekend—closer to Christmas, when Santa will be out, and everything will be more real for him."

"Humph. That makes sense. Have you given any thought to the Christmas cookies I mentioned?"

Yep. He was only making simple conversation, which he easily brought back to work. No need to worry he'd seen her crush or was even trying to be friends. She was safe.

"The gingerbread men?"

He nodded.

"Found three recipes online. I gave them to Louis Joubert. He'll make all three. You can do the taste test to choose the one you want."

"Good."

They drove the rest of the way discussing the project. So many details that Erin's head began to spin. Now that she knew the hotel had belonged to his family during its heyday, his surety of what he wanted didn't surprise her. But her heart tugged when it occurred to her that he could be recreating his past.

The memory of Hugo asking about gingerbread men popped into her brain. At the time, she'd held back a laugh, thinking that must have been one of his childhood favorites. But what if they'd actually been a big part of the Christmas Eve celebrations of the past? And what if it had been his mom, not the chef, who'd made them?

What if those had been the cookies he and his mom had set on a plate for Santa?

Emotion swamped her and the sense of connection rose again. It was almost as if she could see him as a child.

She shook her head to clear it, but realization also hit her. Now that she understood the hotel had once belonged to his family, she'd be making all sorts of connections like this—

And whether she wanted to or not, she'd be getting to know him.

Her breath stalled. She did not want to like him! He'd deserted his family—

But she didn't want to hate him either. That would make working together difficult. And the truth was it didn't matter what he'd done in the past with his family. She was a subcontractor. Someone who worked for him. She'd do her best to keep enough distance that even if she did learn things about him, it wouldn't matter.

He. Was. Her. Boss.

The limo pulled up to her building and Hugo slid out of the car, motioning for her to exit.

Finishing the work discussion, she said, "Tomorrow morning, I'll send Dave and Terry on a scouting mission in the attic. We may find old lamps or paintings. Things we can use to draw out the ambience of the hotel when it was popular. Honestly, I think everything you want will be easy to accomplish."

He winced. "Even getting my brother and sister to hang ornaments with me?"

She slid the strap of her purse farther up her shoulder. Guessing that must have been one of their family traditions, she wished she could promise that, if only from a professional standpoint. But she didn't know much about his brother and sister except that he'd abandoned them, and she wouldn't promise something she couldn't deliver. She certainly wouldn't blame them if they wanted no part of hanging ornaments with him, as if everything was peachy keen and hunky-dory.

"Let me touch base with them before I commit."

He gestured for her to walk up the sidewalk to the building, and she frowned.

"I want to see your quarters. I was under the impression they'd found you something nice and close to the hotel. Since they blew the close-to-the-hotel part, I need to see what they rented for you."

Surprised by his concern, she said, "It's fine."

"I promised you an opportunity to show your son a wonderful holiday. Part of that is having a good place to live."

The odd feeling of connection with him tightened her chest again, maybe because he sounded more like a friend than a boss. "We do have good living quarters. Actually, they're wonderful."

"Let me be the judge of that."

They ambled up to the three-story building, which reminded Erin of some of New York's brownstones. He opened the main door for her, and she turned to the right to enter the first apartment.

As she opened the door, Noah jumped off the sofa and ran to her. "Mom!"

She scooped him up, turning to Hugo. "See? Perfectly comfortable."

He glanced around at the gray walls, white kitchen cabinets and solid hardwood floor in the living room and said, "It is nice." Then he looked at Noah, his eyes lit and his lips lifted into a smile. "How do you like it?"

Noah turned his face into his mom's shoulder.

"He's just shy," Erin said, as more conflicting feelings rippled through her. She hadn't expected all-business Hugo Harrington to be interested in her child. Estranged from his family, he was even more of a lone wolf than she'd originally thought. But judging from his expression, Noah intrigued him.

Still, everybody liked her adorable son.

"That's okay. When he sees the Christmas gift I told Santa to bring him, he's going to love me."

The little boy's head slowly lifted from Erin's shoulder. "Santa brings presents."

"And he takes special orders from bosses of little kids' moms."

Her heart began to soften at his unexpected kindness, but she stopped it. She liked not having a crush on him. She might have been righteously indignant on behalf of his family, but it made working for him so much easier.

She could not let a few kind words drag her back. Not when she had evidence that he wasn't a nice guy.

She kissed Noah's cheek then slid him to the floor. "Go sit with Grandma a sec, and then we'll watch a Christmas movie before bedtime."

Noah obediently did as he was told.

"He's a great kid."

"Thanks. He's a sweetheart. Barely a ripple of badness when he hit the terrible twos."

Hugo laughed. Then he glanced around again. "I'm satisfied with your quarters." He walked to the door and she followed him, seeing him out.

He turned to her, and their eyes met. Her blasted attraction tried to rise again. She reminded herself he'd abandoned his family, told herself anything nice he said about Noah was because Noah was adorable, and her defenses returned.

"See you tomorrow."

She murmured, "See you tomorrow." And almost felt guilty that she now knew enough about him that her feelings couldn't simply be neutral. She was either wondering what it would be like to kiss him or sitting on the edge of totally disliking him.

Still, smart women did not mess around with guys who thought so little of their families. No matter how good-looking he was or how strong her curiosity about what it would be like to kiss him.

what had sounded like *I have to be careful on the edges* *to avoid disturbing the carpeting.*

Adroll. Smart women did not mess around with guys who thought was okay to have an affair, then enter a new world consisting of naval behavior. Her opinion about what it would be like to be in Hugo's

CHAPTER TWO

THE NEXT DAY, meeting with Erin as she quickly reported on the progress of the details of the Christmas Eve celebration, Hugo was in awe. She was every bit as shrewd as he was in getting her own way and every bit as tough of a negotiator.

But something had happened the night before. Every time he'd looked at her, a weird sensation had shuffled through him. At first, he'd taken it as a continuation of his surprise to discover her disrespectful remarks amused him. But the more he'd stood in her quarters, the more times their gazes linked, the more he noticed odd little things about her. Things he *liked*.

Sitting in front of his desk, notebook on her lap, pen in hand, glasses perched on her nose, she went on with their meeting, totally oblivious to his confusing thoughts.

"The Christmas trees are ordered. Even the huge one for the ballroom."

Taking in her simple blue T-shirt that outlined nice-sized breasts and her worn jeans, he told himself that it was okay to agree that she could wear work clothes in a dusty hotel that was being renovated. But the nice-sized breasts observation was one of those unexpected things again.

Not that she wasn't attractive. She was. Maybe too attractive.

Seeing she was waiting for a response, he said, "Great. The trees are very important to the overall scheme of things."

"I saw that. I got the general idea of the size for each one from the old photos you gave to the contractor recreating the rooms and lobby."

Her hair caught up in a ponytail was also cute. Though it was abundantly practical when working in a construction zone, he liked it. He also loved that she hadn't lost one iota of her stunning beauty when she quit wearing makeup. The dusty environment had probably forced that too. But it had made his breath catch to see her skin clean and shiny, her bright eyes every bit as luminous without shadows and liners or whatever it was women used to make themselves pretty.

She needed none of it.

And it was confusingly odd that he reacted to that too.

"I've been in the attic with Terry and Dave and we've uncovered a treasure trove of decorations."

All thoughts of how pretty she was fled at the mention of decorations. He sat up. "The originals?"

Her blue eyes shone with victory. "I'm not a hundred percent sure, but they've been up there a long time, as if put in storage when the hotel changed hands and never used after that. With your brother and sister both out of the country, I'm going to need you to come up to the attic to look at them. Because you're only in the hotel a few hours a day, I called your assistant and made an appointment with you for this afternoon at one."

He laughed. "You made an appointment with me?"

She peeked up at him again. "You're a busy man. I don't assume you'll be free. I knew we had too much to discuss to squeeze it in this morning, so I called your assistant."

Which was another thing that made her so successful. She left nothing to chance. He adored that about her.

Actually, he now liked a lot of things about her. Too many. Especially for a guy who didn't date—

No, that wasn't true. He dated a lot. He didn't have relationships. Erin was a relationship kind of girl. He might not have known she had a child, but he knew she'd been married and was a widow.

A widow.

Not the kind of woman a man dated for fun.

His thoughts about how much he liked her fled in the wake of that reality and pulled him out of the haze of whatever the hell seemed to be happening to him when he looked at her. With his brain back on track, they finished the meeting and she left his office, her arms stacked with papers.

After shrugging into his overcoat, he walked out to his limo, but rather than step inside, he turned and glanced at the hotel again. He'd put Erin in Harrington Park, instead of with his staff, because he wanted her to get a feel for the building. As the renovations were completed, he'd wanted her to breathe in the ambience.

Now he wondered if it wasn't a good idea for them to be separated. He didn't normally feel attractions like this one. Having space between them worked.

That afternoon, Hugo was back at the hotel for the meeting Erin had set with him. He exited his limo under the portico and raced into the lobby of the building, happy to see most of the scaffolding was gone. Probably moved to another section of the hotel. That meant the lobby painting was done. Now the registration desk would be sanded and stained to match the one from decades ago. Soon lighting fixtures would be installed like the ones from when his parents owned the hotel. Flooring would be next. Then the custom drapes. Then area rugs. All things that would bring his past to life again.

When Erin met him in front of his office door, strange tingling feelings of delight washed over him. Because they were wrong, he convinced himself he wasn't happy to see her but happy to be going to the attic, hopefully confirming that all the beautiful ornaments really had been stored and could be shined and hung on this year's tree.

"Give me two minutes to put my briefcase on my desk."

"You can take off your overcoat too." She winced, but her smile ruined the feelings of contrition he was sure she aimed to display. "You should probably ditch your suit jacket as well."

He did more than that. He took off his suit coat, loosened his tie and rolled up the sleeves of his white shirt. He knew the attic would be dusty and should have thought of this himself.

"How's this?"

"Magnificent," she said as she led him to the elevator that took them to the top floor of the hotel and down the hall to the hidden stairway to the attic.

When she opened the door, his past twinkled at him.

He took the last few stairs into the room filled with cobwebs, dust and memories, and his heart chugged to a stop.

She'd had Terry and Dave string the lights along the beams of the roof so he could easily identify them. Heirloom ornaments were displayed on long tables she'd commandeered from the kitchen.

Memories assaulted him. Christmas memories. He shoved away the visions of the night his stepfather had kicked him out and his mother had stood by passively, her silence telling him more than her words ever could have. He focused instead on the childhood memories of waking up Christmas Eve morning, filled with excitement

over that night's party. The visit from Santa. The laughter
of his parents—his dad alive and so full of enthusiasm it
rippled from their living quarters through the hotel lobby,
down the halls, into the kitchen, the ballrooms, the guest
rooms, filling everyone with unbridled joy.

There'd been secrets, like the one Christmas Eve when
a powerful businessman stopped the dancing at the ball to
propose to his longtime girlfriend, making every guest a
part of his proposal. Everyone had laughed with joy and
toasted with champagne. Or the time a guest had received
word she was pregnant after a decade of trying. Everyone
had cried with happiness for her.

Because guests had been repeat visitors. Year after year,
they'd gotten to know each other, become like family.

He touched the ornaments. Bright reds, golds and
greens to be put on a green tree with gold tinsel and a
gold star, all of which accented the special ornaments he,
his brother and his sister had put on the tree. A new one
for every year.

The plan had been for the special family ornaments to
eventually replace the red, gold and green decorations,
and for the tree to be filled with only ornaments placed
by the siblings—

Then their father had died.

He cleared his throat, let the sadness wash through him
until it thinned out and disappeared. Then he glanced at
Erin. "Yes. These are all for the tree. Only white lights,
though. The red and green strands were for the doorways
of the lobby. We'll need live garland. Especially for the
main stairway."

He pointed at a box of all red ornaments. "Those decorate the garland on the banister."

He could see it. His dad bigger than life. His mum always laughing, involving her children. The best mum in the world because she'd loved them—

He'd always believed she loved *him*.

He closed his eyes and took a breath hoping to stop the memories, but they seeped into his thoughts, into his psyche, like ghosts with nowhere to go, so they haunted his soul.

Holding on to his composure by a thread, he pointed at a box of green and gold. "And those go on garland hung on the reception desk."

She frowned. "Hmmm…it's not done. It's not even stained yet—"

Overcome with emotion, he turned on his heel and headed for the stairway. "It will be. It will all be ready on Christmas Eve."

He strode to his office, fighting the emptiness of missing his parents and the confusion of his last night with his mum, wishing his life had been different and longing to rebuild his relationship with his siblings. He'd been their older brother, their protector. And then suddenly he was nothing.

No one.

He sat behind his desk, still reeling from seeing the decorations, and closed his eyes. Not in despair, but in confusion. He knew seeing everything would bring back memories, but he'd genuinely believed he had gotten beyond his mother asking him to leave. He'd become a man, a success. Why did he care?

Two taps on his door forced his eyelids up, shoving him back to the present. "Come in."

The door opened and Erin gingerly stepped inside. "Are you okay?"

The very question raised his nerve endings like porcupine quills. He didn't like being weak, confused. Worse, he didn't want his staff to see it. "Of course, I'm okay."

"Mr. Harrington—Hugo—I've seen you angry, and though you scared Terry and Dave when you stormed out of the attic, that wasn't anger."

He sat back, took a slow breath. "Didn't fool you, huh?"

She ventured a few more steps into the room. "It was close. And then I asked myself who gets angry over gorgeous antique ornaments? No one."

"So, you answered yourself?"

"If you're trying to make me think I'm crazy for talking to myself, that's not going to work either." She took another two steps. "Something's very wrong here. And I'm worried that I'm going to spend the next two weeks creating a wonderful event only to have you ruin it."

"Me?" He gaped at her. "Ruin it?" He pointed at his chest. "*I'm* going to ruin it?"

"I know when something's bubbling under the surface."

Only one of his eyebrows rose.

She huffed out a breath. "Seriously, you dragged me to London for a project that's almost too big to pull off. *You're* a bundle of nerves. And the press is watching you. Which will mean if you snap and the big Christmas Eve grand opening fails... Guess whose name will be ruined in London and probably Manhattan because you're such a hot item all over the globe?"

He said nothing.

"I don't fail, Hugo. If you're pushing to prove something, that's a recipe for disaster and I want no part of it."

"I'm not pushing to prove something." He sat back. "And I won't snap."

"Says every person right before they snap."

He would have laughed except he could see in her eyes that she was serious. He also knew why. She had a child to support. If this failed and her business suffered, her income would nosedive.

He tried to envision anyone else capable of accomplishing the grand opening celebration he wanted and knew there was no one else. They had not quite two weeks left, and she was knee-deep in the details. He couldn't bring in another person. He had to keep her.

He also had to make sure she didn't fail. He'd never forgive himself if he took food out of the mouth of a child. He'd been hungry one too many times himself in those weeks after he'd been kicked out. He knew that anguish just a little too well.

He rose and walked to the closet, where he grabbed his jacket and his overcoat. "All right. You're right. I *am* tense. But I probably just need a release valve." He didn't exactly want to talk, but if he did, what better person to vent to than someone he only saw every few months? Not even an employee, but a *subcontractor*. Someone who had more reason to keep his secrets than spill them.

"But not here." If he did let loose, he didn't want anyone to overhear. "Have you been sightseeing yet?"

She frowned at him. "I'm at the hotel twelve hours a day. Home in time to put Noah to bed, as you promised. But not home in time to sightsee."

"Do you like hot cocoa?"

"Everyone likes hot cocoa."

"Get your coat and meet me outside. I'll show you the one place you're going to want to be sure to take your son."

They rode in his limo to the Southbank. It wasn't a long trip, but it was long enough that Erin about broke her neck, her head moving from side to side, as she tried to take it all in.

He laughed, and for the first time since he'd been to

the attic, some of his tension released. "London has a lot to see."

"I know." She smiled at him. "I can't wait."

More of his tension abated. "It's a beautiful city."

The car let them off and he pointed out Westminster Bridge and Big Ben as they began their walk along the Thames.

She gasped. "There is no feeling to describe being places that you thought you'd only see in pictures. It's surreal! Almost like I can't believe I'm here."

He glanced at the bridge, then Big Ben again, viewing both with fresh eyes. "I guess you're right." He breathed in the crisp air—Christmas air. He could suddenly feel the holiday coming to life around him, overriding his memories.

More of his tension ebbed. His head cleared.

Maybe he'd just needed some fresh air?

When they reached the Beltane&Pop van, he directed her to look at the flavors and asked what she wanted.

Her mouth opened in surprise and finally she laughed. "You know what? Just plain old hot cocoa."

He ordered two and they began their walk again in the crisp air. The sun was bright, but dark clouds eased in. Soon snow would be falling.

She took a sip and groaned. "This is fabulous."

Calm settled over him, along with the unexpected sense that he was happy to be out of the office, a sure sign of overwork, not overwhelm. Meaning, he was fine. "We like to think it's the best in the world."

Her head tilted as she turned to look at him. "That's the first time you've ever referred to London in a way that makes me think it's your home."

"You saw the newspaper article. I didn't leave on the best of terms."

"Is that what's bothering you?"

He shrugged, took a sip of his own hot cocoa and said, "Honestly? I think I've been pushing too hard and it all came to the surface this afternoon."

"That's interesting because I thought maybe you were trying to recreate something you worry can't be recreated."

Her comment hit him right in the heart. He'd never verbalized it to himself, but deep down that was his fear. Not merely because his father was the engine of their joyous Christmas Eve celebrations, but because his brother seemed to have accepted his return only grudgingly, and his sister clearly hated him.

But as much as he trusted Erin, he wouldn't tell her that. He'd stick with his story that he'd been working too hard. Because coming outside had proved it to be true. The walk had cleared his head, and he wasn't noticing those odd things about Erin—

Which was the real reason it would be incredibly foolish to confide in her. He liked her. And she wasn't right for him. Or maybe he wasn't right for her. A woman with a child needed a relationship, not a one-night stand. And he was Mr. One-Night Stand.

"Yes and no." He peeked at her. "The project is ambitious and tied to some memories. It would be wonderful to recreate them, but I know there are things that I can't get exactly right. So, I only need to get close to what we had." He took a breath, then smiled. "When have you ever known me to fail?"

Erin studied the confident expression on his face. Whatever had upset him, it was gone. Or tucked away to pop out when they least needed it? Like the day of the grand opening?

"Come on. You said you wanted to talk."

"No. You said I *needed* to talk. But I don't. I'm fine. You saw the newspaper article. I'm heartless."

Before the trip to the attic she had believed that. But watching his happiness at seeing the family ornaments morph into something deep and profound, something that looked like amazement colored with sadness, she wasn't so sure.

Here they were, at a crossroads, a place where he could talk, confide a fact or two or keep everything bottled up, and he picked silence.

She took another sip of the perfect hot cocoa as they walked into a market dedicated to Christmas. Light and color winked at her. Part of her simply wanted to enjoy the break. To let him be the stubborn man he always was.

The other part—the part that knew this could blow up in their faces—tried one more time. "I don't think you're heartless."

"What? You mean all that anger you had for me after reading the article about the hotel was fake?"

Her face reddened. "It's the first personal thing I'd ever read about you."

"And you chose to believe it. Out of hand. No other facts at your disposal, after working with me for two and a half years, you chose to believe it."

"It's not like I really stopped and made a choice—"

"No kidding." He turned around. "We have our cocoa and you know to bring your son here on your sightseeing day. Plus, we both have tons of work." He smiled but the sentiment didn't reach his eyes. "It's time we got back."

He started walking without waiting to see if she'd follow him.

She did, of course. He was her most important client and her ride back to the hotel.

But regret and something else followed her to the waiting

limo, as the wind kicked up and the once-blue sky quickly darkened. There was absolutely no reason in the world why a successful, important guy like Hugo Harrington would care what she thought of him. But she cared about her own behavior. And he was right. After enjoying working for him for two and a half years, she shouldn't have let one article sway her opinion of him.

Of course, her original thoughts about him hadn't exactly been flattering, either. She believed him to be a hard worker, but a taskmaster. A *gorgeous* taskmaster, but still a taskmaster. Though she would let him light up any fantasy, even she admitted she wouldn't want him in real life.

That seemed so horribly wrong. The flashes of kindness she saw in him almost demanded she admit that something was out of sync in his life. And if she wanted to make sure they pulled off the grand and glorious Christmas Eve reopening celebration he'd planned, she might need to know what it was to make sure they didn't fail.

She almost winced. Did she really want to know a guy who'd set the world on fire professionally but had a huge rift with his family?

If it got the project done right—and on time—and to accolades, not condemnation, then, yeah. She was going to have to get to know the real Hugo Harrington enough that she could keep a lid on whatever emotion had almost pushed him over the edge that afternoon.

CHAPTER THREE

A LITTLE AFTER SIX, Hugo texted his driver, ready to go to his flat on the other side of town. Then he texted Erin, telling her she could ride home with him. The afternoon's darkening clouds had unleashed wet snow that turned into thick white flakes that now fell in earnest. Hugo wouldn't force her to wait for a bus when he had a limo at his disposal.

Erin sent him a text thanking him and telling him she was in the attic and would be down soon.

He told her that was no problem as his driver hadn't arrived, then waited another five minutes before he texted Ronnie again.

No answer.

After twenty minutes, he finally got a text informing him that roads had closed. As Hugo had sat in his office working that afternoon, six inches of snow had fallen. Ronnie had spent the time since his last text checking all the routes out of the city. He was sorry but Hugo was stuck at the hotel that night.

He texted back.

No problem. The top floor penthouse suite is ready for guests.

Plus…he had work. He always had work.

For some reason that didn't sit right. It should have made him happy to know he'd be busy. Instead, discontent shimmered through him.

Ronnie bade him good-night. He promised to keep a watch on the condition of the roads and be at the hotel as soon as he could the next morning to take Hugo to the office set up for his Manhattan staff.

Hugo thanked him and rose from his seat. After opening the drapes behind the desk to watch the snow pouring down, he stretched the kinks out of his back.

The office door burst open. "Hey. Sorry, I took longer than a few minutes, I—"

Erin stopped abruptly, staring at him as he stretched. Her eyes wide. A breathy gasp escaping.

Tingles rippled through him, setting a little fire in his blood. He ignored it. He'd forgotten her when he'd so easily told Ronnie it was no problem for him to stay at the hotel. No matter. Erin wasn't going anywhere either. Plus, there were two master suites in the penthouse. He and Erin might be attracted, but he'd already decided not to do anything about it.

"I think I'm the one who has to say sorry. I knew it was snowing but forgot to check on road conditions. My driver can't find a way to get here to pick us up or take us home."

She ventured a little farther into the room. "Even buses aren't running?"

"Ronnie tells me they've closed the roads. It's all good, though, because the top floor of the hotel is a penthouse. There's a little kitchen, a huge sitting room and two bedrooms that are suites." He accented the word *two*. "The place didn't need much repair work, mostly just cleaning. It was done first so I could use it the weeks before I bought my London flat. I'll bet the bar is even stocked."

She stared at him.

He opened his hands in supplication. "Come on. I'm sorry. Really, I've been up to my neck in work. Normal things like snow and bad roads don't always register on my radar."

She took a breath. "That's okay. In all fairness, I didn't notice it either. Give me two minutes to call my mom and say good-night to Noah and I'm all yours."

His blood surged when she said she would be all his. He scolded himself as he reached for his jacket and overcoat while she stood in the hall, talking to her mum and son.

Her call complete, she turned to face him with a smile that about knocked his socks off. Oh, this was dangerous. She was beautiful and smart and everything he looked for in a woman—

To sleep with.

He didn't do relationships. And she needed a relationship.

That reminder firmly in place, he headed toward the door and she smiled again, sending another whoosh of sexual energy through him. Enough voltage that his conclusion waivered.

Was he really sure she needed a relationship? Just because she'd been in a marriage and had a child, that didn't mean she didn't like fun—

Did it?

Good grief! What was wrong with him that he couldn't stop thinking about sleeping with her?

Once again, he reminded himself that she wasn't someone to trifle with. Especially when he needed her. She might not technically be an employee, but she was still working for him.

They rode to the top floor in silence. The doors parted and he motioned for her to step out into the open–floor plan room. A small white-and-marble kitchen sat to the left. A navy-blue-and-sage sitting area took up most of the available space with sofas, chairs, area rugs, a bar and even a piano. Two white doors in the back led to the sleeping suites.

"See? It's big. Plenty of room for both of us." He pointed at the doors. "And two bedrooms."

All right, maybe he'd said that a little too emphatically, making his voice squeak and himself sound like he wasn't as calm and casual about them staying the night as he should be.

Pulling himself together, he strode to the sitting room wet bar that fronted the windows in the back. He pulled out a bottle of bourbon. "Bar's been stocked."

She ventured another step or two inside.

He headed to the kitchen, marched to the refrigerator and swung open the door with relish, ready to show her a stocked fridge. Unfortunately, it was empty.

"Oh."

She finished the walk to the center island. "Actually, we don't have to worry about food." She pulled a plastic bag of grapes and one of cheese out of her briefcase.

He frowned. "I am not a woodland creature who can survive on grapes and cheese."

"Now, don't be snooty." She rummaged in her briefcase again and pulled out another container. This one looked like a lunch sack made of a happy floral print.

"There are two sandwiches in here."

He gaped at her small form. "You eat two sandwiches for lunch?"

"No. Usually I eat one for lunch and one around six at night." She peeked at him sheepishly. "That's when I get hungry. So that's my dinner. I don't wait to go home to eat."

He crossed his arms on his chest. "A sandwich is your dinner?"

"Yes."

"Every day?"

"Yes."

"Is that really healthy?"

Her eyes narrowed. "Look. Are you hungry or not?"

"I guess it depends on what the sandwiches are."

"Turkey and mustard."

Surprise made him smile. "I like turkey and mustard."

"Then you are in luck. Add a few grapes and some cheese and you have dinner."

He slid out of his jacket and took the sandwich she handed him. "Why didn't you eat lunch today?"

"Busy. Later, when we went for our drive, the hot cocoa filled me up."

He remembered their time in the attic. Remembered that she'd more or less talked him down from the ledge when ghosts of Christmas Eves past filled him with sadness and questions. And though he hadn't confided in her, getting out of the office had certainly helped him regain his equilibrium.

"That was good hot chocolate."

"It was," she agreed, then took a seat at the kitchen island that served as a breakfast bar.

He sat beside her. She opened the bag of grapes and the bag of cheese, setting each in the center, an invitation for him to help himself.

He felt odd having Erin share her last food with him. Not that he thought they would be stuck in the hotel for days without sustenance. It was the kindness of the gesture that struck him.

Usually, people didn't care about him. Oh, his driver asked him if he wanted to stop for dinner every night or coffee every morning, but that was more of a logistics thing. Ronnie needed to know if he'd have to pull over at a coffee shop or restaurant.

Erin sharing her food was pure kindness, a gesture that reached into his chest and softened his heart, even as it made him warm all over, made him want to be close to her—

He jumped off his chair. "How about a drink?"

She sniffed a laugh. "What?"

"The bar fridge is stocked with beer and mixers. I'm not a bartender but I can look up anything you want and make it." He smiled. "How hard could it be?"

"I guess not too hard." She licked her lips. "You know, it's been a while since I had a drink. I'm not even sure what I'd like."

"There are various martinis that are popular."

"No. I'm not a fan of hard liquor." Her face brightened. "You know what I want? A glass of wine."

"White or red?"

She giggled. "I can't believe I'm having a drink."

"Well, you don't have to be awake or alert for your son tonight. So, if I were you, I'd take advantage."

"Okay, then I'll have a glass of white."

He brought the bottle to the kitchen island along with two glasses, poured one for each of them and handed the first to her.

She sipped cautiously, then savored. "Anyone who says kids don't really change your life is lying."

He burst out laughing. "I don't think anyone's ever said that."

"Good, because it would be a lie."

The warmth of companionship swelled. That subtle feeling of total relief at being with someone you don't have to put on airs for.

Oh, Lord.

He really liked her.

Which was why he wanted more. He did like her. And they had a whole night—

The thought filled him with longing for things that went far beyond sex. Something he'd never felt before.

He ignored it. If he'd never experienced it before it had to be wrong. Plus, he could be friendly and withstand an attraction.

Couldn't he?

Their gazes caught and his chest expanded. Part of him wondered why he was fighting this. The other part simply couldn't get enough of looking at her.

That was the part that seemed to be taking control.

And he wondered again why he was fighting this.

When their sandwiches were gone and their second glass of wine was almost a memory, Hugo picked up the bottle and directed them to the sofa. Erin couldn't believe her luck in getting to spend time alone with him. To keep this project from imploding, she needed to get to know him. Needed to understand whatever it was that might cause him to snap. He was softening to her and any minute now she expected him to start confiding.

He refilled their wineglasses and sat beside her. Not close. But not far enough away either. She could smell his aftershave and see every muscle move beneath his white shirt.

Not that she was looking.

Oh, hell, who was she kidding? She *was* looking. Being stuck together and having the best-tasting wine on the planet had softened her. Maybe even lowered her inhibitions. If she hadn't been spending time with him for such a good cause—getting to know him, hoping to discover his secret so it didn't tumble out at the wrong time and ruin their grand reopening—she'd be scrambling out of here. At least, excusing herself to go to her room, away from the hypnotic power of those beautiful gray eyes.

But wouldn't that be a waste? They had a bottle of delicious wine. He was chitchatting like a friend. For the first time since she'd had Noah, she was having fun.

Fun.

With grouchy pants Hugo Harrington.

She laughed at her Noah-age reference.

"What's funny?"

Caught, she remembered her no-lie rule and said, "Something popped into my head."

He smiled at her. Simply. Beautifully. "What?"

She swallowed. It had to be the wine, but he was behaving like the man in her dreams. "Something Noah says when my mom's having a bad day."

His smile warmed, grew.

She cleared her throat. Lord, he was gorgeous. And so muscled and male. She swore she felt heat radiating from him.

"Is it hot in here?"

He laughed. "Actually, yes."

"Whew, because I'm definitely feeling warm."

He slowly caught her gaze. "Top floor. Heat rises. I could turn on the air conditioning."

He was only being considerate, but her chest tightened. Her mouth watered. Visions of things that had never really happened filled her head. Could things she'd imagined doing with him for so long actually be coming true? Her breath caught.

She shook her head slightly. Thinking of those things—those fantasies right now—really, really wasn't smart.

But something pulsed between them. With their gazes locked, he leaned in and brushed his lips across hers. Her heart fluttered. The wineglass between her fingers slipped a notch.

He caught it and set it on the coffee table in front of the sofa, along with his glass. Then he leaned in again. One hand on the back of the sofa, the other at his side, he slid his lips across hers again.

Arousal hit in a wave of longing so strong it made her bold. She slid one hand to his shoulder. He slid his hand to her waist, tugging her closer. His mouth moved over hers seductively, drawing her in, and she fell into the kiss, exactly as he lured her to with his clever mouth. Her other hand moved to his shoulder, and this time she was the one to pull him closer.

The kiss changed, deepened. With just enough wine to lower her inhibitions, she let her fantasies meld with reality and tumbled into the warmth surrounding them. Adrenaline competed with arousal for control. When his fingers went to the hem of her T-shirt, anticipation raced through her, and she shifted so he could pull it over her head. He tossed it behind him.

His palm met the soft flesh of her belly, and her blood tingled. When his smooth fingers slid beneath the lace of her yellow bra, it jumped to boiling. Glad she'd worn the pretty bra, she reached behind her to unhook it. As she slipped it off, Hugo rose and took off his shirt. Without giving either of them time to think, he lowered himself to the sofa again, this time on top of her, his thigh between her legs as their bare chests met.

Emotions rushed through her. She wanted to touch him everywhere at once, but slowed her pace, memorizing the feel of his solid skin and those wonderful muscles beneath her hands. He ran his lips along her arms, her shoulders, her chest until he reached her breasts.

From there everything became the frantic motion of two

desperate lovers. She knew her excuse. It had been years since she'd been with a man. But she doubted the great Hugo Harrington went years without company.

His desperation would have confused her except their joining was probably the most perfect physical thing she'd ever experienced, and she didn't let confusion or questions mar it.

When they reached the end, she lay beneath him, sated and dumbfounded. Not just from the pleasure, but because she'd never done anything like this...and with her boss?

She waited for embarrassment or regret. None came.

"You okay?"

She looked up into his smoky gray eyes and smiled. "Honest to Pete, I don't think I have ever been better."

He laughed and she felt the rich rumble in his chest against hers. "That's exactly what a guy likes to hear."

He levered himself to sit beside her, then held out his hand to help her sit.

When they were side by side, he quietly said, "I don't usually lose control like that." He ran his hand along the back of his neck. "But I'm glad I did. That was pretty amazing for me too."

Pride fluttered through Erin. Dumbfounded that she'd so thoroughly pleased him, she had no idea what to say.

He shrugged into his shirt before grabbing the wine bottle. "We could fumble our way through excuses and say it won't happen again because tomorrow we have to work together, and it probably shouldn't happen again. But we still have the rest of tonight. We could go back there." He pointed at the last door. "And not worry about tomorrow until tomorrow."

Part of her knew the next day probably would be awkward. The other part realized this was a once in a lifetime opportunity. A chance for a fantasy to play itself out.

A chance to just be a woman, not an ambitious business owner, not a daughter helping support her mom, not the mother of a feisty three-year-old. Thanks to a blanket of snow, she could simply be a woman for a few more hours.

With the sexiest man she'd ever met.

He bent and cruised his lips along her neck.

Oh, yeah. She wasn't letting this chance get away.

She woke nestled into his side and her heart swelled. He was perfect. He'd shown her another side of himself the night before. A sexy side, a demanding side—mixed with unexpected softness. He'd touched her with a reverence that stole her breath and made her wonder—

Was there more to Hugo Harrington than a guy driven to succeed? When she added their night together to his emotion when he'd seen the decorations in the attic, she knew that deep down he was a normal guy. And she wondered if she'd only seen his harder, secretive side because that's all he showed his employees.

"Good morning."

His words tiptoed across the pillows to her.

Here it was. The moment of truth. She wished he would be sexy, sweet Hugo. But the night before he basically told her there would only be one night—

He raised himself up and onto his side, then ran his lips across hers in a soft kiss that melted her heart. But he quickly pulled back, turned away from her and grabbed his phone from the bedside table.

"Roads are cleared."

Her heart sambaed. Sweet, sexy Hugo was gone.

A wish that things could be different tried to form but she stopped it. He'd spelled things out after the first time they'd made love. But she'd wanted her fantasy lover. And she'd gotten him. The fact that he'd been better in reality than he had in her daydreams didn't change who he was: cool, aloof Hugo Harrington, keeping the nice guy side of himself hidden, probably because he was a man with secrets.

Still.

He hadn't told her one personal thing the night before.

"You can go home and change, if you want." He didn't look up from his phone. "I won't tell your boss."

A thousand emotions sparred in her brain. Everything about the guy he'd been the night before had been perfect. But she also knew she'd never get involved with another man with secrets, another man who didn't understand intimacy. A man who only let the nice guy out when he needed or wanted something.

She swallowed. "I think I'll be okay in my clothes from yesterday, after I get a shower."

Damn her voice for stuttering with confusion.

He set his phone down with a sigh. "Sorry if I seem grouchy to you. I'm not in the habit of sleeping with women I like."

The fact that he liked her revved her heart, but it also didn't make sense.

"You only sleep with women you don't like?"

"I only sleep with women who know I'm not the kind of guy to make a commitment."

His voice was so casual, so confident that her spine stiffened. "Are you accusing me of falling in love with you overnight?"

He had the good graces to look sheepish. "No." He paused and combed his fingers through his tousled hair, turning back into her Hugo from the night before. "I'm saying you're special. Nice. A good person. And the last thing I want to do is hurt you."

The admission hadn't been easy for him and her soul melted. The sense that spending more time together might turn him into her Hugo forever raced through her brain, but she stopped it. He was a workaholic who had secrets—

Maybe lots of them.

Plus, his project was at stake. She hadn't been hired to keep him sane, but in a way that's what event planners did. They took care of details so the people who hired them could relax. She'd realized the day before that he had memories that haunted him. She'd been grateful for getting stranded together because it was an opportunity to get to know him well enough to make sure he didn't have a meltdown. Even though he really hadn't told her any secrets—

But maybe he didn't have to? He might not have shared a specific secret, but spending time with him had shown her he had some soft spots. The chink in his armor wasn't *one* thing—one memory about his past—that she had to keep him away from. It was *him.* The nice guy inside him who appeared when he thought of his past.

In a way, that made things easier. She didn't have to probe and ponder, trying to figure out one big secret. All she had to do was make sure he didn't linger too long thinking about his past.

He glanced over. "Want to call room service for breakfast?"

She frowned. "We could have had room service last night?"

He laughed. "Probably not. I'm guessing the kitchen staff that's been experimenting with recipes had already gone for the day. But we could have found something to eat. Still, because you provided dinner, I'd like to repay you with breakfast."

She peered around. She didn't really want the chef and/ or waitstaff to come up to the penthouse and find her with Hugo. More than that, though, she'd figured out what she had to do to protect his project. There was no point hanging out too long, getting attached, hoping for something that wouldn't happen.

Saddened by that, but realizing the truth of it, she turned toward the shower again. "I've got a lot of work to do."

He smiled. "Okay." But he rose from the bed. Before she reached the bathroom door, he did. Gloriously naked, he made her heart pitter-patter and some of the better parts of their night together played in her head. Then he caught her upper arms and kissed her gently, and everything inside her told her to forget about work. They only needed more time together for sweet Hugo to come out of hiding and stay out—

But a picture of life with him, another man with secrets, popped into her head, along with the feelings of inadequacy because Josh hadn't confided in her. It might be years before Hugo got comfortable enough that he'd let all of his guard down.

She remembered all the lonely days of living with a guy who had a secret and the horrible pain when she'd realized he *had* confided in someone else.

No.

She didn't want that. Not any of it.

When she finally was ready to date, she'd be looking for someone who treated her like an equal. Someone who trusted her. Someone she could trust.

Sexy—gorgeous—as Hugo Harrington was, he was not the guy for her, and thinking she could change him was foolish.

She eased away and entered the bathroom, ending their one-night stand.

When the penthouse elevator dinged to take Erin downstairs, Hugo headed to the shower.

That had gone well. Not only had he and Erin enjoyed

the evening, but her departure made him believe she was on his wavelength. No pouting. No flirting to extend their time. A nice, clean break.

He frowned. Why did that give him an empty feeling in his chest?

Just as she hadn't fallen in love with him overnight, he hadn't fallen for her.

Had he?

Of course not. He wasn't accusing himself of falling in love, but maybe entering those initial stages of liking someone—

No. He'd liked her before last night. And he knew making love added to those feelings, but he was a smart guy. Not about protecting himself but protecting *her*.

He'd stay in line to protect her.

He stepped into the shower. After a quick scrubbing, he got out and redressed in the clothes from the day before, but when he picked up his shirt a memory slid through him. The lightness of joy that had filled him when she hadn't protested him yanking her T-shirt over her head or when he'd reached for the buttons on this very white shirt.

The memory shivered through him and he shook his head. He had to stop that. He wasn't the kind of guy to dwell on a one-night stand. Especially not one that had gone exactly as it should have. They'd enjoyed each other. But they both knew this shouldn't go any further.

The empty feeling filled his chest again.

Confused, he stopped those crazy thoughts, called the kitchen to order breakfast, texted Ronnie telling him he wouldn't be leaving for the Manhattan team office for another hour, then scrolled through the news on his phone. An hour and a half later, he was with his New York staff, working.

But he couldn't get past the never-before-experienced

regret that he really could only have that one night with Erin. His brain edged toward trying to come up with ways or reasons they could spend another night together, and when he realized he was thinking about her again, he stopped it.

Because it was wrong. She was a mum. She had responsibilities. And he was a lone wolf. His own brother and sister were wary of him because he had left them. Even his mother had let him go. Proving some people weren't made to be loved. Some people were born to be successful, so strong they were off-putting.

Not in a horrible, villainous way. But simply in a way that didn't give them enough time for relationships, enough mental energy.

And Erin absolutely deserved someone who would love her completely.

The thought dinged his heart again, but he ignored it. He was not the guy she needed.

CHAPTER FOUR

ERIN WORKED HARD all morning, happy when her mom brought Noah to her office a little after noon with lunch and a change of clothes.

"Thanks. Not only do I need to get into something clean, but I was starving!"

"No breakfast, I'm guessing," her mom said as she handed Erin her lunch bag full of goodies.

Erin's face reddened. "No. Got right to work."

Her mom glanced around. "Where'd you sleep?"

"There are some finished rooms on the top floor. Hugo took one. I took the other." She blanched internally at the fact that she hadn't mentioned they were part of a penthouse suite. But, really, her no-lying rule was getting ridiculous. Surely there had to be a middle ground.

"I showered, but putting the same clothes back on was icky."

Marge laughed. "You should be glad you had a shower. Not everybody is so lucky to be stranded in a hotel."

"Right." She bit into her sandwich and groaned with pleasure. "So good."

"You really are starving."

"Yes. I'm guessing the roads are clear if the buses are running."

"London road crews might have needed a little time, but they got the job done."

"Or the snow on the streets melted," Hugo said, entering the office.

His beautiful gray eyes met Erin's and damned if she didn't blush again.

"London weather is odd." He faced Marge. "I see you brought lunch for Erin."

Her mom all but swooned. She'd probably be thrilled if Erin told her they'd spent the night together. "Yes. And lucky thing too since she was starving."

"She shouldn't be. The kitchen is filled with chefs and helpers trying out recipes for the grand opening. They could probably feed her for a week."

He turned to Erin. "When you're through, I'd like to see you in my office."

She nodded and he left.

Marge watched him go. "Have you at least *tried* flirting with him?"

Erin squeezed her eyes shut. She wasn't embarrassed that she'd slept with Hugo. But most grown women didn't tell their mom about their lovers.

"Mom! Seriously! The guy is devoted to work. Even if I fell madly in love with him, he's not the kind to settle down."

"Yeah but think of the fun you could have—and practice for when you are ready for a relationship."

Why did having a no-strings-attached affair suddenly sound like the perfect plan?

Erin shook her head to clear it of the ridiculous thought. She had to get herself back on neutral ground with him so she could watch for those memories that hit him the hardest and steer him away from them.

Plus, no matter what the situation, she would not discuss her sex life with her mother. "Please stop."

Noah toddled up to her and she pulled him onto her lap. They talked about snow and the story his grandmother had read to him the night before. Then Erin told them she really had to get back to work. But she'd be home that night at the regular time.

When they were gone, she raced to a restroom to change into her clean clothes, sighing with relief when she finally felt normal.

But her "normal" quickly disappeared when she reached Hugo's office and hesitated by the door. She really could have some fun times with him—

No. She knew herself. She wasn't the kind of woman who became someone's lover. She'd always been a romantic looking for true love. Even more now that Josh's betrayals had almost pushed her to believe love didn't exist. It did. It had to. She had friends who had found it. And now that she was actually letting herself think about this, she wanted what they had. Though an affair sounded appealing and logical, eventually she'd fall in love and he wouldn't.

Then she'd be hurt…and he wouldn't.

Her resolve in place, she knocked on his door.

"Come in, Erin."

"Just wanted to make sure I wasn't interrupting."

"I told you to come to my office. That's the definition of not interrupting."

She took the few steps to the chair in front of his desk, looking at his glossy hair, his broad shoulders, and suppressed a sigh. Fantasy Hugo had definitely disappeared some time during the night and Real Hugo was back.

But that was good. They needed to return to the place where he saw her as he had the day before. Someone he employed, but also someone he could trust. Someone he could talk to.

She sat on the chair and opened her notebook. He got right to the ideas he'd come up with the night before.

The night before?

Seriously?

While she was sleeping, sated and happy, nestled against him, he'd gotten out his phone and made notes?

Maybe she'd inspired him?

Maybe she was his muse?

It was such a romantic notion. Being his muse, she'd be like the other half of him. Yin to his yang—

"Erin? Did you get that?"

She snapped to attention, embarrassed to have been caught daydreaming about something she'd already dismissed. "I'm sorry. I got the part about oranges but didn't hear the other thing."

The tips of his ears turned red.

Let him ignore the reason for her lapse in concentration and get them back to work. Please do not let him ask what had her distracted.

"I said my brother remembered the name of the shop where our mum bought stockings that were stuffed for all the kids in attendance."

She sat up. "You talked to your brother?"

"Briefly."

Forgetting all about being his muse, she looked for signs of distress. Anger. Sadness. Anything that might throw him off his game. "This morning?"

His eyes met hers. "Yes."

Her soul forgot to breathe. Those eyes were so rich with emotion and whether it was a good idea, she and Hugo had connected the day before. First getting cocoa, then sleeping together. She knew the significance of him speaking with someone from his family. Family he was having trouble getting along with—

Was that his big worry? Not that a sad memory would spoil his Christmas Eve celebration, but that his family might?

She sucked in a deep draft of air. He might not out and out admit it. But she saw it now. So clearly it amazed her that it took her so long.

He'd mentioned hanging ornaments with his brother and sister. Even asked if she thought they'd come to the Christmas Eve celebration—

"Oh, my gosh. You're worried your brother and sister won't show up."

Hugo gaped at her. She looked cute and huggable in her jeans and sweatshirt and his heart had done a somersault when she'd entered his office, but her words sucked all the air out of his lungs.

"Do you think I shouldn't be?"

"I don't know." She caught his gaze. "It could be a real embarrassment if you have Ornament Hanging Ceremony in the program for your Christmas Eve event but your brother and sister don't attend."

He tapped his pencil on the desk. It was a problem he knew existed but not something he let himself think about too much because he *hoped* they'd see his dedication to the hotel and show up.

Yet she'd homed in on it.

"You know, you could just hang an ornament yourself."

He frowned. "And leave the other two sitting on the table? For everybody to see? An obvious reminder that my brother and sister didn't come?"

"If they decide not to attend, you can gloss right over it by making a big deal out of choosing one of the three ornaments as if it's a last-minute decision, part of the ceremony. Not that all three ornaments need to be hung. Then once you walk away, I'll swoop in and scoop up the other two and whisk them away."

He took a breath, thinking that through. It was perfect and it solved one of his worst worries.

Some of the tightness in his spine loosened. "Okay. That'll work."

"Now, back to the stockings. I can call your brother for the store's name, but I'm going to need at least an estimate of how many I'll need."

Weirdness settled over him. She'd relieved one of his biggest fears and moved on to the next item on her to-do list as if nothing had happened?

He cleared his throat. "You'll need to check with the reservations crew to get the number of kids who will be attending, and that will give you an accurate count for the stockings."

She scribbled some notes. "I might also poke around upstairs a bit, dig around for either an actual stocking or pictures of the stockings."

She looked up and caught his gaze. A bubble of something formed in his chest. She was a pro. So good at what she did, she didn't even realize how fast and how easily she'd helped him.

Joy skipped along his skin, sensitizing it. And he suddenly knew why he kept thinking about her, about their one-night stand. Their time together had been perfect. Spontaneous. Open. Immensely enjoyable.

His aggressive self, the one that always went after what he wanted, wanted her. Again. And maybe again and again.

Maybe every night she was here, in London.

Erin said, "I'm thinking we should get ten or twelve extra stockings in case there are walk-ins on Christmas Eve."

Hugo's bubble burst. He might want her. But she didn't even appear to be thinking about him. About the possibility of another night together.

"There'll be no walk-ins. We hope to have the place booked."

Her attention fully focused on the notepad she held, she said, "Okay. I'll check with reservations today and every day until the actual event."

He said, "Good thinking," but his pride was a little bruised. While he fought a hellish battle to get himself to stop dwelling on her, she had no problem talking about stockings?

Which was exactly what needed to be happening for the grand opening. The biggest project of his life. The goal he'd been working toward since his stepfather kicked him out.

Plus, she obviously didn't feel the same way he did. He could see himself longing to be with her, if she showed even one sign that she wanted to be with him. But she was a pro. And he was behaving like a smitten fool.

Annoyed with himself, he said, "I'm also toying with the idea of taking the celebration out to the courtyard garden."

Her eyes widened with excitement. "Wow."

"My parents' celebration was wonderful. Warm and cozy. Though I definitely want those elements in our party… I also want a fresh spin. Does taking it to the garden seem like it would be a fresh spin or sound like too much?"

"What if you have the dinner exactly as it used to be in the ballroom, then have everyone go outside for the visit from Santa?"

He loved her idea but couldn't believe he'd asked for her opinion. He never needed anyone's opinion. If he had an idea, he either used it or he chucked it. Fighting his desire to sleep with her again had knocked him off his game.

Which was another reason to get himself beyond this. To stop wanting something he couldn't have.

He waved his hand, dismissing her. "Anyway, that's it for now."

She smiled and rose from her seat, closing her spiral notebook. He glanced at it, wondering why she didn't take notes on her phone, then realized she had an actual, physical record of everything they discussed, the theme of the event and the work she had done. If something happened to her, her staff probably knew to find that book.

She wasn't merely beautiful and sexy; she was smart. And today he was finding her intelligence every bit as sexy and her shiny red hair—

"I can go?"

"Yes! Yes!" He bounced from his seat and hit his knee on the top of the desk. Damn his wandering thoughts. He was behaving like an idiot.

This stopped now. No more rambling. No more noticing things about her.

They'd had a one-night stand. They worked together. He *employed* her. His mind should have already moved on to other things.

She turned and walked out without so much as a good-bye or a smile and his pride dinged again.

This time he did groan as he lowered himself to his seat. He decided his weird reaction was a result of the pressure of the project and didn't think about it for the rest of the day.

But when it came time to leave the hotel that evening, his thoughts jumped back to her. It wasn't right for her to ride a bus after a twelve-hour day. He couldn't break his promise to make her stay comfortable just because he needed time away from her.

When Erin left the hotel that night, Hugo leaned against his limo door. He looked like a teenage boy waiting for the girl from math class to come out so he could talk to her. The urge to tease him rose in her, along with a yearning to simply be with him.

But she said nothing. They'd had a night of fun. Neither intended for it to go any further than it had. She needed to keep the objectivity going that she'd cultivated that day— no matter how difficult it was to get their night together out of her head.

"Are you taking me home?"

He opened the door. "Yes. I promised you a nice stay in London. I'm not marring that with late-night bus trips."

"Okay." She slid into the limo.

He got in beside her and reached out to close the glass that separated the passengers from the driver. She frowned. Why would he care if his driver heard their conversation?

She wondered if she'd done something wrong. Except, she hadn't. She made sure every bit of work she did for him was as good as it could be. Her actions always spoke louder than her words. She hadn't done anything wrong.

So what wouldn't he want his driver to hear?

They made the two turns that would take them to her apartment and the limo stayed silent.

Silent. He didn't even say, *How was your day? Any problems with the project? Anything you want to discuss?*

The car stayed quiet.

So she said, "How was your day?"

He glanced over at her with a frown. "What?"

She sighed. "Just making conversation."

"Oh. Okay, then. My day was fine." He smiled briefly, a weird, fake smile. "How was your day?"

"Um…good. I guess. Getting a lot of things done."

"Good."

She took a breath. "And I'm glad your day was fine too."

"Yes. I was too."

The conversation died, but that was better than enduring the stilted discussion of how their days had gone.

She suddenly missed romantic Hugo. That guy knew exactly what to say. But maybe this was for the best? This stilted, emotionless guy was the real Hugo, and no matter how much she yearned for things to be different, *this* was reality.

She tried to shove that truth into her brain so hard it stuck, but memories of him being sweet and kind, sexy and romantic kept writing over them.

It was going to be harder than she thought to forget about their one-night stand.

CHAPTER FIVE

THE NEXT MORNING, Erin immediately went to the attic to search for stockings. Stooped in front of a big box, she might have stopped at the first sample she'd found, but it wasn't alone. Two different stockings had been stored together.

She rocked back on her heels. She should ask Hugo if the hotel purchased one kind of stocking for boys and one for girls. Or one for older kids and one for younger kids. Or a different kind of stocking every year, making each year's offering a keepsake.

But, frankly, she wasn't in the mood to see him.

She told herself that wasn't good. The guy was her biggest client. It shouldn't matter one way or another if they hadn't been able to have a decent conversation in his limo the night before. Or that the horrible attempt at chitchat had actually made her long for romantic Hugo.

She squeezed her eyes shut. *It doesn't matter.*

Except she was back to thinking about him again, wishing things could be different when she knew they couldn't.

And she had a job to do.

She snatched the two stockings from the floor as she rose and headed to the attic door.

She would set their relationship right simply by going to his office and asking about the stockings. She would be the nicest person on the planet to him. She would not fail. *He* would not fail.

Because, damn it, that's what she did! Made everything perfect for her clients.

She stormed to the general manager's space Hugo used when he was in the hotel, but he hadn't arrived yet. His habit was to come in around ten or so and stay a few hours, but that schedule wasn't etched in stone. If he needed time with the staff in charge of the renovations, he'd stay with the team of New York employees as long as he needed. If he needed to come back to the hotel in the afternoon, he did that. He floated around, being where he had to be to get things done. And he wasn't here now. Apparently, he didn't need to be.

She turned to leave as the office phone rang.

Pivoting to face the desk again, she stared at it. She hadn't realized the landlines had been hooked up. Everybody was using their cell, if only for convenience. Running back and forth between the hotel and office, Hugo was easier to reach that way. And she could be reached anywhere in the hotel, or at the florists, the bakery or any one of her vendors.

The phone rang again.

She inched into the room. It seemed rude not to answer it. Especially since it could be Hugo calling…

No. He'd call her cell. He wouldn't even know she was in this room.

It rang again.

Damn it! She wasn't the kind of person who didn't answer a ringing phone.

She raced to the desk, catching the receiver as the phone rang one more time. "Hello?"

"Who is this?" a female voice asked. "Isn't this the Harrington Park Hotel?"

"Yes. I'm sorry. I'm not a receptionist. I just happened to be in the office waiting for…someone when you called."

"Would that someone be my brother Hugo?"

Erin's breath caught. *Hugo's sister?*

"Yes. He's usually at the hotel by now, but he must have gotten tied up with his regular staff at the office."

"Aren't you in an office?"

She winced. "I'm in an office at the hotel. I'm Erin Hunter, the event planner organizing the Christmas Eve celebration."

"Ah, you're the miracle worker he hired."

Erin frowned at the phone. "I wouldn't know about miracle worker, but I do like to get things done."

"Don't mind my mood. I'm Sally, by the way. I'm not usually this grumpy but things are progressing weirdly on the garden."

Intrigued, Erin sat. "Anything I can do to help?"

"No. But I need to talk to my brother. Can you have him ring me?"

"Sure." She frowned again. "Why not just call his cell?"

Sally cleared her throat. "He gave me the number, but I threw it away."

Erin's heart broke a little. She knew how much Hugo wanted his sister at the ornament ceremony and she'd tossed away his number. Still, having Hugo call Sally might be a good first step to settling their differences.

"Okay. Sure. I'll have him call you." She paused, then said, "Does he have *your* number?"

"Yes. My cell." She laughed. "Unless he tossed it."

Erin waited a second as Sally rattled off her number. "Thanks… Um… I could give you his number if you'd like."

Sally paused a little too long. Giving Erin the sense she didn't want any part of Hugo in her life.

Finally, she said, "You know what? I'm just going to send him an email. And, Erin… Don't let my brother run you off the way he does most other people."

Something about that hit Erin oddly. But the quiet in the limo ride home the night before suddenly made sense. Had he been trying to run her off? Not as a subcontractor. He'd made it abundantly clear that he liked her work and wanted her to stay.

Running her off was personal.

"Actually, we've worked together for years."

"So that must be the secret to getting along with him. Have something he wants."

Erin almost said, "Maybe." But decided against it. Hugo was her boss and she wouldn't badmouth him to his family. In fact, everything about the conversation seemed wrong. Hugo should have been the one talking to Sally, not her.

She said, "I'll give him your number."

"No. No. I'll email him."

Erin said, "Okay. Fine." Then she and Sally said their goodbyes.

Though she had tons of work to do, her mind spun with possibilities of what Sally might want. She was still in Hugo's seat when he walked into the office.

"Problem?"

Caught, she bounced to attention. "No… Yes. Maybe. I—" She stopped her babbling. "Two things. I have a question and your sister, Sally, called."

She handed him the slip of paper with Sally's number and his lips lifted into a smile as he glanced down to read it. But when he saw only Sally's number, he frowned and looked up at Erin again.

"She has my number." His frown grew. "Yet she called on the landline?"

"Yes." The troubled expression on his face wouldn't let her tell him that Sally had tossed his cell number.

"We didn't really chat." Damn it. She suddenly found herself in choppy waters again. Holding back information. Downplaying the call. When she'd sworn to herself that she'd always be honest. Painfully honest.

She took a breath. "Your sister was confused because I'd answered the phone that she'd thought you'd answer. That's all."

That and Sally had clearly let Erin know she wasn't Hugo's biggest fan.

Damn it. No matter how honest she wanted to be, she couldn't say that. Wasn't there some sort of etiquette about this? Like: if you can't say something nice, don't say anything at all?

Yes! That was it! Her mom had said that all the time when Erin was a little girl.

Plus, if she really wanted to get bottom-line honest on this… Getting Sally to the Christmas Eve celebration might fall under Erin's purview, but Hugo's relationship with his sister was none of her business. She had no responsibility to tell Hugo her conclusions and suspicions.

It wasn't like holding back a cancer diagnosis.

She took another breath as her thoughts simultaneously cleared about Sally and muddled about Josh. The pain of his holding that back rolled through her once again. No matter how hard she tried, or how many other circumstances she compared it to, his not telling her had been unforgiveable.

"Anyway, she said she'd email you to discuss the garden. And I wanted to talk about the Christmas stockings."

He rounded the desk as she scooted to the front. "What about the stockings?"

"I found two styles of stockings in a box. If they had

been in two different boxes, I might have assumed your parents bought a unique stocking for every year...sort of like a keepsake. But they were in the same box, making me wonder if younger kids and older kids got different stockings or boys and girls?"

"Different stockings every year. All kids get the same one."

"So, they are like a keepsake?"

He dropped to his seat. "I guess. I never saved mine..."

"Maybe your mother did?"

His frown deepened as he glanced at some papers on his desk, as if his attention was off the stockings and moving on because he had too much work to do to dawdle.

"I think those are requisitions dropped off by subcontractors."

"I know what they are."

His tone caused her to step back, as she reminded herself that he was working to create emotional distance between them—

Except he was also a guy whose sister had tossed his cell number.

She remembered the happily surprised expression on his face when he'd been told his sister had called and how it had shifted when he saw she'd only left a number for him to return her call. What if that had really hurt him? Erin knew he wanted his sister and brother at the Christmas Eve celebration.

He was renovating the family hotel.

He'd given his siblings a role in the new hotel.

What if he wanted to reunite? What if he'd spent millions of dollars buying this run-down building and millions more renovating it? Not just to recreate his past, but to reunite his family?

The truth of it hit so hard, she almost had to sit.

"Erin?"

"What?" She shook her head to bring herself back to the present. "I'm sorry. What were you saying?"

She glanced at his face and saw lines she'd missed before this. She saw sadness in his gray eyes. Not the emptiness of not caring as she'd always believed. But a bone-deep sadness.

"I said we get new stockings every year. Go crazy picking out a new design or find the stockings from the first year and buy those." He frowned. "Though I'm not sure how you'd know which stocking had been chosen for the first year my parents had this celebration."

"Boxes aren't marked."

He dismissed her by looking down at his work again. "Figure it out. It doesn't matter either way. A new stocking type or find the first one."

She backed up, inching toward the open door. "Okay."

"Close that."

She nodded, but as she closed the door her heart hurt, and guilt tiptoed through her for being so angry with him for making things difficult in the limo the night before.

A man who'd been estranged from his family for so long might not know how to make a connection.

Of course, he was the one who'd left his family. So, wasn't it true that he had no one to blame but himself?

Thursday afternoon concluded with a short meeting with the subcontractors doing the renovation work. Hugo strode into the conference room, his jacket off, his tie loose and his sleeves rolled up. This was the real work. Jay had the kitchen and menu under control. Sally had some problems with the courtyard garden, but he had every confidence in her. His brother and sister had become remarkable adults.

And Erin would make the celebration perfect.

Even as he thought the last, he saw her sitting on one of the chairs around the conference table, laughing with the construction supervisor.

Annoyance skittered through him at the sight of her so easygoing and happy with another man, along with that silly joy he always felt when she was around. The joy he had to fight so hard to ignore he could only talk about work with her. Which made riding home in the limo quiet and awkward.

"Good afternoon, everyone."

The men and women at the conference table came to attention at the sound of his voice.

"I hope everyone's got a good report for me."

General murmurs of agreement floated around him as he sat.

"Except for Ms. Hunter, whose presence confuses me."

"I need reports too," Erin said, totally unaffected by his negativism. "I need to know when rooms will be done so I can assign decorating crews." She caught his gaze. Her blue eyes held an emotion that confused him. She should be on her high horse, her pride radiating like the rays of the sun because he'd questioned her presence. Instead, she studied him as if he were a bug under a microscope.

"Plus, I want to check their pics from other Christmas Eve celebrations to see if I can piece together which photos are from the first party...and if any one of them shows the Christmas stockings."

His breath stuttered. He'd told her it didn't matter if she figured out which of the stockings were from the first celebration, but it did. He wanted to do this right and, as always, she understood that and was trying to make it happen.

She smiled slightly, knowing she'd pleased him.

His heart warmed and that silly joy filled him to overflowing. He cleared his throat, but the warmth stayed with him. His voice was gruff when he said, "Everybody hand over their pictures. Let Erin examine them."

"I'll get them back to you," she promised with a smile, as the supervisors who had the pictures pulled them from clipboards or file folders and passed them down the table.

Hugo's head tilted. He'd seen charming people finagle their own way all the time. He'd seen bossy people force their way on others. But he'd never seen anyone softly, sweetly lure everyone in the way Erin did.

She smiled at him and gave him a quick nod as if to say he could go on to the first item on his list, and for a few seconds he only stared at her.

Everything about her was so damned easy. Even making love had been so natural and simple that maybe he'd missed part of the beauty of it.

With a shake of his head, he told himself he was crazy or going soft and that could not happen. He had a job to do. He asked a question of the general contractor who began to give his report, but Hugo's gaze strayed to Erin again.

He'd been rude to her the night before. Snippy with her that morning. Yet here she was, her normal self.

No. She'd realized the Christmas stockings from the first celebration had meaning for him and she was going out of her way to find them.

People were always trying to please him. Employees. Subcontractors. Vendors. But this was personal. He could feel it.

He knew it when she sent him a soft smile when she noticed him staring at her.

His heart flipped in his chest. A million confusing thoughts assaulted him. But the one that stuck was that he'd like to be back in bed with her. His head on a pillow, his arm around her shoulders tucking her beside him.

Crazy.

Seriously. He was protecting *her*. Why couldn't he get a handle on this?

"And that's where we stand, big picture-wise."

Arnie Simmons leaned back in his chair, ending his report, and Hugo leaned back too. He'd missed every damned word the man had said because he'd been fixating on Erin.

The painting supervisor went up next and Hugo paid attention as if his life depended on it. The truth was, he'd sleep with Erin again in a New York minute. Hell, he'd sleep with her every day until the project was over and maybe once or twice in Manhattan after they returned.

But he wouldn't ever settle down and that would hurt her.

And in that moment, he made a vow never, ever to hurt her. In every possible way, she was too good for him.

Sadness replaced the longing that had filled him, but he accepted the pain of it. He knew who he was. Knew there were a lot of things he'd never have because he didn't make those kinds of commitments.

CHAPTER SIX

FRIDAY MORNING, HUGO strode into the Harrington Park Hotel feeling better. Scaffolding had been moved from the lobby to the ballroom where painting had begun. Yet another step was complete. Things were proceeding on schedule. Not a ripple of change had been made in the original plan, and that bolstered his belief that they really were going to do this. They would have the hotel up and running and the most amazing Christmas Eve celebration.

And nothing anyone said or did that day could ruin his mood.

Then he saw Erin bounding down the hall toward him, her movements easy and fluid in her blue jeans and simple gray T-shirt.

Her smile was quick and genuine. "Can I have five minutes?"

He forced a smile so she wouldn't notice his heart burst with that damned joy again. He'd had this conversation with himself yesterday. His inability to get ahold of himself was an aberration. Once he set his mind to something, he did it.

"Sure. Follow me into the office." He walked in, tossed his briefcase on the desk and took off his overcoat.

"I have a delivery scheduled for tomorrow."

"So?" He knew the next day was Saturday, but *she* knew

working Saturdays was always on the table with a deadline this close.

"I promised Noah I'd take him sightseeing tomorrow. If I can't, I'm not sure how I'll make it up to him. So I thought I'd simply switch days. There's not a lot on today's agenda for me. I'd like to take today to show him the sights and work tomorrow."

It made perfect sense. And if he hadn't been distracted by the way her hair seemed to pick up light and make it shimmer, he might have immediately said yes. Now he had to fake annoyance.

"There are always things you can do here."

"Or I could take my son to see the sights on a day that's light with work, as you promised I could."

Thank goodness he'd made the promise. He looked down at his work. He gruffly said, "Okay, fine." But he felt a little guilty for kind of punishing her for something that was his problem. He was the one having trouble being around her. She was fine. It was time to act accordingly.

He glanced up at her. "You know what? You're right. Today's a perfect day to take him sightseeing."

Her face filled with surprise. "Really?"

"Yeah. I'm always semiprepared for bad news. That's why I reacted poorly. Don't mind me."

And that was as close as he would get to either an apology or an explanation. He did have a reputation for being a grouch to protect.

But he also realized that it wasn't her fault that he was so drawn to her. Plus, he was the one who had seduced her, and look at how easily she'd adapted to it meaning nothing even though what they'd shared had been *something*.

It really had.

She said, "Thanks. I'll see you tomorrow."

"And, Erin, don't forget to take Noah to Southbank."

"That's the first place we're going."

"Good. We'll talk tomorrow."

She walked out of his office. Knowing she couldn't see, he watched the sway of her hips, remembering the way they'd felt beneath his hands.

Everything about her and that night had been perfect. If he were a sappier kind of guy, he might have mooned over her.

Wait—

Wasn't that what he was doing? Noticing light dancing in her hair. Jealous when one of his supervisors had made her laugh. Watching her graceful walk.

Identifying the problem put everything into perspective and he settled in to work. Telling himself that now that he'd figured things out, he'd be better. He especially hoped she had a great time with Noah and that Noah enjoyed the sights.

He frowned, wondering if she'd know where to take her son other than Southbank. After all, she spent twelve to fourteen hours a day in *this hotel*. She hadn't seen any sights herself. Probably didn't know anything about London—

He remembered how she'd loved Southbank.

What a great day that had been. How nice it had felt to be outside. How nice it had been to think about Christmas, see it blossoming all around them, without relating it back to the hotel.

He'd spent the last decades thinking of nothing but acquiring the family hotel and reuniting with his brother and sister, and it was working. Sally might be standoffish, but he swore he'd win her over. But suddenly today, he wondered how much of life he'd missed. What had passed him by because he'd been consumed by this hotel?

His skin began to itch. The room felt small and tight.

He thought of Erin again. If he closed his eyes and let himself go, he could feel her smooth skin against his. He could remember her laugh. He also recalled his promise to her that she'd show her son a different view of Christmas and though she could do that all by herself, the strange sense that he owed her overwhelmed him. Not only had he promised, but also he'd been grumpy with her when he was the one who couldn't get *her* out of his mind.

That had been so wrong.

He sprang out of his seat. He couldn't let her go on thinking he was a grinch. And he knew how to fix it. His workload was broader and more encompassing than Erin's, but he could afford a day off too.

He had his driver take him to Southbank, knowing he might be early or that he might not even find her in the crowd. Then his cell phone buzzed with a text from a subcontractor and he smiled. He could find her. All he had to do was call her and ask where she was.

Erin stared at the phone after finishing her call with Hugo.

He *wanted* to make sure she and Noah saw all the right things?

More unexpected, he was taking the day off…for *her*?

She pushed Noah's stroller in the direction of Jubilee Park, where they'd arranged to meet.

When he walked up to her, still in his suit for work and cashmere overcoat, her heart skipped a beat. He might only be playing the role of kind boss, or honest negotiator who intended to keep his promise, but when she looked at him, her thoughts drifted back to their night together.

When he'd laughed.

When he'd kissed her with abandon and loved her like a man starved for intimacy.

And maybe he was. Watching him so closely these past

few days, she'd noticed things he couldn't hide and drawn conclusions about his longing to recreate his past. Then, having spoken with Sally, she understood his fears. While he labored to bring his family together, there was no guarantee that his family wanted *him* in their lives.

She almost couldn't comprehend that. Her father had divorced her mom when Erin was too young to remember, leaving her without an extended family because her dad remarried and moved on. Plus, her mom had been the only child of a couple who had emigrated from Ireland. They'd been alone until Josh. Erin had thought she'd begun building the family she and her mom had yearned for. Then Josh had died.

She'd always believed people with siblings were lucky because siblings were close, there for each other.

But something had happened to ruin the Harringtons. Not just their hotel. And whether Hugo was the perpetrator of the disaster or the victim wasn't as cut-and-dried as she'd originally thought.

Unless he was sorry that he'd broken up his family? And not trying to recreate an idyllic past but trying to make amends?

"Hey."

She smiled at him. Evil villain or misunderstood, tormented soul, she didn't know. But she *was* happy to have someone who knew London to show her and her son around.

And maybe—just maybe—he'd explain some of his life.

"Hey."

He stooped to Noah's level. "And how are you today?"

Noah glanced down and mumbled, "Good."

Erin said, "He'll be happy once we start moving."

Hugo rose. "I get that. He's a man of action."

For some reason that made Noah giggle. Hugo's face

transformed. He glanced down at the little boy as if he were an absolute miracle and Erin's heart stuttered. She suddenly saw not a successful guy or an exacting, grouchy boss, but a guy who'd lived his entire adult life without a connection to anyone.

He pointed to the building behind them. "There's a sea-life aquarium in there. I think he'll love it."

Erin pushed the stroller toward the building with Hugo lifting the front end to make short work of the steps. He paid their admission and Erin decided not to argue. While things were good between them, she had the perfect opportunity to observe. Or maybe just enjoy his company.

But only two minutes into the aquarium, Noah began to fuss. Hugo glanced down at him and Erin held her breath. He looked away from Noah, around the space, and said, "In that stroller, he's two feet below everything." He reached down and loosened the straps. "Hey, bud. Do you want to walk, or do you want me to carry you?"

Amazed, Erin said, "It might do him good to walk around a bit."

When they had Noah on his feet, Hugo frowned. "But he's still too short to see."

"How about if we let him walk until we reach an exhibit. Then we can take turns lifting him to see."

Hugo nodded. "Sounds like a plan."

The time in the aquarium passed quickly. They'd started off taking turns holding Noah and showing him the sea life, but soon Hugo simply kept him. The little boy and happy man bonded right before her eyes, making her heart ache. Noah needed a male influence as much as Hugo needed a family. And if he were anybody else, she'd believe this was fate. But she couldn't forget he might be the villain in his family drama.

They took Noah outside to a vendor for lunch, which

they ate at a table under a tent. But after that, Noah began to fuss again. Erin didn't blame him. She might like the shops and opportunity to look for gifts for her mom, but her son was obviously bored.

"I guess neither one of us thought about how interested a three-year-old would be sitting in a stroller while I browsed through shops."

Hugo laughed. "Actually, I have the perfect place to take him. Trust me?"

Seeing him so happy, she smiled. "Sure."

After calling Hugo's driver, they put the stroller into the trunk of the limo and headed off. When the car stopped in front of Hamleys toy store, Erin gasped. "It's adorable!"

The red facade and red awnings were dressed for the holiday. As she stepped out of the limo, waiting for Ronnie to bring Noah's stroller, she paused and breathed in the cold December air. All this time she'd been worried about Hugo, but she suddenly realized how much she'd needed a break too.

Hugo and Ronnie took over the job of getting Noah into his stroller, and then Hugo pushed him to the store, Erin on his heels.

Joy warmed her. She forgot all about Hugo's troubles because he had. Noah laughed and looked from side to side, amazed by all the toys and people.

They followed the crowd, slowing down to let Noah examine a toy or laugh at the magician. When they reached a set of stairs, Hugo lifted Noah out of his stroller, then texted Ronnie to come in and get the stroller and stow it in the limo.

"He needs to be up high to see all this," Hugo said as they climbed the steps.

Noah seemed to be in awe. The toys and Christmas carols had lulled him into a state of blissful shock. They spent a few minutes in a room with elves who helped him write his Christmas list for Santa, and then they took the short walk into the room where the man himself sat on a throne.

"Come on back, young man."

Hugo slid Noah to the floor and urged him to go see Santa. He shyly stepped forward until he reached the man with the red suit and white beard.

Erin said, "You can sit on his lap."

But Noah didn't look predisposed to doing that and took two steps back.

Santa laughed. "Oh, that's okay." He winked. "If you just want to tell me your list I'll remember."

Still dumbstruck, Noah handed Santa the list he'd created with the elves and when Santa took it, he raced back to his mom.

Hugo laughed. "I like his style. He gets right to the point. His list has what he wants. No need for technicalities like sitting on his lap."

Erin scooped him up. "Did you like Santa?"

The little boy grinned.

They waved goodbye and Santa said, "Ho! Ho! Ho!"

Noah beamed, clearly pleased with the experience.

As they turned to leave, Hugo said, "Did you happen to take note of what was on that list?"

"Memorized it."

"Good. I had something in mind to get him, but if you'd rather I buy him one of the toys on the list, I'm okay with that."

Her heart tugged but warning bells went off. He was behaving like a guy dating Noah's mom. That wasn't their deal. Especially since he'd said they'd only have one night and then made a point to distance himself from her. "You don't have to get him a gift."

"Are you kidding? He's the first kid I've had in my life in… I don't know how long. The first chance I've ever had to buy a child's gift. I want it."

Erin peeked at him as they headed toward the stairs and to the limo. It was the most telling thing he'd ever said. Even if he had been the villain in his family drama, he'd obviously suffered for what he'd done.

They piled into the car and Hugo glanced at his watch. "I'm guessing he needs to get home."

"Yes."

He looked over at her. "This was actually a very fun day for me. Thank you."

"Thank you!" Erin said. "I might have eventually figured out to take him to see Santa, but having a limo makes everything easier."

Hugo laughed and her heart tugged again. She'd never seen him this relaxed. And this might be the perfect time to get him to talk.

"I'd be happy to make you dinner to pay you back."

He faced her. His eyes softened, but he shook his head. "That's okay. I'm going to go to the hotel to see if there were any problems today."

"Yeah." Erin winced. "That might be a good idea."

"Besides, your mum probably missed you two and she'll want some time."

Erin rolled her eyes. "A few days ago, my mom realized how close we were to Ireland and she became obsessed with finding her relatives."

"She has relatives in Ireland?"

"Her parents moved to the US when they got married. Mom was born in the United States and her parents eventually became citizens, but both sides of her extended family are in Ireland."

"Oh."

"When she and my dad divorced, she stayed in the United States to give me a chance to get to know my dad. But he was never really interested. When he remarried and started another family, he totally dropped me, and my mom and I sort of became a team. But now that I'm working and have Noah, some days I think she feels alone... She wants to know where she came from. Who her people are."

Hugo's face saddened. "I get that."

Erin could have kicked herself. Of course, he understood that! He'd lost his family too.

"Anyway," she said, trying to get the conversation away from things that clearly upset him. "She'll probably jibber jabber all night about what she discovered today. Best for you to get away before she bores you to tears."

He chuckled. "I think it's great."

Warmth filled her. This was the real Hugo. The normal Hugo. The guy he was when he wasn't everybody's boss. The guy she liked. The guy she suspected he wanted to be...but couldn't.

But why couldn't he be? What stopped him?

The limo pulled up to her building, and she and Noah got out as Hugo and Ronnie retrieved the stroller.

"Don't open it. I'll carry him up."

Hugo turned to Ronnie. "And I'll carry the stroller."

They headed into the building, walked into the foyer and turned toward the first apartment on the right.

She opened the door and let Noah run inside, into her mom's arms. Closing the door, she looked up at Hugo and smiled. "Thank you for a lovely day."

"It was my pleasure."

She could see from the light in his eyes that it had been his pleasure. Time spun out between them. The day had been perfect, and they weren't strangers. They'd been lovers. A kiss would be the normal way to end their time together.

But he'd made it clear that their one night was their one night—

He leaned the stroller against the wall by the door, then bent down and touched his lips to hers.

Her lungs froze, but her heart bumped to life. His mouth was familiar, his kiss like coming home. Pure bliss poured through her.

He pulled away. Their gazes clung. Caught in a haze of happiness, she couldn't speak.

Then she realized he was as ecstatic as she was. Her brooding, wounded, confusing boss grinned at her.

"I'll see you tomorrow."

Her smile grew. "Yeah. Tomorrow."

Happiness morphed into something more. A feeling so deep and rich it filled all the empty corners of her soul, as Hugo turned away and headed for the exit.

Dazed, she opened the door and walked into her apartment.

Clearly waiting for her, her mother bounced off the sofa. "Oh, Erin! It's the most wonderful thing! Not only do my parents' relatives remember them…they want to meet me."

Acutely aware of the importance of family acceptance because of Hugo, she said, "That's great."

"They're so kind and so happy that I found them, they're paying for me to go to Ireland. I leave tomorrow!"

Erin blinked. "Tomorrow?"

"Don't worry. They're also making arrangements for Noah. They want to meet him too. And you, when you're not busy with the hotel."

Having trouble keeping up with her mother's news after Hugo's sweet kiss, Erin slid out of her coat. "That's even better."

Her mom studied her face. "What's wrong?"

"Nothing!" She should be confused. But she wasn't. She liked Hugo and he really liked her. She felt like a high school girl after her first real date. A little awed this was happening, but so happy it didn't matter.

"Well, whatever the case, kiss Noah goodbye tomorrow. We'll be gone a few days... But the tickets are open-ended in case my relatives are crazy or we don't get along."

Erin laughed and her mother left the room in a flurry of excitement, wanting to pack.

To keep herself from thinking about how she'd miss Noah, Erin focused on putting her little boy to bed, then the work she needed to do on Saturday, but as soon as she thought of her job, she remembered she'd be seeing Hugo and her heart stopped.

Her mom and son would be gone for four days.

She had no reason not to spend every second of every night with Hugo.

Except, in the end, what if what they felt came to nothing? They'd go their separate ways. And she'd be—

Empty again.

Her heart ached just thinking about it. Josh might have been gone for over three years, but she keenly remembered the pain of losing him. She might lose Hugo for a totally different reason, but a loss was a loss.

Still—

What if what they felt was real?

What if they spent the next few days together and all these crazy emotions floating around in her turned into something real?

Love.

With a guy she would have sworn didn't know what love was.

But maybe being alone for so long had taught him the

importance of connection? She'd always believed that if they spent enough time together, he'd tell her his secrets, and after today she was sure of it.

And maybe it would be the biggest mistake of her life not to take this chance?

CHAPTER SEVEN

HUGO SILENTLY RODE in the back of his limo, his thoughts jumbled, the sights and sounds of London passing unnoticed.

When he kissed Erin, his troubles disappeared... Hell, the world disappeared. Totally in the moment, he felt sensations and desires that he never even knew existed.

But as much as he liked her, the emotions, the *needs* scared him. He longed to be with her, to tell her things, to do things—like watch her son's reaction at the hotel's Christmas Eve celebration. But he knew part of that was the intrinsic yearning for a family, a place to belong.

His heart stumbled at the thought. He'd dedicated his life to getting wealthy enough to buy Harrington Park Hotel, to reuniting the family that had rejected him, but what if his real need was to create his own family? Jay spoke to him, worked with him, but there was a reserve, a distance there. And Sally—well, Sally might always hate him.

He didn't really understand his siblings' side of the story. How could he? How could he know what Nick had told them about why he'd left? The man had cleverly framed him for the embezzlement he himself had committed. Nick hadn't done that merely to save his skin. Getting Hugo out of the way would have been the perfect foil. He'd cleared his name and most likely manu-factured leverage with the twins. Instead of having them pine for their older brother, Nick had clearly given them reason to hate him.

All those years of sending Christmas cards filled with his hope that someday the family could be together again had fallen on deaf ears and minds set against him. With Sally continuing to keep her distance, he was beginning to wonder if his true path might be to create his own family.

But two things were off about that. First, he loved Jay and Sally. He'd loved being a big brother. The bonds of family shouldn't be so easily snapped. Yet theirs had been.

Second, wasn't he shortchanging Erin to "decide" to create a family, so he chose her—

His limo stopped at his building, and he bade Ronnie good-night and stepped out. Walking inside, he snorted at his thoughts. He wasn't deciding to create a new family, so he chose Erin. Erin made him long for all the things he'd yearned for his entire life. She wasn't by any stretch of the imagination a simple choice. The feelings she inspired were like dynamite, blasting him out of his set ways to con-sider a kind of life he'd never believed was right for him.

He rode the elevator and stepped into the luxurious penthouse, but that only tripped a whoosh of longing. He had everything—absolutely everything a man could want—except someone to share it with.

And this woman who set his blood on fire, even as she tempted him with a sense of family, a sense of belonging, closeness, intimacy, was the one he wanted to bring here, to spoil, to share with.

Everything got so confused that he reached for his phone the second he shrugged out of his overcoat.

He hit the contact for Jay. The phone rang twice, and then his younger brother answered.

"Hey, Hugo! What's up?"

Slowly lowering himself to his sofa, he said, "Nothing... really."

"Oh, that's a tone of voice I've never heard from you. Something's definitely up. And it's not nothing."

He took a breath. "I don't know. I just feel weird."

Jay laughed. "Weird?"

"Out of sorts."

"Maybe the project is getting to you. You gave us one hell of a deadline. Maybe the pressure is finally over the top?"

"No. Believe it or not, I've handled worse."

"Seriously?"

"Yes." Loosening his tie, Hugo leaned back and settled on the sofa. This was what he needed. A conversation with the twin who was at least willing to give their family a chance. If this didn't get him back to normal, nothing would.

Jay said, "So how are things going at the hotel?"

"Everything's organized chaos. Though it looks like a Greek tragedy, it's actually on schedule."

"How about the party?"

"Erin's on top of it. Even the ridiculous details. And I can be exacting, but that doesn't bother her. She is so attuned to me that even when I assure her that the type of stocking that she chooses for the kids isn't that important, she knows it is and she works to get me what I want."

There was a pause before Jay said, "You like her."

"Of course, I like her. If all my employees were as able to please me as she is, I'd never have a care in the world."

Jay laughed. "No. I mean, I recognize that you like working with her, but you like her as more."

Hugo ran his hand down his face. "Is it that obvious?"

"Maybe not to an outsider, but I think I know you a little better than most people. You had a sense of responsibility when you worked at the hotel back when Mum and Dad owned it, but you always had time for Sally and me."

He had.

He sank a little deeper into the sofa, as his memories of being a big brother flowed through him and he remembered why he was so eager to bring his family back together. Not just for himself, but for his brother and sister too.

"You don't want to have feelings for this woman?"

"I don't think now is the time." He sighed. It should have felt odd talking about things he usually didn't discuss. But he'd once been close to Jay and confiding in his younger brother felt so right, he couldn't stop himself. "There have always been women in my life but not someone I feel these odd things for."

"Maybe it does have something to do with the project?"

He laughed.

"I'm serious. Maybe things seem different because you're under a lot of pressure and you need to let off steam."

"That sounds kind of callous toward the woman."

"No. No. I'm not saying use her. I'm just saying if the two of you like each other why not run with it? Is she having as much fun as you are?"

He remembered their night together, then the trip that afternoon with her son, and he smiled. "Of course."

"Then you're not hurting anybody. And you should let go a little bit."

It might not seem callous, but it did seem risky. He'd never, ever even considered having a serious relationship with a woman and if he tried and failed, he'd hurt her. "I don't think so."

"I do!"

"I don't want to hurt her."

"What if you don't?" Jay sighed. "What if this is the real thing?"

"What if it's not?"

"Did you ever stop to think she's available too because she needs the break as much as you do?"

Feeling his resolve weakening, Hugo closed his eyes. "She probably does. I can be pretty demanding."

Jay laughed. "That's an understatement if I've ever heard one. Look at this like a mutually satisfying agreement. If you ever get the sense that she's uncomfortable, back off. But as long as you're both having fun... For God's sake, have some fun."

"That is how I usually look at things." But those women weren't widows with children.

"Good. Then get back to that. Have some fun. I know how hard you work. You simply need a little bit of down-time."

He chuckled. Talking things out with Jay had made him feel much better. Stronger. In control. He and Jay talked a bit about the hotel, both careful not to mention Sally, who was a touchy subject, and then they said good-night.

Hugo went to bed refusing to think about Erin. Their night together had been amazing. The day with her son had been wonderful. But he was a businessman. The hotel had to come first.

He fell into a deep, rich sleep and woke Saturday morning feeling like a tiger, a man a week away from the biggest success of his life.

His conversation with his brother had more than bolstered him. It had made him realize that he and Jay were growing close again. Even if he didn't turn his family back into the tight unit they'd been before Nick entered the picture, he and Jay would be okay. And he would have his sister in his life somehow—

He shouldn't give up on his plan to make the Harrington family whole again.

After a quick shower and breakfast, he was driven to the office with his New York staff, most of whom were growing eager to go home. He gave a short, inspirational speech, thanked them for helping him complete the project that had always been closest to his heart, urged them to hang in there and sent everyone back to his or her desk ready to do their best work.

Riding the limo to the hotel and walking through the almost complete lobby, he was refreshed. Renewed. His old self. Ready to take on the world.

He sat at his desk and dived into the stack of papers in front of him. Then Erin walked in and a whoosh of desire burned through him, even as his heart did a funny flip.

The temptation was strong to rise and kiss her senseless, which not only confused him, it pushed him back to the place he was before, before he'd spoken with Jay. Filled with a need so intense—something that braided sexual desire, a longing for intimacy and a yearning to create something special with her—he stayed in his seat, dumbfounded.

"Good morning, Hugo."

Her bright, chipper voice warmed his heart, which stuttered to a stop. She was gorgeous even in her jeans and T-shirt. Her kisses were sweet. Making love with her had been amazing…

But her friendship was important to him. And the hotel even more so. He had to get himself back on track.

He cleared his throat. "It's Saturday. Though we took yesterday off, you know it would have been okay to come in late today."

She shrugged. "I have that delivery plus a few other things to do. If I get through them all, I probably won't have to come in tomorrow—Sunday. Sunday's a better day off."

His stuttering heart faltered even more. He used the same principle to get himself to go the extra mile, work harder, get things done.

His voice was thin and gruff when he said, "That's fine. But don't stay all day. I'm sure Noah would like more than a peek at you before bedtime."

She took the seat in front of his desk. For a good thirty seconds she said nothing. Then she raised her gaze to Hugo's and said, "Noah's not home. Neither is my mom." She paused as if letting that information sink in. "You know those Irish relatives I told you she was searching for?"

Confused, he nodded.

"She found them. They got her and Noah tickets to fly to Dublin where a gaggle of them are apparently going to pick her up and take her to their small town."

He blinked. Not just because it seemed sudden that Marge had found her people and wanted time with them, but because he knew why Erin was unexpectedly nervous. She had no responsibilities at home for days. If he wanted, he could be with her every night that her little family was in Ireland.

His brain immediately said, *Yes.* But his throat tightened, and his chest froze. His conversation with Jay played in his head. If they both needed some fun, some stress relief in this final week before the grand opening, they could have days and nights together. Alone. Happy. And no one had to be any the wiser.

Their gazes held a few seconds more as all the possibilities rolled through him, luxurious dinners, passionate nights—

The want of it overwhelmed him and he couldn't stop himself from saying, "So, does this mean we can have dinner at Alain Ducasse?"

Her eyes widened. "Are you kidding?"

He frowned. "I'm not sure if that's a yes or a no."

"I didn't bring the clothes for it."

Her hesitation brought the tiger back—the guy who didn't let anything get in the way of what he wanted. Yes, he remembered that she had a child and that he might hurt her, but, as Jay said, this should be about fun.

For them both.

"I have a personal shopper who can get you anything you need."

When she hesitated, he said, "Please. We've both worked so hard, I think we deserve a night." *A night.* Two words that clarified his intentions. She would know what she was agreeing to.

She shook her head. "Okay. But only if I pay for the dress and shoes."

A thrill raced through him. "You don't have to—"

"I do. I always get myself a Christmas gift. So this will be it."

Not giving her a chance to change her mind, he called his personal shopper to tell her Erin would be in touch. When he got off the call, he gave Erin her number. She left his office with his personal shopper's info clutched in her hand.

Even as the joy of getting what he wanted filled him, nerves jumped in his stomach. The whole date had been arranged so simply one would have thought he could settle into work and forget it until time to pick her up at her flat.

But he'd never been so excited about taking someone to dinner. Never had this shaky feeling over knowing she could be his—all his—for two or three or even four days.

One day at a time. One invitation at a time.

As long as they were having fun. If it ever looked like she was getting serious when he wasn't, he'd know to shut it off.

But he didn't believe it would go that far. Their time together came with a shelf life. Though she was spending Christmas Day in London, he'd be on a plane back to Manhattan. And they wouldn't see each other again for months.

She had to realize that.

CHAPTER EIGHT

EAGER NOW, WISHING the day was over so he could have time with Erin, Hugo bounced out of his seat and walked into what he considered ground central. Things were progressing. Painting done in some places, on target in others.

He saw one of the specialty plasterers and walked over to talk about design. But before they got into their conversation, he saw Sally heading toward him. He'd known she was in the hotel today, but as had been his practice, he let his brother and sister work alone, at their own speed. And while Jay phoned him with updates, Sally still preferred the more impersonal method of emailing.

She looked hesitant walking to him. Then her steps faltered, and he noticed that her color was off. Her face a pasty white.

His chest tightened with fear and he sped up his steps as she reached out her hand. "Hugo!" she said, her knees buckling.

He caught her just as she fell.

An ambulance was called, and Hugo had to fight with the attendant to be able to ride with Sally. But he won. After she was seen by the doctor, he'd waited for her to awaken, but the conversation they'd had hadn't pleased him.

She was pregnant and not intending to marry the baby's father.

Because she wanted to be independent.

The words cut through him like a knife. Not because his little sister had grown up to be strong and capable, but because underlying those words was a worry that having her father die, her older brother desert her and her stepfather cheat her had given her the wrong impression of all men.

Which was why, when he ran into Edward Chen in the Harrington Park lobby on his way out of the hotel to dress for his date with Erin, he almost took the man's head off. He had to be the baby's father. Hugo hadn't seen Sally with anyone else. Not that he saw a lot of her. She rarely told him when she was in the hotel—

But Edward was the guy she'd been staying with when she'd traveled to Tianlipin.

"So? You're just going to drop your responsibilities to my sister?"

Edward gaped at him. Tall and dark-eyed, Edward quietly said, "Drop what responsibilities?"

"To your child!"

Edward eased back a step. "I don't believe this is any of your business."

"Oh, do not kid yourself. My sister and I might not have seen each other for a long time, but she is still my sister and I want to know your intentions."

Edward turned on his heel. "Right now, my intention is to go to the hospital. If you'll excuse me."

With that, he was out the door, and Hugo counted to thirty-five. It wasn't that he didn't believe he had a right to confront Edward. It was more that when Sally found out he'd yelled at her baby's father, she was likely to hit him.

But a weird happiness filled him. His sister was pregnant and no matter who liked it and who didn't, he had held the father accountable.

All right. Edward didn't look like the kind of guy who

would abandon his responsibilities. But Hugo had finally been able to step up as big brother again.

Erin stared at the three dresses on the bed. She'd encouraged Hugo's personal shopper to bargain hunt. Though the request had sounded odd to the store managers Kathleen had called, she had found three dresses for about a third of their original cost.

The first was a simple red sheath with a cardigan that could go anywhere. A restaurant or a Christmas party.

The black one was more sleek, sophisticated. That one definitely had Christmas party or gallery opening written all over it.

The blue one was a good dinner choice.

But if Hugo only wanted tonight, she'd be sending back the two dresses she really liked.

Of course, if things went as well as they had the last time she and Hugo were alone…he'd spend every day with her.

Her thoughts drifted back to the night they were stranded at the hotel and eagerness raced through her. When she stopped thinking of things in terms of "permanent," everything was perfect. They laughed. The sex was amazing. And there had been no hurt feelings.

No expectations did that to a person.

She hadn't thought she'd expected too much from her late husband, but maybe she had. And maybe that was the lesson? She wouldn't *attach* herself to anyone who couldn't give her his whole heart and soul, but she could date them. That opened the door to having fun with someone who didn't want to commit, and Hugo was definitely fun.

And probably unable to commit. He hadn't told her much about his life, his family, how they'd become estranged. She'd pieced things together, but he didn't talk, and she was finally beginning to realize that would be for the best, if they were simply together to have fun.

She decided to think positive and slid into the blue dress. It dipped low enough in the front to be alluring, but not so much that it was provocative. Better, though, it brought out the best in her straight red hair. With a little makeup and a pair of black high-heeled pumps, she was ready when the doorbell rang.

She raced to answer it, then forced herself to slow down. Whatever she and Hugo were doing, it was only about fun. A woman only having fun did not race to the door.

The second she opened it, Hugo caught her upper arms and brought her to him for a long, sensual kiss that made her dizzy.

"Wow."

"You're so beautiful."

And just like that, he took an evening that could have started out awkward and brought them both out of work mode and into romance. Happiness tingled through her. *She liked him.* She liked being with him. When there was no discussion, no expectation, no tomorrow guaranteed for them, he was a warm, loving guy.

And from the way his gaze moved from her face down the lines of her dress, she knew he liked her too.

"I'm going to have to congratulate Kathleen on her choice of outfits."

She almost said, *Just wait. There are two more. Each one better than the last.* But she bit her tongue. There was no guarantee they'd have more than this date. She refused to ruin it by putting him in an odd spot.

She rose on tiptoe to give him a quick kiss. "Thanks."

He took a slow breath. "You're welcome." His gaze rippled down her figure again. "We better get to the limo before I convince you we don't need dinner."

The expression on his face sent her head spinning and arousal careening through her blood. "Maybe we don't."

He laughed. "I'm not starting my third date with you by not feeding you or buying lunch from a vendor the way I did our first and second."

Walking to the limo, she realized he counted their being stuck in the hotel as a date and then him showing her and Noah around as their second, and her heart warmed. Mostly because he liked her son, was easy and casual around her son, like a man who adored children—

Then she reminded herself this was only about fun, and she pulled herself together. He wanted to wine and dine her. Wasn't that what fun was supposed to be about? Enjoying each other's company, not just falling into bed.

Ronnie opened the limo door. As she entered, Hugo said, "I saw my sister this afternoon."

His simple statement broke the argument in her head. "You did?"

He settled beside her on the long, comfortable seat. "Yes. She fainted in my arms and I called an ambulance."

"I thought I heard scuttlebutt about an ambulance coming to the hotel."

His gaze jumped to hers. "Just scuttlebutt. No out and out gossip?"

"There might have been." She shrugged. "You know me. I don't interrupt the workers unless I need to. Plus, I stay in my own little corner." Cautious because she didn't want to push, she carefully said, "So, what happened?"

"I sort of got to be a big brother."

The pride in his voice made her laugh. "What?"

"It's a complicated situation...and some of it I don't feel comfortable revealing."

"Oh." Confusion jolted through her. Sometimes they were so close, and their conversations seemed so open, that his pulling back was like a bolt of lightning. A hot little sizzle that singed her nerve endings.

"It's about her health." He winced. "Obviously, since she went to the hospital, but suffice to say she's fine. Better than fine. Fit and healthy and probably going home tomorrow."

Erin listened carefully, noting how close he came to telling her something about his family without telling her anything. Still, it was more than he ever said. Even if he was keeping a lot of his life close to the vest, the fact that he'd said anything at all pleased her.

She reminded herself she hadn't entered this relationship to find a husband or even a real boyfriend. She was determined not to be hurt by things he said or didn't say.

"Because the twins are seven years younger than I am, I felt like their protector." He winced. "And by default, something of a teacher. Showing them the ropes about life."

She laughed, warmed again by his sharing with her. "How old were you when you were their guru?"

He thought a second. "I left at seventeen." His head tilted. "So, probably from when I was ten and they were three. At the time I thought I was wise. Turns out I didn't know a damned thing really."

"No seventeen-year-old knows everything." After laughing with him a bit more about how much he liked being a big brother, they entered the restaurant and she shifted the conversation to something light and friendly. Books they'd read. Movies each had seen—mostly on internet platforms because with his schedule, Hugo didn't go out much.

The way he so casually mentioned it, Erin knew it was true. She desperately tried not to let her brain leap to the conclusion that he didn't have much of a social life, which meant there wasn't a woman waiting for him back in Manhattan—

not even a dependable date for social events he needed to attend—and she had to stop that too.

Keeping things light and casual in a relationship didn't happen as naturally as Erin thought it would. Her inclination seemed to be to jump to the future and this wasn't about the future. It was about now.

Still, she liked him. She liked this relaxed version of Hugo who could now trust her with tidbits about his family and converse about simple, mundane things. And dinner was divine. The venue was luxurious and just pretentious enough to demonstrate that she was dating "up" from her own class.

But Hugo never made her feel less than. In fact, he made her feel like the most beautiful woman in the room. Their conversations were filled with intelligence and laughter. Walking out of the restaurant to the limo, warm with wine and happiness, they linked arms.

Ronnie opened the door with a smile and an odd look to Hugo.

Hugo turned her to face him, locking his eyes with hers. "Will you come back to my penthouse with me?"

She didn't hesitate. "Yes."

Ronnie smiled. After they'd entered the limo, he closed the door on them. Cocooning them in the warm, private back seat.

They kissed the entire drive to his building. Kissed in the elevator going up to the penthouse and kissed their way down the hall to the master bedroom. But once they got into the bedroom, both removed their winter coats and he reached for the zipper on her dress.

Abundantly glad she had a fetish for pretty undergarments, she stood still as he peeled away her dress and revealed the pink bra and panties. He kissed her reverently as she loosened his tie and undid the buttons of his white shirt.

He broke their kiss to get rid of his clothes, then rolled her to the bed with him onto silk sheets that slid sensuously against her skin. Her breathing slowed, even as her thoughts jumped to double time, taking it all in. The fierceness of his kiss, the solidness of his muscles beneath her palms. She wanted to remember every little detail for cold Manhattan nights, if only because this was a temporary fling.

But her brain shut down when his fingers skimmed her flesh and his mouth found her breast. Her breathing stuttered as heat and need flowed through her veins, pooling at a point just below her belly. What started out slow and easy quickly heated to boiling. Their joining was swift and intense. Kisses became hot and desperate. Until a stunning climax roared through her and she felt his follow.

For a few seconds she simply let herself breathe. Then he raised himself to smile down into her eyes, and something inside her heart cracked and opened. But she caught it just in time, before those haunted gray eyes of his could soften her to the point that she felt things she knew she wasn't allowed to feel.

The emotions were there, right on the surface, and she longed to indulge them. Instead, she ignored them.

She wouldn't let herself fall for another man with secrets. Though he might not have realized it, he'd drawn a line that day by only taking her so far into his confidence about his sister.

But remembering that would keep her from getting her heart broken and help her to simply enjoy what they had.

She woke the next morning so sated and happy that she decided to make him breakfast in bed. In a relationship that was only about fun, there was no room for second-guessing her every move. There was no way she could be too forward.

No worry that she'd scare him off and there'd be no more dates. She had no idea if he'd want to see her that night, if he'd chase her home so he could get some work done this morning or if they'd spend the day—Sunday—together. She also didn't care.

A little voice inside her brain said that wasn't true, but she shoved it aside. She and Hugo were not a match made in heaven. Even if he somehow gave her the magical sign that she meant something to him, she should be smart enough to give returning his feelings a lot of thought. He was a man with secrets and an odd past. A smart woman wouldn't want to get involved with that. At least not permanently. So right now, she had no expectations. She liked him. She loved talking with him and he was a fabulous lover whose generosity made her a better lover because she wasn't afraid of messing up what they had. They had nothing. Except that moment.

Having no expectations was a beautiful thing.

With bacon frying on the stove and bagels in the toaster, Erin had her back to the open area of the penthouse when Hugo walked up behind her, slid his arms around her waist and kissed her neck.

She laughed. "You better step back or you'll get splashed with bacon grease."

"I have a robe on...since someone stole my shirt."

She winced. "Sorry, didn't want to put on my new dress to cook bacon."

He nibbled the back of her neck. "I like you in my shirt... I like you better in my bed."

"After we eat. Last night was amazing, but we drained every drop of energy I have. We need to power up."

"Good thinking." He slid away from her. "Anything I can do?"

"Nope. I only found bacon, cream cheese and bagels. No eggs. So maybe bacon sandwiches?"

"Sounds great."

"Get some plates and napkins while I take the bacon out of the pan and we'll be set."

He did what he was told but when they sat at the breakfast bar, they both got quiet. After a few bites of bagel, he said, "So you weren't upset about your mum taking your son and running away to Ireland?"

She laughed, licking some cream cheese off her thumb. He might not be able to tell her much about himself, but her life was not a secret. She had no qualms telling him anything.

"No. My mom has never had extended family around. Since my parents' divorce, my mom's been pretty much alone. Except for me. I got married and my husband died before I had Noah. So, though we have a Noah, who we didn't have before, my mom and I are back to being pretty much alone."

"Where's your dad?"

She shrugged. "Don't know. I invited him to my wedding, but he declined. Luckily, by that point my mom and I didn't care. I was so thrilled to be marrying Josh that having my dad refuse to walk me down the aisle just made room for my mom to do it."

Erin glanced down at her bacon when she said her husband's name, and Hugo fought a battle with jealousy. The man was gone, but it was clear there was still a boatload of emotion there.

He wanted to ask what the man—Josh—was like. What he'd done for a living. How he'd died. Partly out of curiosity. Partly because he longed to find a rift, a flaw, something he could identify and use to make the jealousy go away.

But he reminded himself that his relationship with Erin was a temporary thing. And hearing Erin say her husband had died, her dad had deserted her, her mum and son were her only people, he knew she needed some fun in her life.

Maybe more than he did. And maybe he was looking at this relationship all wrong. It might be casual, but that didn't mean they couldn't share their troubles. Their lives had a few similarities and it wouldn't hurt to admit that.

He took a breath. "Your mum's obsession with finding her Irish relatives reminds me of me trying to get my family back together."

Her gaze jumped to his. He understood why. He'd never really said those words to anyone. She might have guessed. He might have hinted. But he'd never actually come right out and said it.

"I think it's a biological imperative to be connected."

She bobbed her head. "I suppose."

"And while she fulfills that need and hopefully really does find her roots, her place—" he leaned in and wrapped his arms around her waist "—you and I can enjoy ourselves."

Her smile was quick and genuine. "What do you have in mind?"

"A sightseeing tour."

Her eyes widened. "Really?"

"The adult version."

Her eyes widened even more, and he laughed. "I don't mean sex on the lawn of Buckingham Palace. I mean there won't be any stops to see Santa."

She laughed. "Whew. I'm okay with being adventurous, but I don't want to be arrested in a foreign country."

This time he laughed. Long and loud. In a way he couldn't remember laughing for a long time. His sister was okay. Pregnant. But okay. He'd got to be a big brother the day before. And the woman he desired was at his fingertips. Not just for bed, but to really enjoy the day.

"The limo will have to take me back to my apartment to dress."

He rose from his stool by the breakfast bar. "Sounds good. I'll call Ronnie, get a shower and dress. Then we'll drive to your apartment."

He kissed her quickly. "Your phone's in the master bedroom. So's the shower. You could come back there with me for some really adult fun before I clean up. Then you might want to give your mum and Noah a call."

She smiled. "Sounds perfect."

CHAPTER NINE

It *WAS* PERFECT. All of it. The drive through London gave her a real feel for the city. The stops at Buckingham Palace for a closer look and the Thames Path—Hampton Court to Albert Bridge—were especially nice. A late lunch at an out-of-the-way bistro ended their outing and they returned to her flat for her to change again.

It seemed oddly foolish to keep stopping at her home to grab her things for the quiet evening in his penthouse that they'd agreed to, but the alternative was for him to say, *Just pack a bag*, and he wasn't sure what message that would send.

When she came out to the apartment's main room, her overnight case in hand, she walked to him, rose on tiptoe and kissed him. "Let's go."

And he suddenly didn't care what kind of message it sent, except by the time he thought to suggest she get more clothes, she was already in the hall.

They returned to his penthouse to find Louis Joubert and his staff working in the kitchen.

She turned to him with a smile. "What's this?"

"A special dinner."

"Thought we were going to have a quiet evening?"

"This is quiet. He's going to let us sample Christmas Eve dinner."

She faced Louis. "How nice."

"It never hurts to be sure the boss is pleased with your creation," Louis said.

Hugo laughed. "Jay chose you. I know how picky he is. Which means I also know you'll be phenomenal."

"And you'll get to tell me so, once you taste the goose."

An hour later, Hugo and Erin sat down to a dinner of goose, ham and chocolate mousse, with side dishes of mashed potatoes and green beans almandine, as well as hot rolls.

"There'll also be chocolate cake, if anyone dislikes mousse," Louis said, when he came in for a final bow at the end of the meal.

Erin said, "It was amazing. All of it."

"Absolutely perfect," Hugo agreed.

Louis took his bow, then exited the dining area. Hugo and Erin retired to the living room where they watched a movie on the large-screen TV, as Louis and his staff cleaned the kitchen and gathered their things.

But as they filed out of the penthouse, Hugo's phone rang. Recognizing Jay's number, he answered. "Jay. What's up?"

"Where have you been? I've been trying to reach you all day."

He winced. "I had my phone off because I took Erin sightseeing. Why?"

"It's Sally. She was at the hospital yesterday."

"I know. I'm the one went with her in the ambulance."

"You did?"

Hugo sat back. "Did she tell you she was pregnant? I had to have a word with the baby's father. I hope he steps up like he promised."

"Did you know he's wealthy?"

"Neither of them told me that. But it doesn't matter

how much money he has. No man should desert a woman he got pregnant."

"Don't get your knickers in a twist. Sally told me today that they're getting married."

Hugo sat up. "Married?"

"Yes."

"That's great news. If that's what she wants."

"You're sounding a little too proud."

Feeling like his big brother speech had hit home, Hugo laughed. "I'm relieved my intervention helped."

"You must not have done any damage if they got engaged."

"Or maybe I can take credit."

Jay laughed. "Don't go that far."

"Sure. Fine. Whatever. But if I get invited to the wedding, I'm taking credit in a dinner toast."

Jay laughed again and they said their goodbyes.

As he tossed his phone to the end table beside the sofa, Erin slid her arm beneath his and nestled against him. "So, your sister is pregnant?"

He grimaced. "Yeah."

"And you feel like you had a hand in your future brother-in-law's proposal?"

He laughed. "He came to the hotel yesterday looking for her and I didn't hold back."

She sat up. "The intervention you told Jay about?"

"Yes. I told him I didn't think very much of a guy who gets a woman pregnant and deserts her." He grinned. "Then he proposed. You don't think that was my doing?"

She shook her head. "You *really* enjoy being a big brother."

"Yeah," he said with another grin, but he quickly sobered. "But, honestly, with all the lost years between us, I don't have a clue what I'm doing."

"Well, this time, you did great." She snorted a laugh. "In an odd kind of way, your yelling at the guy proves to Sally you'll be there for her. And maybe that's all she needed to hear."

"I'm not even sure he would have told her. For all I know, he went into her hospital room and proposed as if it were his idea."

She arched a brow. "Maybe it was."

Proud, he sat up. "I'm taking credit."

"Yeah, I can see that. But it looks to me like you needed that confrontation more than their relationship did."

"*I* did?"

"Yes." Her eyes were soft and serious as she added, "It's proof of how much you still want to be a big brother. Plus, that's how people step into a role they aren't sure of. They say and do the right thing over and over until it's part of their life. You haven't defended your sister before, so yesterday it was new. If you guys ever get your troubles straightened out, you're already one step into the game."

He studied her face, realizing not just how much he'd told her about himself with a few throwaway comments, but how well she listened—how much she cared. "You're awfully smart for someone so young."

She laughed. "I'm not that young." She took a breath. "I've also had some hard lessons."

He knew she had, and said nothing for a few seconds, but in the silence, all of Hugo's questions about her husband came pouring back and he couldn't stop them. "Because of losing your husband?"

"Yes." She took another breath, this one much longer as if she were debating telling him anything about her past. He supposed he deserved it, but the itchy feeling wouldn't go away. He desperately wanted to know about the man who had won her heart.

"I imagine losing your spouse is the worst thing in the world."

"It is. But in my case, not for the reasons you think."

Confusion brought him up short. "You weren't sad when he died?"

"I was devastated when he died. The devastation was made worse when I discovered he'd been sick for a while and had been getting experimental treatments for terminal cancer."

"Terminal cancer?" Hugo's stomach fell. "But you made it sound like you didn't know he was sick."

"I didn't. He was only getting treatments for a few weeks before they weakened his heart, and he had a heart attack and died. Knowing what was coming, he'd shaved his head, telling me it was the style. When he lost weight, he told me he'd joined a gym."

Concern for her squeezed his lungs, his heart, even as confusion almost rendered him speechless. "Why didn't he tell you?"

"He claimed he'd done it to spare me. Because I was pregnant, he didn't want me to worry about his health too."

"That makes a weird kind of sense..."

"But you don't think it was right, do you?"

When he didn't answer—was so flabbergasted he didn't know what to think, let alone say—she shook her head.

"Marriage is a partnership. It's like your hotel investments. You commit to certain things but when you begin a project, you have no idea what kinds of problems will be thrown at you."

"I have some idea because I do a great deal of investigating before I make any commitments."

"But there are no guarantees you won't find something unexpected."

"There are never any guarantees."

"Marriage is the same. You go into it with a plan, expectations, then things happen. People lose jobs. Houses are difficult to find and afford—all kinds of things. In our case, Josh got sick when I was pregnant."

"But didn't tell you. So you couldn't fulfill your end of the bargain and it hurt you."

"Yes. But it was more. I didn't find out he needed me until he was already dead. Do you know how guilty that made me feel? And how much worse I felt when I discovered there was someone he confided in?"

"Please tell me it wasn't another woman."

"It was. She was a coworker. My mother believes he needed someone to talk to or someone to help with his workload and he turned to someone he could trust."

He realized how isolated they were and how the darkness of the room must have either made her bold or comfortable. So he spoke his mind. "And that was the real betrayal. In finding someone else, he all but said he didn't trust you."

"That's what I felt. And that's why I understand the importance of trust. Of saying and doing what you're supposed to be saying and doing. Josh might have believed it was the worst time in the world to be sick. Especially since my pregnancy was difficult. But that didn't change the fact that he was terminally ill. He robbed us of the opportunity to face it together, to make videos for his son... Most of all he robbed me of a voice in his decision to try an experimental treatment."

"I understand." He did. "My stepdad—Nick—robbed me of almost two decades of time with my siblings. I missed my own mother's funeral because no one told me she'd died."

"I'm so sorry."

He shook his head. Erin not being trusted by her husband mirrored his not being wanted by his family. The pain of it wasn't a big, angry wound. It was a huge, open hole that he didn't know what to do with.

That Erin didn't know what to do with.

Empty Christmases. Solitary birthdays. Blank spaces where people should have been. True, Erin had her mum and son, but in some ways, he wondered if that didn't make her husband's loss more obvious.

"The thing is, I don't merely understand your loss. I kind of understand why your husband didn't tell you. I kept some secrets." He took a breath. "I should have told my mum the very first time I suspected Nick was embezzling."

"He embezzled?"

"Yes, and blamed me." He ran his hand along the back of his neck. "I don't want to get into all of it, but I do understand why your husband didn't tell you. When you love someone that much, it's like you'd give your life to keep them safe." He pictured Erin pregnant, enduring difficulties. Then he put himself in the place of the man he didn't know and easily recognized why he'd believed he couldn't tell her.

"He was sheltering you. Trying to protect you while he fought a battle to save his own life."

She studied his face. "You make it sound very noble."

"To him it was."

"I guess I never really tried to see his side."

"You should."

She leaned back on the sofa again. Her shoulder brushed his and confusion flooded his brain.

Now that he understood her husband, it seemed callous to be taking his widow back to his bedroom to have meaningless sex.

But he thought again about those gaping holes in her life. Because he knew them too. Understood the empty places where people should have been. Understood the sorrow that overshadowed holidays.

He swore he wasn't using her. *Knew* he wasn't using her—

Because they were having fun. *She* was having fun.

And it sounded like she needed it.

Still, he took his time easing them into the rest of their night. They drank wine, talked a little more, and kissed slowly, easily. He had absolutely no idea what he was doing, except Erin was a wonderful woman…a wonderful person. He had been privileged to spend time with her and if it killed him he would make sure their being together filled up her empty places, shored up her defenses and warmed her with the knowledge that she was special and wonderful. So that when she was ready to find a real relationship, she would have the confidence of a Greek goddess.

Even though they went to work on Monday, Erin had the odd sense that they were on their honeymoon. Sightseeing? Romantic dinners? Long, meaningful talks? Sex every time they were alone? That was a honeymoon.

She could confess that to Hugo, and he'd break the spell with hard truths, hard reality. Then she'd get her thoughts straightened out. But she couldn't do it. Something had changed after he'd taken Sally to the hospital or maybe after she'd told Hugo about Josh and Hugo had understood—helped *her* to understand. She hadn't meant to so easily spill her big secret. She'd meant to show him that there were many ways people could betray each other, hurt each other. And she had. But telling that one small truth had also brought them closer—

After he'd admitted to yelling at the father of Sally's child and let her see that he was inordinately proud.

He'd let her see. He'd let her in.

So she'd let him in.

Now she had no idea what they were doing. Making love really had become making love the night before. The things they'd done, the way they'd kissed had formed some kind of connection. They'd bonded.

They'd bonded.

Her heart jolted with fear.

Oh, God. Now, she would be so hurt when this ended!

Except, after their discussion, it didn't feel like it was going to end. Which should have scared her silly. Bonded to a man whose past she didn't understand? A man who still had secrets?

It was exactly what she didn't want.

But every time he looked her in the eye when he listened, every time he took her in his arms and kissed her—

Nothing had ever felt more right.

"So, you're looking bright and chipper!"

Marge's voice interrupted her thoughts. After her mom called saying she and Noah were returning, Hugo had arranged for Ronnie to drive Erin to the airport to pick them up. With Noah strapped into the car seat Hugo had bought and her mom right beside her, Erin couldn't evade the implied question.

"I had a nice weekend."

"Re-e-all-y…"

"Mom. Stop. Seriously."

"Well, if you don't want to talk about Hugo—"

"What makes you think my mood has anything to do with Hugo?"

Her mother blinked. "What else could it be? You light up like a Christmas tree when he's around. But today, even though he's not here, your cheeks are pink. And there's something about your posture…" Her mom gave her a quick once-over. "It wasn't that you slouched before." She snapped her fingers. "I know. You were too stiff. Now you're sitting straight and tall, but in a relaxed way."

Erin gaped at her. "What?"

"I don't know." Marge shrugged. "You're normal. Back to normal."

"Normal as compared to what?"

"The woman who had to have a child alone because she believed her husband betrayed her." Marge studied her face. "Have you forgiven Josh?"

Erin pulled her fingers through her hair. But when she tried to say no, or to tell her mom it was irrelevant, she realized she *had* forgiven Josh. Somewhere, somehow in spilling her guts to Hugo and having him explain why Josh had kept his secret, she'd let it all go.

Her heart expanded and filled her chest. Having Hugo identify with Josh had eased her into looking at her past, and she had seen Josh as Josh. Not blinded by her own needs, her own hurts, she understood his fears. But also, hearing Hugo talk about his family, and seeing his fight to bring them back together, she understood Josh's sense of responsibility. Just as Hugo was now putting his own feelings aside, Josh had ruthlessly put his feelings aside—

Her head spun. She had finally gotten beyond it. And she had Hugo to thank.

Grumpy Hugo Harrington.

No...*wounded* Hugo Harrington.

"Are you okay?"

"Yeah, Mom. I'm fine. I'm just finally seeing Josh's side of things."

Her mom's eyes narrowed. "Really?"

"I did spend time with Hugo while you were gone. He told me he went to the hospital with his sister, who is pregnant. He was so thrilled to get to play the part of big brother for her that it was amazing. He never said it, but he put his own needs aside, his own questions about what happened when he and his siblings were younger, and just reacted, protecting his sister."

"That's lovely." Her mom's voice was soft, compassionate.

Erin smiled. "He's had a rough life."

"Hugo or Josh?"

"Both, I guess. They are nothing alike. But they have a sense of responsibility and some sort of weird male pride that makes them think they are in charge of everything. I saw Josh through Hugo. Trying to spare everybody by taking on all the burden himself."

"What about him telling the other woman?"

She licked her lips. "Everybody has a breaking point." She didn't tell her mom that she suddenly realized she was "the woman to confide in" in Hugo's story. No matter how wonderful their time together, she knew he'd hit his breaking point the day they went into the attic to look at decorations. She'd forced him into a corner, and he'd decided they should leave the office—go for hot cocoa. But she'd set up the scenario.

Josh's female friend had sworn that Josh had simply needed a release valve, someone to talk to, and now Erin totally understood that. Even as forgiveness for Josh filled her soul and gave her peace, her relationship with Hugo came into perspective.

While she was worrying that she was falling in love, he was working out his past, probably appreciating that he could drop a tidbit here and there and not fear that she would judge, because she'd endured hardship too.

He might never explain the whole of it, but he was talking to her. She would always be the woman who helped him through the hardest days of his life, but he would

never love her. She would always remind him of his terrible past.

Even if she was the person who helped him fix it.

This wasn't the beginning of something wonderful. It
was the end of something horrible for Hugo.

And if it was the beginning of anything, it was a heartache for her.

CHAPTER TEN

WHEN RONNIE RETURNED Erin to the Harrington Park Hotel, Hugo stood at the door, waiting for her.

"How was their trip?"

She looked up at him, her gaze locking with his for a few seconds as she stared into his eyes. Then she glanced away. "Good. She loves everybody. Had it not been for Noah getting cranky, missing me, I think she could have stayed forever."

Feeling as if something was off, but not able to identify it, Hugo carefully said, "That's good, right?"

"Yeah. Sure." She sighed and shook her head. "Actually, it's excellent. I know how she's longed for her family, and you bringing us here gave her a chance we never would have had without you, if only because we couldn't afford it."

He casually put his arm around her, feeling, for some reason or another, that she needed reassurance. "Nonsense, you're the best. Some day your business is going to really take off and you're going to be the 'it' girl for events in Manhattan."

She smiled, but the smile didn't reach her eyes. "That'll be great."

What she said was good, but like her eyes, her voice didn't back up the sentiment of it. Not knowing what to do, he left her, veering off when they reached his office. But sitting at his desk, reading progress reports, the feeling that he had to fix this overtook him. He didn't like that something was troubling Erin. He also realized that with her mum and son home, they wouldn't sleep together tonight. His big bed would be cold and lonely, but this feeling he had wasn't about him.

Erin was off. She couldn't be unhappy. Her son was home. She'd probably hugged and kissed him a million times.

So, what the hell was it?

After an hour of contemplation, he was still stymied. He couldn't stand the thought that something was wrong and shoved himself out of his desk chair and headed to the kitchen, where he instructed Louis to send up a sample tray of everything he and his staff had created that day. Then he called Erin and told her to meet him in the penthouse.

When the elevator opened for her to enter, the little penthouse kitchen was filled with everything from lobster to pudding.

She sniffed the air and groaned with pleasure. "What's all this?"

"Food to sample. Louis doesn't just have to feed a hotel filled with guests on Christmas Eve. He's got to make breakfasts, lunches and dinners for their entire stays." He motioned to the counter lined with samples. "What you see right here is him trying to pin down his restaurant menu."

She walked over and sniffed the air. "And we're the guinea pigs?"

He laughed. "Or you could say we're the lucky people who get to taste test." He picked up a bit of lobster, dipped it in butter and popped it in his mouth. "The man is a genius."

She laughed. "And we're both going to have to join

a gym when we get back to Manhattan—" Her breath caught slightly.

And Hugo knew why. Mentioning Manhattan shoved them back to reality, back to being a businessman and the woman he employed to plan his events.

Even as his heart jolted at the thought of not seeing her after this wonderful affair, he wondered if they really did have to part. Maybe what had started out as an affair had turned into something solid? Something real?

Maybe that was what she was feeling? The confusion of a temporary arrangement edging over into something permanent.

It should have scared him. He'd never believed he was the kind of guy who'd find love. He didn't think he had time for love or a big enough place in his life. But what he experienced with her was so different, so important, it filled his heart.

The shock of it should have made him at least pause and consider the consequences. Instead, the longing he'd been battling since she'd arrived in London had him patting the stool beside his. Taking a chance. "Sit."

With a nervous laugh, she did as he said.

But the laugh confirmed his suspicions. She'd never been nervous around him before. Recognizing that, he concluded the shift in their situation had to be the problem. Still, he didn't have any answers. He was as baffled as she was.

There was only one way to handle this. Just keep doing what they'd been doing—enjoying each other's company— and see what happened.

"Why don't we play a food game? You close your eyes and I'll feed you a bite of something and you try to guess what it is."

She rolled her eyes. "Hugo…really…"

"Close your eyes."

Skeptical, she nonetheless closed her eyes. Using a slim seafood fork, he took a piece of lobster, dipped it in butter and said, "Open your mouth."

She opened her mouth and he set the lobster on her tongue.

She groaned with pleasure. "Mmm…lobster."

"That one was easy." He paused. "You've got a little butter on your mouth." He leaned in, kissed it away.

Her eyes opened and she smiled. Hugo's chest filled. He'd hated to see her sad, and in ten minutes he'd brought his Erin back.

"Close your eyes again. I don't want you peeping."

She laughed. He chose a small bite of filet mignon. "Open your mouth."

She shook her head, fanning her beautiful red hair along her shoulders, but opened her mouth, and he set the filet on her tongue.

"Oh, God, that's good. Perfect."

"Louis is a genius."

Her eyelids lifted and again she smiled. "So you've said."

He leaned in. "I think I see sauce on your lips."

"There was no sauce on the steak…" She stopped when his lips met hers. This time he put his arm around her waist, pulling her close, deepening the kiss.

He'd never felt so powerful or so happy that he could make someone smile. He enticed her nearer and nearer until she was on his lap. Then he kissed them both into oblivion, as he removed her T-shirt and she got rid of his jacket and tie.

He could have taken her right there in the kitchen, but with elevator doors that could open for anyone who had the code, he decided against that and drew her back to the bedroom with him.

After they made love, she fell asleep beside him, and that indescribable joy filled him again. The thought that he had found his place, his purpose, tiptoed through his brain, and for once he didn't argue.

The beep of his phone floated back from the main living area, interrupting his thoughts. He eased out of bed, careful not to wake Erin as he slipped into his shirt and pants. He couldn't believe he'd got so involved that he didn't realize he'd left his phone behind and shook his head at the strength of whatever it was between him and Erin.

He grabbed a bite of watermelon from the fruit salad Louis had prepared and walked to the coffee table, where he'd left his phone. He hit a button and saw eight missed calls.

Eight missed calls?

And one voice mail.

"Hey, Hugo. Not sure what's going on, but Sally's gone back to Tianlipin. She'd thought you might have come to the hospital when she was released on Sunday and was surprised you hadn't." There was a pause, and then Jay added, "It's odd. It's as if she expects to see you now and again."

Hugo's heart stopped and he fell to the sofa in the seating area. Sally had talked about him? Expected to see him?

He slammed his phone on the sofa cushion with an unsatisfying thud and bounced up to pace, his thoughts going a million miles a second. Then he realized he'd been showing Erin around London on Sunday. He'd never followed up with Sally about her hospital stay because Jay had called him and given him a report.

He hadn't given Sally a passing thought.

He bent and grabbed the phone again, calling Jay. "It never entered my mind to see her off on Sunday."

Jay laughed. "No biggie."

But it was a biggie to Hugo. A door had opened—

No. He'd opened a door by taking Sally to the hospital, talking to her, yelling at her now-fiancé, and then he'd forgotten about it.

"I wasn't there either. She'd called telling me she was home. I'm assuming that's Tianlipin. Look. Don't make too much of this."

Easy for Jay to say. He wasn't the one on the outside looking in. Hoping for an opening. Praying for a way to show Sally his intentions were genuine and that he'd spent years missing her and Jay.

He'd found it, and then he'd walked away.

Still, he wouldn't let Jay see his annoyance with himself. "Okay. Fine. Whatever."

Erin strolled out of the bedroom, saw he was on the phone and motioned to the center island still filled with Louis's goodies.

He watched the gentle sway of her hips and his mouth watered, the way it did every time he looked at her.

He told himself not to make too much of that either. Though he'd had all kinds of thoughts of permanency with her, those couldn't be real. Not when he had so much else on his mind. He was in the middle of trying to renovate his family's hotel and reconcile with his brother and sister…he didn't have the mental energy left to get involved with a woman.

Which was the entire state of his life. Strong feelings or not, he was a ridiculously busy man. He could have fun with her, yes. But when they returned to Manhattan his life would get crazy again. Hotels would go up for sale. His brand would need reinforcing. And if he was lucky, his brother and sister would want him in their world.

Those were the things he'd worked his entire life for.

Those were his goals.

The things that had filled him with purpose and kept

him from sinking into a black pit of despair after his mum had kicked him out.

He couldn't abandon them because of a few days. Especially since Erin's odd mood might have been because she was also recognizing their time together was ending.

He finished the call with Jay, went back to the food and stayed in the moment as he and Erin ate lunch.

He reminded himself that this wasn't a relationship. It was fun. And those thoughts he'd had when he'd called her to come up to the penthouse? They were foolish musings of a guy having a really great time with a very special woman. She was sad. He wanted to make her happy. Because that was what their relationship was about. Fun. Nothing more.

When she left the penthouse to go back to work, he returned to the office with his New York staff.

He didn't wonder if she'd got home safely. At the end of her workday, he sent the limo to take her to her flat. But he didn't call to see how she was. Didn't go to the hotel first thing in the morning. He went back to the office with his staff, where he belonged.

Moving boxes was not how Erin had intended to spend her Wednesday morning, but with her workstation now overtaken by the painters, she had no choice. The mountains of paperwork on the desk Hugo used when he was in the hotel prevented her from usurping that area. So she'd had some workmen bring her small desk downstairs into Hugo's office, but they'd dropped it in the middle of everything.

She shoved boxes against the walls, carving out a place where she could push the desk, and was thrilled when she had everything arranged. But a box fell off the old-fashioned filing cabinet and dumped its contents all over the floor.

"Stupid clutter!" She crouched to pick up the papers, file folders and envelopes scattered around. She knew she was out of sorts because her time with Hugo continually confused her. She shouldn't like him, shouldn't enjoy his company, but lately he'd been damned near irresistible, baffling her. Making her long for things she couldn't have because as soon as they returned to Manhattan, he'd associate her with trouble, not success. And he wouldn't want to see her anymore.

She almost launched the papers and file folders across the room, if only to get them out of the way. "Why do people save everything?"

But when she saw Sally Harrington neatly printed on the front of one of the red envelopes and Hugo Harrington's name in the space for the return address, she stopped cold.

She looked at the postal stamp cancellation to see the date, then rifled through at least twenty dusty red and green envelopes—probably Christmas cards—with Hugo's return address, mailed to James and Sally. *His brother and sister.*

Gobsmacked, she sat on the cluttered floor. He'd tried to get in touch with his brother and sister, but the cards had never gotten to the twins. Someone had held them back.

More secrets.

Her heart stuttered. She'd never had the feelings for another person that she had for Hugo Harrington. He was sweet, caring, and more fun-loving than she'd ever expected him to be. He'd sensed her mood the day before and dispelled all her fears, and dear God in heaven, she was falling for him—

Had fallen for him.

She loved him. Loved a man who would undoubtedly dump her when they returned to New York. Loved a man with secrets. And in her hand, she held another one. He'd tried to stay in touch.

She blew the dust off one of the green cards, staring at it as if expecting it to give her the answer. In a way, it did. Whoever hid the cards might not have wanted Sally and Jay to have them, but he or she hadn't been able to toss them away either.

His mother?

Most likely. The stepfather who'd brought their hotel to ruins wouldn't have been sentimental enough to keep them. But a mom trying to protect the twins from whatever Hugo might have said? She'd keep the cards. She might not have had courage enough to open them, but she clearly wanted the connection to Hugo and might have even hoped something good was inside. So, though she hadn't summoned the nerve to open them, she'd kept them.

Erin stared at the small stack of cards, sadness permeating her soul. If Hugo had wanted to leave his family, had wanted his freedom, wanted the clean break, would he have tried to keep in touch?

Probably not.

The only conclusion that could be drawn from Hugo reaching out was that he had wanted to stay connected. And if he had wanted to stay connected, was it so farfetched to believe that he might not have wanted to leave at all?

Did that explain why he'd bought this hotel—*waited* to buy this hotel?

And if he hadn't wanted to leave, it had to have been his stepfather who'd pushed him out. A mother unable to part with cards from her son couldn't have been the one to shove him out. But a stepfather who didn't want an older child around, a child smart enough to remember the past and strong enough to make his wishes known, would definitely kick him to the curb. Especially since Hugo had said he'd caught his stepfather embezzling.

Poor Hugo!

Her heart squeezed. But she took a breath. She was only making assumptions.

She stared at the dusty envelopes. As an employee, it was none of her business. As his lover? He hadn't told her the whole story of his past, but he'd told her enough that she knew she had to show him these cards.

She shoved them into the big manila envelope, set it on top of a filing cabinet and went back to work.

Twenty minutes later, she had her desk arranged. Her head down, she focused on last-minute details for the big Christmas Eve celebration, especially deliveries. Food was arriving now. Chefs were reconciling the purchase orders against packing slips, but so was she. Everything was checked and double-checked.

"Knock! Knock!"

Erin glanced up to see her mom at the door, sliding Noah to the floor. He ran to her. "Mum!"

Erin laughed as she hoisted him into her arms. "Since when do you call me Mum?"

Her mom sauntered in. "He's been picking up the language subtleties like a little parrot."

She pulled his cap off his head and smoothed his static-filled red hair before he bounced off her lap to explore the office. "What brings you here?"

Marge said, "I have an errand and can't take Noah." She winced. "I was hoping you could keep him for a few hours."

Rising from her seat, she hesitated. Pretending the envelope of Hugo's Christmas cards was no big deal, she slid it off the filing cabinet and into the empty top drawer. Everything was too chaotic to show them to Hugo today.

Or worse, for him to find them. She should probably wait until after the holiday—

No. Hugo being able to show these cards to his brother and sister might be the thing that helped Sally and Jay see he'd been forced out of their lives. She had to do it today... or maybe tonight? Maybe she could entice *him* up to the penthouse before she went home?

"Can you keep him? I swear I won't be long."

Pulled out of her reverie, she turned her attention to her mom again.

Though most construction had been finished, the hotel was a beehive of activity and everyone was tense. It might not be a good idea to have Noah underfoot.

But when her little boy smiled at her, with his baby teeth all in a straight white row and his blue eyes gleaming, she ruffled his hair. "Sure. Why not?"

"Why not what?" Hugo asked, walking past her mom to come into the office. He stopped short when he saw her desk. "What's this?"

"They're painting my office. I got the workmen to bring my desk down here. I don't want to mess up any of the clean spaces. And if I go to another room that's in line to be painted, I'll just be moving again."

He grunted. "Good point."

Her mom said, "So it's okay if Noah stays?"

Hugo pivoted to face Marge. "What?"

Before her mom could speak, Erin quickly said, "I was just getting settled when my mom came with Noah and asked if I could keep him for a few hours."

Fear had her heart beating so fast she almost couldn't breathe. Up to now, she hadn't thought too much about whether Hugo liked Noah. Now, suddenly, it was the most important thing in the world.

Hugo surprised her. "Actually, that might be a good

idea. There are a few things I'd like to see a child's reaction to."

Erin's lungs filled with air again. "Really?"

"Sure." He smiled at Marge. "You go. He'll be fine here."

With a kiss on Noah's cheek, Marge scampered off.

Hugo stooped in front of Noah. "You remember me, right?"

Noah nodded.

"I'm going to show you something really special. Will you come with me?"

He nodded eagerly.

Hands on Noah's waist, Hugo lifted him as he rose. "I want to see his reaction to the courtyard garden."

"Sure," Erin said, so confused she would have liked to sit again. It almost seemed like the guy she knew in Manhattan was gone. The man she'd thought had a heart of stone had taken to her son as if he loved him. He'd sent cards to his brother and sister that were never delivered. He was good to her mom…and to her. Very, very good to her.

Her heart stumbled with hope.

Maybe it hadn't been a mistake to fall in love with him?

CHAPTER ELEVEN

THEY MADE THEIR way to the ballroom, Hugo holding Noah and Noah giggling with excitement.

He glanced down at the little boy and the strangest feelings rippled through him. This little boy needed a father. Another reason for him to make sure he backed off his relationship with Erin when they returned to Manhattan. If something serious ever happened between him and Erin, he would be Noah's stepfather.

His breath stuttered. He'd had the *worst* example of a stepfather imaginable.

Of course, that could mean he knew what not to do.

He shook his head, telling himself these thoughts were pointless. He wasn't made for a family. He was a businessman. Someone who worked at all hours of the night if he had to. Plus, his goal of getting his family together was in reach.

He couldn't divide his attention and miss that opportunity. Jay's call on Monday had shown him how easily his own family could slip through his fingers. His goals could turn to dust. The hole in his heart could remain cold and barren simply because he lost focus.

They walked through the clean space, newly painted, floors redone and round tables being set up around the dance floor. When the doors opened on to the garden, his breath stalled. Plants that had been put into place fully grown were dewy from the mist that spritzed down on them every morning. A miniforest with fir trees, winterberry shrubs and snow surrounded a skating rink that looked like a frozen lake. Tiles created walkways between the plants and two sections had been arranged: the skating rink and the area housing Santa's throne.

His lungs couldn't seem to fill. It would be the perfect addition to the Christmas Eve launch party for the restored Harrington Park.

"Do you see that chair over there?" he said to Noah, pointing across the garden. "That's actually a throne."

Noah only looked at him, waiting for more information.

Their eyes locked for a few seconds and a strange connection began to form. It was as if the little boy was checking him out to see if he was worthy of liking.

Finally, Hugo said, "Because he's so special, Santa sits on a throne."

Noah gasped. "Santa?"

The little squeal broke the spell of connection. Hugo wondered if he'd imagined it, but he also got the feeling he'd just scored major points with Noah. "Yes. Santa will be here."

Noah squirmed to be put down and Hugo lowered him to the floor. He scampered over to the throne, a tall-backed chair with a red velvet seat and trimmed with gold paint.

Catching Hugo's gaze, Noah said, "I saw Santa."

"I know. I was with you, remember?"

"Noah also saw him in Ireland." Erin walked over to the throne. "I think he's confused because he's already seen him twice, and I'm sure Irish Santa spoke with an accent."

Connection wove around and through them. Him to Erin. Erin to Noah. Noah back to Hugo again. It was almost as rich and deep as the feelings he'd had around his family when his father had been alive. He blamed it on the space. The throne they were using for Santa had been around since his father had planned the Christmas Eve event.

He cautiously answered Erin. "I'm sure he did have a bit of a brogue."

Erin stooped in front of Noah. "Santa can be many places." She winced and faced Hugo again. "Won't the kids wonder what Santa's doing at the hotel when he's supposed to be delivering presents?"

"My dad always told them that he didn't start his rounds until midnight. Then our Santa would make a big deal out of leaving. He'd wave and say he had lots of work to do and every kid in the room would get big-eyed with anticipation."

He could see it in his mind, feel the excitement from all those years ago, but with Erin and Noah added in, as if they belonged.

She smiled. "Sounds nice." Rising, she said, "Look at what you've done, Hugo. Everything is beautiful."

He took a breath, easing thoughts of Erin and Noah aside, unexpectedly afraid Jay and Sally might not see it as he did. "My brother and sister loved the original trees and the Santa throne. Maybe changing things isn't a good idea?"

"You think they aren't going to approve?" She laughed. "After everything Sally did to create this place?"

Their gazes connected and he quietly said, "Yes."

She might not see it because she didn't know his entire past.

"I guess if it isn't quite right, we can always change it back next year."

She smiled. "Hey, look at you, being all flexible."

He laughed. That was one of the things he liked about

her. Even when the past grabbed him, she lured him to see the future. His long-held beliefs about himself, his life, shivered through him, but they didn't have their usual power. They were weak. Insubstantial.

"I do have my moments when I recognize flexibility helps."

Noah ran over and put his little arms up for Hugo to hold him, and the future leaped to his brain again. Teaching this boy to throw a ball. Helping him with homework. Reading bedtime stories—

Then relaxing in the master bedroom with his mother.

He'd never seen anything so clearly. Never wanted anything so badly. And while his smart, powerful self knew he could bring it about, his cautious side told him there was always trouble lurking somewhere. He'd spent his entire life believing he was made for boardrooms, takeovers and decision-making. How could one woman make him think he'd changed?

They took Noah to the kitchen, and Hugo made a production out of Noah being the taste tester for the gingerbread that would create the enormous gingerbread house centerpiece for the goody table, but also the gingerbread men to be served with vanilla ice cream like sundaes. And, again, the whole experience was so natural, so easy that like a child longing for there to be a real Santa, Hugo could have believed.

But he recognized that was because he *wanted* to believe.

And that's when a man got into trouble. Wanting something, anything, too much was dangerous.

After they returned the office and Erin's mum had taken Noah home, Erin settled into the seat behind her desk. "So? Dinner tonight?"

She might have casually issued the invitation, but there

was something in her voice. A hesitation. As if she was as unsure of their situation as he was.

But that was good. It meant she knew as well as he did that their relationship wasn't a sure thing.

He pulled in a breath. "The chef's trying recipes, so we could have anything we want from the menu."

"That sounds perfect."

He heard it again. This time he wouldn't dub it hesitation. There was more of a professional tone to her voice. Like they were getting together to talk about something pertaining to the hotel, not to make love.

Hugo gave their dinner request to the chef, who, as always, was thrilled to have Hugo tasting the food before guests began arriving the day before Christmas Eve. But as he and Erin rode the elevator to the penthouse, where the chef would deliver their meals, he frowned at her briefcase and coat.

She'd never brought her coat and briefcase up to the room, a blatant reminder that she'd be leaving him alone in the big bed or to go home to his own cold, empty penthouse.

He reminded himself that shouldn't bother him. Even if they really were beginning a relationship, they were in the early stages. Right now, what they were doing was supposed to be casual. Not important. Feeling as if he were bonding with Noah that afternoon, he'd made too much of it. It was time to get them back to the easy relationship they both wanted. If something developed after they returned to Manhattan, that would be great. If it didn't, he would survive. But that was why he wanted this now. Something easy. Something fun.

He walked over, pulled her to him and kissed her. "The chef says we have forty minutes."

She slid her hands to his shoulders. "Oh, yeah?"

"Yeah. Wanna make good use of it?"

She laughed, then kissed him. Long and sweet. The thing he always felt with her stirred in his soul. He took them deeper, delving into her mouth with his tongue, pulling her so close the clothes that separated them didn't matter.

When he broke the kiss, he walked to the bar, retrieving a bottle of wine and two glasses, before he caught her hand and led her back to the bedroom.

They removed their clothes slowly, between kisses that felt different. He knew it was because of his thoughts that afternoon and decided to roll with it. Then he realized she was leading him, her feelings evident in every press of her lips, ever lick of her tongue. Before he could stop it, longing swelled inside him, a need so intense and pure it stole his breath. He couldn't imagine living his life without this, without *her*.

Telling himself to stop thinking that way, he almost swiped control from her. A few shifts, a few touches would have done it. But he liked this feeling. Not a loss of control, but a chance to be himself, let her love him.

His heart stuttered. *Let her love him?*

The thought rippled through him, tiptoed into his brain. She clearly loved him. Nothing was ever as sweetly innocent as the touch of her tongue on his skin, the smooth movement of her palm as it roamed over his flesh, seeking sensitive spots, luring him into the spell she created.

Confused, he lay back, let her explore until the profound perfection of her touch build a fire inside him that would only be assuaged one way. He caught her shoulders and rolled her beneath him, entering her with a thrust that made her gasp.

She'd shown him her curious side. Now he would show her his demanding side. They rode a wave of intense arousal that shattered them. Then she fell asleep at his side and he took a long, slow breath, his heart so soft he knew she held it in the palm of her hand. His soul so open he could feel the fresh air of liberation filling it.

He closed his eyes.

He'd fallen in love and he didn't merely want a life with her. He yearned for it. He wasn't even sure how this had happened. He had a past that told him he wasn't a relationship person. He liked work. He liked success. He liked control.

Nothing that he felt with her was stable or secure. It was fragile and scary and so insubstantial it was almost liquid.

But it was also bliss. Maybe worth more than a sister who didn't like him and a brother who might never really trust him?

Or maybe he'd been right the day before when he realized being with her was so distracting that it might ruin the plan that had been the only thing to keep him sane since his mother asked him to leave?

CHAPTER TWELVE

DINNER—LOBSTER FRA DIAVOLO, flavored with clam juice on cognac—melted in Hugo's mouth. Erin seemed to enjoy hers, but the odd behavior he'd noticed before they'd made love had returned.

She was nervous. Not out of sorts the way she had been the day he'd fed her lobster and filet mignon. But jumpy about something.

His thoughts after making love returned and he realized that whatever they were doing, having fun or falling in love, it snagged all his mental energy and could ruin his plan to get his family back together. Not because she was demanding, but because the feelings he'd had when she made love to him made everything else in the world seem irrelevant.

And his brother and sister could not be irrelevant. His past had to be cleared or he'd live with the shadow of secrets and lies his entire life.

When they finished dessert, she rose from the table that the wait staff had set up in the sitting room and walked to the chair where she'd left her briefcase.

Conflicting emotions skittered through him. If she left so quickly, so easily, it would confirm that what they were doing was only about sex. Irrelevant. And his focus could return to where it should be. On his plan to fix his family. Clear his name.

But what she had done in that bedroom hadn't felt irrelevant.

He said nothing. Leaning back. Watching her. The feeling in the air confounded him. The mood had shifted from the intense warmth of what they'd just shared to something disjointed and jagged.

"I have something for you."

He still said nothing. The tone of her voice said it wasn't a gift.

"Something I found."

"Found? Where?"

She faced him. "In a box." She winced. "Actually, as I was moving junk out of that corner so I could set up my desk, it fell." She pulled a manila envelope from her briefcase. "This spilled out."

She held it out to him, and he took it, his heart thundering in his chest. Would she have made love to him so sweetly if she'd found the evidence Nick had trumped up to make it appear Hugo had been the one who'd embezzled?

She might. Especially if what he'd believed was profound emotion was her goodbye.

Their gazes held.

She whispered, "Open it."

His emotions a knot of chaos, he poured out the contents of the envelope. Smaller red and green envelopes greeted him. "What's this?"

She swallowed without answering, and curiosity compelled him to look down again at the envelopes—

Addressed to Sally and James.

His gaze leaped to the return address. *His.*

"What the hell?" He glanced up at her, then back at the cards. "I sent these to my brother and sister. And they're—" he peered down again "—not even opened."

"They were all together in the box. As if someone had intercepted them and stashed them away."

"That jerk, Nick!"

She shook her head once, quickly. "Wouldn't you assume Nick would have destroyed them?"

His face fell. "You think my *mother*…kept these from the twins?"

"I think she intercepted them in the mail. Whatever her reasons, she didn't give them to your brother and sister. But I also believe she couldn't throw away the only part of you she still had."

He slammed the handful of cards to the table beside his empty plate. "She didn't have any problem tossing the whole me away. Why keep these?"

She shrugged.

Hugo scrubbed his hand across his mouth, his head spinning, his heart so heavy it hurt to breathe.

Watching myriad emotions race across Hugo's face, Erin held her breath, wanting to understand how he felt and to reconcile the man he was beginning to show her sparingly to the one he showed the world. The guy who'd barely paid a whit of attention to her in two and a half years and now suddenly couldn't keep his hands off her. The guy who'd been sweet and kind to Noah that afternoon. The guy who'd laughed with her.

The guy she was trying not to love but couldn't help herself. He held so many secrets and they hurt him, and she couldn't love another man with secrets. She couldn't let the chance to get answers to her questions pass.

"Hugo, what happened to make you leave? You say your mom tossed you out and she clearly kept these cards from your brother and sister. But she also couldn't throw them away." She spread her hands imploringly. "Every time you tell me about your Christmas Eves, I see the perfect family. What happened?"

He took a breath. "My dad died."

"You didn't leave when your dad died." That much she'd gleaned from the newspaper in his desk drawer.

"No. My dad dying changed everything. He was the engine behind our great Christmas Eves." He ran his hands down his face. "He was the engine behind everything. When he died, our mother couldn't cope. She was a fantastic mum, but Dad was the one with the business sense. I was too young to realize it, but she was failing. When she started dating Nick—he'd been a frequent guest at the hotel—she saw salvation. She married him and essentially let him take over."

"That's…" She almost said *sad*, but remembering her state after Josh died, how hard it was sometimes to simply put one foot in front of the other to get herself to work, she changed her mind. "Actually, Hugo, as a widow myself, it makes sense to me."

"Well, I was a teenage boy who saw it all differently. It felt like a betrayal."

"You gave him a hard time?"

"I tried to get along until things got bad. I started hearing innuendos in everything he said. Thinly veiled threats to kick us *all* out. The reminder that we'd be homeless, living on the street without him. Especially after Mum gifted the hotel to him as a Christmas present."

Erin gasped. "She gave him the hotel?"

"Yes. It was jaw-dropping. Odd. Everyone thought it was a gift of love, but I had this horrible sense there was more to it. By then I was seventeen, and decently smart because I'd worked at Harrington Park since I was young. My dad had even begun showing me the inner workings like employee schedules and bookkeeping. So I sneaked a peek at the books and realized Nick was cooking them. Money supposedly spent on renovations for Harrington Park was actually being siphoned off and going to his other busi-nesses…most of which were failing. He did this for so long and so consistently that he'd bled Harrington Park dry."

"You left because he was embezzling?"

"No, like a fool, I went to him. Told him what I'd found. Gave him a chance to come clean with my mother." He sniffed a laugh. "That's the enthusiasm of a teenager. Or maybe the naivete. That night my mum called me into the office and confronted me with evidence that showed I was the one siphoning off the money. Nick's money, she'd said, because he was the one who owned the hotel. She wanted to know where it was. I told her that I hadn't taken it, Nick had. But Nick was older, smarter and probably accustomed to hiding his deeds. He bested me at every turn. Even threatened me with arrest. And the ongoing hints were also in there. Suggestions that with the hotel being his, if my mum took my side I wouldn't just go to jail, but she and the twins would be out on the street. The silence was so thick in the room, the click of a pen would have sounded like thunder. Eventually, my mother told me to leave."

"Oh, my God. He framed you!"

"He *used* me. I gave him just enough information and time to turn the tables and, in the process, turn my mother against me."

Erin held out one of the Christmas cards. "She still loved you."

"Right. Keeping a few Christmas cards proves she loved me? I think her not giving them to Jay and Sally proves she didn't." He combed his fingers through his hair. "For a while I toyed with calling the police myself. The real ac-counting had to be somewhere. All they had to do was find it. But I looked at Nick's face and I knew if I didn't leave,

Nick would throw my mother and my brother and sister out into the street. That night. Christmas Eve."

The penthouse fell silent again. Even Erin could feel the ghosts of Christmas Eves past haunting the quiet room.

She walked to Hugo, putting her hands on his forearms and sliding them up his biceps, but he shrugged her off.

"No," he said, stepping and turning away. "Stop."

She retreated, feeling and seeing the reserved Hugo returning. Not about to let that happen, she said, "I still say she loved you."

He spun to face her. "Oh, really? She never once tried to contact me, and she kept my messages to my brother and sister away from them. How do you get love out of that when it's pretty clear she didn't want me in her life?"

"You yourself said she was under a lot of pressure—"

He remembered that. Remembered her fearful eyes. Remembered how he'd wanted to help her—

Suddenly he was seventeen again. As fearful for his mother as she was for herself. He glanced at the cards. Pictured himself at eighteen, addressing the first ones to Jay and Sally. So hopeful. He'd been that way every year. Choosing just the right cards, penning a personal message, absolutely positive that year would be the year he'd get an answering card or letter.

It was only after his cards began coming back to him marked "addressee unknown" and he knew his brother and sister no longer lived at Harrington Park that he'd stopped sending cards and begun making plans to buy the hotel. He'd known the only way to bring his family back together would be to buy Harrington Park.

And that was working…sort of. Jay was trying. Sally was cool. But she had fashioned the garden. She wanted to be part of the hotel.

She simply didn't want any part of him. For years he hadn't let that hurt him, but these past weeks it had. Because he'd gone soft. Wanting things he'd known all along he couldn't have. He was the strong businessman, older brother. Not their peer. Not someone who begged them to like him.

"Let me help you through this."

He also wasn't a man who let himself be vulnerable. Erin was so beautiful and so loving, it had been tempting to succumb—but he suddenly saw it wasn't right.

It was not who he was—not who he could be if he wanted to bring his family together again.

"I'm fine."

She laughed sadly. "No. You're not."

Anger whipped through him. She wanted him weak? She wanted him humble?

"I'm fine." He didn't care that his voice was loud, his tone impatient. "In fact, I'm glad my mother didn't show them these cards. I'm not going to show them either. I was a sad, lonely kid, trying to make amends. But Jay and Sally didn't need a friend. They needed the strong big brother who should have protected them. *That's* the family we all want back."

"No. What you want is honesty. Honest relationships."

"No, what *you* want is an honest relationship. Josh hurt you, so you think everybody in your life has to be soft and vulnerable about everything. That's not how some of us are made. Some of us are made to be strong, made to absorb pain and solve problems—"

"Hugo! No!"

His resolve strengthened along with his disappointment in her. How could she not see? Or was being with her the problem?

"Yes. That's who I was made to be." He pulled in a determined breath, feeling like himself as his lungs filled with air and his muscles solidified. "Actually, I think it's time for you to leave."

"Okay. I do need to get home to put Noah to bed."

He shook his head. "No. I think what I'm saying is that you and I need to back off. You're soft and sweet and you see the world a certain way. But I can't be that way."

Her face twisted in confusion. "You're breaking up with me? Over a simple argument?"

"It's not simple for me. This is my family—my *life*. And if you want to split hairs, we never really were together."

She blinked. "It felt like it to me."

"And that's the difference between us. Something always held me back, made me question everything about us. Now I know what it was." He motioned around. "This. I don't want to be soft."

Saying that aloud filled him with certainty. No longer confused or angry, he turned toward the master bedroom and his jacket and phone. "I'll see you in the morning. We have a lot to do to make sure this project is on track...the way it's supposed to be."

CHAPTER THIRTEEN

SEEING HUGO WAS not only serious, he was determined, Erin punched the button for the elevator, confusion making her breath stutter. Those cards had triggered something in him she couldn't quite put her finger on, but he'd changed right before her eyes—

And meant it.

Just as she had feared, she'd landed in the middle not merely of his personal battle, but also of his fight to fix his past and reunite his family.

She raced through the lobby with tears in her eyes, avoiding Ronnie's gaze as he opened the limo door for her, and just barely had herself composed when she walked into her apartment.

"Hey, Erin." Her mom rose from the sofa. "Noah's done nothing but talk nonstop about seeing Santa on Christmas Eve. He's so excited. He even calls Hugo, Ugo."

Halfway through shrugging out of her coat, Erin stopped dead in her tracks. Hugo's reaction had been unexpected. She knew he was smarting from finding that his mother had kept the cards from Sally and Jay. She'd thought she could talk him through it. But he'd turned back into businessman Hugo so fast she hadn't been able to keep up. And though he hadn't blamed her for what his mother had done, in the heat of the moment he had ended their relationship.

She could think that—maybe—he'd feel differently in the morning. But their romance had happened so fast, they hadn't built any real trust, and at their first problem, he'd pulled away from her.

What he'd really done was yanked himself away—dropped her—so he could go back to being himself. The guy who didn't need anybody. The guy who didn't *want* to need anybody.

Maybe that was the thing that always bothered her about them, the thing that wouldn't quite let either of them believe their relationship would last? He didn't *want* to need anybody because the first people in his life, the people he longed to have in his life, had asked him to leave. And that hadn't merely hurt, it had forged who he was.

He couldn't make a commitment, fall in love, because he was always afraid it would be snatched away. So he'd always hold something back.

No matter how much she loved him, Josh had taught her the pain of living with someone who always held something back.

If he hadn't broken it off, she should have—

They were not right for each other.

The realization that she'd really lost Hugo, permanently this time, stole her breath, filled her eyes with tears. When things between them were good, they were perfect. But life had taught her some hard lessons. Still, no matter how logical, losing him hurt. He might not have loved her, but she had loved him.

She still loved him.

She almost told her mom she was thinking about not attending the Christmas Eve celebration, but there were things she had to do at the hotel the next day.

Forcing a smile for her mom, she said, "Ugo? That's funny." Then she faced Noah. "Okay, little friend, let's get you into bed."

She slid Noah into pajamas and closed her eyes when he gave her a good-night kiss on the cheek.

He pulled back and with a happy grin said, "I love you."

Her eyes filled with tears. Though his coloring was hers, his bone structure and facial features belonged to his father. She'd made peace with Josh, with his death, with his secrets, because Hugo had helped her to understand him.

How could it be that they weren't right for each other—

She didn't need to figure it out. The truth was like a neon sign. She and Hugo did not belong together.

Now she had to figure out how to get through the next few days, especially the Christmas Eve celebration. Then she could go home and try to heal.

Because this hurt. It hurt worse than losing Josh. She felt like a part of her soul was being ripped from her. But how could that be when he'd never really trusted her?

Hugo returned to the first floor to get his laptop so he could do some work in the penthouse that evening. He wasn't going to his London flat. He had to get the celebration back on track. Get his game face on. Whip this hotel into shape so that nothing, not even the color of the smallest ribbon, was wrong.

The elevator opened on the lobby, dressed up in evergreen branches, lights, ornaments. The scent of pine mixing with the smell of fresh paint took him back decades. Every December, his dad had the hotel repainted for the big Christmas Eve celebration.

If he closed his eyes, he could picture it.

He expected a flood of joy. But for the first time, picturing those old Christmas Eve parties didn't feel right.

He didn't feel right.

He stopped in the center of everything. The perfect recreation of his past shimmered around him.

And he didn't feel right?

He'd put his world back into place after seeing those cards. He'd pulled himself together, more determined than ever to fix his family—

His phone rang. Thinking it might be Erin, he slid it from his pocket to refuse the call, but the caller wasn't Erin. It was Jay.

He clicked to take the call. "Yes?"

"Well, you're in a chipper mood."

Those weird feelings that something was off tumbled through Hugo again.

"No matter. What I have to tell you will cheer you right up. When Sally said she was going home, I assumed Tianlipin. Turns out she meant her flat in Kensington. She's definitely attending the Christmas Eve celebration."

And just like that, the weirdness disappeared. Sally and Jay would both be at the Christmas Eve party.

"That's great."

"Yes," Jay happily replied. "Everything will be perfect."

Hugo started to answer, but the odd feeling returned. He and Jay had always been eager to work things out, but how could their relationship be real if his brother and sister didn't know a big piece of their family puzzle? That he'd sent them cards and their mum had held them back.

He took a breath and suddenly realized the oddness he'd been feeling was about those cards. He couldn't withhold the knowledge that his mother had kept his Christmas cards from them. He and his siblings needed to talk this out. All of it.

His brother and sister had to know he hadn't deserted

them. He didn't really want to paint his mother in a poor light, but maybe he was simply tired of being the bad guy.

He arrived at work the next morning lost in thought. Now that most of the hotel renovations were complete, his staff had gone back to New York to be with their families for Christmas. He'd offered them the chance to attend the celebration, but most had wanted to go home.

He walked through the renovated lobby, beautifully decorated, and the odd feeling he had the night before was gone. Confirming that his decision to show Jay and Sally his Christmas cards was essential to getting the three of them back together as a family.

He glanced at a red ribbon with gold trim and his heart stuttered. He remembered his mother choosing that ribbon, then realized Erin had spotted the detail and recreated it—

His heart swelled with emotion, but he took a breath. It was her job to please him. And it was his job to do this right. Not be soft. Be strong. Be the guy who could hold his family together.

He stepped into his office and stopped short when he saw Erin sitting at the small desk in the corner.

His heart tried to kick-start again, but he remembered his decision the night before. To show his siblings those cards. To set this past right. To not be soft.

To forget the happiness he'd found with her.

To forget the thought that he might be falling in love with her.

To get back to being himself. Hugo Harrington. Smart, savvy, successful.

The last thing he wanted was to compromise who he was.

He considered telling Erin she could go home, to end the weird parade of thoughts he had around her, but practicality wouldn't let him. There were things to be done. Not to mention last-minute disasters. Problems she'd need to handle. Especially if his siblings' reactions were good. Then his party could be the event he'd longed for.

The businessman in him would not let her go home.

He very casually said, "Good morning."

Erin didn't even look up. "Good morning."

Her cool reply went through him like a knife. But he hadn't changed his mind about their relationship. The next day or so would be incredibly awkward. But he deserved it. He'd known better than to start something with her. He hadn't been able to resist temptation.

He shrugged out of his cashmere overcoat. "The lobby is gorgeous."

Her attention focused on whatever she was reading, she said, "I got it as close to the pictures as I could."

"Yes. You did. Thank you."

Then he didn't say anything else.

The room filled with silence, but there was no way around it. He loved her son, might even love *her*…but he couldn't be the guy she needed. He didn't want to be the guy she needed.

Smart, strong Hugo would reunite his family, build hotels all over the globe, rule his world.

Erin blinked back tears and rose from her seat. She reminded herself they weren't right for each other, but it didn't help. She kept seeing him funny and happy, and part of her knew that was the guy he was supposed to be.

The guy he didn't want to be.

"If you need me, I'll be in the ballroom and courtyard garden, checking on a few things."

With that she walked out of the office she'd now be sharing with the guy who'd just shattered her heart.

Guests had begun arriving, filling the lobby with laughter in anticipation of what Hugo had done with his family's hotel. That bolstered her mood a bit as she pulled herself together walking to the ballroom and the courtyard garden.

Hugo's sister had done a remarkable job.

His brother had found the chef.

And Hugo had proof that he'd tried to keep in touch with them, yet all he saw was evidence that his mother hadn't loved him.

She had to work not to sympathize with him. Those cards had broken him, but she couldn't care. No matter how much she wanted to hug him and remind him he was one of the smartest, most wonderful people in the world, she couldn't. Not only did he not want to hear it, but she had to save herself. If she didn't pull away, she might end up not able to get away. In love with a man who wouldn't return her love.

It was unthinkable. Yet somehow her heart kept drawing her back. And she knew what she had to do.

Sitting on a bench in the serene garden, she pulled out her phone and called her mother. "What would you think about returning to Manhattan for Christmas?"

Her mom groaned. "Erin, all of Noah's gifts are here. We have a tree I'll have to take down. Not to mention packing!"

"Doesn't matter. As long as we can get it all done by Christmas Eve and find a flight for the three of us to go home that day, it'll be fine."

"You don't want to stay for Hugo's big party?"

"No." She almost said Hugo didn't want her to stay for his big party. But that wasn't true. He'd want her around for last-minute problems, and she'd keep seeing the happy man inside him desperate to get out. She couldn't risk getting soft again.

She needed to go home. To think of Harrington Park Hotel as just another job. To be in her own home with her son and her mom. To have a normal Christmas and then throw herself into the work of making sure her clients for New Year's Eve parties were taken care of.

Because if she let herself stop too long, she'd feel the pain in her bleeding heart, and she didn't have the strength for that.

She'd lost enough already in her still-young life, suffered enough. Being widowed, having her son alone, raising her son alone—

She just wanted to go home.

CHAPTER FOURTEEN

Knowing Sally was in town, Hugo phoned her and requested her presence at the hotel. Then he called Jay and told him the same thing, making it sound like hotel business that needed to be discussed, not something personal.

Aware that Erin was buzzing around, working on last-minute details as if her life depended on it, he shoved down the self-loathing at hurting her by reminding himself it was for the best. One way or another, his family situation would resolve itself over his Christmas cards. He simply wanted it done. So he could go back to being a hotel magnate. Someone who found his sense of purpose by making other people happy.

Refusing to even let himself think about Erin, he waited for his brother and sister in the penthouse. When the doors opened on Jay, he asked him if he'd like some coffee or a drink, and though Jay chose coffee, Hugo poured himself a glass of bourbon.

Sally arrived a few minutes later, glowing and wearing a ring on the third finger of her left hand.

"I see congratulations are in order."

She gleefully said, "Yes!"

Hugo hugged her, his spirit lifting. He'd been a strong big brother when she needed it. He had to continue behaving that way.

Sally and Jay sat on the sofa and Hugo lowered himself to the chair across from them. He picked up the manila envelope from the coffee table and slowly poured out the Christmas cards.

Jay said, "What's this?"

"Christmas cards. Addressed to you and Sally. All are postmarked, which proves I didn't desert you." He met Sally's gaze, then Jay's. "I tried to keep in touch."

Sally glanced at the red and green envelopes, then looked up at Hugo.

Jay rummaged through, finding the cards addressed to him and pulling them out. "There are so many cards here."

"I didn't give up until my cards started being returned by the post office."

Sally murmured, "That was probably when we were sent away to school."

A shaft of pain pierced Hugo's heart. It was no wonder it was so difficult for him to get through to them. They'd been as betrayed as he had been.

Jay laughed nervously. "Do we get to read these?"

Hugo leaned back in his chair. "Yes, but I need you to understand that I was lonely and missing you too. If I sound weak, that's why. But trust me, I'm back to being the big brother you knew. I had a few rough years, but I used them to make myself strong."

Sally quietly said, "You want us to read them now?"

His confidence fully in place, he met Sally's gaze. "No. You can take them home with you, if that would be more comfortable for you."

Having scooped his up, Jay said, "Okay." His smile was warm when he said, "I can't wait."

Hugo laughed. "Remember I was just a kid when I wrote some of those cards."

Jay laughed. "I know. I know. You're back to being big brother Hugo now."

But Sally shook her head. "You think sending us a few cards absolves you of everything?" She took a disgusted breath, squeezing her eyes shut. "All this talk about you being weak? When were you *ever* weak? You seemed pretty strong when you left us! Left our mum. If you truly believed that Nick was so bad, you should have stayed!"

She stormed to the elevator. Because the little car had just brought her up to the penthouse, it opened the minute that she tapped the button. Before Hugo could say anything, she was gone.

But Jay stayed behind. His hand hovered above Sally's cards.

His eyes rose and he caught Hugo's gaze. "You sent us a card every year?"

"Yes. And I didn't leave. I was pushed. Nick fabricated evidence that I'd stolen from the hotel."

"Young as I was, I still remember the whispers about money being missing."

"Nick took it." Hugo sucked in a long breath. As long as Jay listened, he intended to talk. "I'd found the evidence and confronted him. I gave him time to come clean with Mum. I never thought the bastard would use the time to frame me."

"So, you did nothing wrong?"

"I did nothing wrong." Hugo waited a few seconds then said, "Go ahead and take the ones addressed to Sally. She might not want them this very minute, but in a day or so she might have a change of heart." Strong, honest, he smiled at Jay. "You have a better chance of getting her to read them than I would."

After Jay left, Hugo strode to his office, his head swimming. Part of him still couldn't believe his mother hadn't given his Christmas messages to his brother and sister. The pain of it rose again and tried to weaken him but he refused to let it. All those years he'd waited for even a simple acknowledgment of the cards and mourned when he didn't receive so much as a thank-you. But no response had come because his mother hadn't given the twins his cards.

And now Sally wouldn't read hers and was still hurt and angry. Not that he blamed her. She had been a kid, left by her big brother, living in a house filled with tension.

Alone in the office, he looked at the outdated filing cabinets that lined the right wall, fighting back his anger with Nick. Death had taken his father, then grief had stolen his mother. Only a shell of herself, she'd married because she'd needed help, needed a partner. And what had she got? A thief. A thief so clever he'd edged out the only person who really knew him.

The bastard was a liar and a thief who had caused the people in Hugo's life to believe *he* was the thief. The people who should have known him best—

Erin knew him.

The idea tiptoed through his brain as soft as a feather. As real as warm summer rain.

He groaned. Erin was wonderful. But he couldn't have her. He wasn't himself with her—

But he'd liked the guy he had been with her.

The thought entered his brain softly again, as if afraid to form. And he knew why. Ever since he'd bought this hotel he'd been confused, trying to reunite his family and renovate a hotel so old a lesser man might have bulldozed it.

Yet he hadn't been as preoccupied with the hotel as he should have been because he liked being with Erin so much more—

Fury burst like a volcano and he swept his arm along the cluttered top of the row of cabinets, sending papers flying.

Angry with himself for losing control when Erin could walk in any minute, he bent to pick up the debris. He had two armloads of unmitigated junk—stuff so dated it should have been tossed a decade ago—when his gaze fell to an old Harrington Park Hotel manila envelope.

He might have simply stacked it up and thrown it back to the top of the cabinets, except his name was scrawled across the front... *Hugo.*

Could there have been another Hugo associated with the hotel?

Maybe.

But his heart sped up as his curiosity piqued. The envelope was so old...

He rose and took the envelope to the desk. Using a letter opener, he sliced the seam and reached inside for the contents.

Ten cards tumbled out.

The first had his full name and one of his former addresses on it. He scrambled to read the others. Each had his name and one of his addresses.

His mother's name and the hotel information had been scrawled in the return address space of the envelope.

He couldn't breathe. His mother had tried to send him things?

His heart thundered, tightening his chest.

Fear tried to tell him that the contents of those envelopes might not be good. She might have sent him threatening letters, trying to get her money back—

He shook his head, setting aside the fear. It wouldn't matter if they were threatening letters. He already believed his mother hated him. They couldn't do any more damage than that.

But if these were happy letters, Christmas cards, even letters expressing sadness that she hadn't defended him, then he wanted to see.

No. He *needed* to see.

He ripped them open. And read the most wonderful words he had ever seen in his life.

She was desperate.

She was sorry.

She loved him.

He read each card, then read the more memorable ones again and again, his heart lifting with every swipe of his eyes across her brokenhearted words.

He wished for a moment that he could have had confidence enough to see her desperation and that he'd swooped in and rescued his family. But wishes to change the past were fruitless.

And he hadn't been unloved.

He sat back on his seat, the whole situation of his leaving played before him, except differently. He saw his mother's pain, saw her love for him.

Things could not have turned out any differently. As a seventeen-year-old without an education, he couldn't have supported his family. His mother didn't have skills enough to get a job that would pay her enough to support a family.

She'd had to let him go. And he'd done very well by himself.

He straightened in his chair.

He *had* done very well for himself. He'd educated himself, worked his way up the ranks of companies…

He'd created a wonderful life for himself, and now he could make it better by bringing in his brother and sister. Not as the superstrong older brother—

Just as their brother.

A strange relief filled him, along with thoughts of Erin.

And Noah and even Marge. They'd never once wanted him to be anything other than what he was. And if his brother and sister wanted him to be something more, a superstrong brother for them to lean on…was that right?

Wasn't the world supposed to be more like the one he and Erin had been creating?

The thought confounded him. Instinctively he knew it was right. But he'd spent his entire life believing otherwise. Believing he had to be tough and focused. Not made for the softness, the comfort, the ease Erin had brought into his life.

And this was his moment of truth.

He pulled his phone from his pocket and texted both Sally and Jay for another meeting, this one in his office.

Each came scurrying in, again thinking there was a crisis with the hotel. Jay immediately took a seat in front of his desk. Sally stopped cold when she looked at him, her distrust so evident he could finally see her pain.

But he'd been gone, out of the family, for seventeen years, and so young when he'd been forced out that he suddenly wondered how any of them could believe any of this was his fault.

Nodding for her to take a seat, he said, "Sally, I see that all this hurt you. Maybe even more than me. I was seventeen, old enough to plan a future and work my way into it. You were a scared kid."

Looking at her hands, she said nothing.

Hugo took a slow breath and said something he never thought he'd say. "That's why we need each other. Not as me being the white knight older brother who swoops in and fixes everything. I'm not that guy." His shoulders relaxed as he said the words, and the relief that filled him rained down as if straight from heaven. "But I would love to have you both in my life as my brother and sister. Just simple family." He picked up three of the cards, all of which contained heartrending letters from their mum. "These are from Mum. I'm going to leave you two alone to read these, to process everything."

With that he left. If Sally didn't understand after reading their mother's letters, she never would. But at least he could let her go with a clear conscience.

He stepped out of the office, closing the door behind him. Erin approached, frowning. "I have stuff in there I need. I hope you didn't lock it."

He stared at her. If he hadn't spent these past days with her, he would have seen his mother's letters as vindication but still believed he somehow had to be more than he was, more than what Sally and Jay legitimately had a right to expect.

She was the first person in his life to let him be himself.

Love for her poured through him. He was pretty sure he'd loved her from their first night together. He'd simply been alone so long he hadn't recognized it, and when he'd come close to seeing it, his past had filled him with fear.

He took a breath, ready to shout it from the rooftops, but he remembered that he'd hurt her—had broken things off with her—and he knew he'd have to make it up to her.

He might even have to win her back.

Seeing the stern expression on her face, he realized he'd definitely have to win her back. He just wasn't sure how.

So when his mouth opened, he didn't say, "I love you." He said, "Sally and Jay are in there. The door's not locked, but I would ask that you give them at least fifteen minutes of privacy."

"Oh." She frowned. "Something I should know?"

He laughed. "No. The celebration's not going to blow up in your face. I'm not going to melt down. In fact," he said, bending to kiss her cheek, "things are finally on track."

* * *

Erin didn't know if she should be insulted or heartened by Hugo's kiss on her cheek. So she refused to think about it.

The next day—Christmas Eve—with a flight back to New York booked for that evening, Erin rushed to pack her remaining things before she could get her mom and Noah into a taxi to go to the airport.

Noah didn't want to leave. He had it in his head that Santa knew he was in his new house and wouldn't find him. He crossed his arms and sat on the sofa, refusing to move.

Her mom didn't want to leave either.

"I finally feel like I've found my place in the world now that I've connected with my parents' families. If anything, I think we should scrape together the cash to rent this place in January."

Erin's heart hurt. "I hear what you're saying, and I love that you're finding a place in the world." She tossed the shirt she was folding onto the sofa and closed her eyes. "You were right about me and Hugo. We did start something, but he broke up with me the day before yesterday."

Her mom scampered over. "Oh, Erin! I'm so sorry. He's an idiot!"

"He's not an idiot. When I moved into his office, I found some things. Things that more or less gave him a big piece of the puzzle to his past. It made him angry and he told me our relationship had gotten in the way of his plans for his family. As if what we'd shared had been me dragging him away from his purpose."

Tears filled her eyes and her mom hugged her. "You always said he had trouble with feelings."

She sniffed. "That's why I want to leave before the party. How could I stay here, in love with someone who'd dismissed me so easily, once I'd discovered his secrets?"

She pulled in a breath, all the feelings she'd been suppressing suddenly pouring out of her. "What is it about me that no one trusts me? That no one wants to share their secrets and dreams with me?"

"Oh, honey, that's not it. You might have found some things about Hugo's past. But you've told me a hundred times the man didn't have feelings."

He did have feelings.

Erin had seen them. She'd watched him go from being a man so careful that even his hellos were guarded to someone who let her take the lead in bed. There was something there. Something strong and precious. But he didn't want to be that guy. He wanted to hold back part of himself.

The way Josh had.

Even if Hugo wanted her back, that was the real bottom line. He might be nothing like Josh, but they had a few similar beliefs. Beliefs she couldn't live with.

Her mom heaved herself up from the sofa. "Come on. Let's pack."

"What about your relatives?"

"I can just as easily save some money to come back next summer." She winced. "It'll mean you'll have to find day care for Noah."

"Not a problem," she said automatically because that was her thing. Just as Hugo could be cold and distant, businesslike when pain overwhelmed him, she became accommodating, not letting anyone see her hurt, upset or confusion.

Maybe it was time for that to stop. Maybe she was tired of being the one everybody counted on. Tired of being the one who always did the right thing.

And maybe that was the lesson in losing her husband. It was time to stand up for herself.

Her phone pinged with a text.

Where are you? I can't find you. Someone said they thought you'd left.

Hugo.

He was probably looking for her because he'd decided he wanted more icing on the gingerbread cookies…or no icing…or more flowers…or fewer flowers. A detail that shouldn't matter. But he was a fussbudget.

She debated not answering him.

But no matter what she decided about herself personally, he was still her boss. Her employer. She would do her duty.

I'm at home. We're packing to leave.

Leave? You're not coming to the party?

She took a second. She'd spent the past weeks working her butt off to make this the perfect Christmas Eve. Part of her had envisioned Noah chitchatting with Santa. Her mom had bought a beautiful party dress. She'd used Hugo's shopper again to get a wonderful red velvet dress to wear. But every time she pictured herself at the celebration of Hugo's greatest success, she saw him coolly greeting her, then shipping her and her family to a far corner. Because they weren't anybody. The family of a subcontractor. Not even an employee.

No.

Erin! You have to come!

Not really. We're homesick. Eager to be in our own space.

For ten minutes there was no reply.

Then…

I'm sending the limo to bring you to the hotel. After that, if you still want to leave, Ronnie will drive you all to the airport.

She almost politely refused but realized very business-like Hugo had made her a proposition she couldn't refuse. An easy limo ride to the airport? Rather than a cab when she wasn't even sure all her suitcases would fit in the trunk?

Okay.

Her little family was completely packed when Ronnie showed up at her door.

"I've been instructed to leave your mum and son. After you assist Hugo, we'll come back and get them."

"We have to leave for the airport by three."

Ronnie nodded. "Then we'd best be going."

He took her directly to the Harrington Park lobby doors and dropped her off. A light snow began to fall as she ducked under the portico and into the hotel that bustled with the activity of newly arrived guests.

Her heart swelled. These were the people she'd created Hugo's vision for. Parents who had brought their kids all those years ago were now grandparents with adult children and little ones tucked at their sides.

She skirted the long check-in line and headed to the office, but one of the registration clerks stopped her. "Mr. Harrington is in the penthouse. He instructed me to tell you to go up."

She sighed. Surely to God he didn't want her to decorate the penthouse for some sort of private party for business associates?

Annoyed, she rode the elevator to the penthouse, only to have the doors open on a fully decorated sitting room. Holly and fir branches hung over doors. Christmas lights edged the kitchen island. A decorated tree stood in front of the wall of windows, half hiding the view of London.

She looked around in awe. "What's this? Are you having a party up here later?"

He handed her a glass of champagne. "I thought Noah might like it. Especially if he stays over tonight."

"We're not coming to the Christmas Eve party. We'll be over the Atlantic and in our own beds in a few hours."

He set his glass on the kitchen island. "Look, I know I handled everything poorly."

"You did a great job of getting this hotel renovated and the perfect party planned. And you know it."

He winced. "Reverting back to our business relationship?"

"You've said it yourself. You're my biggest client."

"I'm also the guy who loves you."

Her gaze jumped to his.

"I felt it that day. The day you found the envelopes. It didn't sneak up on me. It sort of whooshed through me when we were making love. But I lost it, or maybe it confused me, when you showed me those cards."

"I shouldn't have. They were none of my business."

"They were definitely your business. But the pain of my past had to be dealt with first." He paused, peeked over at her. "I found a second batch of cards. Same place you probably found the first batch. These were from my mum to me." He paused again, then quietly said, "She vindicated me."

Everything she thought about him, this meeting, her own feelings of hurt, fell out of her head. "She vindicated you?"

"Yes. She believed me. She believed Nick had bled Harrington Park dry. She knew she'd made a mistake giving it to him and a worse mistake asking me to leave. But he'd scared the hell out of her. I got the feeling she was the victim of emotional abuse."

"Oh, Hugo."

"I know. I also know that I was too young to have seen it. And in my last conversation with Jay and Sally, I told them it was time we had a normal relationship. Not some trumped up thing where I'm their knight in shining armor."

"I'm so sorry."

"Jay and Sally are fine. More settled than I am. They don't need a domineering big brother to fix everything for them. They just need a big brother who loves them." He took a breath. "I think my family has suffered enough and it's time for us to let go. I'm going to tell Jay and Sally that tonight."

Erin whispered, "I think you're right." Not only because she agreed with him but because he was telling her—first—before he told Jay and Sally. Confiding in her. Warmth pooled in her heart. Her head cleared. Everything that had happened in the past two days disappeared and her feelings for Hugo rose and bloomed.

"I love you, you know." He ran his hand through his hair. "I'm not sure how that happened. I was so broken that I'd spent over a decade believing I was a stoic businessman who wasn't meant for love. It was easier to believe that than to deal with the possibility that I'd failed and couldn't get my family back together again. Turns out, I don't have all the responsibility. Some of it is up to Jay and Sally."

"I'm so sorry you had to go through all this, Hugo."

"You have nothing to be sorry for. I'm grateful we fell

in love despite the mess my life was in." He laughed and held out his arms to her. "I'm so sorry you got caught in the middle of all this."

She'd realized it would happen. She'd known that she'd become part of him dealing with a messy past. She'd tried to prepare for it. But suddenly it didn't matter. She raced into his arms, let him pull her against his solid chest, and breathed in the feeling of being loved, being wanted, being trusted.

"Nothing like that will ever happen again."

"I certainly hope not. Losing your dad, your mom struggling, a thief coming into your life…that's too much for a family to go through twice."

"Agreed."

He glanced down at her and she looked up at him. Both smiled, and then Hugo laughed. "I can't believe I found you."

"I was always there. Right under your nose."

He frowned. "Really?"

"I had the biggest crush on you."

"You didn't!"

"I did. You should have seen the fantasies I created about us."

"You'll have to tell me some day when we have time."

"Or maybe we could recreate one or two."

He laughed, then kissed her. She rose on tiptoe to kiss him fully, and he held her against him so tightly he knew he'd never let her go.

That thought reminded him of the ring in his jacket pocket, and he broke the kiss. Without any word of explanation, he reached for it as he got down on one knee.

"I think it's time we make it official." He opened the ring box, displaying the three-carat diamond solitaire.

Her eyes widened. "Oh, Hugo!"

"Will you marry me?"

"But we haven't known each other long enough to—"

He slid the ring on her finger. "To what? Fall in love? We both know we did. And we both know we've gone through a lifetime of experiences these past two weeks. Enough that we can be sure." He smiled at her. "Say yes."

She pressed her lips together to hold back a flood of emotion, then said, "Yes! Yes! A thousand times yes."

He rose and took her into his arms, kissing her until their kisses turned hot and steamy and he pulled away. "Bedroom?"

"Yes. But first, we have to call my mom. She's undoubtedly got her coat on and is standing by a mountain of luggage."

"We could send Ronnie over there to get them, luggage and all. Then we could come up here after the Christmas Eve celebration and have Christmas morning together... all of us watching Noah open his gifts."

She kissed him. "It sounds perfect."

It did to Hugo too. His brother and sister would always be in his life, but Erin was the woman with whom he'd make a family.

EPILOGUE

THE DOUBLE DOORS to the courtyard garden were pulled apart and Hugo took a breath. "Ready?"

Erin glanced at the stunning garden. He could see her taking in the fir trees and winterberry shrubs. The skating rink was rimmed with lights and would be opened for skating the following day.

She smiled up at Hugo. Her red velvet gown fit her curves to perfection. The white boa-like trim around the sweetheart neckline gave just the slightest peek at the swell of her breasts. The diamond shimmering at her throat winked at him. His Christmas gift to her.

His heart constricted. He'd spent years wanting only to reconnect with his brother and sister. Though his parents had modeled real love for him, somehow that hadn't registered in his brain enough for him to realize that was what he really needed. Someone who cared for him on a level he could neither define nor describe, but a place in his heart so deep and so pure it lifted his soul.

"As ready as I'll ever be."

He took her hand, the diamond on her ring finger nestled against his palm, and he smiled. She was his. And he was hers. They'd never be alone again.

The doormen at the entry sent a signal to the band,

which abruptly stopped playing. The MC scrambled to the stage, taking the mic.

"May I introduce the third of the Harrington siblings, Hugo Harrington, and his fiancée, Erin Hunter."

The crowd parted as they walked to the stage. Familiar faces of people who'd attended the original Harrington Park Christmas Eve celebrations smiled at him. There were new faces too. Not new people. The children who'd accompanied their parents to the magical wonderland of Harrington Park Hotel were now adults, attending with *their* kids.

He accepted congratulations and a few handshakes as he walked to the stage and stopped at the mic. Erin stood by his side.

"This was my father's dream," he began quietly. "He'd made that dream a reality for many years before his life ended too soon. We mourned his loss and eventually the loss of our legacy, but we have it back now. And we intend to make every Christmas Eve the highlight of our lives. Thank you all for coming."

He and Erin left the stage to thunderous applause and the ringing laughter of children. He scanned the crowd and found Erin's mum with Noah, standing by the tree waiting for them.

He'd never realized how much he wanted children, but looking at the elaborate celebration with Christmas gifts piled high under the tree, an entire table of Christmas treats and an upcoming visit from Santa, he longed to be a father. Not just to Erin's son—soon to be his son—but to a few new children.

They walked over to the grove of fir trees where Sally and Jay awaited them.

Jay laughed. "Nothing like a grand entrance."

"This is a grand hotel," Hugo said, unable to stop the

smile that rose like the sun in the spring. "It deserved a grand reopening." He looked from Sally to Jay. "Ready?"

Jay reached for the ornament with his name on it, but Sally put her hand on Hugo's forearm. "Not quite." She glanced down, then caught Hugo's gaze again. "I need to apologize."

Hugo brushed that off. "No. Sally. Really. All that's over. We start fresh tonight."

"Yes. I agree. But there are some things that need to be said. I was duped by our stepfather. Mother was too. It didn't take me years to figure it out, but it did take until now for me to realize how much he hurt you. Saying I'm sorry doesn't change things. But I think it's a step we all need in order to be able to put the past behind us."

Hugo's breath caught. He hadn't realized how much he'd yearned for someone to say that. "Thank you." Not wanting to linger on the past, he lifted his ornament. "Now, let's officially start over."

Agreeing, Sally smiled. She picked up her ornament. Jay had his.

Hugo faced the audience. "Every year, my siblings and I would place a new ornament on the tree. The idea was that eventually family ornaments would replace all those red and green balls," he said, pointing to the simple red and green ornaments. "Tonight, we pick up that tradition where it left off."

As they turned to place their ornaments on the tree, someone in the crowd cried, "Hear! Hear!"

Waiters in tuxes and white gloves brought out trays of champagne. When they reached Hugo, Jay and Sally, each took a flute, Jay handing his to his fiancée, Chloe, and Sally handing hers to Prince Edward Chen, the love of her life. Hugo handed his to Erin and all three commandeered another flute—Sally's filled with orange juice because of her pregnancy.

"To Harrington Park!" Hugo shouted, raising his glass.

The crowd echoed, "To Harrington Park!"

With the toasts made, the crowd dispersed. Hugo had instructed the band to take a ten-minute break. As parents led children to the goody table that lined the far wall or over to the tree to peruse the gifts, he turned to Sally and Jay.

"There is one more thing."

About to take Sally's hand, tall, sophisticated Edward stepped back. One of Chloe's eyebrows rose. Hugo wasn't sure what the betrotheds of his siblings were expecting of this night, so rather than have their nerves frazzle, he quickly reached into his pocket.

He pulled out two envelopes and handed them to Jay and Sally. "I'd like you to be joint owners in the hotel with me."

Sally gasped.

A quick burst of laughter came from Jay. "Are you kidding?"

"This hotel was all of our legacy. It's about family. It belongs to all of us. Not just me."

Sally murmured, "I don't know what to say."

"I think you said it before." Before she knew he would be giving her one third of the hotel. She hadn't apologized because he'd given her fair share to her. She'd done that out of truth and love.

His gaze met Sally's and she smiled.

They really were getting a chance to start over. As family.

He reached over and slid his arm around Erin's waist. "Besides, I'm going to be a little busy."

Erin laughed. "He's taking me to see all of his hotels."

"And Noah," Hugo agreed, taking Erin's son from Marge's arms. The little boy grinned at him.

"While I spend some time with my relatives," Marge said with a laugh. "I love Ireland and feel like I'm home."

"I feel the same way about Tianlipin," Sally said.

"Which makes me and Chloe the official family no-mads." Jay laughed.

"And that means we're going to have to divide the responsibilities for running the hotel."

Jay said, "All three of us? I thought you'd want to run it."

Erin smiled. "Hugo and I *have* decided to move to London."

Jay gasped. "That's great!"

"But I own a lot of other hotels," Hugo said. "That's why we all have to help with the Christmas Eve celebration. All promise to attend."

Sally shook her head at Hugo. "As if we'd miss it."

Jay raised his glass for another toast. "We're a family again."

Warmth flooded Hugo. He had his siblings back, a fiancée, a little boy and a soon-to-be mother-in-law, and he was returning to London. Returning to the person he was supposed to be all along. A little wiser. A lot more compassionate. And very happy.

His life could not be better.

* * * * *

A COWBOY'S CHRISTMAS CAROL

BRENDA HARLEN

This book is dedicated with love to Connor,
who brought Worf home.

And with thanks for research assistance, including
"how to bury a body in the backyard."

Chapter One

Desperately Seeking Daisy.

Desperately seeking a woman named Daisy who was born in 1945 to teenage parents and placed for adoption somewhere in Montana. Your birth family would like to meet you! Please contact the Abernathy family at the Ambling A Ranch, Bronco Heights, Montana. Time is of the essence!

Evan Cruise clicked his mouse to close the open window on his desktop that displayed the company's Twitter feed. It was at least the tenth time in three days that he'd spotted the notice on different social media sites, and something about it made the back of his neck itch, though he wasn't eager to dig deep and figure out what that *something* was.

Of course, he'd lived in Bronco his whole life, so he was familiar with the Abernathy name and knew the location of their ranch. What he didn't know was why the Abernathys were suddenly searching for an apparently long-lost relative. In any event, he didn't have time to waste worrying about some decades-old mystery that he'd decided, despite the itch at the back of his neck, had no connection to him. He had a business to run.

He moved his cursor over the desktop to click on the icon labeled This Week. The seven-day calendar popped up to reveal each of the scheduled tour slots highlighted in pink, indicating that it was fully booked. He clicked to advance to the next week and saw all the dates in pink again and had to smile, despite the fact that it was the middle of November, which meant that the holidays—and all the hoopla that went along with them—were just around the corner. Because pink translated to more money in the bank, and more money was the surest sign of success.

Of course, he only ran tours three days a week during what was considered the off-season for Bronco Ghost Tours. Still, the numbers had convinced him there was interest enough to justify adding a fourth weekly tour through to the new year. The extra tour, along with the supplemental income he made selling Bronco Ghost Tours merchandise in-store and online, guaranteed a very healthy bottom line for his business.

Lucky for Evan, everyone seemed to enjoy a good story, and quite a few of those liked scary stories. Since even more got excited about the holidays, he'd come up with the idea of a seasonal Yuletide Ghost Tour. Just because he didn't share their enthusiasm didn't mean he couldn't capitalize on it.

Eager to sell this tour as something different, he'd committed to finding new legends and venues rather than just adding a seasonal spin to the locations visited on some of his other tours. It was a happy coincidence that he happened to overhear a group of old-timers chatting at the coffee shop near his office the previous week—more specifically the mention of "ghost horses" at "the old Whispering Willows Ranch" and the claim that they "always kick up a fuss this time of year."

Though Evan habitually drank his coffee black, he'd taken his time adding cream and sugar to his to-go cup that morning and, at the same time, making careful mental notes as he listened to the men.

When he got back to the office, he jotted down the brief details for his assistant to dig deeper into the story and determine if the old Whispering Willows Ranch might be a suitable addition to his tour. Considering that the first Yuletide Ghost Tour was scheduled for the Friday after Thanksgiving—only nine days away—he needed to finalize not just the destinations and the route but the story line to entice his guests every step of the way.

As if on cue, a tentative knock sounded on the open door, and he glanced up to see his assistant hovering in the entranceway.

"What is it, Kelly?"

"It's Callie, sir."

"What's Callie?"

"My name is Callie," she clarified.

Another man might have been embarrassed by the slip, but Evan wasn't one to dwell on emotion. Besides, it was hardly his fault that he couldn't keep straight the names of the assistants who seemed to rotate through his office as if they were in a revolving door. No, the fault could be laid squarely at the feet of Brittany Brandt. Since she'd abandoned her position at Bronco Ghost Tours early in the spring, he'd been at the mercy of a local temp agency that sent a different candidate every couple of months—and sometimes even more frequently than that.

Apparently his former assistant was now an event planner for Bronco Heights Elite Parties and making quite a name for herself. In fact, she was reputed to be the talent behind the recent Denim and Diamonds fundraiser that had been hosted by Cornelius Taylor and his third wife, Jessica, to benefit programs for low-income families in Bronco Valley. Evan knew that he should be happy for Brittany, who'd moved on to a career that she obviously loved—and had fallen in love and married, too—but he was still a little annoyed that she'd left him with only two weeks' notice and an explanation that still rankled: *You're impatient and demanding and it's not a lot of fun to work here.*

"What is it, *Callie*?" he asked the temp still hovering in his doorway, looking as if she was standing on the edge of a cliff without a safety harness.

He tried to be patient, but honestly, he felt as if he'd wasted so much time training new employees over the past six months that he might have been further ahead if he'd done the work himself. But this one had been a quick learner, and at least when she wore skirts to the office, they covered more than just the curve of her bottom, and with shoes that were more serviceable than sexy. Her immediate predecessor had been more interested in earning the title "missus" than "administrative assistant" and had flirted outrageously with any man who walked into the office—including her boss! Sure, she was attractive, and Evan might have been flattered if he wasn't terrified of a sexual harassment suit, which he told her from a safe distance on the other side of his desk.

"I finished the research you wanted on the former Whispering Willows Ranch," Callie said.

He held out his hand because, more important than either her skirts or her shoes, she was smart and a hard worker, if a little on the timid side.

She stepped into the room to offer him the sheaf of papers.

There were a lot of pages, attesting to the thoroughness of her research, which he appreciated. However, he had a meeting in less than an hour, so he asked, "Can you summarize for me?"

She nodded and immediately began. "In 1912 the Milton family bought the property on which they operated a cattle ranch for almost fifty years. Just before Thanksgiving 1960—"

"Wait." He held up a hand. "Are you sure about the date?"

Because the way the old guys in the coffee shop had been talking, it was as if the property had been haunted for more than a hundred years. Not that the timing mattered, really. All that mattered was that there was some corroboration of the haunted part.

"Yes, sir," she said, her head bobbing for emphasis.

"Okay, then." He gestured for her to carry on.

"Just before Thanksgiving in 1960," she continued, picking up where she'd left off, "Henry and Thelma returned home from a trip into town to find the barn engulfed in flames. The firefighters would later describe the horrifying screams of the dying animals that they couldn't save, but no one knew that Alice had also been trapped in the barn…perhaps having raced in after the fire started to save the horses…until her charred remains were found in the wreckage the following day.

"Her father—inconsolable over the loss of the daughter—took his own life a week later."

Evan had been flipping through the pages as she recited the facts, but he looked up now, his brows drawing together as he spotted a glint of silver on her shoulder. "Is that *tinsel*?" he demanded.

"What?" She followed the direction of his gaze. "Oh, um, yes." But she removed the offending metallic strip from her shirt and scrunched it in her hand. "Other local businesses have started to decorate for the holidays, so I thought Bronco Ghost Tours should get into the spirit, too."

"I don't pay you to decorate," he said.

"Of course not, sir," she agreed. "I only put a few things up while I was on my lunch break."

"Okay then," he harrumphed, understanding that he couldn't dictate how she spent her free time.

But he would absolutely put his foot down if he heard Christmas carols coming out of the speaker by her workstation.

"Now tell me what you found out about the ghost horses," he said, returning to the matter at hand. "Has anyone claimed to see shimmery apparitions or hear unusual noises?"

She nodded. "The most recent former owner apparently decided to sell the ranch because he was creeped out by the sound of horses whinnying in the dark—and he didn't have any horses."

"That's what I'm talking about," Evan said, rubbing his hands together. But then he wondered aloud, "Who buys a ranch without having any horses?"

"Some Hollywood stunt double who wanted a quiet retreat to get away from it all," Callie told him. "Until he realized it wasn't so quiet after all.

"Neighbors and passersby have also claimed to hear the horses, usually at night, and some have even reported smelling wood smoke, as if something was burning."

"What about the current owner?" he prompted. "Has he heard anything?"

"The current owner is Daphne Taylor. *She* acquired the property almost six years ago."

"Cornelius Taylor's daughter?"

Kelly—*Callie*—nodded.

"Hmm…" He considered this complication. Not that he had any issue with the wealthiest family in town, but he suspected they might not be thrilled to have rumors of ghosts associated with their property. "I forgot that she started an animal sanctuary."

"Yes, sir," she confirmed. "Whispering Willows is called Happy Hearts now."

"Do you have contact information for Daphne Taylor?"

"It's on the front page."

He handed the papers back to her. "Give her a call and set up a meeting. Tell her I want to discuss a business proposition as soon as possible."

"Yes, sir," she said again, turning to make her way back to the door.

It wouldn't hurt to say "thank you" every once in a while.

They were the words Brittany had said to him as she was packing up her belongings on her last day of work, and they echoed in his head now.

And to let your employees know you're grateful for their efforts—if you are.

Apparently he needed to remind himself that sometimes, a paycheck wasn't appreciation enough.

With the echo of Brittany's words in his head, he said, "Kel—Callie?"

His new assistant pivoted on her heel to face him, her expression set as if she was braced for a reprimand.

"Thanks," he said. "You did a good job on the research."

Her eyes went wide, as if she wasn't quite sure she could believe what she was hearing, then her lips slowly curved into an appreciative smile. "Thank you, sir."

He nodded. "And don't forget to unpack the delivery from BrandYou before you leave today. We can't sell Yuletide Ghost Tour merchandise if it isn't on the shelves."

Daphne Taylor lived and breathed Happy Hearts Animal Sanctuary. It wasn't just her job or even her home, it was her passion. And while she felt good about the work she did and the life she was living on the purportedly haunted property, that didn't prevent her from dreaming sometimes about being stretched out on a white sand beach under a tropical sky with a fruity drink in her hand and a handsome man rubbing sunscreen over her body.

She frowned as she shoved the pitchfork into the

soiled straw and transferred it to the waiting wheelbarrow, acknowledging that it wasn't really possible to enjoy a drink at the same time as a sensual massage. Since her shoulders and back felt tight and stiff, she set the imaginary drink aside and focused on the fictional man with magic hands.

An impatient grunt interrupted her mental fantasy.

"Don't worry, Tiny Tim." She took one gloved hand off the fork to rub his bristly head affectionately. "You and Barkley are still my favorite guys."

After a few more rubs, the potbellied pig lumbered past her to his pen, with the heated pad on the floor, a rooting box to keep him busy, and lots of hay and water.

She thought wistfully of her own living room, where she was usually curled up with a mug of hot tea and a couple of cookies and her devoted yellow Lab by her chair at this time of day. But she usually had a lot more help on the farm than she'd had today, without which she was a few hours behind schedule.

It was her own fault for not remembering that it was Career Day at the high school and that her co-op students wouldn't be showing up for their afternoon chores. She glanced at the clock on the wall again, unable to shake the feeling that she wasn't just running behind schedule but actually late for something.

She had a calendar app on her phone—and she used it, but she sometimes forgot to schedule reminders along with appointments. A careless oversight that had resulted in the end of her previous relationship when Boyd Watkins had shown up to take her out for their six-month anniversary and discovered that she'd completely forgotten their date and the significance of it.

In the two years that had passed since then, she'd purposely limited romance to her fantasies because the men in her dreams never protested being forgotten when the animals needed her attention. And the animals always needed her attention, which was why a vacation to Hawaii—or anywhere else—wasn't on her agenda in either the near or distant future.

And that was totally okay because Happy Hearts was as much a joy as a responsibility. But every once in a while—and maybe a little more often since her oldest brother had announced his engagement—she found herself wishing she had someone special in her life with whom to share the joys and responsibilities. Someone she could love and who would love her back, like Jordan loved Camilla.

"If wishes were horses," she mused wryly, and forced herself to refocus on her task.

As the hands on the clock inched closer to three o'clock, she finished clearing out the soiled straw and dumped it behind the barn. She looked around for Barkley, who didn't usually venture too far away, then remembered that Elaine, one of the volunteers, had borrowed Daphne's canine companion to help socialize some of the other dogs in the adoption center this afternoon.

She returned to spread fresh straw in the stalls,

still racking her brain in an effort to remember what task or appointment she was certainly forgetting.

"Knock, knock," a male voice called out from the front of the barn. "Is anyone home?"

She turned automatically, pitchfork still in hand.

"In here," she responded, waiting for the visitor to make his way to her.

When he finally stepped out of the shadows and into the light created by the late-afternoon sun slanting through the windows, he appeared almost luminescent, like an angel—or a ghost.

Daphne shook off the thought as every hormone in her body came to full alert to remind her that she wasn't just alive but a woman—and one who hadn't experienced such an immediate and visceral attraction to a man in a very long time. If ever.

Because…wow. He was definitely the best-looking guy to set foot on the farm in all the time that she'd lived there. Brown hair, neatly trimmed but long enough that she could see the natural wave in it; darker brown eyes with tiny crinkles at the corners; a square jaw with the two days' growth that so many guys seemed to be sporting these days but that looked *really good* on this one.

Straight, dark brows rose as his gaze zeroed in on the implement in her hands and he slowly lifted his own in a gesture of surrender. "I come in peace," he promised.

Flustered to realize she was holding the pitchfork as if it was a weapon, she lowered her arms and pushed the prongs into the straw at her feet. "How can I help you?" she asked.

"I'm looking for Daphne Taylor."

"And now you've found her," she said, and sent a silent thank-you to the universe that her prayers had finally been answered—and in such spectacular fashion. Even deducting points for what was obviously a leather jacket worn open over a navy sweater with dark jeans, the guy was almost heart-stoppingly good-looking.

But apparently he wasn't as entranced as she was, because his brow furrowed and his tone held a note of disbelief when he said, "*You're* Daphne Taylor?"

Of course, he was impeccably dressed while she was wearing a pair of oversize coveralls and clunky rubber boots, not to mention there were several strands of hair falling out of her ponytail to frame a sweaty face devoid of makeup.

"Welcome to Happy Hearts," she said with a forced smile.

"I'm sorry." His apology was quick, if a little gruff. "I just didn't expect to find the owner of the sanctuary mucking out stalls."

"Around here, everyone pitches in to do whatever work needs to be done."

"Makes sense," he said, and added a curt nod before finally introducing himself. "I'm Evan Cruise. We have a three o'clock meeting."

"Yes, we do." She suddenly remembered and

winced as she glanced at the clock. "Sorry. I'm a little short-staffed today and fell behind on my chores."

She pulled off her gloves and tucked them into the back pocket of her coveralls to accept his proffered hand. Heat jolted through her system in response to the contact, tempting her to snuggle up and melt against him. But she managed to hold her ground as she lifted her gaze to his, wondering if he'd felt something, too.

She couldn't tell from his neutral expression, but she thought his eyes had gotten a little bit darker, and he definitely held on to her hand for another few beats of her racing heart.

"Your assistant said something about a business proposition when I spoke to her yesterday, but she caught me in the middle of feeding the animals and I didn't have a chance to ask for any more details."

"I own and operate Bronco Ghost Tours," he said.

Which she knew, of course, because one of her friends used to work for him. And while she recalled Brittany grumbling that her boss was a tyrant, she'd been unprepared to discover that the tyrant was unbelievably hot.

And now that Daphne had put the pieces together, she was certain she knew why he was there, though she wasn't eager to admit as much.

"What do you think I can do for you, Mr. Cruise?" she asked instead.

"Evan," he said, then added a smile that started her heart racing again.

Yes, he was good-looking, and just being near him was making her feel things she'd almost forgotten she was capable of feeling. But she had no intention of letting her farm be a sideshow to his circus.

She was about to repeat her question when the sound of a bell preceded the appearance of a fleecy not-so-white sheep hobbling toward them.

"You never can resist an open door, can you, Winnie?" Daphne asked, her tone laced with affection and exasperation.

Baaaa.

"Even though you know very well that you're not supposed to be in here," she continued.

The sheep ignored her admonishment and moved past the humans toward Tiny Tim's pen at the back of the barn, her casted back leg dragging slightly behind her.

Daphne wasn't sure how or when it had happened, but the pig and the sheep had become good friends. And while she didn't object to the visit, she did move past Evan to close the door so that no other animals would wander inside.

"What happened to her leg?" he asked.

"She got it caught in an electrified fence at the wool farm where she used to live. The farmer tried to treat the injury with home remedies at first, obviously unsuccessfully, and when she finally called the vet and learned that Winnie would need surgery— and the cost of that surgery—she decided it would be cheaper to euthanize her."

It required a concerted effort for Daphne to recite the details in a neutral tone, because her blood still boiled to think that Winnie's life could easily have been snuffed out because some farmer—whose negligence was responsible for the injury—didn't appreciate the value of it.

"Thankfully, the vet suggested that she bring Winnie to Happy Hearts instead," she continued.

"It must be expensive," he mused, "caring for sick and injured animals."

His tone was sympathetic and sincere, and Daphne found her guard dropping, just a little.

"The bills add up," she acknowledged. "But I know you didn't come here for the educational tour, so why don't you tell me how you think I can help Bronco Ghost Tours?"

"Actually—" he flashed another smile, and her guard dropped a little further "—I think we can help each other."

Chapter Two

Evan's employees might think he was a taskmaster, but he knew how to turn on the charm when he wanted to—or when he wanted something. And what he wanted, more than anything else, was for his business to be successful. The research had convinced him that Happy Hearts could be the highlight of his Yuletide Ghost Tour, and the moment he'd pulled into the long drive of the animal sanctuary, he knew he was right.

He didn't usually make business decisions on the basis of emotion, but he couldn't deny that he had a feeling about this place. When he'd parked his SUV and stepped out onto the snow-covered ground, he felt confident that this was where he was meant to be. For the purposes of his holiday tour, he assured himself, shaking off the sensation that the feeling might mean something more.

So he was doing his best to charm the owner of Happy Hearts, and though he would have sworn there was a spark between them, his efforts didn't appear to be having much of an impact on Daphne Taylor. Obviously he needed to kick it up a notch, so he rested his forearm on top of the gate of the nearest stall and leaned a little closer.

Her blue eyes widened, perhaps with wariness as much as awareness, and he realized that she might not be as much of a pushover as he'd initially suspected. He was generally opposed to wasting time, because time was money. But he knew that impatience wouldn't help overcome her reticence, so he'd take his time and slowly lure her in. After all, he didn't have anywhere else he needed to be this afternoon, and it wasn't exactly a hardship to spend some time flirting with a pretty lady.

And once he'd managed to look past the baggy coveralls and muddy (*please let it be mud*) boots, she really was an attractive woman—even with her strawberry blond hair tied back in a messy ponytail and her face bare of makeup.

"How, precisely, do you think we can help one another, Mr. Cruise?" she asked him now.

"Is there somewhere we can talk?" he asked, aiming for a hopeful tone. "Maybe over a cup of coffee?"

"There's an office at the back," she said.

"That would work," he agreed, eager to demonstrate cooperation.

She propped the pitchfork against a support post and led him deeper into the barn. He was a city boy through and through, but he didn't mind the scent of fresh hay that permeated the building. Sure, he could smell the sweat of animals, too, but it wasn't an entirely offensive smell.

He followed Daphne into the office: a simple room with a wide desk, a couple of chairs and a minifridge on top of which sat a single-serve coffee maker and half a dozen mugs. The outside wall had two windows to let in natural light, an adjacent wall had built-in shelves and cupboards, while the two remaining walls were covered in whiteboards upon which were scrawled notes about the behavior, habits and feeding of various animals.

He scanned the notes while Daphne got a coffee pod out of the fridge and made his coffee. She offered him the first mug before making her own.

"Cream and sugar are in the fridge," she said.

"Why do you keep sugar and coffee pods in the fridge?" he wondered aloud.

"We try to keep everything behind closed doors and away from curious creatures," she said. "Goats, in particular, will eat anything."

"Do all of the animals have free rein around here?"

"Of course not," she said. "That wouldn't be safe for any of them, but we try to restrict their freedom as little as possible. Happy Hearts is a sanctuary, not a zoo."

"It's also, according to rumors heard around town, haunted."

She lifted her mug to her lips, sipped. "Also, according to rumors heard around town, Gordon Toole is the illegitimate half brother of the queen of England. Do you believe that, too?" she challenged.

He chuckled at her mention of the retired mechanic from Bronco Valley who pretended to live off-the-grid so the British government couldn't find him. "I believe Gordon Toole lives in a different reality than the rest of us. Thankfully, that reality is harmless."

Her lips curved then, just a little, as they shared a moment of amusement.

"But back to the reason I'm here," he said, eager to push ahead with his agenda. "You must be familiar with the stories about ghost horses that can be heard whinnying at night—or maybe you've even heard them."

He was hoping for some kind of reaction to confirm or deny the supposition, but her expression remained neutral.

Deliberately neutral, he surmised, and his curiosity immediately piqued.

"No doubt those stories are the reason you were able to snap up this prime piece of real estate for well below market value almost six years ago," he continued.

"Isn't market value, by its very definition, the

amount for which something can be sold in the open market?" she asked.

He suspected she wasn't interested in economics as a topic of conversation so much as she was unwilling to acknowledge that her farm might be haunted.

"A comparable piece of property located not too far from here sold a few weeks later for almost twice what you paid," he noted. "You can't honestly expect me to believe that the discrepancy is simply because of fluctuations in the market."

"I don't expect you to believe anything," she said. "You're the one who spins stories out of whispers and rumors in an effort to convince others that they're true."

"I'm not twisting any arms to get people to buy tickets," he said, perhaps a little defensively.

"And I'm not turning my farm into a tourist attraction—and risking it being overrun with ghost hunters again—for the sake of your ticket sales."

"Again?" he echoed curiously.

"It was long before I bought the farm," she said. "A whole group of pseudoscientists trampled all over the property with electronic devices and cameras, trying to document evidence of paranormal activity."

"Did they have any luck?" He was surprised that he hadn't heard about the ghost hunting—unless, most likely, it had happened when he was away at school.

"They claimed to hear horses whinnying and smell fire burning, but those are the same claims locals have been making for years without any real evidence to back them up."

"So the hunt for ghosts was a dead end," he said, hoping she might crack a smile at his pun.

She didn't.

Evan decided to push a more practical angle.

"I've visited your website and viewed your postings on social media," he told her. "And it seems to me that you're trying really hard to drive traffic not just to your online sites but your actual door. You want people to visit so that you can educate them about the compassionate care of animals, and you want them to donate money so that you can continue to provide that care."

She sipped her coffee again, her expression still not giving anything away.

But even if she wasn't yet buying into his plan, she hadn't completely shut him down, either.

"Bronco Ghost Tours will bring people to your door," he assured her.

"And potentially distress the animals," she countered, obviously displeased by the prospect. "And some of them have already experienced far more stress and trauma in their lives than any creature ever should."

"You welcome visitors here all the time," he countered reasonably.

"During specific hours," she clarified. "We don't have nighttime visitors and perhaps I'm wrong, but

I'm assuming something promoted as a ghost tour would have more ambience in the dark."

"Tours start at eight o'clock in the winter months," he acknowledged. "Nine o'clock in the summer."

"The animals aren't accustomed to people walking around after dark."

"We'd follow whatever guidelines you establish to minimize any disturbance," he promised. "And if you agree to let Happy Hearts be a featured site on our Yuletide Ghost Tour, it will raise the sanctuary's public profile, resulting in increased donations."

"An unproven supposition," she said.

But he sensed that she was wavering, and he leaned closer again, turning up the charm another notch. "Come on, Daphne. Let's do this together."

She finished her coffee and set the empty mug down on her desk. "What would you tell your customers—"

"Guests," he interjected. "At Bronco Ghost Tours we invite our *guests* to come with us on a journey of mystery and discovery."

"What would you tell your *guests* about Happy Hearts?" she asked, obviously worried about potential negative spin.

"I haven't finalized the details of the story yet, but I was planning to focus on the fire that burned down the barn, killing not only three horses but the rancher's daughter, his only child."

"And her lover," Daphne said.

That gave him pause.

"My research didn't reveal anything about any-one else dying in the fire," he admitted. But he was surprised—and intrigued—by this revelation of an-other detail that would add to the poignancy of the tale.

"Maybe they were even star-crossed lovers," he mused aloud. "People enjoy a tragic love story almost as much as a happy one."

"Whatever sells tickets?" she guessed, still sound-ing a little uneasy.

"Actually, I was thinking more in terms of a nar-rative that will engage my guests. I want them to be drawn in, to feel for the characters and under-stand why their spirits might continue to linger in this world."

"Isn't the loss of life tragic enough?"

"It can be," he agreed.

"I have to admit, I'm a little concerned that any attention generated by the inclusion of Happy Hearts on your tour might be more negative than positive."

"We don't have to say that the property is haunted," he said. "Instead, we could suggest that the spirits of the horses remain to watch over the animals who live here now."

"That's a unique perspective," she said. "Or a load of horse manure."

Apparently she remained unconvinced, and now that both their mugs were empty, he sensed his time was running out.

"It's obvious that you still have questions and concerns," he acknowledged. "So tell me what you need to know to make this happen."

"I need to know that the animals will benefit from this proposed partnership, and the only way to ensure that happens is for Bronco Ghost Tours to donate a percentage of the ticket sales to Happy Hearts."

He frowned, not sure he'd heard her correctly. "You want a portion of my ticket sales?"

"Not from all your tours," she said. "Just the groups that come to the farm."

"You're serious," he realized, torn between irritation and admiration. He might have thought she was a bleeding heart animal lover, but apparently she was a savvy negotiator, too.

"You bet I'm serious," she said. "How many guests would be in a tour group?"

"Usually twelve, though we sometimes stretch to fifteen to accommodate groups of friends or family members, but we don't allow guests under the age of twelve, so there wouldn't be any little kids running around in the dark."

"And what's the cost of a ticket?"

"It depends on the date and the tour," he hedged. "There are also discount prices for families and groups."

"But at least fifty bucks a ticket?"

"That's not all profit," he protested. "I've got overhead and expenses to pay."

She nodded. "Believe me, I know about overhead

and expenses. Still, I think five dollars from every ticket would be a reasonable contribution."

"Five dollars from every ticket?" he echoed.

"I'm sure the money will make a lot more difference to the animals than it will to you," she said. "Come on—I'll give you a tour of the facility, so you can meet them."

So he followed her from barn to barn, and she introduced him to various cows, horses and sheep, an ornery goat named Agatha and a rooster named Reggie. Along the way, Evan found himself impressed by not only the work Daphne did at the farm but her skills as a guide.

"If you ever want to moonlight for Bronco Ghost Tours, let me know," he said as they left the adoption center, where numerous dogs and cats—and even a couple of lop-eared rabbits—waited for interested visitors to take them home.

"I don't think I'd be an asset to your company," she said, turning in response to the sound of a dog's bark.

"Because you don't believe there's any truth to the rumors that the barn is haunted by the spirits of the lovers and horses?" he asked.

"I'm definitely more comfortable working with creatures living in the here and now," she said, crouching to greet the yellow Lab that raced toward her.

Which, he noted, wasn't actually a denial.

"You've seen or heard something, here on the farm," he guessed.

"Just rumors and gossip," she said.

He wasn't sure he believed her, but he decided not to push her. Hopefully, if they agreed on terms to include Happy Hearts on the Yuletide Ghost Tour, he'd have plenty of time later to get answers to his questions.

"Who's this friendly guy?" he asked when the dog moved away from Daphne—and shoved his nose into Evan's crotch.

"Barkley," she said sharply, admonishing the animal and answering his question at the same time. "He's usually more shy than friendly—and obviously still learning his manners."

Evan crouched as she'd done to interact with the dog on its level and prevent any more indignities to his manhood. "How long have you had him?"

"Seven months."

He rubbed the soft fur beneath Barkley's chin, and the dog panted happily. "What's his story?" he asked, because he knew now that every animal on the farm had one.

"His mom was dropped off here only a few days before she gave birth to five puppies. We had ten times that number of adoption applications, and at eight weeks, they all went to new homes."

"I'm sure puppies are always popular."

She nodded. "Barkley was the very first of the litter to go home with his new family. And then, three days later, they brought him back again."

"What happened?"

"It turned out the four-year-old son of the couple who'd adopted him was severely allergic. Barkley didn't seem too bothered when they dropped him off, because the shelter was familiar. And he ran around excitedly, looking for his brothers and sisters. But, of course, they were all gone. When I put him into the empty enclosure, his whimpering broke my heart. I probably should have walked away, but I couldn't leave him like that. So I took him to the house—just for one night—with the intention of reviewing the adoption applications again the next morning to find him a new family."

"Just for one night, huh?" he asked, amused.

"That was the plan," she said. "But one night turned into two and now, seven months later, I'm his as much as he's mine."

"Then I guess you both got lucky."

"I know I did," she agreed.

"You've got an eclectic assortment of animals," he remarked now. "Do you ever turn any away?"

"Only if we don't have the ability to house and care for them," she said.

"Has that ever happened?"

She nodded. "We were contacted last spring about a couple of black bear cubs. We referred the caller to Montana Fish, Wildlife & Parks. They have a wildlife center in Helena where they care for orphaned and abandoned cubs and then return them to the wild."

"Even without bears, there's a lot going on here,"

he noted as they circled back to where they'd started. "How do you manage it all on your own?"

"I don't," she told him. "I'm lucky to have the help of regular volunteers plus high school students who work here half a day, Monday through Friday, for a co-op credit."

"Still, you don't hesitate to do what needs to be done—and you're not afraid to get your hands dirty."

"I sometimes wonder if they'll ever be clean."

He chuckled at that. "But truthfully, what you've done—and continue to do—is amazing."

Amazing? Was that spreading it on too thick?

Perhaps he should have said *admirable*.

That was probably a more appropriate word, but he couldn't backtrack now.

"I don't know that it's all that," she said, "but thank you."

"Take it from somebody who's never attempted to care for anything more demanding than a houseplant—it's not just impressive but awe-inspiring."

Impressive was good, he decided. *Awe-inspiring* might be a little over the top.

"How did the houseplant fare?" she wondered.

He winced. "Not very well."

Now she laughed. "I don't have much of a green thumb, either. And while we do pots of flowers and hanging baskets for curb appeal in the summer, Elaine—one of the regular volunteers—is in charge of those."

"So you're not perfect," he mused.

"Not even close."

"Are we close to a deal?" he asked, eager to finalize the terms and conclude their business.

"Are you going to donate five dollars from every ticket sold to Happy Hearts?" she asked, obviously just as stubborn and determined as he.

"I think—"

He halted midstride, every muscle in his body going still as an unexpected chill crept up his spine.

"Do you hear that?"

Daphne stopped beside him at the exact same moment, making him suspect that she'd heard it, too.

But she looked at him curiously and asked, "Hear what?"

He started to shake his head, but then the sound came again, a little bit louder this time, and the cold spread through his veins.

"That," he said. "It sounds like someone…a woman…crying."

She tilted her head, as if listening, then shrugged. "Sometimes a coyote—or even a red fox—can sound like a woman screaming."

But what he'd heard wasn't screaming, it was weeping. And though the sound had already faded away, the feeling of grief lingered inside him.

"Or maybe you've been telling ghost stories for so long, you're starting to believe them," she suggested as an alternative.

"Yeah, maybe that's it," he agreed, unwilling

to confide the truth—which was that the owner of Bronco Ghost Tours didn't actually believe in ghosts.

Not anymore.

Maybe he'd gone through a stage during his early adolescence during which he'd thought he could sense the lingering presence of those who had supposedly departed. He'd definitely felt a chill in his bones whenever he passed the downtown library— supposedly the site of a brutal murder more than a hundred years earlier—or the historic courthouse where the library killer was hanged. But as his awareness of supposedly paranormal activity began about six months after his dad left, his mom believed that he was making up stories in a bid for attention.

Two years later, when he hadn't outgrown what she'd hoped was only a phase, Wanda had taken him to see a child psychologist. Dr. Henson had confirmed that it wasn't uncommon for children who'd experienced some kind of emotional trauma—such as parental separation—to search for meaning in the chaos, often seeing things that weren't there as a way of explaining the unexpected event and feeling more in control of the situation.

Apparently Evan was seeing ghosts because it was easier for him to believe that his dad had been scared away by something that didn't exist than accept the simple truth that Andrew Cruise had chosen to abandon his family. In any event, a few more sessions with the psychologist convinced Evan that he wasn't sensing spirits of the departed—he was just using his imagination to help him cope with the grief of losing his dad. And eventually he stopped seeing and hearing things that weren't there.

Until now.

Shaking off the sudden feeling of melancholy, he returned his attention to their earlier topic of conversation. Ordinarily he'd try to dicker, to whittle her five-dollar request down to half that. But right now, he just wanted to get the deal done so that he could get out of there.

"You must have inherited some of your father's legendary negotiating skills, because you drive a hard bargain, Daphne Taylor," he said.

An unexpected shadow darkened her expression and, when she responded, her voice had lost some of its earlier warmth. "My father didn't teach me anything."

Realizing that he'd touched a nerve, Evan immediately backed off. "Well, five dollars a ticket it is."

"Really?" Now her lips curved, and he decided that the amount she'd demanded was a small price to pay for a smile that lit up her whole face. "We have a deal?"

"We have a deal," he confirmed.

This time, she proffered her hand.

And this time, he was prepared for the frisson of awareness that skittered through his veins as his palm came into contact with hers. Maybe he was undecided as to what, if anything, he intended to do about the obvious and mutual attraction between them, but he was sincerely looking forward to their partnership.

Daphne watched as Evan Cruise's SUV disappeared down the laneway, her emotions tangled up in a messy ball inside her. Before she could even begin to sort out her feelings, another vehicle pulled in. Recognition was immediately followed by joy—a simple and welcome emotion.

"Did I know you were going to be stopping by?" she asked, when the truck had parked beside the barn and her oldest brother slid out from behind the steering wheel.

"I didn't know until I texted Camilla from the feed store and she suggested I pick up a bag of those pellets that Tiny Tim likes," Jordan responded.

"I think your fiancée loves that pig as much as she loves you," she teased.

"Maybe more," he acknowledged, as he lifted the bag out of the back of his truck and propped it on his shoulder. "But she's wearing *my* ring on her finger."

"Well, Tiny Tim says thank you." She brushed her lips against his cheek. "And so do I."

"You want it up in the hayloft?" he asked, knowing that was where she stored her feed inventory.

"Yes, please."

Daphne fell into step beside her brother and carefully closed the door behind them so that Winnie—recently returned to her pen with the other sheep—didn't escape and come wandering in again.

While Jordan climbed the ladder, she checked on the horses, making sure they had water in their buckets.

"Hey, there," she said, surprised and pleased to see Star's head appear above his gate. She slowly lifted a hand and gently stroked the gelding's cheek. His ears pulled back and his eyes showed white, but he held himself still, allowing if not welcoming her touch.

"That's a good boy," she crooned softly, pulling an Apple Snap out of her pocket and offering it to him. He gently plucked the treat from her open palm and munched on it.

"You've come a long way in just a few months," she told him. "I know it's been slow going, but that's okay. Neither of us is in a hurry."

"You really need to get out and interact with *people*," Jordan said, teasing.

"I interact with people," she said. "In fact, I met someone today."

"Visitors to the farm don't count," he told her.

"This one does." She hadn't intended to tell him—or anyone—about Evan's visit. She wanted to savor the excitement for a while first, but the words spilled out as if of their own volition. "Because he's not just someone, I think he might actually be *the* one."

"The one *what*?" her brother asked cautiously.

"The one I've been waiting for." And okay, maybe it sounded a little crazy when she said it aloud, but that didn't shake the conviction in her heart.

"Did you fall down and hit your head?" Jordan sounded genuinely concerned.

Daphne huffed out a breath. "No, I did not."

"Are you sure?" He leaned closer, as if checking her pupils. "Because you're talking a little bit crazy," he said, though not without affection.

"Says the man who fell head over heels the first night he met the woman who's now his fiancée," she pointed out. "Maybe I should have checked *your* pupils at the Denim and Diamonds Gala."

"And maybe that's the reason you want to believe your attraction to this man is something more," he said gently. "Because in the past few months, you've witnessed several people around you fall in love."

"And I was happy for all of them, so why can't you be happy for me?"

"I just want you to be careful," he said.

"I appreciate that you're looking out for me," she said, because he'd been doing so for as long as she could remember. "But I'm thirty-one years old now and capable of standing on my own two feet."

"It's not your feet I'm worried about. You've got the biggest heart of anyone I know, and I don't want it to end up dented or bruised."

"But if I don't follow my heart, it will never be as full of love and joy as I know it can be."

He sighed, a wordless concession to her point. "Just don't rush into anything."

"It's taken thirty-one years for me to feel this way. I hardly think I'm rushing into anything."

"But you just met this guy," Jordan reminded her.

She nodded, because it was true. And because she

knew her head-over-heels-in-love brother would still try to convince her that love at first sight didn't exist.

Not that she believed she was in love with Evan Cruise, but there was definitely something there. An awareness and attraction, at the very least.

And maybe more.

Daphne was sure of it.

And judging by what had happened during his visit, so was her so-called ghost, Alice Milton.

Chapter Three

Evan didn't believe in love at first sight.

He wasn't sure that he believed in romantic love at all.

But familial love was something different altogether, and his affection for his mother, his sister and his grandmother was real and deep. And if he was, perhaps, a little bit hyperfocused on the success of his business, it was because he needed to know that he could take care of them. To know that he had sufficient funds in reserve to ensure that they'd never again be forced out their home.

Of course, the most important women in his life would balk at that idea and insist they could take care of themselves, and Evan wouldn't disagree. They were all smart, strong and capable, but as the man of the proverbial house—as he'd been since his father walked out when he was ten years old—they were his responsibility. And nobody—not his mother or his sister or even his grandmother—was going to convince him otherwise.

He was thinking about his family as he drove away from Happy Hearts Animal Sanctuary and toward his mother's tidy three-bedroom bungalow. Wanda Cruise had lived in the same small house for more than twenty years now, having been forced to downsize after her husband disappeared with all of the money in their joint checking account, leaving her with a mortgage she couldn't afford and two children who couldn't understand why their daddy didn't come home.

Vanessa had been a toddler when Andrew Cruise walked out on his family, and Evan knew it bothered his little sister that she had no memories of their father. Personally, he thought she was lucky not to remember anything of the first three years of her life. Because if she couldn't remember how it felt to be part of a real family, then she wouldn't feel a sense of loss when that family no longer existed.

She also wasn't burdened with the memory of how much their mom had cried in the early days after the separation. At first, Evan had thought the tears were a sign that she missed her husband as much as he missed his dad. It was only later, when he overheard his mom talking to her parents, that he realized she was worried about keeping a roof over their heads and food on their table.

His grandparents wanted to help, but Wanda had refused to let them dip into their savings to bail her out. She was happy for them to pitch in with the kids, but she wouldn't take their money.

Wanda had worked part-time as a legal secretary throughout her marriage. After the separation, the law firm agreed to upgrade her status to full-time. Of course, more hours at the office meant fewer at home with her children. That was where her parents stepped in, so that she didn't have to work extra hours to pay for day care for Vanessa and after-school care for Evan. And when Wanda was looking for a new home that she could afford on her budget, she'd been lucky to find one just a few doors down from her mom and dad.

Dorothea and Michael McGowan had been more than grandparents to Evan and Vanessa—they'd been surrogate parents. They were there when their grandchildren got home from school, they helped with homework and assignments, and they attended school assemblies and sporting events. They more than filled the gap created by their former son-in-law's disappearance, they filled Evan's and Vanessa's lives with love and laughter.

Though Evan had spent a lot of time with both of them, there had always been a special bond with his grandmother. She seemed to understand what he was thinking and feeling even when he was unable to express those thoughts and feelings. And through all the years that had passed, their closeness remained constant.

Evan pulled into his mother's driveway, shaking his head as he parked behind her ancient minivan. More than once, he'd offered to buy her a new car, but Wanda wouldn't hear of it, insisting that her Honda, despite showing signs of age, got her where she needed to go. He'd offered to buy her a new house, too, something bigger and nicer, perhaps in Bronco Heights instead of Bronco Valley. But she refused to even consider moving, assuring him that she was happy in the little bungalow filled with memories of her family.

He wondered if it was true, if she was somehow able to focus on the good times they'd shared together rather than the financial burden she'd shouldered alone for far too many years. He thought it probably was, because she smiled a lot and laughed easily these days, but it continued to be a source of frustration to Evan that she wouldn't let him make some sort of grand gesture to show his appreciation for all the sacrifices she'd made.

The ghost tour business was surprisingly lucrative, and he'd made some smart investments when he'd had the money to do so. The decision to expand into merchandising had been a boon, too, and now the storefront booking office was also a gift shop, selling hats and T-shirts and a wide assortment of other items branded with the company logo. He even had Christmas ornaments this year, though those had been his mom's idea.

He didn't understand why anyone would want a glass ball advertising Bronco Ghost Tours, but Wanda had insisted that decorating the tree was, for many families, a happy trip down memory lane. He knew she was right, even if it was a trip he preferred not to take.

Shoving aside the unwelcome thought, Evan knocked on the door to announce his arrival, then used his key in the lock. After removing his boots at the back door, he strolled into the kitchen and sniffed the air appreciatively.

"Something smells good."

"I'm cooking a pork roast with those little potatoes you like," Wanda said, stirring something in a pot on the stove.

"You shouldn't go to so much trouble," he protested, bending down to kiss her cheek.

"It's no trouble at all. And I only worked half a day today."

When Vanessa had finished college, Wanda had decided that she could afford to cut back her hours again. Now she worked full days on Mondays and Wednesdays and every other Friday, and half days on Tuesdays and Thursdays.

"But—" she glanced at the clock "—you're early."

"I had an appointment out of the office this afternoon, so I came straight here after."

"And I'm happy to see you," she said. "But you're in my way, so get yourself a drink and go into the living room to visit with your grandmother until dinner's ready."

"I could do that," he said. "Or I could give you a hand in here."

"The two I've got are plenty. I just need you out of my space."

"Okay," he relented, opening the refrigerator to retrieve a can of cola for himself and one of ginger ale for his grandmother. Then he filled a glass with ice, knowing that she didn't like to drink out of the can.

Grandma Daisy looked up when he walked into the room, her hazel eyes lighting with pleasure. She'd moved into the bungalow after Grandpa Mike passed away three years earlier, not because she wasn't capable of living on her own, as she made very clear to her family, but because she didn't want to. And Wanda, feeling a little melancholy over the fact that her nest was empty now that Evan had a place of his own and Vanessa was living and teaching in Billings, had been glad for the company.

"There's my favorite grandson," Grandma Daisy greeted him now.

"You always say that when I'm the only one around," he remarked in a dry tone.

"And that's why you're the smart one, too," she said with a wink.

He couldn't help but chuckle as he handed her the can of soda and the glass.

"Thank you." She turned her head, offering her cheek.

He obediently touched his lips to the soft skin, breathing in the familiar scent of her White Shoulders perfume and shoving the niggling memory of that social media post firmly to the back of his mind.

"Now hand me my tote," she said.

"You have a sudden urge to sketch my picture?" he teased, reaching for the bag.

"Cheeky boy," she chastised, sliding her hand into the side pocket and pulling out the flask of Irish whiskey she kept stashed there.

He only grinned as she unscrewed the cap and added a generous splash to her glass of ice before topping it with the soda. He'd heard that seventy-five was the new sixty-five and couldn't imagine anyone who personified that theory better than Grandma Daisy with her ageless style, endless energy and quick wit.

"And just for that—" she returned the flask to its not-so-secret hiding place "—I'm not going to tell you that I made apple crisp for dessert."

"You don't have to tell me—I saw it on the counter. But now I'm wondering…pork roast for dinner and apple crisp for dessert? What's the occasion?"

"We knew that you were coming for dinner."

"Because I'm here almost every Thursday."

Grandma Daisy sipped her drink rather than point out that he tended to make more excuses than visits between Thanksgiving—coming up the following week—and the end of the year. "Now tell me about this Yuletide Ghost Tour I heard you're going to be operating."

In addition to teaching art at the local senior center, his grandmother belonged to a book club that met every Monday night and took a yoga class three days a week. As a result, she had a network of sources that ensured she was privy to all the latest gossip in town.

And because Grandma Daisy, more than anyone else in the family, seemed genuinely intrigued by his tall tales of alleged supernatural happenings and psychic events, he told her, even including details of his visit to Happy Hearts and the story of the ghost horses.

He stopped short of mentioning that he'd heard something that sounded like a woman crying when he was at the farm. Maybe because Callie's meticulous research hadn't turned up any mention of the spirit of the rancher's daughter lingering, and in that moment, he'd been certain she was the woman he'd heard crying. But now that he was away from Happy Hearts, he wasn't entirely sure that what he'd heard was anything worth mentioning.

It was quite possible, after all, that what he'd heard was a wild animal, as Daphne had suggested.

Or the wind.

Or maybe a creaky gate.

Or the wind moving a creaky gate.

There were all kinds of reasonable and rational explanations for what he'd heard, and not one of them was a ghost.

So he shook off the discomfort he'd experienced, because ignoring and denying his feelings was one of the things he did best.

* * *

"You didn't tell him," Dorothea admonished Wanda after dinner had been eaten and Evan had gone, taking a container of leftover apple crisp with him.

"I know." Her daughter sighed as she folded the tea towel over the handle of the oven door. "I was going to… I wanted to…but he seemed a little pre-occupied tonight."

"He's always preoccupied, always thinking about the business," she pointed out.

"He works hard," Wanda acknowledged. "Maybe too hard."

"He learned that from you," Dorothea said. "And maybe, if he knew that you were finally enjoying life a little, he might be encouraged to do so, too."

"Or he might freak out to hear that his mother has a boyfriend." She shook her head. "Truthfully, it freaks me out a little. A boyfriend? At my age?"

"You're fifty-five and, if you want my opinion, you've spent far too many of those fifty-five years alone."

Dorothea had enjoyed five wonderful decades with her Michael before he was taken from her, and she was counting on the memories of those years to help her through however many she had left.

In addition to love, they'd been blessed with chil-dren, each one a joy—and occasionally a trial. Wanda had given them the least amount of grief. Sure, there had been some rough patches during her adolescence and teenage years but, on the whole, they'd had no major cause for complaint. And when Wanda started dating, they'd tried not to interfere, letting her make her own choices—even when she'd chosen Andrew Cruise.

Still, despite the end of the marriage, Dorothea knew her daughter had no regrets about the relationship that had given her two amazing children. And everything Wanda had done, she'd done in the best interests of her son and daughter. Though Evan and Vanessa were both grown now, it was a mother's prerogative to worry, and she continued to do so.

"I wasn't alone," Wanda said now. "I was lucky to have both my kids and my parents."

"And now you've got a man to remind you that you're not just a mother and a daughter but a woman, too," Dorothea said. "And you need to tell Evan about Sean before he hears about him from someone else."

"He's not going to hear about him from someone else."

"Don't be so sure," she cautioned. "Because if you don't tell him, I will."

Wanda sighed again. "I just wish Evan would find someone special to share his life with. Of course, he'd have to have a life first."

"He'll figure things out eventually," Dorothea said, wanting to assuage her daughter's worries.

"Working so many nights can't be conducive to building a relationship," her daughter noted. "Do you think he'll ever turn his attention to a more…mainstream kind of business?"

"Why would he want to when the business he has now is successful and growing?" she challenged.

"I probably shouldn't be surprised that he managed to turn his penchant for scary stories into a vocation," Wanda mused. "Do you remember how he used to terrify Vanessa when she was little? She slept in my bed almost every night for three years because she was afraid of ghosts coming into her room."

"I remember that you thought Evan was making up the stories for attention after Andrew left."

"Because he was. Even the doctor agreed. Thankfully, Vanessa stopped having nightmares when we moved in here—because Evan told her the house was too new to be haunted. Of course, that was after he refused to even step foot inside that cute split-level on West Street, insisting that something really bad had happened inside." She shook her head. "He always did have a vivid imagination."

"I think you're forgetting that, almost two years later, the family that bought the house on West Street had a flood in the basement, and when they pulled off the ruined wallboard, they found the mummified corpse of the former owner's mother in the wall."

"I did forget that," Wanda admitted, frowning now. "Are you suggesting that Evan somehow knew there was a human skeleton in the house?"

"I'm not suggesting anything," Dorothea said. "I'm just pointing out that he wasn't wrong to want to stay away."

"I just wish I knew why he's so determined to stay

away from personal entanglements. I just want him to meet somebody special to share his life."

"Don't worry about Evan—when he meets the right woman, he won't stand a chance."

Daphne was nibbling on her thumbnail, a habit from childhood that she told herself she'd kicked a long time ago but occasionally fell into again when she was feeling anxious. The butterflies in her tummy were having trouble flitting through the tangle of knots, a sure sign that she was as nervous as she was excited.

Because tonight was the first presentation of the Yuletide Ghost Tour.

Evan had assured her that her presence wasn't required, but she wanted to be there. Not just to ensure that his guests were respectful of the animals on the property, but to hear him tell the story of the fire— and to know if anyone heard anything else.

She'd been living on the farm for several months before she let herself acknowledge the sound that Evan had heard on his first visit. Of course, she'd tried to dismiss the mournful weeping as something— *anything*—other than a grieving ghost. But more than the sound, it was the feeling of sadness that weighed on Daphne's heart, forcing her to recognize the tragedy that had happened on what was now her land and accept that Alice Milton was not resting in peace.

So she wanted to be there to gauge the reactions

of Evan's guests, but mostly, she just wanted to see him again.

He'd stopped by earlier that day with a contract outlining the terms and conditions of their agreement, including that Happy Hearts Animal Sanctuary would receive five dollars out of every Yuletide Ghost Tour ticket sold, a charitable donation rather than remuneration to ensure that each party would be held harmless in case of accident or injury on the property. But while he'd been reviewing the contract terms, she'd been thinking about how much she wanted him to kiss her.

Just one kiss, so that she'd know for certain that he was *the one*, as she'd told her brother.

Or to prove that she was making something out of nothing, as Jordan had suggested.

And maybe he was right.

Maybe she was starting to feel a little desperate because while she did hope to fall in love, get married and have a family of her own someday, she'd been growing increasingly skeptical that it would ever happen for her in this cattle ranching town. Her own fault, perhaps, for choosing to locate her animal sanctuary in Bronco, but she'd believed the pervasive ranching culture in the area was just one more reason that she needed to be here.

Of course, that knowledge didn't lessen the sting of the whispers that circulated about her in town— and not always quietly. Many of the local residents thought she was a spoiled little rich girl thumbing her nose at Daddy. Worse was knowing that her father apparently believed the same thing, and that he sometimes referred to her shelter as Hippie Hearts, as if it was funny. As if her desire to help animals was nothing more than the punch line of a joke.

Cornelius had always chided his only daughter for her soft heart, warning that she wouldn't survive life on a ranch if she didn't grow a thicker skin. Instead of toughening up, she'd moved out.

But that had done nothing to reduce the tension between Daphne and her father, and whenever they disagreed about anything, he somehow managed to spin it so that he was the injured party. As he'd done the previous day, when she'd suggested bringing portobello mushrooms stuffed with eggplant and Gorgonzola as her contribution to the family's Thanksgiving meal. Cornelius had not only refused her offer, he'd gone on to complain to Jordan that Daphne had demanded their stepmother add vegetarian options to the menu when she'd done no such thing.

So maybe there was some validity to Jordan's concern that she was trying too hard to find love simply because it had thus far proved elusive. At least until Evan showed up at the farm and her heart had started to full-out gallop inside her chest.

Still, a kiss didn't seem like too much to ask as proof that he felt something, too.

Because so far, aside from a little bit of casual flirting, he'd been all about business. But maybe that was because their limited interactions had focused on his business, and hopefully that would change.

So after finishing her chores and feeding the animals, she'd showered and dressed in clean jeans and her favorite knitted turtleneck sweater. She'd dried her hair but left it untied, so that it fell to the middle of her back. After a brief internal debate, she dabbed a little bit of mascara onto her lashes and swiped some gloss over her lips. Not enough to be obvious—she hoped!—but enough to highlight her features. Then she tucked her feet into fleece-lined boots, slid her arms into the sleeves of her puffy coat and headed outside to wait for the van.

She remembered Brittany telling her that Bronco Ghost Tours offered year-round ninety-minute walking tours of the town's haunted sites, but there was a fifteen-passenger van available for use in inclement weather and extreme temperatures. Since Happy Hearts wasn't exactly on the beaten path, she suspected that the group would have come by van even if the air temperature hadn't been well below freezing.

She saw the vehicle's headlights in the distance before she heard the crunch of tires on gravel, and the butterflies in her tummy started fluttering around again. Evan stopped the van beside the house rather than pulling up closer to the barn to avoid disturbing the animals.

When all the guests had disembarked, their tour guide led them to the nearby paddock, where they would be illuminated by the lampposts that lined the path to the barns.

Daphne hovered in the shadows, observing. The guests had lanyards with name tags around their necks, identifying them as members of the group.

"Welcome to Happy Hearts Animal Sanctuary, a registered charity animal rescue that helps farm and companion animals through rescue, adoption and education. It is, for all of the animals that live here now, a happy home—but it wasn't always so.

"Just before Thanksgiving, sixty years ago, a terrible fire ravaged the property known back then as Whispering Willows Ranch. The fire started while Henry and Thelma Milton, the owners of the property, were in town for dinner. They returned to find the barn fully engulfed and the local fire department valiantly battling the flames to keep the fire from spreading to their home—the same home that you see standing right there," Evan said, gesturing toward Daphne's house.

"Obviously they were successful in that effort, but the barns were completely destroyed. Henry and Thelma were devastated by the destruction of the buildings that had stood for nearly fifty years after being erected by Henry's own grandfather, the loss of all the equipment and supplies that had been stored within, but mostly by the tragic deaths of three valued and valuable horses."

There were some sympathetic murmurs in the small crowd as the visitors found themselves caught up in the story told by their tour guide with just the right amount of dramatic flair.

"They stood helplessly by, the rancher holding his wife close, watching as the fire fighters continued to douse the smoldering remnants of the once proud and strong buildings. Friends and neighbors, drawn by the sound of the wailing sirens or the sight of the crimson flames or the acrid scent of the smoke that hung heavy in the air, milled around, asking questions and offering sympathy. And then, as Thelma's mind began to clear and focus on the familiar faces around them, she turned to clutch the lapels of her husband's jacket and asked, 'Where's Alice?'"

The tour group was silent, hanging on his every word, waiting, wondering… And though Daphne knew that he'd likely made up at least half the details he was using to tell the tale, he was definitely giving them their money's worth.

"Alice was their twenty-two-year-old daughter and a teacher at the elementary school in town. Maybe she wasn't invited to join her parents for dinner or maybe she'd declined the invitation—" he shrugged "—who knows? But as Thelma's eyes, burning from the smoke and streaming with tears, moved desperately around the gathering, she knew that her daughter wasn't there. And though it was far too early to believe that Alice might have already gone to bed and somehow not been awakened by the sound of the fire trucks less than a hundred feet from her bedroom window, Thelma raced into the house to look for her, methodically going from room to room to room, screaming for her daughter…but there was no response.

"She ran back outside, asking everyone, 'Have you seen Alice?' and 'Where's Alice?'

"It was a question that would remain unanswered until the following day, when the fire marshal found her charred remains."

Daphne saw one woman discreetly dab at the corner of her eye with a tissue while another tried to blink away her tears as she sniffled.

"After the tragedy of that long-ago night, there were whispers and rumors that horses could be heard whinnying in the night—even when there were no longer any horses in residence here. And some people even claim to have smelled wood smoke when there was no fire burning anywhere in the vicinity."

"Okay, that's creepy." The speaker, whose name tag identified her as Sandra, added a shiver for good measure.

"Isn't it?" her friend agreed, rubbing her hands up and down her arms.

"And though it's believed that the spirits of the three horses remain to this day," Evan continued, wrapping up his story, "local residents claim that the ghost horses have been more settled since the property became an animal sanctuary, and that they no longer haunt the ranch but watch over the animals who now call it home."

His guests all put their hands together, their applause muffled by the mittens or gloves they wore in deference to the frigid temperatures.

"Does anyone have any questions?" he asked, his gaze skimming over the group, looking at each of his guests in turn. Then his eyes landed on Daphne, and his lips curved.

"You folks are lucky tonight," he said. "We have a special guest in our midst."

"A ghost?" the weepy woman asked, half hopefully, half fearfully.

"I wouldn't rule out the possibility," Evan told her, as he gestured for Daphne to come forward. "But I was referring to a real live person in the form of Daphne Taylor, the owner of Happy Hearts and caregiver to all the animals who live here."

Daphne lifted a mittened hand to wave to his guests. "Welcome to Happy Hearts."

And that was how she found herself answering questions about not just the animal sanctuary but the farm's history.

"Do you know anything else about Alice—the rancher's daughter who died in the fire?" The question came from a middle-aged woman wearing dark-rimmed glasses and a bright orange hat on her head.

Daphne shook her head. "In fact, Mr. Cruise filled in some details that, before tonight, I didn't know. But there is a marker in the field over there—" she lifted her arm to point the way "—under the peachleaf willow, where Alice Milton is buried."

"Can we go see it?" one of the guests asked hopefully.

She looked at Evan, not wanting to hijack his tour. He shrugged. "It's your property."

"Then please feel free," Daphne said. "But be careful—the ground is uneven and there might be icy patches in the snow."

She and Evan remained where they were while the tourists made their way across the field.

There was a gasp, then one of the women grabbed the arm of the man beside her. "Did you hear that?" she asked, a slight tremor in her voice. "It sounded like a horse snorting. Do you think maybe it was one of those ghost horses?"

"I think it was more likely one of the live horses in the paddock over there," her companion suggested wryly.

She huffed out a breath. "Honestly, Darrell, you have no imagination."

"That's not true," Darrell denied. "In fact, right now I'm imagining—" He dipped his head then to whisper the rest of the details in the woman's ear, making her giggle.

"An interesting group," Daphne remarked.

"An interesting revelation about the marker," Evan noted. "Why didn't you tell me about it when you gave me the tour of the farm?"

"I guess because I want Alice to be able to rest in peace," she said. "But your guests seemed sincerely interested and respectful."

"Most of them, anyway," he agreed. And then, after

checking to ensure that they were all out of earshot, he asked, "Was it Alice that we heard the other day?"

Daphne shifted her gaze to the peachleaf willow tree in the field. "How am I supposed to know what you think you heard?"

"Did you know that you look away when you're being evasive?" he asked, sounding more amused than disappointed by her response.

She forced herself to meet and hold his gaze. "How am I supposed to know what you think you heard?" she asked again.

His lips curved. "That was a pretty good effort, but I still don't believe that you didn't hear it, too."

"This is a farm with a lot of different animals— it's rarely ever quiet," she said. And then, "So this is your last stop on the tour tonight?"

"It is," he agreed. "And that wasn't at all a subtle change of topic."

"I wasn't trying to be subtle," she said. "I was trying to be quick because your guests are starting to head back this way and I wanted to know if you have any tours tomorrow."

"No. Saturdays are a day off throughout the winter."

"Work-life balance is important," she noted approvingly.

"That's what my employees say," he acknowledged. "And anyway, winters are a slow season in the ghost tour business."

"Well, if you don't have any other plans, we're having an open house here—our fourth annual Christmas at the Farm."

"I appreciate the invitation, but—" he gave a slight shake of his head "—I don't really get into the holidays much."

"Says the guide of the Yuletide Ghost Tour," she remarked in a dry tone.

"That's different," he said. "That's business."

"Oh. Okay," she said, but she couldn't deny that she was more than a little bit disappointed.

Because even if he didn't "really get into the holidays much," the fact that he'd turned down her invitation suggested, more importantly, that he wasn't really into *her*.

"Well, then." She forced a smile. "I guess I'll probably see you next Friday."

But then, after another brief hesitation, Evan surprised her by asking, "What time is this open house thing?"

"Noon till five."

"If I showed up toward the end, do you think your animals would let me take you out for dinner when it was done?"

She had to concentrate on keeping her feet flat on the ground as her heart did a happy dance inside her chest.

"I can't imagine that they'd have any objections," she told him.

"I guess I'll see you tomorrow, then," he said.

She nodded, already looking forward to seeing him again—and to their first date.

Chapter Four

Christmas at the Farm combined two of Daphne's favorite things right in the title. It was an opportunity to not just celebrate the season but shine a spotlight on the many wonderful creatures who were home at Happy Hearts. It was also a pretty big event, which translated into a lot of work in the weeks leading up to it. Every fence and gate and building that was accessible to the public needed to be checked for any potential safety hazards, the walkways needed to be cleared of ice and snow—and thank you, Mother Nature, for deciding to drop another four inches of fluffy white flakes even while Rudy and Samantha, two of her co-op students, were shoveling.

Still, she wasn't really unhappy about the snow,

because it covered everything in a pretty white blanket, making the farm look even more picturesque. Add a few miles of twinkling white lights, a similar length of evergreen boughs and dozens of red velvet bows and it was pretty darn close to perfect—at least until Barkley was let loose to race across the fields.

But she wanted the Lab to have a good run before she shut him up inside again. Though he was usually allowed to come and go as he pleased and got along well with all the other animals, she wasn't comfortable letting him run around with visitors on the property. Because he was still a pup, his excitement often eclipsed his training, and she couldn't risk him knocking someone over and causing a lawsuit she could not afford.

There was no admission charge for the open house, but there were plenty of opportunities for visitors to make donations to support the care and rehabilitation of animals at Happy Hearts. In addition to the donation boxes wrapped up like Christmas gifts and placed at strategic points around the farm, there was a tent set up beside the barn where visitors were encouraged to make a donation—into a box wrapped in smiling Santa paper and topped with a shiny white bow—before helping themselves to a cup of hot mulled apple cider and an assortment of holiday treats.

Under another tent, raffle tickets were being sold for a chance to win various prizes ranging from animal care baskets to children's toys to gift certificates for a local spa to an exquisitely detailed gingerbread village—all of them donated by local residents or businesses. And of course, all of the boxes for deposit of the tickets were done up like Christmas presents, too.

"I've wrapped more boxes already this year than any other Christmas that I can remember, and I haven't even started my shopping," Hillary Beaudoin, one of Happy Hearts' earliest and most dedicated volunteers, said to Daphne.

"I'm more grateful than I can tell you."

"Well, it is for a good cause," her friend acknowledged. "And it was more fun than scrubbing down dog kennels."

"We both know that the real reason you don't like to go into the adoption center is that you want to take all the dogs home with you."

"It's true," Hillary admitted. "And when I went home with Roscoe, my husband said that was it, no more."

"And then you got Toby."

"And threatened with divorce."

"Then Buddy."

"Aaron came home with Buddy," Hillary reminded her. "After he found him abandoned at a gas station on the outskirts of town.

"But yes, I think I've pushed my luck—and Aaron's patience—far enough with the six dogs we've already got."

"Six dogs, four kids, and you somehow still find time to help out here," Daphne marveled.

"I don't find time, I make time," Hillary said. "Because what you're doing here for these animals is important."

Daphne hugged her friend, her eyes misty. "Thank you for saying that, but it's what *we're* doing—all of us."

"And right now, I need to be selling tickets at the raffle tent so that Georgia can get off her feet for a while," Hillary remembered.

"And I'm going to circulate among our visitors to answer questions and encourage them to fill those boxes you wrapped so nicely with lots of money."

"Tell them we want bills—with big numbers on them—not jingly change and pocket lint."

Daphne was smiling as she parted ways with her friend, and though she'd promised herself she wouldn't spend the day staring at her watch, she couldn't resist a quick glance as she moved toward the enclosure where Gretel, a sweet cow formerly resident at a local dairy farm, was calmly enduring the curious stares of passersby.

It was almost four o'clock, and still no sign of Evan. Of course, he'd said that he would show up toward the end, and she had no reason to suspect that he'd changed his mind, but she was eager and anxious nonetheless. Though she'd dressed carefully for the weather, with thermal underwear layered beneath her jeans and sweater, she'd also picked out a dress to change into later, for her dinner date with Evan.

She didn't wear dresses very often—and even less so in the winter months—but she wanted to make an extra effort tonight. She was well aware of the adage "You don't get a second chance to make a first impression," but she was nevertheless hopeful that she might miraculously erase Evan's memory of the coveralls she'd been wearing at their first meeting.

"But I wanna ride a cow!"

The plaintive request came from a little boy who Daphne guessed to be about seven years old, and she pushed all thoughts about the night ahead out of her mind to focus on the present.

"Cows aren't for riding, Jace," his mother admonished.

"They're for milking," a girl—likely the boy's older sister—said.

"And eating," his father added.

Maybe he was trying to be funny.

Or maybe he was just an ass.

Daphne tried not to judge, but she couldn't let the remark pass without comment.

"No one eats our cows," she interjected. "They're former dairy cows that were saved from the slaughterhouse and brought here to live."

"Whatsa slaughterhouse?" Jace wanted to know.

"It's where they turn cows into hamburgers," the boy's dad chimed in again.

Jace looked troubled by this revelation. "I didn't know hamburgers were from cows."

"Duh," his sister said. "Where'd you think they were from?"

"The supermarket."

"We don't say 'duh,' Mia," the mother admonished her daughter.

The little boy tipped his head back to look at Daphne. "If you don't milk 'em and you don't eat 'em, what do you do with 'em?" he asked curiously.

"We take care of them, as a way of saying thank you for all the hard work they did on the dairy farm when they were younger."

"So this is like a retirement home for cows?" Mia guessed.

"Something like that," Daphne agreed.

"Our grandma's in a retirement home," Jace said.

His sister nodded. "And she always says, 'this is the thanks I get for devoting myself to my family.'"

Daphne had to press her lips together to hold back a smile as the mother's cheeks turned pink.

"It's not the same thing," the mom said.

"I know," Jace said. "'Cuz we don't have to pay for her food."

"Oh, believe me, we pay," the dad said. "And a lot more than a couple dollars."

His wife sighed. "Can we go see the pigs now?"

"There's just one pig," Daphne said, not wanting the family to be disappointed. "Tiny Tim."

"Is he really small?" Jace asked.

"No, but he was the runt of the litter when he was born and tiny compared to his brothers and sisters."

"Whatsa runt?"

But his mother took point on that question as she steered her family away.

As Daphne watched them wander off, a deep male voice behind her said, "A day in the life."

She whirled around, a happy smile spreading across her face when she saw Evan. "You came."

"I told you I would."

"You did," she confirmed. "But I didn't get the impression that this was where you wanted to spend your day off."

"I don't have a problem with the 'at the farm' part, I'm just not a big fan of Christmas."

It wasn't the first time he'd said something like that, and the more he professed indifference, the more determined she was to help him experience the joy of the holidays. "You don't believe it's the most wonderful time of the year?"

"I believe it's the most hyped time of the year," he said. "And that children who put their faith in Santa to deliver their heart's desire are doomed to disappointment."

"Why do I get the feeling you're talking about something bigger than a race car track?" she asked, certain the answer to that question was the reason for his lack of holiday cheer.

He just shrugged.

"Apparently I've got my work cut out for me if I'm going to change your attitude about Christmas."

"Let's change the subject instead," he suggested.

"Okay," she relented. "But we're going to circle back around to this one later."

"Forewarned is forearmed."

She tucked her arm through his and drew him toward one of the tents that had been set up near the barn. "Do you want a glass of hot cider? Or a sugar cookie?"

"It's hard to resist cookies, but I don't want to spoil my appetite for dinner," he said.

"Then let's go to the raffle tent," she said, making a slight detour. "There are a lot of great prizes available, and it's only five dollars a ticket."

"That seems to be a theme with you," he noted.

"What?" And then she made the connection and laughed. "Well, Hillary's selling the tickets, so maybe she'll give you a special deal—two for ten."

"A bargain," he agreed as they ducked into the tent.

When he'd gone home after the Yuletide Ghost Tour the previous evening, Evan had found himself second-guessing his impulsive decision to return to the farm today. He really did prefer to steer away from holiday events, not wanting his "bah, humbug" attitude to bring anyone else down. But Daphne had seemed genuinely disappointed when he'd declined her invitation, and he'd hated to be the one to dim her smile. And truthfully, as much as he would have preferred to avoid anything with twinkling lights or jingle bells, he couldn't resist the lure that was Daphne.

And now that he was here, he was sincerely glad that he'd come. There was something about the sparkle in her eyes that seemed to light up everything around her. Though he wasn't a fan of corny sentiments or romantic clichés, he thought Daphne Taylor might truly be one of those people who made the world a better place just by being in it.

If he believed in lucky stars, he might have found himself thanking them for putting him in the coffee shop the day that he'd overheard the conversation about the ghost horses at the former Whispering Willows Ranch, because that had been the first step in the journey that had brought him to her door. But he didn't believe in such things and he didn't like that the thought left an unsettled feeling in his gut.

"You seem to be deep in thought all of a sudden," Daphne remarked.

"Actually, I was just thinking how glad I am that I came here today."

"Imagine that," she said. "Because I was just thinking how glad I am that you came here today, too."

They walked around the tables, browsing the various prizes. He was surprised to find some pretty big-ticket items available, and some unique homemade ones—including a Santa's village made entirely out of gingerbread, complete with Santa's workshop, his house, a toy store, a candy shop and a post office.

"This is incredible," he said, leaning in for a closer look at the intricate details on the buildings.

"Isn't it?" Daphne agreed. "Each year that we've celebrated Christmas at the Farm, Elaine has made a Christmas village for our raffle—and each one has been a little bit different."

"Is this the same Elaine who does your flowers in the summer?"

"You were obviously listening when I was talking," she mused aloud.

"Is that so surprising?"

"I don't know," she admitted. "I usually spend more time talking to animals than people, and I can never be sure how much they understand—though I'm sure it's a lot more than most people give them credit for.

"But yes," she said, finally answering his question. "It's the same Elaine. She was here earlier, but she didn't stay long. She had to get home to finish another gingerbread village for her church bake sale."

"You have to know that you'd make more money if you had people bid on some of these prizes," he said.

"You're not the first person to suggest that," she told him. "But then the prizes would always end up going to whoever has the deepest pockets. This way, everyone who buys a ticket has an equal chance of winning."

He would have focused on maximizing the profits rather than evening the odds, but this was her event, so he kept that thought to himself.

"How many tickets did you buy?" he asked instead.

"None," she said. "I can't deny that I was tempted—and I would have put them all in the box for Elaine's gingerbread village, which, by the way, tastes as good as it looks. But could you imagine how it would look if my ticket was pulled?"

"So it's probably not a good idea for me to buy a bunch of tickets and put your name on them?" he teased.

"No," she confirmed. "But you could buy a bunch in your own name and then gift the village to me if you won it. Even half of the village would make me happy. Or even just a roof off one of the buildings."

He was still chuckling over that when Daphne was snagged by a visitor asking about puppies available for adoption. Promising to be right back, she left him in the raffle tent.

Evan hadn't come here with the intention of spending any money—wasn't it enough that Happy Hearts was getting a portion of his ticket sales? But there were a few prizes that might make decent gifts for his sister or mom or grandma, so he pulled out his wallet.

Still, he was frowning as he exchanged bills for tickets, wondering what had come over him that he was suddenly willing to part with his hard-earned money. Growing up poor had taught him the importance of saving rather than spending, and though it had been a lot of years since he'd had to keep track of every dollar in and out, he still had his own bills to pay.

Then he remembered Winnie, the lame sheep, and acknowledged that, even if he didn't win anything, the raffle was for a good cause.

Evan wasn't surprised that there were still stragglers hanging around well after five o'clock, which was one of the reasons he'd made a reservation at DJ's Deluxe for seven o'clock. Thankfully Daphne had a lot of volunteers on hand to help pack up leftover cookies and unclaimed prizes and break down the tents and other displays. He lent a hand, too, happy to help, and Daphne took advantage of the opportunity to "freshen up" before they went for dinner, inviting him to let himself into her house through the back door when he was finished folding tables and stacking chairs.

He didn't rush. In his experience, a woman who said she only needed five minutes to get ready wasn't likely to appear before thirty minutes had passed. Of course, Daphne wasn't like any other woman he'd dated, so he shouldn't have been surprised when he walked into the mudroom and found her by the door, already sliding her feet into low-heeled boots that were—in his estimation—a definite step up from the serviceable thick-soled boots she'd been tramping around in all day.

But it was the dress that made him say, "Wow."

And the sharp bark that made him jump back.

"Yes, you're a good boy to let me know someone's at the door," Daphne said to the dog. "But when I'm standing right here, you should trust that I can see him, too."

Barkley's tail wagged happily.

Evan crouched down and held out his hand for the dog to sniff. "Do you remember me?"

Barkley sniffed, then licked, then lifted his paw.

"Am I supposed to sniff?" Evan wondered.

Daphne chuckled. "No, you're supposed to shake."

"Well, aren't you a clever boy?" he said, shaking the dog's paw.

Barkley's tail wagged some more.

Evan gave him a pat on the head, then straightened up to his full height and refocused his attention on Daphne. "Did I say 'wow' already?"

She nodded, an unexpectedly tentative smile on her face. "So this is okay? I'm not overdressed?"

He shook his head. "You're perfect."

She exhaled a sigh of relief. "I picked out the dress this morning, and then I spent all day second-guessing my choice because I didn't know where we were going or even what exactly this is tonight."

"What do you mean, you don't know what this is?" he asked, sincerely baffled by her question.

"Well, you invited me to dinner, so I thought maybe it was a date…but then you said you wanted to talk about the tour, so I started wondering if it was supposed to be a business meeting instead."

"I think I understand your confusion," he said. "Now let's see if I can clear it up."

Then he kissed her.

And it was every bit as toe curling as Daphne had hoped it might be.

His arms came around her, holding her loosely as his mouth, warm and firm, moved against hers with masterful skill, making her blood race and her head buzz. She lifted her hands to his shoulders, holding on to him as the world swayed around her.

It was the same every time he kissed her.

Just the touch of his lips against hers made the rest of the world fade away so that there was only the two of them in the here and now. No one and nothing else mattered.

Daphne wondered how it was possible that he could taste so familiar when it was their first kiss. How she could be certain that she'd never felt safer than when she was in his arms when this was the first time he'd held her.

She knew who might have the answers to some of those questions, but she set them aside for the moment to focus on the simple enjoyment of being kissed.

And when Evan finally eased his mouth from hers, they were both a little breathless.

"So…it's a date," she said, her lips still tingling from the pressure of his.

"I sincerely hope so," he said. "And we've got a seven o'clock reservation—" he glanced at the watch on his wrist "—so we need to get going if we're not going to be late."

Daphne said goodbye to Barkley and locked up the house.

"Going where?" she asked, as he opened the passenger side door of his SUV for her.

"DJ's Deluxe."

The upscale barbecue restaurant, boasting an extensive wine and craft beer list in addition to the finest cuts of meat, had been incredibly popular since it opened in the spring. As a result, reservations were a must, with Saturday nights usually booking up several weeks in advance.

She fastened her seat belt as Evan slid behind the wheel and started the engine.

"How did you manage to get a table on such short notice?"

"I lucked out," he said. "Just before I called to make a reservation, someone else had called to cancel theirs."

"That was lucky," she agreed.

He turned into the parking lot and found a vacant spot. "Have you been here before?"

"Once," she said. "My friend Brittany got married here a couple months ago."

He opened her door for her. "Brittany Brandt?"

"She goes by Brandt Dubois now." Daphne took the hand he offered as she slid out of the passenger seat. "But you probably know that, considering that she used to work for you."

He nodded slowly. "And now I'm wondering what my former employee might have said to you about me."

"Nothing that made me hesitate to accept your invitation to dinner," she assured him.

"That's a relief," he said, leading her toward the entrance. "Because I don't think she loved her job at Bronco Ghost Tours."

"Not just because you were a demanding boss," she said teasingly. "But because she always wanted to be an event planner, and now she is."

"Then I'm happy for her," he said, pulling open the door and gesturing for her to enter.

The warmth was a welcome change from the frigid air outside, the air tinged with the scents of grilled meat and sweet barbecue sauce.

"Mmm… I'll bet your mouth is already watering for DJ's famous ribs—or maybe a nice juicy steak," he said. "I know mine is."

Daphne was baffled that he would imagine any such thing—not just because he'd been given a detailed tour of Happy Hearts and met so many of the farm's rescued residents, but because she thought everyone in town knew that her vegetarianism was a major reason for the rift with her cattle ranching father.

He gave his name to the hostess, who immediately showed them to their table for two. The high ceiling with open rafters was undoubtedly a trendy design, if a little stark for her personal taste. She'd much preferred the way the room had looked when it was decorated for Brittany and Daniel's wedding, with lots of greenery and pink tulips and a gorgeous floral arch under which the bride and groom had exchanged their vows.

But she probably shouldn't be thinking about weddings when this was only a first date, so she pushed the romantic image out of her mind as the hostess handed them each a leather folio and set a drink menu on the table.

"Gerald will be with you shortly," she promised.

"Do you want to look at the wine list? They have some great cocktails, too, if that's more your thing," Evan said, handing her the menu.

She perused the offerings, pleased to discover her favorite red was available by the glass, then returned the menu to Evan.

Gerald introduced himself as he poured ice water into the goblets on the table. The server was dressed similarly to his colleagues, in black pants with a white button-down shirt and black butcher-style apron.

"Can I get you anything from the bar while you're looking at the menu?" he asked.

"I'll have a glass of the Brick House Pinot Noir, please," Daphne said.

"And for you, sir?" the server asked Evan.

"I'll try a pint of the Ale Works IPA," he decided.

"Can we get a basket of garlic knots to munch on while we're figuring out what else we want to eat?" Daphne asked, looking to Evan for a sign of agreement.

He nodded. "Sounds good to me."

"Coming right up," Gerald replied.

"I skipped lunch today," Daphne confided after their server had gone. "And the garlic knots here are amazing."

"Why did you skip lunch?"

"Because I was chasing Agatha around the barn."

"Agatha's…a goat?"

She nodded. "A cranky old goat."

"How did she get out?"

"That was my fault," Daphne confided. "I didn't properly latch the gate when I went into her pen to refill her water bowl and she snuck out."

"How long did it take you to catch her?"

"I didn't. Rudy—one of the co-op students—lured her back with a piece of banana."

"She likes bananas?"

"Not usually, but she loves Rudy."

Evan chuckled at that. "Your co-op students work weekends?"

"They aren't required to, but the ones who really enjoy working with animals sometimes come in for a few hours on Saturday and/or Sunday. I was fortunate to have both Rudy and Samantha on hand for most of the day today."

"They must enjoy the work."

"Some parts are more fun than others, but they don't usually grumble too much about the less fun parts."

She smiled her thanks to Gerald when he delivered their drinks, and she'd only taken a first sip of her wine when he was back again with a basket of warm bread and two plates.

Evan nudged the basket closer to Daphne. "Dig in."

"You don't have to tell me twice," she said, pulling out a twist of bread brushed with garlic butter and dusted with parmesan cheese.

She tore off a piece and popped it into her mouth, humming with approval.

"Good?" Evan asked, selecting a garlic knot for himself.

"Sooo good," she said.

He took a bite and nodded his head in agreement.

"It looked like you had a good turnout for Christmas at the Farm today," he noted.

"It was a good turnout," she confirmed. "Every year, it gets just a little bit bigger, which usually means a little bit more money for the animals. And, as an added bonus, we finalized seven adoptions today—four cats and three dogs went to new homes."

"Were they the puppies that you were talking to Hillary about?"

"No, those ones are still too young to be adopted."

"What kind are they?"

"Golden retriever–basset hound mix. Why—are you looking to adopt?" she asked hopefully.

He immediately shook his head. "Don't you remember me telling you about my houseplant?"

"I do," she confirmed, reaching into the basket for

another garlic knot. "But a houseplant doesn't tell you that it needs to be watered."

"It also doesn't chew the furniture or pee on the carpet."

"Fair point," she acknowledged.

"I was only asking because I didn't remember seeing any puppies when you gave me the tour of Happy Hearts last week."

"Right now, they're being fostered off-site."

"So how do visitors know that they're available for adoption?"

"We have pictures on the website," she said. "The adoption tab has a drop-down menu so that visitors can view dogs or cats or other small animals. We've already received more than a dozen adoption applications for the six puppies—four girls and two boys."

"How do you decide who gets one and who doesn't? Or do the puppies simply go to the first six applicants?"

"No, they go to the most suitable applicants, taking into consideration both the family's habits and environment and the animal's needs."

"Are any of the farm animals available for adoption?" he asked.

"Not publicly," she said. "But again, we try to ensure the best environment for each animal. Only a few months after we'd opened, we found a Babydoll lamb tied up at the gate. We cared for him as best we could, but immediately started searching for a suitable adopter who already had one or more Babydolls, because they have a very strong flocking instinct and don't do well on their own. Thankfully, we managed to find a local farmer who was willing to add him to his flock."

"How are the garlic knots?" Gerald asked, when he returned to their table.

"Gone," Evan said.

"But they were delicious," Daphne assured the server.

"Are you ready, then, to order your main courses?" he asked.

"I think we are," Evan said, and gestured for his date to do so.

Daphne opted for the harvest salad bowl and Evan ordered a rib eye steak with a fully loaded baked potato.

"You're not one of those women who thinks a woman shouldn't eat on a date, are you?" he asked when Gerald had gone.

"Did you not see me scarf down three of those garlic knots?"

"So you're telling me that you filled up on bread?"

She sipped her wine and mentally braced herself for his reaction when she said, "I'm telling you that I don't eat meat."

Chapter Five

Evan set his beer glass down on the paper coaster. "You're a vegetarian?"

Daphne nodded. "Yes, I am."

"And I brought you to a restaurant known for its barbecue."

"It's the hottest ticket in town," she acknowledged, hoping he wouldn't make a big deal out of her revelation.

"Why didn't you say anything?" he asked.

"Because you seemed happy that you'd managed to snag a reservation and, having been here before, I knew there were some decent vegetarian options on the menu. Plus—" she shrugged "—I didn't want you to think I was a freak."

"Why would I think you were a freak?"

"Because I'm a vegetarian whose father owns the biggest cattle ranch in town." She kept her tone light so that he wouldn't know how much it hurt her to be at odds with her family.

"I'm guessing that's a source of conflict between you?"

"One of many," she confirmed.

"Well, I think it takes a lot of courage to march to the tune of your own drummer, especially when the rest of the band is moving in the opposite direction."

"Thank you… I think."

"It was a compliment," he assured her as he pushed his chair away from the table. "Excuse me for a minute. I see someone that I need to talk to."

Daphne sipped her wine, relieved that he didn't seem put off by her revelation.

And really, why should he be? Why should he care? The choice to eat or not eat meat was her own—except to hear her father tell it. To Cornelius Taylor, it was a sign of disrespect, a personal affront to who he was and everything he'd given to her. And every time she sat down to a meal with him, he made a point of saying so.

"Do you want another glass of wine?" Evan asked as he returned to his seat.

"Maybe with dinner," she said. "If I have another one now, I might be asleep at the table before our food comes."

"Living on a farm, your mornings must start pretty early," he noted.

"It's not a working farm, so I don't actually have to be up with the sun, but Reggie makes sure that I am."

She'd introduced him to the dark Brahma rooster when she gave him the tour of the farm. Although the average lifespan of a rooster was five to eight years, twelve-year-old Reggie was still going strong.

Gerald returned then, setting a bowl in front of Daphne and a plate in front of Evan. "Enjoy."

Daphne frowned at Evan's meal. Instead of the steak and baked potato that he'd ordered, the plate held a burger with hand-cut fries and coleslaw.

"I think they brought you someone else's order."

"No, they didn't," he said. "I changed my rib eye to a veggie burger."

"You didn't have to do that," she protested. "I've lived my whole life with other people judging me for my choices, so I try really hard not to judge others."

"Which isn't actually the same as not judging them," he noted.

"But I try really hard," she said again, making him laugh.

Then his expression grew serious as he studied her across the table while nibbling on a fry. "You know, you're not at all what I expected, Daphne Taylor."

"What did you expect?"

"I don't know," he confided. "But I didn't expect to find myself so instantly and thoroughly…captivated."

He made the admission reluctantly—and not entirely happily.

"Maybe it was fate that brought you to Happy Hearts last week," she suggested.

"I don't believe in fate," he said.

"You prefer to believe you have control over your destiny?" she asked, dipping her fork into her bowl.

"I'd definitely rather be a driver than a passenger," he confirmed.

"But if your attention is always focused on the road ahead, you might miss other things happening around you," she pointed out.

"I'd still rather drive."

"Fair enough," she decided. "Now tell me how a man with such a pragmatic streak got into the ghost tour business."

"Happenstance, really," he told her. "A few weeks after my college graduation, I was in the library when I heard a couple of teenagers in the stacks talking about how the old building was supposedly haunted."

"Is it?" Daphne asked curiously.

"There are rumors," he said. "But I suspect he was just trying to get her to go down to the basement with him to make out."

"The only reason anyone ever went down to the basement of the library," she noted with amusement.

"Which might be why they now keep the door locked," he said. "In any event, our hopeful Romeo was unsuccessful in luring his Juliet to a subterranean rendezvous, because she said the cold spot in the basement gave her the creeps.

"Even when he pointed out that all basements were cold, she adamantly refused to go down there, claiming it wasn't just chilly but haunted."

"Did he laugh?"

"He did," Evan confirmed. "Because he was clearly too young and stupid to realize that laughing at a girl you're hoping to get to second base with is pretty much a guarantee of striking out."

Daphne couldn't help but laugh at that. "Obviously you are older and wiser."

"I like to think so," he agreed when he'd finished chewing a mouthful of burger. "And while he was teasing her for believing in ghosts, she told him, in a very matter-of-fact tone, that there are haunted sites in almost every town around the world but most people don't realize it—or don't want to admit it. Then she proceeded to tell him about a trip she'd taken the previous summer, to visit a great-aunt who lives in Niagara-on-the-Lake, apparently the most haunted town in Canada."

"What makes it the most haunted town in Canada?" Daphne wondered.

"I'm not sure, but it might have something to do with the fact that there was a lot of bloodshed there during the War of 1812. Whether the haunted reputation is deserved or not, Juliet mentioned that she and her family had gone on a ghost walk there—a well-attended, apparently very successful ghost walk—

and suggested that it would be really cool if there was something like that in Bronco."

"So you stole her idea?"

"She didn't have any plans to start a tour company herself. She just wanted someone to show her the sites. Although she did apply for a job with Bronco Ghost Tours the first summer we were in operation."

"How did you know it was her?" she asked curiously.

"She mentioned the ghost walk in Niagara-on-the-Lake as 'relevant experience.'"

"Did you hire her?"

He nodded. "I did. I figured I owed her that much. But she quit after three weeks, saying it was too scary."

Daphne wasn't surprised. Even she hadn't been immune to the story he'd told about the fire at Whispering Willows, and she'd heard most of it before. But somehow his telling of the tale had created a chill in her bones...and evoked a sadness in her soul similar to what she felt whenever she heard Alice crying.

But she shook off the feeling now and focused on Evan. "You do know how to create atmosphere in your stories."

"Thank you," he said.

"So how many of your stories do you believe are true?"

"All of the accounts are based on reports of eyewitnesses who believe they've seen or heard whatever it is they're reporting."

She sipped her water as she tried to read between the lines of what he was saying. "If you ever want to change your career path, you could go into politics, because that was a perfectly evasive answer."

"Thanks, but I'd rather deal with ghosts than politicians any day." He picked up a fry and gestured with it toward her bowl. "How's your dinner?"

"Really good," she said. "And yours?"

"Better than I expected."

"But definitely not a rib eye."

He shrugged. "I don't always have to have meat and potatoes," he said, then grinned. "Sometimes I have rice instead of potatoes."

"Did anyone leave room for dessert?" Gerald asked, when he came by a little later to clear away their empty plates.

"There's always room for dessert," Daphne said.

"My sentiments exactly," the server agreed, winking as he retrieved a printed dessert menu from the pocket of his apron and set it on the table between them.

"The berry cobbler sounds good to me," Daphne decided. "With a cup of decaf coffee."

"I'm going to go for the Mile-High Mud Pie," Evan said. "And regular coffee."

"So how many supposedly haunted places are there in Bronco? And how do you decide which ones to include on your tour?" she asked, picking up the conversation again while they waited for their last course to be delivered.

"We do a walking tour in the summer, so we stick to the downtown area and usually visit the courthouse, the cemetery and the library, then we walk over the old train bridge to Easterbrook House."

"I've heard that some people claim to hear the creaking of the wood gallows outside the courthouse, which used to be the site of public executions," Daphne said. "But tell me about the cemetery."

"It's where they bury dead people."

She rolled her eyes. "Not that a plot of land filled with skeletons isn't scary enough, but why is it part of your tour?"

"Rumor has it that a grave robber buried himself alive there after being haunted by the deceased victim of his crime."

She shivered. "Maybe we should talk about something else."

"You don't want to know about Easterbrook House?"

"Wasn't John Easterbrook the politician whose wife and daughter were killed during a home invasion while he was at a council meeting?"

Evan nodded. "It's said that he resigned his position on the council after that night and never left the house again—not even after his death."

"A politician *and* a ghost," she mused.

"That's the story," he said.

The server brought their desserts with two spoons on each plate. "In case you want to share."

Of course Daphne wanted to share, and she wasn't

shy about digging into his mud pie with as much enthusiasm as she showed her cobbler.

"This—" she pointed her spoon toward the melting pie "—is why I could never go vegan."

"Mud pie?"

"I was actually referring to dessert in general," she said. "Most cakes and pies include dairy and eggs, and while a lot of restaurants now have vegan options, it's usually some kind of berry sorbet."

"But you like berries."

"I love berries—especially with ice cream. Or whipped cream."

He chuckled.

"At home, I buy my dairy products from a local farmer who subscribes to humane practices."

"I'm not judging," he promised.

"I know, but sometimes I judge myself for not doing more."

"I ate a veggie burger instead of a steak tonight—does that do anything to help balance the scales?"

"Maybe it does," she decided.

"So when and why did you decide to become a vegetarian?" he asked curiously.

"I think I was eight or nine," she said. "My older brothers were outside, watching the branding and castrating of the new calves, but I was expected to stay in the house to help my stepmother with my little brothers."

"I'm guessing that you didn't stay in the house."

"I hated being treated differently from Jordan and

Brandon just because I was a girl. So no, I didn't stay in the house."

But later, she would wish she had, because the sight of those poor baby calves being pinned to the ground and the sound of their desperate bawling had haunted her dreams for far too many years afterward.

"And when I saw what was happening, I flew at my father, fists flailing, screaming for him to stop." She pushed her empty plate away. "He was furious— and probably embarrassed that I would make such a big scene over what was, in his opinion, nothing more than a day in the life of a rancher.

"We had roast for dinner that night, but I refused to touch it. So I went to bed hungry, because if I wasn't going to eat the food that he worked hard to put on the table, then I wasn't going to eat at all."

"So you've been a vegetarian since then?"

She shook her head. "No, it took a few more years for me to realize that he couldn't actually force me to eat meat—though he still hasn't given up trying. Our battle of wills continues to this day, whenever we're in close enough proximity to argue."

"I'm picturing some awkward family get-togethers."

"You have no idea," she told him, thinking again of the confrontation with her father over the Thanksgiving menu. "Which is why I prefer to avoid those events whenever possible."

Gerald discreetly left the check on the corner of the table.

Daphne wanted to split the bill, but Evan was old-fashioned enough to believe that when a man invited a woman out for dinner, he should pay. Still, he appreciated the offer.

After he'd settled up, he helped her with her coat and took her arm as they left the restaurant, in case there were icy patches on the ground. And maybe because it gave him an excuse to touch her.

"Look," she said, tipping her head back to peer up at the night sky. "It's snowing."

"A rare sight in Montana this time of year," he remarked dryly.

She laughed. "You're not a fan of snow?"

He shook his head. "Not when I have to shovel it."

"I'll have to do that in the morning," she acknowledged. "Tonight, I'm just going to enjoy it."

They chatted easily on the drive back to Happy Hearts, though the closer they got to home, the more flutters she felt in her tummy as the butterflies awakened again in anticipation of another kiss.

He pulled right up to the house, so she wouldn't have to walk too far across the slippery ground, and he took her arm again to hold her steady. The security lights turned on automatically as they approached the short flight of stairs that led up to the wraparound porch.

Daphne pulled her keys out of her pocket as they neared the door. She was tempted to invite Evan inside for a drink, but she suspected that if she did, the evening wouldn't end with a drink. And though there was no denying that she was powerfully attracted to him, she wasn't ready to take that next step.

Instead, she simply said, "Thank you for dinner."

"It was my pleasure."

Then he lowered his head to brush his lips against hers.

He tasted of berries and chocolate and man—and the mixture of flavors was more intoxicating than the wine she'd drunk at dinner. And the heat that surged through her veins made her forget that it was only twenty degrees outside. She also forgot that she was holding her keys in her hand, until they slipped through her fingers and dropped onto the porch.

Evan smiled against her mouth, and she knew that he was well aware of the effect he had on her.

Of course he was aware. A guy who kissed like he did obviously had some experience.

Daphne pushed the thought aside to focus on the kiss, but he was already pulling back.

He reached down to scoop up her keys. "You're going to want these," he said, pressing them into her hand.

"So…" She took a moment to catch her breath and gather her thoughts. "I guess I'll see you next Friday?"

He smiled. "You'll see me next Friday."

"Or…maybe before?" she suggested.

"Do you have anything specific in mind?"

"It occurred to me, since you didn't have any trouble choking down that veggie burger, that you might be willing to try some homemade vegetarian cooking."

"Are you offering to make me dinner?"

"I am," she said. "If you're interested and—"

"Oh, I'm definitely interested," he told her.

She felt her cheeks flush with pleasure. "What day works for you?"

"Wednesday?" he suggested.

She nodded. "Six o'clock?"

"Sounds good." He kissed her again, but lightly this time—a casual brush that nevertheless caused tingles to skate through her veins. "I'll see you on Wednesday."

"There's nothing like falling in love, is there?"

Daphne started and pressed a hand to her racing heart.

"You're going to give me a heart attack one of these days."

"You've been living with me for more than five years," Alice pointed out. *"You should be used to me by now."*

"How am I supposed to get used to you when there's no rhyme or reason for when you're suddenly going to show up?"

"I'm always here."

"Okay," she acknowledged. "But could you maybe make yourself scarce when I'm otherwise occupied?"

"You mean, in a passionate lip-lock with a handsome man?"

"At the very least."

"You really like this one, don't you?"

"I really do," she said. "And you really need a hobby."

"I thought people watching was a hobby."

"A *different* hobby," she clarified.

Alice laughed softly.

The sound surprised Daphne, who didn't think the ghost—assuming that was an accurate term for Alice—was ever anything but sad.

"You seem… I don't know that *happier* is the right word," Daphne said. "But your mood definitely feels lighter these days."

"I can see a light in the darkness."

"How can I help?"

"Find Russell."

She sighed wearily. "I don't even know where to begin. All you've ever given me is his name."

"Talk to Evan."

"Why do you think Evan can help me find Russell?"

There was no response to the question, making her wonder if Alice had actually mentioned his name or if Daphne was projecting her own thoughts—because Evan seemed to have taken up permanent residence in her mind since his first visit to the farm.

"If you're not going to give me any more guidance, I'm going inside—it's cold out here."

"Sweet dreams."

But Daphne was too wired to sleep.

Whether it was the conversation with Alice or the residual effect of Evan's kiss, she knew sleep would be a long time in coming. Instead, she sat down at her desk and opened her Twitter feed to review the postings from the open house.

She was pleased with the number of visitors who'd posted photos with #HappyHeartsAnimalSanctuary #ChristmasattheFarm and #AnimalLove. Tiny Tim was the star of many of the snapshots, and he looked suitably festive in his Santa hat and coat, but Winnie and Gretel were close runners-up. Several of the raffle winners who'd been present when their names were drawn at the end of the event had posted pictures of their prizes already, and the winner of the gingerbread village included an image of her kids setting up LEGO figures around it #PlayWithYourFood #ChristmasDessert.

Daphne added a few of her own pictures, then switched over to the Facebook page to check the postings there.

Desperately Seeking Daisy.

It wasn't the first time Daphne had spotted the headline on social media over the past few weeks. Ordinarily she didn't pay much attention to personal ads, but this one had piqued her curiosity, probably because of the date. Because a child born in 1945 would be seventy-five years old now—not a child at all.

Practically speaking, it was entirely possible that the missing Daisy wasn't even alive anymore, in which case the search would not end happily for the Abernathy family. Still, she hoped she was wrong, and that the message would continue to circulate until somebody somewhere made a connection so that Daisy could be reunited with her family.

Because Daphne knew only too well how it felt to be missing a part of her family. Contact with her mom was sporadic at best and communication with her twin half brothers, Dirk and Dustin, from Cornelius's second marriage, was almost nonexistent. But the hardest part was being estranged from her father and Brandon, and she didn't know how to bridge the distance between them. And maybe, stubbornly, she didn't feel that it was her responsibility to do so. Because she hadn't done anything wrong, except maybe to follow her heart.

Was she making the same mistake with Evan?

She didn't like to think so, but so far, her heart had proven remarkably unreliable.

And yet, she didn't regret for a minute what she was doing at Happy Hearts. How could she when she'd been successful in saving so many beautiful creatures? Even if she hadn't succeeded in making her father and uncles change the way things were done at Taylor Ranch, she was making a difference in the lives of the animals who made their home here.

But right now, she had something else on her mind.

She opened up a browser window and started to search for the elusive Russell Kincaid.

"When you invited me to come over for dinner, I didn't expect a three-course meal," Evan said as he lifted the last forkful of cheese and spinach manicotti to his mouth.

The starter had been a salad of baby greens with toasted pumpkin seeds and a vinaigrette dressing, followed by the main course of pasta and warm bread.

"Most people don't consider bread to be a course," Daphne said. "Or did you think the tray of triple-chocolate brownies on the counter is dessert?"

"I was hoping," he said.

"In that case, I just might let you have one," she teased. "Maybe even served warm with vanilla ice cream and chocolate sauce."

"If people knew that you could cook like this, your table would be the hottest reservation in town," he said.

She smiled, obviously pleased by his remark. "I like to experiment with different recipes. Although I don't often take the time to make a meal like this if I'm eating alone."

"That's my excuse for not cooking, too," he told her.

"But I'm sure you don't eat out every night."

"No," he agreed. "But heating up a frozen pizza or throwing some chicken fingers into the air fryer isn't really cooking, is it?"

"You're actually saying that if I opened your

freezer, I'd find only frozen pizzas and chicken fingers?"

"And French fries and ice cream."

"Okay, that's sad," she said. "Except for the ice cream—that's a staple."

He chuckled. "Now I know how to lure you to my apartment—with the promise of ice cream."

"Or you could just invite me to come over sometime." She pushed away from the table to clear their empty plates.

"I could do that," he agreed. "Though there's really not much to see."

"You haven't yet decorated for the holidays?" she guessed, as she cut into the pan of brownies. "I've only just started here, but even the littlest touches go a long way toward putting me in the holiday mood."

"I haven't really decorated at all since I moved in," he admitted.

"When was that?"

"Three—no, four years ago," he said, a little surprised to realize that so much time had passed. Maybe he should do something to spruce up the place a little, except that he'd chosen the apartment because he liked the simplicity of the off-white walls and hardwood floors.

Daphne retrieved the tub of vanilla ice cream from the freezer. "Do you at least put up a tree for Christmas?"

"No."

"Why not?" she asked, seemingly taken aback by his blunt response.

"I told you—Christmas isn't a big deal to me," he said, reluctant to share the reasons why.

She added scoops of ice cream to the brownies, then drizzled chocolate sauce over the top. "Maybe a tree would help get you into the holiday spirit," she suggested.

"The Yuletide Ghost Tour has all the holiday spirits I need."

"I think we're talking about different kinds of spirits." She set the dessert plates on the table and returned to her seat across from him. "So what are your plans for Christmas?"

He picked up his fork and dug into the cake. "I'll have dinner with my mom and grandmother and sister on the twenty-fifth. Nothing special."

"You definitely need someone to remind you what the holidays are all about," she said lightly.

"I've seen the Charlie Brown cartoon," he told her. "I get the gist." And more important, he didn't want to be reminded—he wanted to forget.

She licked chocolate sauce off her lip. "What about your dad? You didn't mention him."

So much for forgetting, he thought ruefully. "I haven't seen him since I was ten."

"Your parents are divorced?"

Now he nodded.

"I'm sorry," she said. "I didn't mean to pry."

"You didn't," he said, although the question had admittedly pried the scab off an old wound. "You asked a question and I answered it. It's just not one that I have a lot to say about."

"My parents are divorced, too," she said. "My mom remarried three and a half years ago, and my dad's currently on wife number three—but you probably knew that because they had a ridiculously splashy wedding to celebrate their nuptials."

"I do remember hearing about the wedding," he acknowledged.

"I wish I'd only heard about it, but as the groom's daughter, I was expected to be there and smile appropriately for the family photos, conveniently disregarding the fact that my father's barely spoken to me for the past five years because I had the gall to open an animal sanctuary in the same town as Taylor Beef."

"He should be proud of you for following your own path," Evan said.

"You'd think," she said. "But he's convinced that I came up with the idea for Happy Hearts either because I wanted attention or just to embarrass him, even after I pointed out that I could have accomplished both of those objectives more easily by getting knocked up."

His lips twitched. "Did you actually say that to your father?"

She nodded, a little sheepishly. "I sometimes lose the filter between my brain and my mouth when I get emotional, and my dad knows just how to push my buttons. Like when he refers to the farm as Hippie Hearts."

"So I guess he's not a donor?"

"No," she said, then her lips started to curve. "Not directly, anyway."

"He gives you money indirectly?"

"As I already mentioned, my parents split up when I was really young and my dad married his second wife, Tania, almost as soon as the ink was dry on the divorce decree. But up until my mom remarried, she was collecting regular alimony checks from my dad.

"Jordan claims the payments were actually child support, because their prenup made her ineligible for spousal support." She shrugged. "Whatever the subject line on the checks, the money was paid by my dad to my mom, and when I told her that I wanted to open a farm-slash-animal sanctuary, she immediately put up a chunk of what she said was his money."

"Does your dad know?" he wondered.

"I haven't told him," she said. "But I wouldn't be surprised if my mom did. She'd get a kick out of watching the vein in his neck pulse."

"I think I'm starting to see where you get your spirit," Evan mused. "Does your mom live in Bronco?"

"No, she and her new husband live in Billings."

"My sister, Vanessa, is a high school science teacher in Billings."

"It's interesting," Daphne remarked, "that your sister's job is science and yours is based on pseudoscience."

"If you asked her, she'd tell you that she decided to go into science because it's based on evidence rather than anecdotes."

"I take it she's not into ghosts?"

His lips curved, just a little. "Not even when she worked at Bronco Ghost Tours."

She smiled then, too. "But you love her, anyway. I can hear it in your voice."

"Yeah, she's all right," he acknowledged, surprised not so much that she'd picked up on his deep affection for his sister but that he'd actually mentioned Vanessa's name.

He was usually reticent to talk about his family— or anything else too personal—with the women he dated. But Daphne was so easy to be with that he seemed to have trouble remembering his own rules, and he had yet to figure out if that was a good thing or bad.

Chapter Six

Daphne had just started to load the dishwasher after dessert when her phone rang. She didn't intend to answer it—she was enjoying getting to know Evan and looking forward to more toe-curling kisses before the night was over—but when she glanced at the screen, more out of habit than interest, she saw that the call was from Bronco Valley Pet Clinic.

"Sorry," she said, "but I have to take this."

"No worries," he assured her, and took over the task while she connected the call.

She appreciated his willingness to pitch in—and the way his jeans hugged his butt when he bent over to position the dessert plates in the rack.

"Daphne?"

The voice in her ear forced her to tear her gaze away from her dinner guest to focus on the call.

Any disappointment that the evening had been interrupted was supplanted by eagerness to help as she listened to the vet outline the situation, and she ended the call with a promise that she'd be at the clinic within the hour.

"That was Dr. Liebert—one of the local vets," she told Evan. "I hate to rush you off, but I have to go pick up a baby goat."

"At eight o'clock on a Wednesday night?"

"It's a twenty-four-hour clinic," she explained. "Animals have emergencies, too. And this little one lost its mom a couple days ago."

"I don't know that I've ever seen a baby goat," he remarked.

"You're welcome to come with me," she said.

Barkley nudged her thigh with his nose.

"Not you," she said regretfully as she scratched him behind the ears. "I know you'll love the baby goat, because you love everyone, but we'll give it a few days to settle in here before we make the introductions."

The dog dropped his head, clearly understanding her tone if not her words.

"But I won't be too long."

Barkley trotted back over to his bed, clearly not appeased by her promise.

At least she had Evan's company on the drive, and she was grateful for it. She was pleased, too, that he seemed to take an interest in her work and impressed by his awareness of some of the issues regarding the treatment of farm animals.

"So tell me more about this baby goat," he said as they got closer to the clinic. "How old is he?"

"Four and a half weeks."

"What happened to the mom?"

"She was attacked and killed by a coyote. Since then, the farmer's been trying to persuade the other goat moms to help out with the orphaned kids, but none of them would bond with this little one."

"So what are you supposed to do?" he wondered.

"I'll take him back to Happy Hearts and we'll bottle-feed him until he's ready to be weaned."

"The farmer couldn't do that?"

"Of course he could, but someone who already works sunup to sundown doesn't usually have the time to give a baby animal the care it needs."

"I guess it's lucky, then, that you have so much time on your hands," he noted dryly.

She laughed at that as she pulled into the parking lot of the twenty-four-hour vet clinic. "Let's go meet the baby."

While Daphne talked to Dr. Liebert and signed the necessary paperwork, she left Evan in charge of the baby goat. Of course, he didn't have a clue what that meant or what he was supposed to do, but one look at the furry creature with the big sad eyes was all it took for his heart to begin to melt.

Letting his instincts—questionable though they

might be—guide him, he lifted the little goat into his arms. It was bonier than a puppy or kitten, with sharp hooves, but the way its skinny body trembled wasn't different from any other animal that had been neglected or abused.

"I hear you've had a rough go of it the past couple of days, and I'm sorry for that," he said. "But I promise, you're going to a better place now, and Daphne will take good care of you."

Of course, the kid didn't respond. It didn't bleat or *baa* or make any sound at all. But it did, after a few minutes, drop its head against Evan's chest and close its eyes.

And only a few minutes after that, Daphne was back and they were on their way again.

She had a crate in the back seat of her truck, specifically for the safe transport of animals, but as soon as she tried to put the baby goat inside, it started making all kinds of noise, bleating as if its heart was breaking.

And maybe it was. The poor little thing had been through so much already, and now he was in an unfamiliar environment with strange people.

"Come on, baby," Daphne crooned softly. "You're not doing yourself any favors by getting all worked up."

But Evan could tell that the animal's distress was causing her distress.

"I'm sure he'll settle down once we're moving," Evan said, wanting to be helpful.

"Do you think so?"

He shrugged. "Isn't that why new parents often take their kids for a drive when they won't sleep?"

"I guess we could give it a shot," she said dubiously.

"Or, since he seems to like being held, he could ride on my lap back to the farm."

"That isn't really safe for you or the animal."

"It's probably safer than you being distracted by his cries."

"Are you sure you don't mind?" she asked. "It's not a short drive."

But he was already reaching into the crate to pick him up.

"I guess not," she decided.

The little goat snuggled into Evan's chest and actually sighed.

"Does he have a name?" he asked when they were finally underway.

Daphne shook her head. "Not yet."

"You should call him Billy—as in Billy the Kid."

"That's a little corny," she said. "Not to mention that the goat you keep referring to as *he* is actually a *she*."

"So spell it *i-e* instead of *y*," he suggested.

Not that it really mattered to him what she called the kid. The baby goat was her responsibility now—he was just along for the ride.

Or so he wanted to believe.

But the truth was, the little creature had already managed to take hold of his heart—and so had Daphne.

* * *

Thursday night, Evan went to his mother's house for dinner, as he did almost every week. Because he was still craving the rib eye he'd given up on Saturday, he let her know that he'd bring the steaks to go along with Wanda's baked potatoes and green salad.

"How was your date Saturday night?" Grandma Daisy asked when they were seated around the table with their food.

Evan stabbed his fork into the cherry tomato on top of his salad. "How did you know I had a date?"

"Your grandmother has spies everywhere," Wanda said.

"I have a social network," his grandmother clarified. "Real people in the real world—none of this virtual nonsense."

"And which member of your spy—I mean, *social* network was at DJ's Saturday night?" he asked.

"My yoga instructor. And she said she saw you with—and this is a direct quote—an attractive young woman who seemed very smitten."

"Is this true?" Wanda asked, sounding as pleased as she was surprised. "Are you dating someone?"

"One dinner doesn't constitute dating," he said, eager to put the brakes on before his mother forged full steam ahead planning his future.

And if he'd admitted that they'd already shared two dinners and a handful of kisses, she would surely think it was the beginning of a relationship.

But Evan didn't do relationships. Because relation-

ships came with expectations, and he never wanted
to disappoint a woman the way he knew his mother
had been disappointed by his father.

"Who is she? When did you meet her? Where did
you meet her?"

"Mom," he said, a single word filled with weari-
ness and warning.

"Well, you can't expect me not to have questions
about the girl you're—you had dinner with," she
quickly corrected herself. "And you can't stop me
from hoping that you might invite her to come home
and meet your mother someday in the not-too-distant
future, even though you never bring home any of the
girls you date anymore."

He sighed. "I don't bring anyone home because
every time I do, you immediately assume she's the
one."

"Twice," she said. "If I made any such assumptions, it was no more than twice because you've only
ever introduced me to two of your girlfriends. And
the last one was four years ago."

He cut into his steak. "Because both times you
were mentally drafting a guest list for the wedding
before we got to dessert."

"I just want you to be happy," she told him.

"I am happy," he said, wishing she could believe
it was true. "I have a busy life—"

"If your definition of *life* is work," Grandma Daisy
chimed in.

"I do enjoy my work," he insisted. "But if you'd

let me continue, I was going to say, 'and a wonder-ful family.'"

"Well, that part goes without saying," she told him.

"At least tell me her name," Wanda urged.

"Why? So you can stalk her on Facebook?"

"You know I quit Facebook when I started getting all those invitations from strange men. And anyway, isn't Instagram all the rage now?"

"Are you on Instagram?" he wondered.

She shook her head. "I'm not interested in taking pictures of my food—or seeing pictures of other peo-ple's food. Although—" she slid her knife through her meat, cutting off another piece "—this steak is really good."

Because he was enjoying the meal, and because not telling her about Daphne seemed to make the relationship—if it even was a relationship—into a bigger deal than it was, he finally relented and said, "Her name is Daphne Taylor."

His mother and grandmother shared a look that suggested they'd both recognized the surname and made the connection to Taylor Beef.

"She's the one with the animal sanctuary," his grandmother realized.

He nodded.

"That must make for interesting conversations around the dinner table," Wanda noted, no doubt thinking about her own siblings, all of whom had moved away from Bronco and rarely bothered to keep in touch.

"Family relationships are never simple," Grandma Daisy agreed. "But good for her for standing up for her convictions."

But his mother had a more pressing question. "When do we get to meet her?"

On Friday, a second-grade class from Mountainview Elementary School took a field trip to Happy Hearts Animal Sanctuary to learn about farm animals. Daphne truly believed that education wasn't just an important part of her work but the key to changing the way other people viewed and interacted with animals, and a school group visit was usually the highlight of her day.

Children were, in her experience, naturally curious and innately kind. Though occasionally she encountered someone like Oliver G., who'd picked up stones off the ground to throw at the animals. His action had resulted in a firm admonishment and the option of spending the rest of the time on the bus or staying close to his teacher. He opted, not very happily, for the latter.

When the group had finished their tour, they were escorted to the education center to eat their lunches and watch a short, age-appropriate film about life on a farm.

Daphne took advantage of the momentary break to deliver some treats to Tiny Tim and listen to a voice mail from her father. The message was characteristically brief, demanding that she "call when you can."

It was their first communication since Thanksgiving, and though she knew better than to expect an apology from Cornelius, it still would have been nice to hear one. Of course, that would require her father to acknowledge that he'd played at least a small part in the conflict, which she knew didn't fit his personal narrative of their relationship.

So she would call him back, but not right now. She wasn't going to let Cornelius spoil her happy mood or distract her from visiting with the pig. After a few minutes with Tim, she exited the barn, halting as she heard the distant sound of soft weeping, a wave of sadness washing over her.

Over the past few years, she'd grown accustomed to both the sound and the sensation, but she wasn't immune to the heaviness of emotion. She didn't know how finding Alice's long-deceased lover would help alleviate her sorrow, but Daphne was trying, because it was what Alice wanted her to do.

She paused when she saw Mrs. Brunswick standing outside the barn with a young girl.

"Chelsey, what are you doing over here?" the teacher asked, understandably concerned that one of her students had managed to get separated from the group. "You're supposed to be in the education center having your lunch."

"I heard the pretty lady crying."

"Who's crying? Where?" Mrs. Brunswick asked, more distracted than concerned. "I don't hear anyone crying."

The wrinkle on the child's brow smoothed out. "That's because she's not crying anymore."

The teacher looked around, but didn't see anyone in distress. "Who's not crying anymore?"

"Alice."

Daphne froze.

"There's no one named Alice in our class," Mrs. Brunswick reminded her student.

"I know."

"So she's another one of your imaginary friends?" the teacher guessed.

The little girl shook her head. "She's not imaginary. She's a ghost."

Mrs. Brunswick sighed. "We've talked about this, Chelsey. And I know your mom's talked to you about this, too. Ghosts aren't real."

"Just because you don't see them doesn't mean they're not there," the child protested, even as she let the teacher lead her away.

Daphne knew that she should get back to the education center, too, but she needed a moment to wrap her head around what had just happened. Though she'd gotten used to the sound of Alice's weeping and even enjoyed the occasional conversation with her, Chelsey's reference to a "pretty lady" suggested that the little girl had not only heard Alice, but seen her, too. A possibility that raised goose bumps on her own arms.

Was it possible that the little girl was like that kid in the movie—the one who could see dead people?

Or was the child only imagining that she'd seen a pretty lady?

"What's going on with you, Alice?" Daphne muttered the question under her breath. "What kind of game are you playing?"

"It's not a game."

Daphne's breath caught in her throat. "I thought you'd gone."

"Where would I go?"

"How am I supposed to know?"

"You're annoyed with me."

"No, I'm not," she denied.

"You are," Alice insisted. *"You're wondering why Chelsey could see me and you can't."*

"Okay, yes," she acknowledged.

For five years, Daphne had worried that she was going crazy, hearing things that no one else seemed to hear. And now, in the space of only a few weeks, the presence—Daphne was reluctant to think of her as a ghost, maybe because she'd always been told there were no such things as ghosts but there was definitely Alice—had let herself be heard by two other people. First by Evan, on his inaugural visit to the farm, and now seven-year-old Chelsey on a class trip.

"And that's why you don't see me—because a part of you still questions the possibility of my existence."

"Are you reading my mind now?"

"Your feelings more than your thoughts."

"That's reassuring," she said, not feeling reassured at all.

"Children are much more open to believing."

Daphne couldn't deny that it was true, and perhaps it did explain why Chelsey was aware of Alice's presence.

"But what about Evan? He doesn't believe in ghosts."

"He only thinks *he doesn't believe in ghosts,"* Alice said, sounding amused.

But Daphne wasn't willing to take her word for it, and she wasn't ready to tell Evan about Alice, let alone ask him to help her find Russell Kincaid.

Because even someone who wasn't afraid of ghosts might be scared off by the discovery that she could communicate with a woman who'd been dead for sixty years.

After a dozen years in the business, Evan still enjoyed taking different tour groups to haunted sites in and around Bronco.

"You mean you enjoy taking their money," his sister would say.

And that was true, too.

He wasn't in business to make people aware of alleged paranormal activity in the area but to pay the bills and take care of his family. It was a bonus, he figured, that he enjoyed operating the tours.

And though every group was different, he'd noticed that there were always one or two die-hard believers, a few maybe-willing-to-be-convinced skeptics, and several others who definitely didn't buy into the paranormal aspects of the stories but were interested in the history and/or willing to be entertained.

Tonight he had a middle-aged couple in his group that hit both ends of the spectrum.

"My aunt went to high school with Alice Milton," Colin Dockray said to his wife. "She came out here after the fire with a bouquet of flowers, and she said there was a heaviness to the air that could only be caused by the presence of restless spirits."

"Or maybe the heaviness was lingering smoke from the two buildings that were destroyed by the fire," Emmaline suggested.

"You really don't feel anything here?" her husband asked, obviously disappointed.

"I feel cold," she said. "It's fifteen degrees outside and I'm standing in ankle-deep snow."

"Close your eyes," Colin suggested. "Breathe in the atmosphere."

"Can I wait in the van instead?"

"Your mind wasn't always so closed to possibilities. What happened?"

"We saw that psychic at the carnival who said you were going to marry a very rich woman, despite the fact that I was right there with you and wearing your ring on my finger," his wife reminded him.

"*Rich* doesn't necessarily refer to material wealth," Colin pointed out.

"I'm going to wait in the van," Emmaline told him. She was halfway there when Daphne came out of the barn with the baby goat wrapped snugly in a fleece blanket in her arms. The adorable kid was too much of a temptation for even Mrs. Dockray to resist, and while his guests shifted their attention to the kid, Evan found his own snagged by the pretty woman who'd rescued it.

She was wearing her customary outfit of jeans and puffy coat with a knitted red hat on her head. Beneath the brim of that hat, her blue eyes sparkled, and when she met his gaze, her lips curved.

The warmth of her smile spread through him, immediately followed by something that might have been panic as he realized he was in serious danger of falling for her. But he managed to keep his voice light when he said, "Way to upstage my tour."

Her smile widened as his guests gathered around to coo over the newest resident of Happy Hearts. "At least I waited until your story was done."

"Thank you for that," he said.

Daphne fielded some questions from the tour group then, mostly sharing information about the animals who lived on the farm with a few questions about the ghost horses and Alice sprinkled in.

"Obviously whatever restless spirits were here before have settled over the years," Colin said to his wife. "Because the animals wouldn't be so happy and content if the property was haunted in a bad way."

Emmaline rubbed her knuckle under Billie's furry chin. "You're suggesting that it's haunted in a good way?"

"I think it's just like Mr. Cruise said—that the spirits of the horses that died in the fire are still here as guardians for the other animals."

Evan was pleased that his guests—or at least some of them—were buying into the story he'd spun about the ghost horses. And though each tour had included one or more guests who swore they could hear the horses or smell the fire, Evan had experienced none of those things.

And yet, with each successive visit to Happy Hearts, he was increasingly convinced that there was something to the story about the farm being haunted.

Or maybe the farm's sweet and sexy owner had put him under her spell.

The following afternoon, as Daphne wrestled with the fragrant balsam fir that had been delivered by a local tree farm, she realized that asking Evan to help set up and decorate her Christmas tree would have been the perfect ruse to get him engaged in preparations for the holiday—because it wouldn't have been a ruse at all. The fact was, trying to maneuver the six-foot tree into the stand was not a one-woman job.

But even with less than three weeks until Christmas, she'd hesitated to enlist his help because she didn't want to appear as if she was hitting him over the head with her holiday spirit.

Aargh.

She rubbed the top of her own head as the tree toppled over on her again.

Barkley announced a visitor at the same time the doorbell sounded—a welcome interruption. She didn't care who was at the door, whether it was a neighbor or volunteer or FedEx delivery person, she was going to beg them to help get the damn tree set up.

Even better, it was Evan.

"Hi," she said.

"Should I apologize for stopping by without calling first?"

"Of course not," she said. "I'm happy to see you."

He reached out then and plucked a fir needle from her hair. And a second and a third. "You look like you've been rolling around on the forest floor."

"Wrestling with a Christmas tree in my living room," she said.

"Ahh, that would explain it."

"And only one of the reasons I'm happy to see you," she said.

He lifted a quizzical brow.

"I could really use a hand."

"Look at that—" he held his up "—I've got two."

She stepped away from the door so he could enter. "Bring them in."

With Evan's help, the tree was quickly set up in its stand. It took a little bit longer, and a lot of cajoling, to convince him to help with the lights after he'd reminded her—yet again—that he wasn't really into Christmas. But finally the branches were wrapped with lights and the real decorating could start.

"You didn't say why you stopped by," Daphne remarked as she hooked a hanger on a shiny glass ball.

"I just wanted to see you," he said.

"Me or Billie the Kid?"

He grinned. "I was happy to hear that you decided to keep the name."

She shrugged. "It's corny, but it fits."

"Is she settling in okay?"

"Seems to be. It helps that Agatha's taken her under her wing."

"Your cranky old goat Agatha?"

Daphne carefully removed the ornament he'd just hung and shifted it four inches to the left. "She has surprisingly strong maternal instincts."

"Imagine that," he mused.

He hung another ornament, and Daphne moved that one, too.

"Why don't I put the hangers on the ornaments and then you can hang them on the tree?" he suggested.

She had the grace to look chastened.

"I'm sorry," she said. "But you had two silver balls hanging side by side."

He didn't ask why that was a problem, he just handed her the next ornament and let her place it on the branch.

He reached into the box again and was surprised to pull out a plastic character in orange overalls with a pink baseball cap over a mass of wild red hair. In deference to its purpose as a holiday decoration, the character was holding a Christmas wreath in her hands.

"You have a Messy Marsha ornament."

"I got that in my stocking when I was a kid." She took it from him now, a smile curving her lips in response to the obviously happy memory. "I've also got the complete set of books."

"I've got the books, too," he said. "All thirty-five of them."

"*You* were a fan of Messy Marsha?"

"Not the stories as much as the pictures," he said. "My grandmother was the illustrator."

"Your grandmother is Dorothea McGowan?"

He nodded. "But if artistic talent is a genetic trait, it definitely skipped me, because I can't draw a stick figure."

"You tell a pretty good story, though," she noted.

"It's easy when you've got a captive audience."

She hung the last ornament on the tree, then stood back to assess the overall effect. "I think it looks pretty good. Certainly not any worse for wear after our wrestling match." She turned to him. "What do you think?"

But he was looking at her instead of the tree. "I think I'm really glad I stopped by today."

She smiled. "Me, too."

"So what are your plans for Christmas?" he asked, after the boxes were put away and they were sitting down to a meal of tofu pad Thai that Daphne had quickly thrown together. His contribution had been setting the table.

"Jordan and Camilla might stop by in the afternoon, if they can squeeze in a quick visit between holiday celebrations with their respective families. I'd be skeptical that they'll have time, except that Camilla told me she has a present for Tiny Tim and I know she'll want to give it to him."

"Your future sister-in-law has a Christmas present for your pig?"

"She fell for him the first time she saw him—kind of like you and Billie."

"It's hardly the same thing," he said. "Billie is an adorable baby goat. Tiny Tim is…big. And…a pig."

She shrugged. "Beauty is in the eye of the beholder."

"You mentioned Jordan," he said, circling back to the original topic of conversation. "But don't you have another brother?"

"Actually, I have three other brothers. Brandon is two years younger than Jordan and two years older than me, then there's Dirk and Dustin, my twin half brothers from my father's second marriage to Tania."

"Will you see any of them on Christmas?"

"Probably not," she said. After the blowup at Thanksgiving, the last thing she wanted was to ruin another holiday for everyone. Based on their recent telephone conversation, her father seemed willing to pretend that their conflict over the menu had never happened, but Daphne had a little more trouble letting go of the hurt. And she had no intention of setting herself up for a repeat performance.

"What about your mom?" he asked.

"We haven't celebrated a holiday together since... I can't even remember when. But I won't be on my own," she was quick to assure him. "I've got Barkley to keep me company and chores to keep me busy."

Okay, maybe her plans did sound a little lame when she said them out loud, but she didn't want Evan to feel sorry for her. If he wanted to include her in his holiday plans, such as they were, that would be great, but she didn't want a pity invitation.

Thankfully, he didn't offer one.

And she wasn't the least bit disappointed—or at least that was what she told herself.

After they'd finished eating, including leftover triple-chocolate brownies for dessert, he helped her tidy up the kitchen. There wasn't a lot of room around the sink, which meant that there was a lot of unintentional—and some not-so-accidental—body contact as they worked side by side. And with each fleeting touch, her awareness of him grew sharper and stronger.

She'd known him a little more than two weeks, but she felt confident that she knew everything she needed to. And as much as she enjoyed the flirting and the kissing, she was more than ready to take their relationship to the next level.

As he was wiping the frying pan with a towel, she glanced through the window over the sink and discovered that it had started to snow again.

"I'm feeling pretty good about our odds for a white

Christmas," she remarked. "They're calling for another four-to-six inches tonight."

"In that case, I should probably be on my way," he said.

Was that a note of regret she heard in his voice?

Or was she projecting her own feelings onto him?

Was it possible that she was the only one who wanted more than a few steamy kisses?

"It's not coming down too hard just yet," she pointed out.

"Not yet," he agreed. "But I'm sure you don't want me to get stuck here."

His words suggested that he was ready to go, but he still made no move toward the door.

And that was what gave her the courage to say, "Actually…I wouldn't mind if you stayed."

Chapter Seven

"Are you inviting me to stay?" Evan asked cautiously, not certain if she was offering him a haven from the coming storm—or something more.

Daphne lifted her gaze to his, her blue eyes dark with awareness. "Do you *want* to stay?"

"Yes," he told her. "Very much."

Her lips curved slowly then. "I'm glad, because that means you can help me feed and water the animals."

Her tone might have been teasing, but he knew that the chores needed to be done. So he bundled up and went with her, in the hope that his extra set of hands would help complete the tasks more quickly.

She let him feed Billie while she dealt with the

rest of the animals, but when they finally got back to the house, trudging through several of the forecasted inches that had already fallen, she seemed more apprehensive than eager.

"It's okay if you've changed your mind," he told her.

"I haven't," she said. "I'm just a little nervous. It's been a long time for me."

"We'll take it slow," he said, a playful note in his voice. "See if that might jog your memory."

"Okay," she said.

Because she would have agreed to anything he wanted. Because all she wanted was Evan. And when he lowered his head to kiss her, she exhaled a quiet sigh of both relief and anticipation.

But he bypassed her lips to brush his own over her temple. Then his mouth touched her cheek... skimmed over her jaw...nibbled on her ear. Every teasing kiss heightened her anticipation, increased her arousal, so that when his mouth finally settled on hers, she was aching for his kiss.

His hands found their way beneath the hem of her sweater, his fingertips gliding over skin. His hands skimmed up the sides of her torso, seeking and finding her breasts, and groaning his appreciation when he discovered she wasn't wearing a bra. His thumbs brushed over the already peaked nipples, sending arrows of heat from the tips to her center, melting her bones.

"We should go upstairs." She whispered the suggestion against his lips.

"Upstairs is too far."

"I've got condoms upstairs."

And now that she thought about it, she should probably check the expiration date on the box because she hadn't been kidding when she'd told him it had been a while.

"I've got one in my wallet," he told her.

"In that case," she relented.

He released her for a moment—just long enough to pull the blanket off the back of the sofa and spread it on the floor beside the Christmas tree, then retrieve the promised square packet and dropped it on the fleece, within easy reach.

He took her hand then and drew her toward him.

"You should see the way your eyes sparkle with the reflection of all the lights."

"I'd rather see yours," she said.

"I've got the better view," he insisted, lifting his other hand to her cheek. "You're so beautiful, Daphne. Sometimes I look at you, and you actually take my breath away."

"You don't have to seduce me with pretty words, Evan."

"I'm not usually good with words," he told her. "But you inspire me…in so many ways."

She was inspired, too, and reached for the hem of her sweater to pull it over her head. His gaze skimmed over her bare upper torso, his pupils growing wide. Then she unfastened the button of her jeans, but it was the rasp of the zipper that mobilized him.

"Let me," he said, and dropped to his knees on the blanket.

Her hands fell away as he hooked his fingers through the belt loops to tug the denim over her hips, and lower, until the fabric was pooled at her ankles. He helped her lift one foot, then the other, then tossed the jeans on top of her already discarded sweater, leaving her clad in only a pair of pink cotton bikini panties.

Evan's hands slid up the back of her legs to cup the curve of her bottom, holding her in place while he pressed his mouth to the fabric at the juncture of her thighs. Daphne's breath hitched in her throat and her knees nearly buckled as he teased her with his tongue through the thin barrier, making her panties wet both inside and out.

"Evan." His name was a plea.

He responded by tightening his hold on her buttocks as he continued to nibble and lick until she was panting and dripping. Just when she was certain her knees would buckle, he eased away, drawing her down onto the blanket and whisking her panties away.

"You're supposed to be naked, too," she pointed out, as he knelt between her legs.

"I will be. But first, I need another few minutes right here," he said, nudging her thighs farther apart and lowering his head again.

He was wrong.

It took less than a minute for his tongue to work

magic on her bare flesh, taking her to unimagined heights of pleasure…and beyond.

She was still shuddering with the aftereffects of a mind-bogglingly intense orgasm when he finally tore off his own clothes, readied himself with the condom and buried himself inside her. And just like that, the glorious tension began to build again.

She lifted her hips off the floor, and their bodies moved together in an easy and familiar rhythm. At the same time, her hands explored the taut skin of his torso, tracing the contours of his muscles. For a man whose daily exercise was primarily spinning stories, he was very nicely built.

He began to thrust faster, deeper. She could feel the tension in him, see it in the set of his jaw. She linked her hands behind his head, drawing his mouth down to hers, opening for his kiss. His tongue slid between her parted lips, mirroring the intimate strokes of his body, stoking the fire that burned between them.

Their mutual pleasure continued to build with each successive stroke until it was almost too much. But still he held himself in check, waiting. Only when the waves of her release began again did he let the tide of his own climax sweep him away.

Jesus, it was hot.

He lifted a hand to brush his hair away from his face dripping with sweat. He could hear something hissing and crackling, could see flickering light even through closed eyes. It was an effort to pry them open, and when he finally did, they immediately wanted to slam shut again as thick, acrid smoke made them burn and water. He tried to draw in a breath, but filled his lungs with smoke instead of air, and pushed it out again in a violent, hacking cough as he hauled himself up into a sitting position.

He squinted through the dense gray fog, desperate to get his bearings. As if from far away, he could hear the horses whinnying as they danced restlessly in their stalls.

That's right—he was in the hayloft.

With Alice.

He put his hand on her shoulder. His skin, darkly tanned from working outside in all seasons, was a stark contrast to hers, pale and soft. Despite the gaping distance between their worlds, they'd somehow found their way to one another and fallen in love. But now was not the time for reminiscing.

He shook her, not at all gently. Because now was not the time for tenderness or subtlety, either.

"Alice. Wake up."

Her eyelashes fluttered, her brow furrowed as her brain registered the heat, the smoke, the flames. She sat up, tugging the corner of the rough wool blanket to cover her naked form.

"Ohmygod. The barn—" The rest of the words were lost in a fit of coughing. She tried again. "The horses—"

"Let's get you out of here first."

He found his discarded T-shirt and offered it to her.

"To cover your face," he said, when she started to pull it over her head.

"Oh." She held the fabric over her nose and mouth.

He nodded his approval, trying to ignore his own rising sense of panic as he listened to the horses below growing more frantic as the fire began to spread across the roof.

"We have to go. Now."

But there was already a wall of flame blocking their path to the ladder—their only means of escape...

He jolted awake, his heart racing, his mind reeling.

He sucked in a deep breath, desperate to draw air into his lungs as his gaze moved frantically around the unfamiliar room.

Where was he?

Who was he?

"Evan?" A gentle touch on his arm. A familiar voice. "Are you okay?"

"Yeah." He scrubbed his hands over his face as his heart rate gradually slowed to something approximating normal. "I just had a weird dream."

"Anything you want to talk about?"

He shook his head. "I don't actually remember the details."

Liar.

"That happens to me all the time." She wrapped her arms around him and pressed her lips to his bare shoulder. "I think it's the subconscious mind's way of protecting us from things we don't want to think about."

"Makes sense."

She hugged him a little tighter. "Do you want me to get you anything? A glass of water? A glass of whiskey?"

He smiled at that. "My grandmother's going to love you."

Every muscle in her body stilled then, and he mentally cursed himself for the offhand remark even as he braced for her to ask when she was going to meet his family.

Considering that he was right now naked in her bed, it wasn't an unreasonable question. But it also wasn't a step he was ready to take.

And maybe Daphne realized that because when she finally spoke again it was only to ask, "Is that a yes to the whiskey?"

"No," he said. "I don't need whiskey. I just need you."

It shouldn't have been an easy admission to make. He wasn't comfortable admitting to anything more than the most basic needs. Then again, he wasn't accustomed to feeling anything more than the most basic needs.

But everything was different with Daphne.

When he was with Daphne, he was where he was supposed to be.

Maybe it was fate that brought you to Happy Hearts.

He'd been quick to dismiss the possibility when she mentioned it, but now, with her warm, naked body pressed against his, he found himself reconsidering.

Then he found her breast with his hand and he let the pursuit of mutual pleasure chase all his thoughts away.

The following morning, Evan followed the scent of French roast to the kitchen where he found Daphne already dressed and standing by the stove, pouring batter onto a frying pan.

"I smelled coffee," he said.

She smiled at him and pointed to a cupboard with the spatula. "Mugs are in there."

He headed in that direction, then paused en route to nuzzle her throat. "You were up early."

"That's life on a farm," she reminded him as she handed him a plate piled with pancakes.

"That's a lot of food," he remarked.

"I figured you burned off a lot of calories last night."

He smiled then. "Maybe after breakfast, we can go back upstairs and burn off some more."

"As tempting as that sounds, I have to open up the adoption center at eleven today."

He poured maple syrup over his pancakes. "You don't even get one day off?"

"Not without arranging in advance for somebody to cover for me."

She carried her own plate, with a much smaller stack of pancakes, to the table.

"What time will you be done?"

"We close at four, but then I usually spend another hour or so with the animals, to make sure they're settled."

"And I have a tour tonight," he noted.

It should have been a relief. They both had things to do and it was important for a relationship to have boundaries. But after knowing Daphne only two and a half weeks, he was having trouble remembering where those boundaries were.

"Do you run tours on Tuesday nights?" she asked him now.

"Not in the winter."

"Good." She sipped her coffee. "Because there's a Christmas concert at Mountainview Elementary School on Tuesday and I'd love for you to go with me. Nothing embodies the pure joy of the season like the sound of children singing."

"Thanks, but I'll pass."

"You're really not interested?" she pressed, obviously disappointed by his response.

A children's Christmas concert?

Definitely not.

"But I'm up for seeing a movie on Tuesday," he suggested as an alternative.

She shook her head. "Sorry. The concert is something I go to every year, and I don't want to miss it."

On second thought...

"What time does it start?" he asked, surprised to hear the words come out of his mouth.

But maybe he shouldn't have been, because as much as he didn't want to go to the concert, he didn't want to give up the opportunity to spend more time with her.

Yeah, he was definitely venturing into dangerous territory here.

And when Daphne rewarded his change of heart with another one of her sweet smiles, he knew that she was the reason he wasn't even trying to navigate toward safer ground.

"Seven o'clock," she said, in answer to his question.

"I'll pick you up at six thirty."

"Can you make it six? I don't want to be stuck standing at the back."

He nodded. "I'll be here at six."

Monday afternoon, Daphne was doing paperwork in her office at the adoption shelter when there was a knock on her door.

"This is a surprise," she said, pushing away from the desk to greet her stepmother with an air-kiss.

"I hope you don't mind that I stopped by, but I wanted to see where you worked," Jessica Taylor said.

"Visitors are always welcome—even family," she said, softening the remark with a smile. "Do you want a tour?"

"Maybe another day," Jessica said. "Today, I wanted to talk about dogs."

"One of my favorite subjects."

Her stepmother offered a tentative smile. "I told your dad that we should have a dog at the ranch, and he agreed."

"Did he?"

Jessica nodded. "So I'm here to get a dog."

"I appreciate that you thought of Happy Hearts," she said cautiously. "But I'm pretty sure when Dad agreed to the idea of a dog, he was thinking you'd get in touch with a breeder."

"I don't care what he was thinking," Jessica said in an uncharacteristic show of backbone. "I refuse to pay way too much money for a pedigree when there are plenty of rescue dogs who need a good home."

Daphne could hardly argue the point, but she still had reservations. "Well, then, let's take a walk around and see if any of our dogs appeal to you—and if they don't, that's okay, too."

As they made their way through the row of enclosures, she pointed out the information sheets that gave each dog's name, breed and approximate age along with details of observed behaviors and personality.

"I can't believe that someone would just abandon a pet," Jessica said after she'd read that status on several of the pages.

"It happens more often than you want to know," Daphne told her. "Some people grow tired of the responsibility, or they don't want to deal with behavioral issues, or they can't afford necessary medical care, so they dump the animal on the side of a road somewhere.

"Boo was tied to the fence at the end of our driveway," she said, gesturing to the three-year-old German shepherd in a nearby enclosure. "Which suggests that even if his previous owners didn't care enough to keep him, they cared enough to ensure he would be looked after by someone else.

"Rousey wasn't nearly so lucky," she said, moving on to the next enclosure. "She was left in a dumpster behind The Bronco Brick Oven."

"That's so completely heartless," Jessica said, crouching in front of the glass for a closer look at the short-haired black-and-white Chihuahua with tan markings.

The dog lifted her head and stared at Jessica with one eye.

"She lost an eye in a fight with a feral cat over food scraps," Daphne told her.

"Is that why you called her Rousey? Because she's a fighter?"

She nodded. "It seemed appropriate."

"Could I change her name?"

"Of course, but—"

"Then I'll call her Button," Jessica said. "Because she's as cute as one."

Daphne was surprised by her stepmother's assessment. Though she admittedly didn't know her father's third wife very well, she'd assumed that a woman whose designer labels were always perfectly coordinated wouldn't look beyond labels. And while she was willing to admit that she might have judged her too harshly, she was certain that her father wouldn't share his wife's assessment of the tiny dog.

"I appreciate your interest in Rousey—"

"Button," Jessica insisted.

"—but I'm not sure she's the right dog for you."

"You mean you don't think she's the right kind of dog for your father?"

"And obviously you agree."

"She probably isn't a dog Cornelius would have chosen, but he's not here," she pointed out. "I am. And I want Button."

Daphne looked at the dog, who was looking back with such a hopeful expression on her face that she knew she couldn't stand in the way of her chance to go to a "furever" home.

Evan arrived promptly at six o'clock to pick Daphne up for the concert Tuesday night. While a holiday show put on by grade-school kids wouldn't have been his first choice for entertainment, he would gladly suffer through it with Daphne by his side.

He'd grown up in Bronco Valley, so he'd never been to the elementary school in Bronco Heights before. Which made it all the more puzzling that, as he followed the directions Daphne gave to him, he could picture not just the exterior of the stone building but the maze of interior corridors and neat rows of desks in a classroom that smelled of chalk dust and poster paint.

"There's a parking spot there," Daphne said, gesturing to the empty slot between a minivan and Mini Cooper.

He ignored the tension that had settled between his shoulder blades and maneuvered his SUV into position.

"Busy place," he noted.

"Parents and grandparents and siblings will be shoulder to shoulder with aunts and uncles and other members of the community," Daphne said as they made their way to the entrance where the cornerstone beside the doors established the date of the building as 1958.

Since she'd invited him, she insisted on paying the admission fee and accepted a program for "A Holiday Celebration" from the teacher who took their money.

Despite their early arrival, they walked into an auditorium already half-full. They found a couple of seats near the middle, and she offered him the program to peruse while they waited for the show to start. The front cover was divided into quadrants, each with a child's illustration of a Christmas tree, a menorah, a kinara and a diya, and the back cover had various holiday greetings in different languages.

"It's a K to five school, so the songs and skits are usually pretty short and simple," Daphne said. "The kindergarten class is always a lot of fun because half the kids are more interested in waving to their parents in the audience than singing, but what they lack in talent they make up for with enthusiasm. The first graders are a little more disciplined, emphasis on…"

Evan knew Daphne was talking to him, but he could no longer hear her words. Instead, it was a man's voice—or maybe the echo of his thoughts—that played inside his head.

She was at the school tonight, for the annual holiday concert. She'd invited him to go, but he knew her parents would be there and, after the big blowup with her family at Thanksgiving, he thought it would probably be best to give her father a wide berth for a few weeks.

He didn't care that Henry Milton didn't like him.

Sure, it would have been nice if her father wasn't such a disapproving bastard, but he'd learned a long time ago not to worry about things he couldn't control. All that mattered was Alice.

And when school let out for the Christmas break, they were going to sneak out of town for a few days and get married.

Only twelve more days now, because yes, he was counting.

Alice had laughingly confided that her colleagues liked to tease her because she was as excited about the holidays as her second-grade students. She didn't deny that it was true, though she didn't tell any of them the real reason. Until the vows had been ex-

changed and she was wearing his ring on her finger, it would be their secret.

"I'll say goodbye to my students as Miss Milton in December, and hello to them as Mrs. Kincaid in January," she'd said.

She'd been disappointed that he was going to miss the concert, and he was sorry to do so. She'd worked hard to prepare her class for their big performance, and all of the students were going to have their noses painted red and wear reindeer antlers they'd made out of construction paper to illustrate the song they'd be singing: "Rudolph the Red-Nosed Reindeer."

Alice had shown him the prototype of the head-wear, and she'd looked so cute with the antlers bobbing on top of her head, he couldn't resist kissing her.

Of course, one kiss had led to another, then another...

He'd never thought it was possible to feel the way he felt about her, and nothing and no one would get in the way of them being together forever.

Not even Henry Milton.

"Evan?"

He started when Daphne laid a hand on his arm.

"Are you all right?"

He shoved the vision or memory or whatever the hell it was out of his mind. "Sure. Why?"

"You looked like you'd seen a ghost."

"Ha ha," he said, because he knew she was making a joke, but her comment had struck a little too close to the truth.

But was it truth or just his imagination?

He wondered what his mother would say if he told her about the connection he seemed to have made with the ghost of Alice Milton's undocumented lover, whether she would think he was making it up for attention—or maybe to bring attention to his business.

Which, now that he thought about it, wasn't an entirely unreasonable supposition. Oftentimes when people claimed to have had encounters with ghosts or experienced other paranormal phenomena, they were trying to capitalize on the event for financial gain—either selling the story to the tabloids or promoting a supposedly haunted B and B.

Maybe he had been telling ghost stories for too long and was seeking a personal experience to make his job more palatable to himself, because every salesperson knew that it was easier to sell a product he believed in.

The group of kids onstage must have finished singing, because the crowd was applauding their effort. Evan put his hands together, too, and determinedly pushed all thoughts of Alice Milton and Russell Kincaid out of his mind.

"I really enjoyed that," Daphne said, as Evan drove them back to Happy Hearts after the concert was over. "And I appreciate you going with me. I would have gone on my own, but it was nice to have company."

"I enjoy spending time with you."

Though the words were appropriate, his tone

sounded stiff, as if he wasn't really focused on their conversation. And even as they chatted more during the drive, she couldn't shake the feeling that his mind was somewhere else.

When he pulled up in front of the house, he got out of his vehicle to walk her to the door, as he always did, but this time, he kept the engine running.

"I made Christmas cookies today," Daphne said. "If you wanted to come in for coffee and cookies?"

She thought—hoped—he'd guess that her offer of "coffee and cookies" was an invitation to more, but whether he did or not, he shook his head.

"Thanks, but I really need to get home."

"Oh. Okay," she said, not just disappointed but a little concerned about his sudden distance.

"But I'll see you Friday," he said, forcing a smile.

She nodded. "Okay."

Then he lowered his head to kiss her goodbye, an effort that seemed more perfunctory than passionate at first. But when he pulled her closer, some of his tension seemed to ease, and he kissed her until they were both breathless. And for just a second, when he looked into her eyes, she thought he might change his mind about the cookies—and other goodies—but he only said, "Good night, Daphne."

Then he was gone.

And she was left standing on the porch, watching his taillights disappear into the darkness.

"Well, that was weird," she said.

"Weirder than the fact that you live on a haunted farm and talk to ghosts?"

So Alice was back.

"Only one ghost," she said.

"Well, then, that's not weird at all."

"You're not being helpful."

"I'm sorry," Alice said, this time sounding sincere. *"Tell me what happened."*

"Didn't you see? He kissed me goodbye and then he just left."

"Ah, you wanted to be tangling the sheets with him again."

"How did you—no," she decided. "I don't want to know."

"I wasn't peeking in the window while you were doing the deed," the ghost assured her. *"But I could tell, seeing the two of you together afterward, that there was a new closeness—a greater intimacy— between you."*

"How could you tell?" she wondered, apparently having changed her mind about not wanting to know.

"Your auras were pink."

"Is that a ghost skill—reading auras?"

"It's hardly specific to those who have passed, but it might be easier for us because we're not so focused on the concrete details of here and now."

While Daphne had never really understood the whole aura thing, she'd been forced to open her mind in a lot of ways since taking up residence at the farm, leading her to ask, "So what does pink symbolize?"

"Love. Happiness. Passion."

"What color was Evan's aura tonight?"

"He's stressed. And confused. His aura is muddied right now."

"Is that my fault?" she asked worriedly. "Am I stressing him out?"

"No, it's not you. He's just dealing with some things that he didn't anticipate ever having to deal with. Otherworldly things."

"Oh, Alice. What have you done?"

"I haven't done anything," the spirit denied. *"But he's connected—whether he wants to be or not."*

"How? Why?"

"Because he's the one you love, and he can bring back the one I love."

Chapter Eight

He was an idiot.

And a coward.

After the concert Tuesday night, Evan had kissed Daphne at the door and walked away instead of taking her to bed and spending long, glorious hours making love with her again, as he really wanted to do. And then last night again, he'd declined her invitation to return after the tour.

Why?

Because he was an idiot and a coward.

Because he was seriously starting to believe that her farm was haunted and he wanted no part of it.

But he couldn't deny that he wanted Daphne.

She was his first thought in the morning and his

last thought at night, and even after only one night together, he couldn't imagine ever wanting anyone else.

But were those feelings real? Or were they somehow tangled up with everything else that was going on? Because there was no longer any doubt in his mind that something else was going on.

Ever since Daphne had mentioned that Alice Milton had a fiancé who'd died with her in the fire, he seemed to be getting caught up in the story, in their lives. And he had no interest in getting tangled up with a bunch of ghosts—especially when he knew that ghosts didn't really exist.

There was alive and there was dead and anything in between only existed in legends and books and movies.

With that thought in mind, Evan turned his attention to the night ahead—and of course he thought of Daphne. He had no doubt that if he showed up at her door, she'd invite him to come in, but he'd decided it would be smarter to keep his distance from Happy Hearts for a few days. To give them both some space to figure things out.

Or maybe he could invite her to come to his place. Maybe if they made love in his bed, in his definitely-not-haunted apartment, it would be easier to separate reality from the crazy dreams and visions that had been playing out in his head.

He opted to try the space thing first and called his mom's house instead.

"How does pizza sound for dinner?" he asked when Grandma Daisy answered.

"Delicious," she said.

"Pepperoni and mushrooms?"

"And hot peppers."

"I'll see you in half an hour," he promised.

Grandma Daisy had the table set for two when he arrived with the pizza box in hand thirty minutes later.

"Isn't Mom eating with us?"

His grandmother shook her head. "She's out."

He frowned at the succinct response. "But her car's in the driveway."

She opened the fridge and pulled out two bottles of beer. "Obviously she didn't take her car."

"It's kind of cold to be out walking."

"She isn't walking." She handed him one of the bottles. "She's out for dinner."

"You didn't mention that when I called," he noted.

"I was afraid you'd change your mind about bringing pizza."

"You know I'd bring anything you want," he told her. "You only ever have to ask."

"I know," she agreed. "But I don't like to ask, because I like to pretend you have better things to do than hang out with your grandmother—especially on a Saturday night."

"And I like to let you have your illusions."

She smiled, but then her expression turned serious. "Did your girlfriend dump you already?"

"No, she didn't dump me, and I didn't dump her, either," he said.

"I didn't think you'd cut her loose—not before your Yuletide Ghost Tour had finished its run, anyway."

He frowned at that. "You think I've been seeing Daphne because she owns Happy Hearts?"

She shrugged. "It's as good a reason as any."

"There are a lot of better reasons," he said.

"Such as?"

"She's beautiful and smart and kind and..."

His words trailed off as his grandmother's lips curved again, smugly this time.

"Why are you smiling?"

"Because I'm happy to see that you recognize not just her attributes but your feelings for her."

"You played me," he realized.

"I've known you your whole life," she reminded him. "And I knew, the first time you mentioned Daphne's name, that she'd made an impression on you."

"She did," he acknowledged. "And so did her farm."

"I checked out her website. She's got information on all of the animals—and every page has a link to make a donation."

"How much did you give?"

"My money's my business," she said.

He smiled at that. "She's doing a lot of good," he acknowledged.

"So why do you sound troubled?"

"It's a long story," he said. "You might want another beer."

She got up and went to the fridge; he shook his head, declining the second bottle that she offered to him.

"I have to drive home," he reminded her.

"Or not," she said. "There's a spare bedroom here."

"With a single bed."

"Your mom and I agreed that we should have a bed if someone needed to stay, but we didn't want anyone staying for too long."

He chuckled. "And that's why I'll be going home tonight."

Grandma Daisy sat down at the table again. "So tell me about the farm."

"Do you remember hearing anything about a fire at Whispering Willows Ranch when you were younger?"

"Of course. It was big news...and such a horrible tragedy." She shook her head sadly. "Alice Milton was only twenty-two years old when she perished in the blaze."

"Along with her fiancé."

His grandmother frowned. "I don't recall hearing that she'd been engaged. And I definitely would have remembered if more than one person had died in the fire."

"Could there have been a cover-up?" he asked.

"Why would anyone want to cover something like that up?"

"Maybe because her parents disapproved of the relationship."

Grandma Daisy sipped her beer. "Is this a theory or do you have any evidence to back it up?"

"Nothing that would stand up in a court of law."

"Tell me anyway," she urged.

So he told her, about the woman he'd heard crying on his first visit to the farm and Daphne's mention that Alice had been engaged, then his dream about the fire and the flashback or vision or whatever it was that had happened at the elementary school.

"I can see why your head's spinning," Daisy admitted. "That's a lot to take in."

"You don't think I'm crazy?"

"I don't think you're crazy," she assured him. "I think there are all kinds of inexplicable things that happen in this world, and that some people are more receptive to seeing and hearing what so many others refuse to acknowledge."

"Do you think it's possible that Henry Milton somehow covered up the fact that Alice wasn't alone when she died?"

"I don't know that he would have been able to do so on his own," she said. "But the Miltons were a wealthy family. Have you tried to access the fire marshal's report?"

"No," he said. "I'm not sure I want to get involved."

"It seems to me that you're involved, whether you want to be or not. And I suspect that this mystery has created another level of connection with Daphne, and it's something you can't control—which is the real reason you're here with me tonight instead of at Happy Hearts with her."

He couldn't deny it. Instead, he said, "And now it's time for me to be heading home."

"You should be heading over to see your girlfriend," Grandma Daisy countered.

"It's late and morning comes early on the farm." As he rose from his seat, a flicker of light speared through the narrow gap between the curtains in the living room, indicating that a vehicle had pulled into the driveway. He made his way to the window and pulled back the covering to peek out into the darkness. "Is that Mom coming home?"

"No, it's my Uber," Grandma Daisy said. "I'm going out clubbing with the girls."

He laughed. "I wouldn't be surprised. You have a much more active social life than I do."

"A sad truth that says a lot more about your social life than it does about mine," she told him.

He watched as the driver of the vehicle got out and came around to the passenger side. The man opened the door and Evan's mom got out.

Grandma Daisy yanked the curtain out of his hand and pulled it shut.

"Are you going to take that leftover pizza home?" she asked, obviously trying to distract him from the fact that his mother had returned home from a date.

"No. You can have it for lunch tomorrow," he said,

making his way to the kitchen again to grab his coat and exit through the back door.

"And I'll enjoy it as much then as I did tonight," she assured him.

He kissed her soft cheek. "Thanks for listening, Grandma Daisy."

"Always."

The easy smile on his face froze when he opened the back door and found his mother in a lip-lock with a stranger.

Evan cleared his throat. Loudly.

Wanda jolted, as if she was a teenager caught making out on the porch by a disapproving father—or mother. But Grandma Daisy, Evan saw when he glanced over his shoulder, had already disappeared into the other room again.

The man who held Evan's mother in his arms was a little slower than Wanda to react. Even when he turned his head to glance at the source of the interruption, he didn't release her—or appear the least bit embarrassed.

His mother drew in a quick breath. "Evan…hi."

"Hello," he said.

"This is, um, Sean. Sean Donohue," she clarified. Then, speaking to the man who was still entirely too close for Evan's liking, she said. "Sean, my son, Evan."

"It's a pleasure to meet you," the man said. "Or maybe I should say meet you again."

Evan took the proffered hand, grateful that manners had at least forced the man to let go of Wanda. "We've met before?"

"A long time ago," the other man said. "When you were playing with building blocks under your mom's desk."

"I'm sorry I don't remember that," Evan responded dryly. But he put two and two together. Sean was the Donohue of Dwight & Donohue, the law firm where his mother worked.

"Well, it was a long time ago," Sean acknowledged with a grin.

Evan didn't smile back.

"Did you want to come in?" Wanda asked Sean.

"I think it would be better if I didn't," he said, obviously sensing the tension between his date and her son. But he took her hand and gave it a gentle squeeze. "I'll call you later."

She nodded. "Thanks again for dinner."

"It's always my pleasure."

"Always?" Evan echoed when the man had gone.

"Do you mind if I come in and take my coat off before you start your interrogation?" his mother asked.

He stepped away from the door, his head still reeling over the discovery of his mother in the arms of a man.

She unzipped her boots and set them on the mat, then unbelted her coat and hung it by the door.

She was wearing a dress, he noted. With a skirt that fell just below her knees and clung to curves he didn't know—*didn't want to know*—his mother had.

Looking at her now, he was suddenly struck by the fact that she wasn't an unattractive woman. Though there were some creases around her eyes and faint lines bracketing her mouth, it was difficult to guess her age. Her dark brown hair, cut in an angled bob, was shiny and sleek with no visible signs of gray.

So maybe he shouldn't be surprised that she had a boyfriend. And he definitely shouldn't overreact to the news, but he couldn't seem to help himself. His mom had always been just that—his mom. And when his dad walked out, upending all their lives, she'd been the one to right things again. She'd been steady and strong, a constant when everything else was changing.

And now she was changing, and the realization left him feeling a little unsteady.

Wanda moved past him to fill the kettle, then set it on the stove to boil. "Do you want a cup of tea?"

He shook his head. "I want to know why you were out for dinner with your boss."

"Sean's not my boss," she said, taking two mugs from the cupboard and dropping a tea bag into each. "I work for Mr. Dwight."

"Is the name Donohue on your paycheck?"

"I don't get a check anymore. All our payroll is done by direct deposit."

He huffed out a breath. "You're missing my point."

"No, I'm making my own point," she said, using her don't-mess-with-your-mother voice. "Which is that my personal relationship with Sean is no one's business but mine and his."

"How can you say that to me?" he demanded. "I'm your son—"

"Yes, you're my son," she acknowledged, as the kettle started to whistle. "And I will always love you with my whole heart, but I don't need or even want your permission to go out with a man whose company I very much enjoy."

"No, you don't," he conceded, as she poured hot water into the two mugs. "But you might have at least given me a heads-up that you were involved with someone."

And then, without giving her a chance to reply, he walked out.

"Well, that went well," Dorothea said, accepting the mug of tea that her daughter handed to her.

Wanda sighed. "Is this the part where you say, 'I told you so'?"

"It might have been, but it's not nearly as satisfying if you know it's coming," she remarked.

"How about if I say you were right? Because you were," her daughter admitted. "I should have told him."

"Why didn't you?" Dorothea asked.

"Because I knew he wouldn't take it well."

"You didn't give him a chance to take it well. He was ambushed by the sight of your boyfriend's hands on your—"

"Okay," Wanda interjected. "We all know where Sean's hands were."

"And Evan's going to need some time—and possibly therapy—to block that image from his mind," she said, trying to tease a smile out of her daughter.

She didn't succeed.

"Plus, you know how he gets around the holidays."

Now Wanda sighed. "I remember when he used to love the holidays."

Dorothea did, too, but Andrew's decision to walk out on his family only days after Christmas had changed that. Since then, all the signs of the season that others anticipated with so much excitement only made her grandson become sullen and withdrawn.

"He'll come around," she assured her daughter.

"Do you really think so?"

"You raised two wonderful children, but even grown-up children sometimes have trouble seeing their mom as anything other than that."

"You're not trying to tell me that you're dating someone, are you?" Wanda asked.

Dorothea chuckled. "No. I was lucky enough to have fifty-two wonderful years with the love of my life, so I've got fifty-two years of memories to keep me company."

Her daughter sighed. "I only ever wanted what you and Dad had. When I married Andrew, I thought we'd be together forever."

"No one ever gets married thinking that there

might be an expiry date on their vows. Well, except maybe people who marry for money."

"If I'd married for money, I might have had at least that to keep me warm at night."

"No amount of money can compete with a good man, and your father was the very best," Dorothea said, her tone a little melancholy.

"Did you ever love anyone else?" Wanda wondered. "When you were younger, I mean."

She shook her head. "No. I met Michael when I was fifteen years old, and that was it for me. There was never a thought of anyone else."

"So who's the man in your sketches?"

Dorothea reached for the sketchbook that was always close at hand and folded back the cover, thumbing through the pages until she got to the section of pictures her daughter was asking about. She studied the face again, as if that might give her the answer to Wanda's question, but could only shake her head. "I don't know."

And the not knowing was frustrating for her, because she felt as if she should know him—as if he was a real person and not merely a construct of her imagination.

"And the woman?"

She flipped a few more pages, and shook her head again.

"She looks vaguely familiar to me," Wanda said. "The man not at all, but the woman... Maybe she's an actress?"

"Maybe," Dorothea allowed.

"And this place?" her daughter asked, reaching over to turn to the page to reveal a sprawling log-style home that had been sketched with great detail.

A deep line was etched between Wanda's brow, a telltale sign that she was worried. No doubt she thought her mother was starting to lose her mind, drawing so many pictures of the same two people and a place that didn't seem to exist.

So instead of answering with the truth—that she didn't have the slightest clue—Dorothea said, "I was just imagining a remote cottage where we might enjoy a summer vacation."

And the line between Wanda's brows smoothed out a little. "A summer vacation would be nice."

She turned back a few pages, looking more closely at the sketches. "You're lucky to have such talent. I sometimes wonder what I'll do when I retire. It's not like being a legal secretary has any skills that translate into a hobby."

"Hopefully by that time you'll have grandbabies to play with," Daisy said.

Wanda's sigh was wistful. "I'm afraid to count on it. Evan shows no indication of wanting to settle down, and Vanessa... I have no idea what's going on in my daughter's personal life and it's entirely possible that if she does get married and have babies, they'll be five hundred miles away."

"Billings isn't five hundred miles away," Dorothea chided. "Plus, you'll be retired, so you'll have the freedom to visit whenever you want."

"I guess that's true," her daughter agreed.

"But you shouldn't worry about that. Vanessa will be home soon."

"For Christmas, you mean?"

"That, too."

"Has Vanessa told you something that she hasn't told me?"

"Vanessa hasn't told me anything. I just got the impression, the last time we talked, that she wasn't really loving her life in Billings these days."

"The job or the boyfriend?"

"Maybe both."

"You've always been good at reading people, and understanding them," Wanda said.

"I try," Dorothea said, though the ability had been, at times, as much a curse as a blessing. Because the ability to empathize deeply meant being open to sharing not just happiness but sorrow.

It was an ability her grandson shared, even if he wasn't ready to admit it.

Evan knew it was entirely possible that he was overreacting. But as he paced restlessly around his apartment, he could think of one person who was likely to commiserate with him and so he pulled his phone out of his pocket and called her.

"She has a boyfriend," he said without preamble when his sister answered.

"I do, too," Vanessa told him. "And he's on his way over, so whatever this is about, please make it quick."

"*Our mother* has a boyfriend," he clarified.

"She finally told you, huh?" Instead of sounding horrified, his sister sounded amused.

"*You knew?*"

"I knew," she confirmed.

"I can't believe she told you and not me. And that you didn't tell me."

"She didn't tell me," Vanessa said. "I stopped by Dwight & Donohue one day in the summer before Mom and I were going for lunch, and it was obvious from the way they looked at each other."

"I don't want to know," he decided.

"But you know the look I'm talking about," she said, ignoring his remark. "The I've-seen-you-naked-and-can't-wait-to-do-so-again look. And sure, it was a little disconcerting to think that our mother had been naked with a man who wasn't our father but—"

"Seriously, Van. *Stop. Please.*"

"Why should I? You never listened when I begged you to stop telling me scary ghost stories when I was a kid."

"None of the stories I told you back then could be half as scary as hearing the words *mother* and *naked* together in the same sentence."

"You don't think she's entitled to have a life?" his sister challenged.

"Of course she is," he said, if not very convincingly.

"Just not a sex life?" Vanessa guessed.

He stopped pacing and banged his head against the wall.

"Maybe it's harder for you," she acknowledged, "because you remember our dad. But I only ever remember Mom being alone, and I'm glad she isn't anymore."

If she was trying to make him feel petty and ashamed, she'd succeeded. Because she was right—their mom had been alone for a long time, and Evan had never considered that she might be lonely.

And if this Sean guy made her happy, then he should be happy for her. Unfortunately, that was probably going to take some effort on his part.

"This has been going on since the summer?"

"At least," she confirmed.

"So much for hoping that he'd be gone by Christmas," he grumbled.

"Because having to set another plate at the table would ruin the holiday, Ebenezer?"

He frowned at that. "Are you implying that I'm a scrooge?"

"To imply means to suggest without explicitly saying—I'm explicitly saying that you're a scrooge."

"Thank you for the vocabulary lesson."

"You're welcome," she said primly.

"Speaking of Christmas," he said, because though it might not be his favorite time of the year, the topic was slightly more palatable than that of his mother's sex life, "when are you coming home for the holidays?"

"Classes finish on the eighteenth, so probably the nineteenth or the twentieth."

"Are you coming alone?"

"Let me guess—Mom asked you to buy the turkey and you want to get a scrawny bird?"

"No," he said. "I'm only asking because you mentioned a boyfriend and maybe I'm interested in what's going on in your life."

"It's strictly casual," Vanessa said. "And way too soon to even be thinking about introducing him to the family."

"Does this one at least have a job?"

"Chaz was between jobs."

"For the whole six months that you dated him," he pointed out.

"At least I've had a relationship that lasted six months," she said. "You've never stuck with a woman for longer than six weeks, and you haven't had a relationship at all in—what has it been? Three years?"

"Actually… I've been seeing someone for the past few weeks."

"A real-life human female?"

Though he knew she was ribbing him, the wording of her question shifted his thoughts from Daphne to Alice, but there was no way he was going to mention a possible ghost to his sister.

"Yes, a real-life human female," he said now.

"So why aren't you with her tonight?" Vanessa asked.

"I don't have to see her every night," he hedged.

"And there it is," she said, sounding a little sad.

"There *what* is?"

"A few weeks and already you're pulling back.

You always pull back when you start to get emotionally involved. Sex is fine, but God forbid you should actually let someone get close."

"I don't pull back," he said.

"Every. Single. Time."

"That's not true."

"And denial isn't going to fix the problem."

He clamped his jaw shut, because telling her that there wasn't a problem was more likely to be seen by his sister as proof of her point than an argument to change her mind.

"You know it's not your fault that he left, don't you?" Vanessa asked, her tone surprisingly gentle now.

"What?"

"I thought that might be why you always leave first—so that you can't be left behind, like we were when Dad walked out."

"Well, this conversation has gone way off track," he decided.

"Just think about it," she said. "And maybe try to give this girl a real chance."

"I will," he said, but it was a lie.

He didn't want to think about his father's disappearance from their lives more than twenty years earlier.

As for Daphne...well, even when he tried not to think about her, he couldn't seem to help himself.

Chapter Nine

Operating an animal sanctuary entailed numerous and various responsibilities. Daphne loved interacting with the animals. She hated being stuck at her desk with paperwork, of which there was often a daunting amount. In addition to keeping daily records of supplies and expenditures, medication logs and behavioral charts, there were funding applications to complete and grant proposals to write in the hope that charitable organizations and government programs might decide to toss some of their money toward Happy Hearts.

So when she finally completed a particularly onerous grant proposal Tuesday afternoon, she rolled the kinks out of her shoulders and decided to reward herself with some playtime in the adoption center.

She'd just finished running Boo through the agility course when she saw a Jeep pull into the parking area beside the shelter. As she hooked a leash onto the dog's collar, she saw a man get out of the driver's seat, then open the back door for a passenger to exit the vehicle.

The passenger, Daphne noted when they came around the front of the SUV, was a little girl wearing a pink coat, purple boots and two pigtails high on her head.

"Hello, there," Daphne said, meeting them en route to the entrance.

The little girl spoke first, looking at the German shepherd with wide, curious eyes. "That's a big dog."

"His name is Boo," Daphne said.

"That's a funny name," the girl said. "Mine's Fiona."

"And I'm her dad, Rick Howard," the man said.

"Welcome to Happy Hearts. Is this your first visit?"

Rick nodded. "Fee discovered your website when she was doing research for a project at school," he explained. "Since then, she's been checking it every day to see the dogs and cats—and begging to visit."

"And get a puppy," Fiona said, since her dad had left out that very important detail.

"Our dogs and cats are always happy to have visitors," Daphne said. "But I'll warn you, some of the dogs get really excited when they see new people, and when they bark it gets pretty loud."

The little girl nodded her head in understanding. "I have a little sister, she gets pretty loud, too."

Daphne chuckled. "Well, then, come on in and take a look around."

While the man and his daughter wandered, Daphne gave Boo a treat and returned him to his enclosure.

A few minutes later, Rick and Fiona tracked her down again.

"I can't find the puppies," the little girl said, sounding distraught. "Where are Barney, Betty, Dino, Fred, Pebbles and Wilma?"

"You memorized all their names?" Daphne was impressed.

"I told you," her dad said, with a wry smile. "She's been on the website every day."

Which likely explained why she'd recited them in alphabetical order.

"Where are they?" Fiona asked again.

"The puppies were really small when they came to us," Daphne said. "So they've been living with a foster family and they'll stay there until they're ready to be adopted."

"When will that be?" the girl asked impatiently.

"The first week of January."

"But that's not until after Christmas, and I really want a puppy for Christmas." Fiona's tone was imploring.

"Everyone wants a puppy," her dad said. "But puppies are a lot of work. They have to be housebroken and—"

The little girl's eyes went wide. "I don't want our house to be broken."

He chuckled. "It's an expression, Fee. It means that they need to be taught to go to the bathroom outside. And to help them learn, you'd have to go outside with them, whether it's raining or snowing, early in the morning or late at night—"

"Even in the dark?" she asked worriedly.

"Even in the dark," he confirmed.

"Maybe we could teach a puppy to go to the bathroom in the bathroom," she suggested as an alternative.

"If you taught a puppy to go to the bathroom in the bathroom, then he'd want to eat at the dinner table. And if you let him eat at the dinner table, then he'd want to help make dinner. And if you let him help make dinner…" He let his words trail off when she giggled.

"You're silly, Daddy. That stuff only happens if you give a mouse a cookie," she said.

"Or a pig a pancake," he pointed out. "Or a moose a muffin."

"I still want a puppy," she said, unwilling to be deterred from her goal.

Daphne flagged down Samantha, who was passing through, and whispered a request for the volunteer to bring out one of the smaller dogs.

Then, taking pity on the girl's obviously wavering father, she said, "Actually, none of our dogs or cats is available for adoption right now."

"How come?" Fiona asked.

"Because it's too close to the holidays."

"And Santa might not know where to bring their presents if they go to a new home?" the child guessed.

She couldn't help but smile. "Something like that."

"And probably because too many pets that were taken home for the holidays were brought back after, when the excitement of having a new pet wore off and the responsibility got real," Rick surmised. "And that would make those dogs and cats really sad."

"That, too," Daphne agreed, grateful that the child's father had understood it wasn't an arbitrary policy but one in the best interests of the animals.

"My brother's a vet in Bozeman," he said. "He volunteers at his local SPCA and is very firmly in the 'adopt, don't shop' camp."

"A vet in the family is lucky," she said. "Caring for a pet can get expensive."

"If we got a puppy, we'd never bring her back," Fee promised. "Except maybe to visit her brothers and sisters, if they were still here."

"We're always happy to have pets come back to visit," Daphne said. Then, when Samantha returned with an adorable little dog on a pink rhinestone-studded leash, she asked, "Have you met Penny?"

Fiona dropped to her knees for a closer look at the dog. "Look, Daddy! A puppy!"

Samantha unhooked Penny's leash, then pulled a small ball out of her pocket and rolled it across the floor. Penny immediately gave chase, pounced on the ball, then returned to drop it at the volunteer's feet.

"She's actually five years old," Daphne told the

dad, who was watching his little girl play with the dog. "But she thinks of herself as a puppy."

"I don't remember seeing her on the website," Rick said.

"She just came in two days ago," she explained. "Her owner died suddenly, and we wanted to make sure no family members wanted to take custody of Penny before we advertised her availability, but her information is going online tomorrow—unless someone happened to put in an adoption application before then."

"What kind of dog is she?"

"A Shih Tzu–poodle cross, otherwise known as a Shih-Poo. She's fully grown, requires only moderate exercise and loves lots of attention."

"But she can't go home with anyone until after the New Year?"

"There are exceptions to every rule," Daphne said. "If your brother the vet is willing to vouch for you, I might be willing to make an exception."

Rick continued to watch Fiona, obviously already head over heels in love with the little dog, and sighed. "We only came in today for a visit."

"And that's okay, too. If you need more time— and you should definitely make sure your wife is on board before you make any final decisions—by all means, take that time."

"My wife sent me over here with our daughter knowing that I have a hard time saying no to her, so I know she wants a dog as much as Fee does."

The little girl's giggle had him sighing again.

"If my application is approved, can I come back to pick her up on Christmas Eve?"

"We don't really have the facilities to take care of children."

He chuckled. "I was referring to the dog."

She smiled. "Let's get the paperwork started."

Evan had no intention of taking relationship advice from his sister, and when he headed over to Happy Hearts Tuesday afternoon, it wasn't because Vanessa had told him to give Daphne a chance—it was simply because he wanted to see her.

"You look happy about something," he said when he encountered Daphne on the path leading from the adoption shelter to the main barn a few minutes later, Barkley trotting along beside her.

"It was a good day—and it just got better." She kissed him lightly. "Did we have plans tonight?"

"No," he said, patting the dog's head to acknowledge him, too. "But I was hoping we could make some."

"What did you have in mind?"

He followed her into the barn. "We could start with dinner," he said. "I'll even let you pick the restaurant this time."

She smiled at that as she made her way down the center aisle, greeting each of the animals by name. "A tempting offer."

"But not a yes," he noted.

She began preparing a bottle for the baby goat. "Because I've got chili in the slow cooker in the house."

"I like chili," he said.

She offered him the bottle. "You feed Billie while I take care of the rest of the animals, and then I'll feed you."

They made quick work of the chores, then closed up the barn. Barkley raced ahead of them to the house, obviously eager for his dinner. They hurried to follow, eager to get out of the cold, their breaths puffing out in clouds and the snow crunching beneath their boots.

"At times like this, I wish I lived in Florida," Daphne confided as she stomped her feet on the porch.

"I'd rather deal with the cold and snow than gators," Evan remarked.

"You might have a point there," she said, hanging her coat.

"Mmm...it smells good," he said as he followed her into the kitchen.

"Almost like real chili, you mean?" she teased.

"Almost," he agreed.

She gave Barkley kibble and fresh water, then washed her hands before filling two bowls from the slow cooker and setting them on the table. He washed his hands, too, and took a seat across from her at the table.

"You haven't been in touch much over the past

few days," she said, her tone deliberately casual as she buttered a slice of crusty bread. "Is everything okay?"

"Yeah. I've just been busy working on a research project."

"What are you researching?"

"The fire at Whispering Willows."

She dipped her spoon into her bowl, a slight furrow creasing her brow. "Any particular reason?"

"I've been wondering about something you said." He lifted his own spoon to blow on the chili. "About how Alice's fiancé died with her in the fire, because in all the research I've done, I can't find any mention of him."

"Well, I must have read it somewhere," she said.

"But you don't remember where?" he pressed.

She shook her head. "Sorry. I do have a folder of old newspaper clippings about the fire—research I did before I bought the property. You're welcome to look through it if you want."

"I might do that," he said. "I did manage to dig up a copy of the fire marshal's official report, but it only mentioned human remains later identified to be those of Alice Milton. There was no mention of anyone else."

She shrugged. "So maybe I was wrong."

"You don't believe that."

And, having done a little more digging into the matter, neither did he. He planned on telling Daphne what he'd learned, of course, but first he wanted to know what she knew—and how she knew it.

"Why all the questions?" she asked, sounding more defensive than curious. "Are you planning to change the narrative for your tour?"

"This doesn't have anything to do with the tour."

"Then what's it about?"

He hesitated. "I've been having some strange dreams recently…since the night I stayed here, in fact."

She pushed away from the table and rose to her feet, apparently needing some time to process this revelation. "Do you want something to drink?"

"I'll have a glass of water," he said, since that was what she was already pouring for herself.

"What's strange about your dreams?" she finally asked, returning to the table with the two glasses.

"For starters, I'm not me in the dreams… I'm Russell Kincaid."

"Who's…oh." Her hand shook slightly as she lifted her glass to her lips.

"You know who he is?"

Daphne nodded and set down her drink to pick up her spoon again. "He's the man Alice Milton was in love with."

"How do you know that?"

"You wouldn't believe me if I told you," she warned, swirling the utensil around in her bowl.

"Try me," he suggested.

She drew in a slow breath, as if to brace herself

before lifting her gaze to look him in the eye. "Alice told me."

He didn't blink. He wasn't even surprised, really. A little unnerved, perhaps, but even more intrigued by her confession. "She talks to you?"

"When she feels like it."

"Since when?" he asked curiously.

"Since…" She paused, as if trying to remember. "I'm not exactly sure when it started—or when I started to believe that the voice I was hearing belonged to Alice."

"The first day I was here—that was Alice crying, wasn't it?"

Daphne hesitated for just a second before nodding. "She's been even more active—and interactive— lately," she confided. "A class of second graders was here on a field trip a couple weeks ago, and one of the little girls not only heard Alice crying, she…saw her."

A chill snaked down his spine. "How do you know she saw her?"

"She referred to her as 'the pretty lady.'"

"Does that describe Alice Milton?" he wondered.

She nodded again. "She was beautiful. There are pictures in the newspaper clippings."

"Did anyone else on the trip see or hear anything?"

Now she shook her head. "Only me. Though I couldn't see her."

He lifted another spoonful of chili to his mouth.

"I thought you'd be more freaked out by all of this," she said.

"I was freaked out the first time I heard her crying," he admitted. "And then… I don't know when it happened, but my curiosity started to outweigh my discomfort. And after I read the fire marshal's report, I decided to track him down."

"Did you have any success?" she asked.

"His name is Stan Jacobs. He lives in Helena now."

"He's still alive?"

He nodded. "And he still remembers the fire."

"After sixty years?" She sounded surprised.

"I think he felt too guilty to ever forget," Evan said. "Because he manipulated some of the details in his report, at the request of Henry Milton, to cover up Russell's death. To ensure that no one would know he was with Alice the night of the fire. Because Henry didn't want his daughter's name to be sullied by her association with a stable hand."

Daphne's eyes filled with moisture. "He didn't believe that she loved Russell. Or maybe he didn't want to believe it, because he hoped she would marry the son of the neighboring landowner, leading to a merger of the two properties."

"Did Alice tell you that, too?"

She nodded. "And when her father found out that she was involved with Russell, he demanded that she terminate the relationship. But Alice refused, and Henry responded by threatening to cut her out of the will, insisting that he'd rather see the ranch burn than let her and her stable hand run it into the ground."

"A rather portentous threat," Evan noted. "And

maybe that's the real reason Henry took his life—not because of grief but guilt."

Daphne brushed an errant tear off her cheek. "So what happened to Russell's remains?"

"Henry told the marshal to dump the body in a hole somewhere. But Mr. Jacobs refused to do that to the man's family. Instead, he delivered it to Russell's parents and encouraged them to make arrangements for a private burial."

Her brow furrowed. "But they must have had questions about where and how their son died."

"Of course, but the fire marshal told them that there was evidence suggesting that Russell started the fire and that Henry Milton was making noises about pressing charges, but that he might be persuaded to let the matter go if they stayed quiet about the fact that their son died at Whispering Willows."

"So they did?"

He nodded. "Apparently."

"But…why would the fire marshal let himself get tangled up in Henry Milton's web of lies?" she wondered.

"I'd guess there were ten thousand reasons."

"He was bribed," she realized.

Growing up in a wealthy family, she'd no doubt learned that people with money didn't have to play by the same rules as everyone else.

Evan nodded again.

"I'm surprised he'd admit it to you."

"He's eighty-eight years old and in failing health,"

he said. "I think he was relieved to finally be able to tell someone the truth."

"What are we supposed to do now?" Daphne asked.

"I've been wondering the same thing. I think Alice is crying because she wants Russell buried with her, as he should have been all those years ago."

"And how are we supposed to make that happen?" she asked dubiously. "I can't imagine Russell Kincaid's living relatives will consent to digging up his grave so that he can be reunited with the woman he planned to marry when they likely knew nothing of his plans or even that he was in a relationship with Alice sixty years ago."

Evan shrugged. "It can't hurt to ask."

The next morning, after a night of thorough and passionate lovemaking, Evan was happy to help Daphne with her morning chores again. Probably because chores for him meant sitting on a bale of hay, holding the bottle of formula for the baby goat that stood in front of him, rapidly emptying it.

"The way she's growing, she probably won't be needing a bottle for very much longer," Evan noted.

"You're right," Daphne confirmed. "She's already drinking water from Agatha's bowl and starting to nibble on hay."

"Speaking of nibbling," he said. "My mom suggested that I might want to invite you to have Christmas dinner with us."

She paused in the act of tucking an errant strand of hair behind her ear, puzzled by his casual delivery of what was, to her mind, a significant piece of information. "Is that an invitation or a recap of your conversation?" she asked, trying to match his tone and not get her hopes up.

"It was meant to be an invitation," he said. And to be clear, he followed up by asking, "Would you like to have Christmas dinner with me at my mom's house?"

More than anything, she thought. But his guarded tone made her suspect that he wasn't as enthused about the prospect as she was, so she proceeded cautiously.

"Are you inviting me because your mom told you to or because you want me there?"

"Both," he admitted. "But mostly because I want you there."

"So why does it sound like you have some reservations?" she wondered aloud.

"Because I do," he told her. "Because they'll make a big deal out of the fact that I've brought you home to meet the family."

"I guess you don't take women home very often?"

"Almost never."

"Would you prefer if I said no, so that you could tell your mom you asked and I declined?"

"No," he said. "I'd like you to meet them—and for them to meet you. I just want you to know what you're getting yourself into."

"In that case, my answer is yes," she said, already looking forward to it.

But then she remembered the thorny issue that inevitably arose when she ate at someone else's table, and asked, "Do you think it would be okay if I brought my chestnut Wellington as a contribution to the meal?"

"That would be great," Evan said, "because the only thing that I can guarantee will be on the menu is turkey. And for dessert—Grandma Daisy's pecan pie."

Daphne stilled. "I thought your grandmother's name was Dorothea."

"That's her given name, but she mostly goes by Daisy."

"Was she born in 1945?" she asked, recalling the social media post that had been circulating in recent weeks.

His mouth thinned. "What is this about?"

"You haven't seen the 'Desperately Seeking Daisy' plea on Facebook or Twitter?"

"I've seen it," he said.

His clipped tone might have been a warning for her to back off, but Daphne forged ahead. "Then it must have occurred to you that your Grandma Daisy might be *the* Daisy that the Abernathy family is looking for."

"Except that my grandmother wasn't adopted," he told her.

"Oh," she said, disappointed. Then, as another

thought occurred to her, "Or maybe she just didn't know that she was adopted."

He folded his arms in front of his chest. "Let it go, Daphne."

But she wasn't dissuaded by his words or his defensive posture. "How can you say that? Aren't you the least bit curious to know if your grandmother is the missing child?"

"She's hardly a child," he pointed out. "And even if she was adopted, why would her birth family have waited so long to reach out?"

"I can't imagine," she admitted.

"Well, I can," he retorted. "And it's because they want something from this long-lost relative, wherever she may be."

"What kind of something?" she asked, curious about his thinking.

"A kidney, liver or lung would be my guess."

"You really believe that?"

He shrugged, but the tension in his body was a marked contradiction to the casual gesture. "It's the only thing that makes sense. They're shaking the family tree to see if a donor will fall out. And there's no way I'm going to let my grandmother be used that way."

"Shouldn't that be your grandmother's decision?" she challenged.

A muscle in his jaw flexed. "And it would be," he said, "if there was any chance that she was this missing child, but there's not."

"Have you mentioned the post to her?" Daphne's tone was gentle even as she pressed for answers he obviously didn't want to give.

"There's no reason to," he insisted.

"Or maybe you're afraid to," she suggested.

"That's ridiculous."

"It's the only explanation that makes sense to me," she said. "You were intrigued by the mystery of Alice and Russell—how can you not be interested in a mystery that might involve your own family?"

Instead of answering her question, he asked his own. "Did you ever do a family tree project in elementary school?"

She nodded. "Of course. I'm sure it's a mandatory part of the curriculum."

"I did, too," he told her. "And Grandma Daisy gave me all the information about her parents and her grandparents. There was no hesitation or evasiveness and no gaps in the history."

"As she understood it," Daphne allowed. "But surely you've considered that closed adoptions were the norm back then and that she might not realize her mother and father weren't her biological parents."

"And if that's true, I'm not going to be the one to destroy her illusions," he said stubbornly.

"You have to tell her about this," she urged. "Even if it's just a possibility, she has a right to know, to decide for herself if she wants to follow up."

"And you have to forgive me for not taking advice

about family matters from a woman who's estranged from most of hers."

Daphne sucked in a breath as the pointed barb struck its target. "Well." She took a step back. "I guess that's clear enough."

And true, too, she acknowledged.

Her strained relationship with her father proved she was anything but an expert when it came to family interactions and dynamics. She hadn't even been back to the Taylor Ranch since Thanksgiving, but at least they were talking again. Or maybe they weren't, she considered, noting that she hadn't heard a word from him since Jessica had visited Happy Hearts—and she'd been certain that he'd have more than a few words to say when his wife introduced him to Button.

But for Evan to use his knowledge of that strained relationship as a weapon against her now, hurt more than she could bear.

"Daphne…"

It was the sincere regret in his tone that made her pause, but when he didn't say anything more, she reached for the lead to hook it on Billie's collar. "I need to get her back to her pen. Agatha gets agitated if they're separated for too long."

At the gate, she glanced over her shoulder.

"You know the way out."

Well, that hadn't gone quite as he'd planned, Evan acknowledged as he drove away from Happy Hearts.

A few weeks and already you're pulling back. You always pull back when you start to get emotionally involved.

He ignored the echo of his sister's voice in his head, and the heaviness in his own heart.

Perhaps he'd done so in the past, but this time, Daphne had told him to go.

Of course, he'd pretty much dared her to tell him off. His remark about her family had been not just insensitive but cruel.

Maybe even unforgivable.

He could have ended the conversation in a lot of different ways, but he'd chosen to be an asshole.

'Tis the season, he thought wryly.

But his reasons for lashing out were about more than just the time of year. They were about his own nagging suspicions that the social media post might, in fact, be about Grandma Daisy. They were also about the strange connection he suddenly seemed to have to Russell Kincaid—a man who'd been dead for sixty years. But mostly they were about his already strong and still growing feelings for Daphne Taylor and his uncertainty about whether those feelings were truly his own or somehow a product of Russell's history with Alice.

When his cell phone rang, he was grateful for the interruption—even when his sister's name popped up on the screen.

"Hey, Van," he said, after instructing Siri to answer the call. "What's up?"

"I was talking to Jayne Kendricks, my friend from high school, this morning, and she mentioned that she'd done your Yuletide Tour last week and really enjoyed it."

"I'm glad to hear it—and I appreciate you letting me know," he said, aware that any discussion that touched on the paranormal made his sister uncomfortable.

"But that's not the only reason I'm calling," she told him.

"You're bringing the boyfriend home for Christmas after all?" he guessed.

"No," she said. "I told you that was casual—and likely to be over soon, anyway."

With the status of his own relationship up in the air, he decided to refrain from commenting on the imminent demise of hers. "So what's the other reason?" he asked instead.

"I wanted to talk to you about a social media post Jayne brought to my attention."

Evan scrubbed a hand wearily over his jaw.

"You know what I'm talking about, don't you?" his sister pressed.

"I can guess," he admitted. "But I don't know why she'd think it would be of any interest to you."

"Maybe because our grandmother's name is Daisy and she was born in 1945."

"No, her *nickname* is Daisy."

"So you don't think Grandma Daisy could be the missing child they're looking for?"

"No." His response was firm and unequivocal. "She would have told us if she was adopted."

"Maybe she was but doesn't know," his sister said.

Which was exactly what Daphne had suggested. Had he been too quick to dismiss the possibility? Too harsh in shutting the conversation down?

Aware that the answer to both of those questions might be "yes," he dug in his heels nevertheless.

"You want to tell Grandma Daisy about some random social media post and potentially undermine everything she's always believed about her life and her family on the strength of a maybe?" he challenged.

"Of course not," Vanessa said. "She'd take the news much better if it came from you."

Evan didn't care how many people badgered him about it—he had no intention of talking to his grandmother about "Desperately Seeking Daisy." He did, however, have another reason for stopping by his mother's house—and it wasn't just a reluctance to return to his empty apartment where he'd be alone with his thoughts and forced to acknowledge that he'd screwed up his relationship with Daphne.

"Evan, this is a surprise," his grandmother said, smiling when she opened the door. "And good timing—I just got back from bowling. Scored one-fifty-five today."

"That's great," he said, having no idea really if it was or wasn't, but she sounded happy, so he assumed it was.

He held up the tool belt that he habitually carried in the back of his SUV, for occasions such as this. "Last week you mentioned the dripping from your bathroom tap was driving you crazy, so I thought I'd come over and take a look at it."

"That's so kind," Daisy said. "But Sean already fixed it."

"Sean," he echoed, as if the name was distasteful. "So that's still going on?"

"I don't know what you think *that* is," she said. "But yes, your mother is still dating Sean. And for your information, she's happier than she's been in a very long time."

"I'm happy she's happy," he said.

"Then try to sound happy," Grandma Daisy suggested. "You're not the only one allowed to have a romance, you know."

"Romance shomance," he muttered.

"Uh-oh." She peered at him more closely now, as if she could see the tension he carried in his shoulders. "Did you and Daphne have a disagreement?"

"I guess that's as good a word as any."

"Which suggests to me that you know you screwed up but realized it too late to unscrew it."

"I might have said something I shouldn't have," he acknowledged. "But she was butting into something that was none of her business."

"Perhaps because she was under the impression that the two of you were building a relationship and, therefore, anything that affects you might affect her, too."

"Relationships are more trouble than they're worth, anyway," he decided.

"Is that a lesson that you learned from your father?"

He physically recoiled from the question. "What?"

"It seems to me that you've spent most of your adult life proving you're responsible and dependable and nothing like Andrew Cruise," she said. "And yet now, when you've finally met a woman who really matters, you walked out on her, just like your father walked out on your mother."

"It's hardly the same thing," he protested.

"Why? Because you're not married? Because you don't have any children together? Because you don't love her?"

"All of the above," he said, though he didn't sound convinced.

"Well, then, I guess your conscience is clear."

"Some real advice might be more helpful than sarcasm," he pointed out.

"Oh, no," she said. "You messed it up without any help from anyone else and you need to fix it the same way."

She was right about the fact that he'd messed it up, he admitted as he walked out of the house. But maybe he didn't need to fix it. Maybe it was better this way.

Why should he open up his heart and risk having it broken?

Because you've never been happier than you've been since you met Daphne.

He scowled at the thought as he slid behind the wheel of his SUV.

And anyway, happiness was overrated as far as he was concerned. He'd been perfectly content with his life before he met Daphne, and he could be perfectly content without her again.

The thought did nothing to reassure him. Not only because he knew contentment wouldn't be enough, but because he didn't want to imagine a life without her in it.

But as he backed out of the driveway, he still wasn't sure which way to turn. Left would take him home; right would lead him back to Happy Hearts.

He was still annoyed that Daphne had pushed him to tell his grandmother about the post, but maybe she had a point. Because he might claim that he didn't want to interfere, but wasn't his refusal to share the information with his grandmother just a different kind of interference?

Yes, Daisy was his grandmother and he wanted only to protect her, but it was *her* life. She should be the one to decide if she wanted to follow up on the posting by contacting the Abernathy family, which she could only do if she knew about it.

So maybe he would tell her about "Desperately Seeking Daisy" and let her decide what next steps, if any, needed to be taken.

But first, he needed to see Daphne.

In the short time that he'd been inside his mother's house, the sky had grown dark. The forecast hadn't called for any more snow, but the gathering of clouds suggested otherwise, and he was almost halfway to Happy Hearts when the snow started to fall.

At first it was just a few lazy flakes dancing harmlessly in the air. But within a few minutes, the snow was coming heavier and faster. Then the wind picked up, blowing the flakes every which way and reducing visibility to almost zero.

He eased his foot off the gas to slow his vehicle, but without warning, the SUV started to spin and slide on the icy road. He tried to steer into the skid, but even with his knuckles white on the steering wheel, he couldn't control the vehicle.

Please stop. Please stop.

But his pleas went unanswered.

Damn it, this was a new SUV. He'd paid good money for it less than six months earlier.

There are more important things in life than money.

He acknowledged the point with a brief nod as the front wheel hit a culvert and the vehicle started to tip.

Living was more important than money.

Telling Daphne he was sorry was more—

He didn't manage to finish that thought before his world went black.

Chapter Ten

After Daphne returned Billie to his pen, she spent some time with Tiny Tim, rolling the pig's new soccer ball back and forth with him. Her porcine companion was more than happy to play, a reminder to Daphne that she hadn't been spending much time with him of late.

"I'm sorry I've been neglecting you in favor of a stupid man," she said, putting her arm around the pig's wide shoulders.

Tiny Tim leaned into her embrace, almost pushing her over with his substantial weight and making her smile despite the fact that her heart was breaking.

"I don't know why I let myself get my hopes up.

Maybe Jordan was right, maybe I'm trying too hard to find love."

"Love cannot be found where it does not exist, nor can it be hidden where it does."

She heard the voice but didn't bother looking around. It was just Alice, once again making herself known. "Are you quoting Shakespeare to me?"

"Paraphrasing."

"Well, poetic words don't change the fact that Evan's a jerk."

"He's not a jerk."

"Really? You're taking his side?"

"I'm not taking sides."

"It sure seems like you're taking sides."

"He's protective of his grandmother, who's been his rock through most of his life."

"How do you know so much about his life?"

"You learn things when you hang around the world for sixty years after your death."

"Apparently," she agreed.

"He'll figure out what he needs to do," the ghost assured her. *"But it's not going to be easy, because he doesn't want to cause his grandmother any pain."*

"But it's okay to hurt me?" she asked, swiping at a tear that spilled onto her cheek.

"Of course not," Alice soothed. *"He just needs some time to understand and accept his emotions, and when he does, he'll be back."*

"I don't want him back."

Daphne was grateful the ghost didn't respond to that, because she didn't want to be called out for lying.

Evan's head hurt.

No, not just his head—his whole body ached.

He squinted his eyes and lifted a hand to shield his gaze against the bright circle of light that appeared in the distance. A light that slowly spread outward, revealing a figure at its center. The woman—draped in an old-fashioned nightdress with billowy sleeves and ruffles at the collar and hem—came closer, until she stood only a few feet away and solemnly said, "I am the Ghost of Christmas Past."

"I've seen several different versions of *A Christmas Carol*," he said, unimpressed. "And I'm not Ebenezer Scrooge and you look nothing like the nefarious Marley, so who are you really?"

"You know who I am," she told him.

And suddenly he did know. "Alice Milton."

The shimmery apparition nodded.

He couldn't see her clearly, but her features were consistent with those of the woman in the photos Daphne had shown to him: long blond hair flowing over her shoulders and wide eyes set in a narrow face.

"But we never knew each other," he pointed out, trying to figure out why she, of all people, would appear to him in what was obviously a dream. Or maybe a nightmare.

"Still we are connected," she said.

"Because I could hear you crying?" he asked dubiously.

"I've been crying for almost sixty years, waiting not just for someone to hear but someone to help. No one ever heard me—not until Daphne…and then you."

"But I've never seen you before. Why am I seeing you now?"

"I'm here to take you on a journey, to remind you of the joys you experienced in Christmases past and reflect on the choices you've made since then. Because your name might not be Scrooge, but your obsession with money is the same."

"Wanting my business to be successful doesn't make it an obsession," he argued.

"You're a con artist," she said. "Selling ghost stories to those willing to pay the price of admission without believing in ghosts yourself."

"I've recently been rethinking my beliefs," he assured her.

"Come," she said, offering her hand. "There is much for you to see."

"Are you taking me into the light? Am I dying?"

"No, but you're killing my patience."

"A ghost with a sense of humor," he mused.

Alice took his hand and led him down a long, dark hallway. There was no light, except that which surrounded the ghost. At the end of the corridor was a door that slowly opened as they drew nearer.

The tableau was familiar: a winter wonderland scene set up in the center court of a shopping mall, a long line of excited and impatient children, a fancy throne-style chair upon which was perched a plump old man in a red velvet suit.

He recognized his mother first, then glanced at the child holding tightly to her hand. It was him. About five years old then, Evan guessed. Probably not his first visit with Santa, but his earliest memory of the jolly elf.

As they inched forward in the line, the little boy's heart raced with excitement—and maybe just a hint of fear. Because Santa knew who was naughty and who was nice, and as much as he tried really hard to be nice, there had been a few times when his actions might have tipped over to the other side of the line.

But Santa had been kind, and after the visit Evan had eagerly counted down the days until Christmas, excited to see what presents might have been left for him under the tree.

The scene shifted then to that eagerly awaited morning, the setting a child's bedroom, complete with a rumpled spread on the bed, a random sock peeking out from beneath it, and an overflowing toy box in the corner. A man and a woman appeared in the doorway.

"What kid sleeps in on Christmas morning?" his mom asked.

"Only ours," his dad responded.

The sound of their voices roused the child, who sat up in bed and blinked sleepily.

"Merry Christmas, Evan," his mom said.

His eyes popped open wide then. "It's Christmas? Did Santa come?"

"Let's go take a look," his dad suggested.

He slid out of bed and raced out of the room.

The scene shifted again, and Evan took a step back.

"I've seen enough."

"Not yet," Alice said.

He wanted to look away, but instead his gaze moved around the room, from the boughs of holly to the ceramic snowmen decorations and presents under the tree. It was Christmas again, but this year, there was no joy in his heart.

The three stockings hanging over the fireplace told him everything he needed to know. His father was gone.

"Look, Evan!" Four-year-old Vanessa's eyes sparkled with happiness. "Look at all the presents! Santa must've knowed I was really good this year!"

"Yeah, 'cause some old guy keeping tabs on little kids isn't creepy at all," he said.

"Don't," his mom admonished sharply.

Evan folded his arms over his chest and slumped down on the sofa.

"This one's for you," his sister said, sliding a festively wrapped box across the floor toward him.

"Thanks," he said, but made no move to reach for it.

"Aren't you gonna open it?" Vanessa asked.

"Let's see what you got first," he said instead.

It was all the encouragement she needed.

He sat and watched while she opened her gifts, envious of her happiness. Santa hadn't brought everything on her list, but he'd hit the major highlights and Vanessa was overjoyed.

Evan was angry and frustrated, and the real reason he wasn't interested in opening any of the presents with his name on the tag was that none of them was big enough to be hiding his dad, and that was the only thing he'd asked Santa for that year.

Not that he believed in Santa anymore by then, because he was ten and only little kids believed in Santa. But his mom had insisted that they take Vanessa to the mall to see the fat man in the red suit and Evan had decided that, since he was there anyway, it wouldn't hurt to ask.

The man in the fake beard had seemed as uncomfortable with the request as the boy, and Evan had known, even as he walked away with a broken candy cane in his hand, that he wasn't going to get what he wanted that year.

So while his father's absence on Christmas morning wasn't really a surprise, it had extinguished the last vestige of hope that lived in the little boy's heart. And when his grandfather had called him out for his attitude, he'd picked up the first thing he could grab and threw it at the wall with all of his might.

It was one of Vanessa's new toys, and when it broke, she cried.

Later, he'd gone into the kitchen to get a drink and

found his mom sitting at the table, her face in her hands, her shoulders shaking with silent sobs. And he knew that her tears were his fault, too.

"Thanks for the walk down memory lane," he said to the ghost. "But I think we're done here now."

Alice shook her head. "Your journey has only just begun."

Daphne wasn't surprised when her father showed up at Happy Hearts following his wife's visit to the farm. She was surprised that it had taken him only nine days to do so.

And she was annoyed that he'd caught her on what was already a crappy day, on her knees in Gretel's stall, applying a clay treatment to an abscess on the cow's belly.

But he let her finish the task and wash up before he said, "I'm sure you can guess why I'm here."

"Hello, Dad. How are you?"

Cornelius's mouth thinned. "Is the chitchat really necessary?"

"No, it's not necessary, but it's considered courteous," she admonished lightly.

"I'm doing well," he said tightly. "How are you?"

"Busy," she said. "But happy—and surprised—to see you."

The words weren't just lip service—she *was* happy to see him, perhaps foolishly willing to hope that his presence at Happy Hearts meant that he was taking an interest in her work. But she was apprehensive, too, that this visit would take an unfortunate turn, as most of their recent interactions had done. She really didn't want their relationship to end the way Alice and Henry Milton's had—with the last words they'd exchanged being harsh ones.

"Now, why don't you tell me why you're here?" she suggested.

"Because I need you to take that—" he made a face, as if struggling to find the right word "—ratlike creature back."

"Are you referring to the Chihuahua that your wife recently adopted?" She lifted her coat off a hook by the door and slid her arms into the sleeves.

"You know I am," he said, pulling the door open for her.

She blinked against the brightness of the sun reflecting on the snow. "What seems to be the problem?"

In the distance, Barkley gave a happy bark and immediately began loping across the field toward her.

"It's not suitable," Cornelius said bluntly.

"For what purpose?"

"For any purpose," he snapped. "It's barely even a dog—proven by the fact that it was beaten up by a cat."

"A feral cat," she pointed out.

"I don't care. I don't want it."

"Then it's a good thing Button isn't yours," she said.

"The name's just as ridiculous as the animal," he grumbled.

"Because an animal without a pedigree isn't worthy enough to live on the Taylor Ranch?" she challenged. "And if something—or someone—isn't worthy, you simply get rid of it. Out of sight, out of mind, right?"

The vein in his neck began to pulse. "Can you please just come out to the ranch and get the damn dog?"

"No, I can't," she told him. "An animal isn't like an unwanted sweater to be exchanged, and Jessica and Button both seemed very happy when they left here together."

"I don't know how you did it, but I'm sure you conned her into taking the ugliest mutt you had just to embarrass me."

"You might find this hard to believe, Dad, but not everything is about you."

"There's no way she chose that dog."

"Actually, she did," Daphne said. "And I'll admit, it surprised me, too. But maybe she's learned that what's in someone's heart is more important than their appearance."

Other than narrowing his gaze, he let that pointed remark slide.

"When she said she wanted a dog for the ranch, I expected her to come home with something more like—" he pointed to the Lab now trotting along at her side "—that."

"His name's Barkley," she told him. "And he's mine."

"Do you have any more like him?"

"I'm not taking Button back," she said again. "And I suspect that you knew I wouldn't or else you would have brought her with you."

"Jessica took it shopping," he said. "She wanted to buy it an ugly Christmas sweater."

Daphne didn't even try to hold back the smile that curved her lips. "I'd love to see that."

"Stop by on Christmas and you will."

It wasn't the most gracious invitation she'd ever received, but she decided that she would give it some consideration, especially since her plans with Evan seemed to have fallen through.

"In the meantime," he continued, "maybe you could show me what other dogs you've got?"

"You really want another dog?"

"Jessica's right—a ranch needs a dog," he said.

"Then let's find one for you," she agreed.

She took him around the shelter, not just to introduce him to the animals that were available but to show off the facilities. Because she was proud of what she'd built here, and maybe it was naive, but she hoped he'd be proud, too. Not that she ever expected him to say as much, so she was pleased when he remarked positively on the organization and cleanliness of the space.

He didn't give any of the smaller dogs more than a cursory glance, but he did linger for a moment in front of Sully's enclosure. She suspected he might have asked about the blue labradoodle—a breed known to be friendly and intelligent—if not for the pink bow Samantha had affixed to the top of Sully's head. Instead, he moved on, turning his attention to Boo, the three-year-old German shepherd. The dog was big and strong and had lots of energy, and Daphne had no doubt Boo would be happy at Taylor Ranch.

Still, she wasn't going to make it too easy for her father to get what he wanted. "He's going to cost you a thousand dollars."

He immediately pulled out his checkbook and pen. "I assume I make it payable to Happy Hearts?"

She nodded, but her conscience kicked in as he filled in the name on the check. "But I was kidding about the amount. The adoption fee is a hundred dollars, not a thousand."

He shrugged and continued writing. "The money will go to help the animals, right?"

"Of course," she said.

"Then a thousand dollars doesn't seem like too much," he said, tearing the check out of the book. "Besides, it likely would have cost me more than that if Jessica had decided to get a dog from a breeder."

Because he was right, she felt no guilt when she took the check and slid it into her deposit envelope. "Congratulations on the new addition to your family."

Evan felt as if he'd been put through an emotional wringer, but apparently his nightmare had only just begun, because Alice had no sooner faded away than another woman took her place. This one he recognized immediately, even if he'd never seen her dressed as she was now, in a dark green velvet dress with a crown of flowers on her head and a glowing torch in her hand, perusing a buffet table set with heavy platters of food and punch bowls filled with drink.

"Are you the Ghost of Christmas Present?" he asked Brittany Brandt Dubois.

His former employee laughed. "Of course not. I'd have to be dead to be a ghost, and I've never felt more alive—or been happier."

"Then why are you here?" he asked.

"I'm your *Guide* of Christmas Present," she told him.

He closed his eyes. "This is a dream. It has to be a dream. No, a nightmare," he decided. "And when I open my eyes, you're going to be gone and I'm going to be home in my bed."

He cautiously lifted one eyelid, just far enough to peek through and see that Brittany was still there, smirking at him.

"You're not at home," she pointed out. "You were on your way to Happy Hearts when your car went off the road."

"That's right," he remembered. "There was a sudden snow squall and—" He broke off to swallow the panic that rose up inside him. "Maybe I am dead."

"Though some would question whether you even have a heart, I assure you, it's still pumping blood through your veins," Brittany said.

"Have you always been this sarcastic?"

"Yes, but you wouldn't know, because you don't pay any attention to your employees except to bark orders at them."

"I don't bark," he denied. "And how would you possibly know anything about what's been going on with my business—or in my life—since you quit your job nine months ago?"

"I made the choice that was best for me and I don't have any regrets. But if you don't start showing some appreciation for the people who work for you, you're going to have trouble holding on to employees."

"Callie seems to be working out pretty well."

"Don't you mean Kelly?"

Damn it. Was it Kelly? Or—

The smirk on her face clued him in to the fact that she was messing with him.

"No, I mean Callie," he said.

"Well, good for you for knowing the name of the woman who's been at your beck and call for the past five weeks."

She waved her hand then, and suddenly they were in the hayloft at Happy Hearts Animal Sanctuary, watching from above as he walked into the barn to meet Daphne for the first time.

He experienced the same range of emotions now that he'd felt then. Annoyance that he was on time and no one was there to meet him. Surprise that the stable boy mucking out stalls turned out to be a woman—a very attractive woman. And a deeper emotion, one he wasn't willing to name, that spread warmth through his chest.

"There was something there, the first moment you met her," Brittany noted.

"The physical attraction between a man and a woman is hardly a mystery."

"The mystery was that she liked you, too," his guide teased.

The scene shifted from their introduction to the tour of Happy Hearts, then his return for the Yuletide Ghost Tour, followed by Christmas at the Farm and their first kiss.

"You've got some decent moves," Brittany said approvingly.

"If I'd known my technique was going to be scored, I would have practiced," he replied dryly.

His guide only grinned.

Then she waved her arms again, like a conductor leading an orchestra, and a montage of clips from the last few weeks played out: brief scenes of everything from decorating Daphne's Christmas tree to Evan bottle-feeding Billie the Kid earlier that same morning. There were more kisses and lots of laughter in between, until he mentioned Grandma Daisy and they argued about the damn social media posts.

And then, after he'd gone, Daphne swiping at the tears that slid down her cheeks.

Watching her cry, knowing he was responsible, made his own heart ache. "I didn't mean to hurt her."

"The road to hell is paved with good intentions," Brittany noted as the scene changed again.

They were at his office now, though the only light on was over Callie's desk. His assistant's fingers moved rapidly over the keyboard as she input data. A man he didn't know was on the other side of the desk, pacing back and forth impatiently.

"Why do you have to do this now?" he asked her.

"Because I didn't get it finished yesterday, Zach."

"But we've got tickets for a movie that starts in—" he glanced at his watch "—thirty minutes."

"I only need ten," she said, as she turned the page. "Maybe fifteen."

"You don't get paid enough to work weekends."

"It's enough to pay my bills," she said. "And it so happens that I like my job."

"Your boss is a taskmaster who thinks that just because he has no life, no one who works for him should, either."

"He's not so bad," Callie said. "I think he's just unhappy…because he's alone."

"Maybe he's alone because he makes everyone around him unhappy," Zach remarked.

Brittany handed Evan a shiny red apple. "Food for thought."

Daphne was pleased when Elaine showed up only a short while after Cornelius and Boo had gone, despite the fact that she wasn't on the schedule for today. Happy Hearts was lucky to have a roster of enthusiastic helpers, and Daphne tried to spread out the schedule and responsibilities so that no one ever felt overwhelmed by the expectations. But it wasn't unusual for volunteers to show up at other times, just to lend a hand wherever it was needed.

Today, Elaine helped bathe a filthy—and very unhappy—Bernese mountain dog that had been picked up while digging through the contents of a garbage can in a local park.

"Is everything okay?" Elaine asked, when the dog that they'd dubbed Rufus was mostly clean and chowing down on a bowl of kibble.

"Sure. Why?"

"You seem a little distracted today."

"I've just got a lot on my mind," she said. "There's barely a week and a half until Christmas, and I still have so much to do."

"*You're* behind schedule?" Elaine's tone was filled with disbelief. "You're the most organized person I know."

"Apparently organizational skills don't help add hours to a day."

"Or maybe it's the hunky ghost hunter who's been hanging around that's responsible for taking up a lot of those hours."

"I've been spending some time with Evan," she admitted.

And she'd been looking forward to spending at least some of Christmas Day with him and meeting his family, but considering the way they'd parted, she didn't think that was likely to happen this year.

Or any year.

Her cell phone rang then, jolting her out of her reverie.

Her heart skipped again when she saw Evan's name on the screen.

"Excuse me a minute," she said to Elaine, stepping away to connect the call.

But it wasn't Evan on the other end of the line, it was a woman who identified herself as Dorothea McGowan.

"There's been an accident," Evan's grandmother said without further preamble, and everything inside Daphne went cold.

"Is he..." She hesitated, not sure what she wanted to ask.

...hurt?

Of course, he was hurt, or he'd be the one making the call.

...dead?

No.

She couldn't ask that. She wouldn't even let herself *think* it.

"He's at the hospital," Dorothea said, answering the unfinished question. "The doctor doesn't think his injuries are serious, but he's unconscious."

"I'm on my way," Daphne said.

"What is it?" Elaine asked when she'd managed to disconnect the call with shaking hands.

"Evan was in an accident."

"How bad?" her friend asked hesitantly.

"I don't know." And the not knowing terrified her. "They took him by ambulance to the hospital…unconscious…" She felt her throat tighten. "I have to go. I have to be there."

"Of course," Elaine agreed. "Do you want me to take you?"

"No." She shook her head, fighting to maintain control of her emotions. "I can drive. But I need to feed the animals and—"

"I can take care of all that," the other woman reminded her. "Go."

"Are you sure?"

Her friend nodded and gave her a quick hug. "Drive safely. And let me know if there's anything you need."

I need Evan to be okay.

Of course, her friend couldn't guarantee that, so Daphne prayed all the way to the hospital.

Chapter Eleven

"Evan Cruise?" Daphne was breathless, having run all the way from the hospital parking lot to the nurse's station. "He was in a car accident…brought here by ambulance."

"Are you family?"

Her heart sank as she realized her frantic rush to get to Evan's side was likely going to end right here.

"No," she reluctantly admitted.

At the same time another voice said, "Yes."

She turned around to see a seventy-something woman with short, stylish gray hair and sparkling hazel eyes. Though the color was different, Daphne recognized Evan's eyes in his grandmother's face.

"Or she will be soon enough," Dorothea clarified with a conspiratorial wink for Daphne.

She wanted to protest that Evan's grandmother was obviously misinformed about their relationship, but she bit her tongue because she knew the little white lie was probably her only hope of getting past the nurse's desk.

"I'll take her back to the family lounge," the older woman continued, hooking her arm through Daphne's.

"The signs says only two visitors per patient in the waiting area, Mrs. McGowan," the nurse pointed out. "And only one in the patient's room."

"I can read," Evan's grandmother said with a friendly wink. "It's math that always gave me trouble."

The nurse shook her head, even as a smile tugged at her lips. "Just so long as Dr. Ruczinski knows that you were informed of our visitation policy."

"I'll be sure to let the doctor know that we were informed," Dorothea promised.

"I don't want to get anyone in trouble," Daphne said, walking beside Evan's grandmother through the sterile corridor. "I could just wait in the coffee shop until—"

"You'll wait with the family." The older woman's tone brooked no argument. "Evan's going to want to see you when he wakes up."

"I'm not so sure about that," she heard herself confide. "The last time we talked… Well, I think we both said some things we probably shouldn't have."

"Relationships have their ups and downs, just like

roller coasters," Dorothea said philosophically. "Both the highs and the lows are easier to handle if you stay on the ride together."

"He might want to jump out of the car if he wakes up to rumors of an engagement," Daphne cautioned.

"Then we'll try to keep that little detail quiet… for now."

As his Guide of Christmas Present faded away, Evan breathed in the scent of his grandmother's perfume.

"Grandma Daisy?" He blinked, not sure if he was still dreaming or if this was real. "What are *you* doing here?"

"I am your Guide of Christmas Yet to Come."

He sighed. "For one very brief moment, I was starting to believe this nightmare might finally be over."

"Then you obviously weren't paying close enough attention when I read Dickens to you," his grandmother chided.

"Let me guess—you're here to show me how bleak and lonely my life will be if I don't mend my ways."

"If that was my only purpose and you apparently know it already, then my work here would be done," she said. "But it's not."

"All right, then," he said. "Let's get this over with."

She shook her head despairingly even as she took his hand. "You were always a good boy, willing to listen, eager to please. Well, almost always."

Having so recently been reminded of some less-than-stellar moments from his past, he could hardly argue the point.

"And you've grown into a fine young man, even if you sometimes have trouble seeing the big picture," she continued.

"What is the big picture that you think I'm missing?"

"That the richness of your life has nothing to do with the balance in your bank account."

"Maybe not," he acknowledged. "But being poor sucks."

"How would you know?" she challenged. "Have you ever gone to bed with an empty belly? Have you ever been without a bed to lie down on?"

"No," he admitted. "But I know Mom worried about those things, especially in the first few years after my dad left."

"She worried even more about the fact that you would grow up without a father," Grandma Daisy confided. "And later, that the failure of her marriage was the reason you hold yourself back from falling in love—because opening up your heart means risking heartbreak."

She paused, giving him a moment to think about that.

"But then you met Daphne."

And suddenly she was there, almost close enough for Evan to touch if he reached out.

And he was tempted, but as the light that shone on Daphne spread outward, he saw that she wasn't alone.

She was with a man, though not someone he recognized, and their hands were joined as they made their way toward the church, its bells ringing to call worshippers to the Christmas Eve service. It was only when they turned to walk up the steps that he saw the swell of her belly beneath her coat.

She was pregnant.

The joy that had filled his heart when she first appeared, spilled out now and drained away.

"Does she...love him?" he asked.

"Not yet," Grandma Daisy said. "In the present-day world, she hasn't even met him. But she will... and very soon. He'll be immediately smitten with her—and why not? She's a beautiful girl, inside and out. He'll ask if he can buy her a cup of coffee, but she'll turn down this first invitation, because she's still tending to the bruises you left on her heart.

"But if you don't find a way to fix things with her, she'll eventually realize there's no future for the two of you together, and the next time he asks, she'll say yes."

"I was on the way to Happy Hearts when my SUV went off the road," he pointed out.

"But you were still angry with her. You still believed that she'd crossed a line, as if lines should exist between a man and a woman who love each other."

"I've never been very good at sorting through my emotions."

"Instead, you buried them deep. Focusing on your business rather than personal relationships."

She waved a hand, and they were standing on a

sidewalk downtown, facing a wide storefront with the words Bronco Ghost Tours painted on the glass.

"In this future, Bronco Ghost Tours is a national chain, with tours running in more than one hundred towns, from Juneau to San Diego to Tampa to Bar Harbor."

"I'm not seeing anything but an upside here," Evan noted, pleased that at least something seemed to have gone right in his future.

"When you realized that you'd destroyed your relationship with Daphne, you refocused all your attention on the business."

"Obviously my hard work paid off."

"But at what cost?"

He didn't know how to answer that as he watched himself—some twenty years older—scan a card to unlock the door and step inside the wide-open office space.

The older Evan frowned as he noted the empty desks while he stomped the snow off his boots and shrugged out of his coat. "Where the hell is everyone?"

An unfamiliar figure—young and female—moved toward him, a mug of steaming coffee in hand. "Everyone is home today, sir," she said.

"Is it some kind of holiday?"

"Yes, sir. It's Christmas."

Christmas.

How could he have forgotten?

Easily, because years earlier he'd made it clear to

his employees that he wasn't a fan of seasonal decorations and wouldn't tolerate holiday music being
played in the office. Maybe the Christmas card he'd
received from his sister, now married and living on
the east coast with her family, should have been a
clue, but he hadn't given it that much thought.

Why would he when he didn't like to celebrate and
there was nobody left in his life to celebrate with,
anyway?

He took the mug from her, his brow furrowing
as he tried to remember her name. Heather? Heidi?
Margot? Maddie? The names and faces of various
assistants who'd come and gone were all blurred together in his mind.

"So why are you here?" he asked her.

She shrugged. "I don't have any family or anywhere else to be."

"Right," he said, and carried his coffee into his
office. "Well, send me the fourth-quarter reports."

"I'll get right on that, sir."

"That's Brooke," Grandma Daisy said. "Your third
assistant in the past six months. The first two quit
because they said you were a tyrant—a common observation of your employees."

"But none of this is real," he pointed out. "There's
no way I'd actually forget it was Christmas."

"You chose to forgo the joy and celebration of the
season a long time ago," she pointed out. "The *to-
getherness*. It's hardly a jump from that to forgetting
about the holiday altogether."

"Okay, I get it," he said. "I have to appreciate the people in my life and remember the true meaning of Christmas. Are we done here now?"

"Not quite," she said. "Because it's not only Daphne's and your lives that will be different…"

The scene changed again to show Grandma Daisy alone in a rocking chair by the window, clutching her sketchbook against her chest, tears tracking slowly down her cheeks.

Evan couldn't remember ever seeing his grandmother cry. She was always so strong and steady. Even when Grandpa Mike died, Grandma Daisy had held it together. He didn't doubt that she'd grieved deeply, but she'd done so privately. And the sight of her tears now weighed on his heart.

"Why are you crying?" he asked.

"I just found out—too late—that Josiah Abernathy died."

He swallowed. "Did you know him?"

She shook her head. "I never had the chance to meet my biological father. Or my mother."

"But you had parents who adored you," he reminded her. "And you always talked about them with so much love."

"Clarence and Frances Hollister were wonderful parents," she agreed. "They gave me everything they could—except the truth of where I came from."

"Why is it my responsibility to fill in the blanks of a story written long before I was ever born?" he challenged.

"Because you know that the story is incomplete."

"I don't know anything," he denied. "I just happened to see a social media post that mentioned someone named Daisy."

"You should have told me about it," his grandmother insisted.

"I didn't want to be caught in the middle," he protested.

"But that's where you are."

For the first time in a very long time, emotion threatened to overwhelm him—but he fought to hold it at bay. "Daphne wanted me to tell you…that's what we fought about."

"Life is about connections, Evan," she said gently. "And those connections should be embraced and cherished. Even—or maybe especially—when they make you feel uncomfortable."

"I made some mistakes. A lot of mistakes." He swallowed around the tightness in his throat. "But I can do better. I can make things right. I will make things right—if you give me a chance."

"It's not up to me," Grandma Daisy said. "It's up to you—it always has been."

And with those parting words, she disappeared into the circle of light.

"Daphne."

Her name was little more than a whisper from his lips, but Daphne jolted when she heard him speak, relief spreading through her veins. She was already perched on the edge of the hard plastic chair beside his bed, but she leaned closer now. "I'm here, Evan."

His eyelids flickered, then opened.

"You're here."

"Of course, I'm here."

He lifted a hand to touch her face, frowning when he saw the hospital bracelet on his wrist. His gaze moved past her then, taking in his surroundings. "Why am I in the hospital?"

"You were in an accident," she said.

The furrow in his brow deepened, as if he was trying to remember.

"I couldn't see, because of the snow," he recalled. "And then my vehicle started to spin—everything seemed to be spinning out of control...but I don't remember anything after that."

She tried to blink away the tears that filled her eyes as she realized, yet again, how much worse the accident could have been and that she might have lost him forever. "Apparently a driver passing by saw your SUV in the ditch and called 9-1-1."

"I thought... Did I hear Grandma Daisy's voice?"

"Probably," she said. "Right now she's in the lounge with your mom, but she was in here earlier. The hospital has a one-visitor-at-a-time policy, so we've been taking turns sitting by your bed, waiting for you to wake up."

Sean Donohue was there, too, offering moral support to Wanda, who'd immediately left the office when she learned of the accident. But understanding that Evan had mixed feelings about his mother's relationship, Daphne held back on mentioning the man's presence.

"I should go now," she said instead, "and let them know that you're awake."

He caught her hand as she started to rise. "How long have I been here?"

"A few hours."

"Did they give me drugs?"

"No. The doctor didn't want to give you anything until you regained consciousness. Why? Do you want something now? Are you in a lot of pain?"

"No," he said, even as he winced. "I just had some really weird dreams that I figured must have been chemically induced."

"Do you want to tell me about them?"

"Yeah, but first I have to know…do you think I'm a scrooge?"

She frowned. "Where is that coming from?"

"You didn't immediately say 'no,'" he noted.

"No," she said now. "I don't think you're a scrooge. You might need a little help remembering the true meaning of Christmas, but I think we've started to make some progress on that."

"Are you still willing to help?"

"If that's what you want," she said cautiously.

"I want to be with you, Daphne."

"Does that mean I'm still invited to Christmas dinner at your mom's house?"

"You are definitely still invited to Christmas

dinner." He squeezed her hand tighter. "I love you, Daphne."

"You've got a head injury," she reminded him—and maybe herself. "You don't know what you're saying."

"There are a lot of things I don't know, but I do know how I feel." His tone was quieter now, his gaze direct. "And I love you."

She hesitated, not because she didn't feel the same way but because she was afraid to believe that the feelings he professed to have were real.

"I don't need you to say it back," he said. "I just need you to know that it's true."

"I want to say it back," she told him. Because she could no longer deny the truth that was in her own heart and, still reeling from the knowledge that she could have lost him, she didn't want to. "Because I love you, too,"

He smiled then. "I know there are still a lot of things we need to figure out, but right now, I need to talk to Grandma Daisy."

But Wanda insisted on coming in first to see for herself that her son was okay. She cried, relieved to confirm that he was, then scolded him for scaring her half to death, then cried some more.

"I love you, Mom."

She sniffled. "I know you do."

"Still, I should say it more often."

"I wouldn't object to that," she told him. Then, "I

finally got to meet Daphne. I wish it hadn't happened in a hospital waiting room, but at least it happened."

"It would have happened in a few days."

"You invited her for Christmas dinner?"

He nodded, then winced when the movement exacerbated the pounding inside his head.

Wanda smiled. "I need to get a Tofurky."

"A what?" he asked.

"It's a tofu turkey."

"A regular turkey is fine," he said. "Daphne offered to make a vegetarian dish. Something with chestnuts."

"I can't have a guest bring her own dinner." His mother sounded horrified by the very thought.

"I'll leave it to you and her to hammer out those details," he said. "In fact, why don't you go do that now so I can talk to Grandma Daisy?"

Of course, his mother was only too happy to leave him then, and he felt only a little bit guilty about using Daphne to distract her. After all, if this was going to be the first of many holidays together, she was going to have to get used to his family.

"You gave us all a pretty good scare," Grandma Daisy said, settling into the chair his mother had recently vacated.

"Sorry about that," he said.

"Well, don't do it again."

"I won't." He crossed his heart with his finger, making her smile.

"So what did you want to talk about that couldn't wait until you got out of here?"

"Contacting Josiah Abernathy."

She looked at him blankly. "Who?"

"Sorry." He gave his head a slight shake, then winced at the pain that shot through his skull, a not-at-all-subtle warning to stop doing that. "I had a really weird dream while I was unconscious, and you were there so I assumed you'd know what I was talking about."

"I think you're going to have to go back to the beginning."

So he did, starting with the uneasy feeling he had when he first saw the social media post and the internal battle he'd been waging ever since about whether or not to bring it to her attention, even admitting that it was what he and Daphne had argued about.

"It seems to me that you caused yourself a lot of grief over something that's probably nothing," she said. "The name Daisy isn't all that uncommon."

"I know," he agreed. "But the name and the birth date together with the fact that you've lived your whole life in the same town as the Abernathys?"

"That does seem like a remarkable coincidence."

"And maybe that's all it is," he said.

But they both knew that she wouldn't ever be certain unless and until she got in touch with the Abernathy family.

Chapter Twelve

Dorothea wished she could take some time to figure out whether or not she really wanted to open up
what might turn out to be a can of worms. But after
Evan had shown her the social media post that ended
with "Time is of the essence!" she couldn't help but
worry that it might already be too late.

As she stared through the minivan's windshield
at the Ambling A Ranch, beautifully decorated for
the holidays, Wanda reached across the console and
took her hand. Dorothea knew that her daughter was
still worried about Evan, who'd been released from
the hospital just that morning to stay at Happy Hearts
with Daphne. No doubt Wanda would have preferred
to have him home with her, where she could fuss over

him to her heart's content, but with Vanessa scheduled to arrive the following day, there wasn't really room for him. And even if there had been somewhere for him to sleep, everyone knew that his preference would be to stay with the woman he'd finally admitted he loved.

It was interesting, Dorothea thought, that her grandson's life finally seemed to be settling down and her own was possibly on the verge of being upended.

"You don't have to do this," Wanda said to her now.

She appreciated her daughter's support, but Dorothea knew that she was wrong. "If I don't, I'll always wonder."

"And I can't help worrying that if it turns out you were adopted, the knowledge will change your memories of your relationship with your parents."

"It won't," Dorothea said. And then another thought occurred to her. "But this could change things for you, too. If I was adopted, it means you have a whole other family out there, too."

"I'm not worried about me," Wanda said. "Because I had two of the most wonderful parents who ever walked the face of this earth."

"Out of all my kids, you always were the biggest suck-up."

Her daughter laughed. "Your favorite, you mean."

"A mother doesn't have favorites," she said, because it was true.

It was also true that there had always been a special bond between Dorothea and Wanda and, by extension, Wanda's children.

And she was grateful for her daughter's support now as she reached for the handle of the door and said, "Let's do this."

Gabe Abernathy had obviously been watching for their arrival, because he pulled open the door before they had a chance to knock.

"Thank you so much for coming," he said, ushering them into a parlor fragrant with the scent of pine, courtesy of the towering tree in front of the window.

"Melanie's going to be sorry she missed you," Gabe said, after they were all seated. "My fiancée's been spearheading the search for Daisy, but she had a work meeting she couldn't miss this afternoon."

"You're going to have to start at the beginning," Dorothea told him. "We don't really know anything more than what was written in those few lines we read on Facebook."

So that was what Gabe did. He told them about Melanie's discovery of the letter, written by his great-grandfather to his first love, and within it the reference to a daughter given up for adoption seventy-five years earlier. The letter had given them more questions than answers, and unfortunately Josiah, in the late stages of dementia, wasn't able to answer any of them. But with the help of Malone, the Abernathy's longtime family cook, they'd managed to piece together a little bit more history.

"It was at my sister Erica's wedding, when the

organist played 'Bicycle Built for Two,' that Malone suddenly remembered Josiah referring to his long-lost daughter, Daisy," Gabe said.

"I'm not familiar with that song," Wanda admitted.

"I know it," Dorothea said. "And I remember— at least I think I remember—a man singing it to me when I was a little girl."

"Then you have to be the Daisy we've been look-ing for," Gabe said excitedly. "I thought the social media post was a long shot at first. And after a few days, I thought it was a mistake." He shook his head ruefully. "You wouldn't believe some of the crazy calls we got. But we followed up every single one, despite the fact that none of them presented any real leads—until now."

"I think it's a pretty big leap from coincidental names and birth dates to such a conclusion," Wanda told him.

"Maybe it is," he said. "But—"

"I want to see Josiah," Dorothea interjected.

Her daughter looked worried. "Are you sure that's a good idea?"

"No," she admitted. "But I feel strongly that it's something I have to do."

"I'll call Snowy Mountain and add your name to the visitor list," Gabe said.

"And now we're all going to Snowy Mountain on Saturday to meet Josiah Abernathy," Evan explained to Daphne later that day, after he'd spoken to his mother and been advised of the plan.

"Who's all?" she wondered as she continued to tidy up the kitchen after dinner.

Evan had wanted to help, but Daphne was determined to see that he adhered to the doctor's order to rest.

"Grandma Daisy, my mom, Vanessa, me—and you, if you want to come."

"I've got a thousand and one things to do here," she said. "And truthfully—"

"Truthfully, *what*?" he prompted.

She shook her head. "Nothing. It's not really any of my business."

He reached out for her hand and slowly drew her toward him. "Please tell me what you're thinking."

"If you really want my opinion—"

"I do," he interrupted to assure her.

"I'm not sure you should be going, either."

"Well, since you won't let me help with any of those thousand and one things you mentioned—"

"Because you're recovering from a head injury," she said, interrupting him this time.

"—there's no reason for me to hang around here."

"How about the fact that you're recovering from a head injury?" she asked as he drew her down onto his lap. "And you're here because, when the doctor released you from the hospital this morning, he said you shouldn't be alone for the next forty-eight hours."

"Which doesn't mean that you have to ask me every five minutes how I'm feeling."

"I haven't been asking every five minutes." More like every thirty. "And how else am I supposed to know if you're experiencing any headaches, dizziness or nausea?"

"I'll let you know," he promised, sliding his hands under her sweater. "And by the way, I'm feeling much better now."

"I don't think that's what you're feeling," she said, even as her blood began to heat from his touch. She tried to refocus on the subject at hand. "Are you sure you feel up to taking a road trip with your whole family?"

"The idea should be enough to give me a headache," he acknowledged. "But Snowy Mountain is just north of town—hardly a road trip."

"How is your grandmother handling all of this?"

"Are you trying to kill the mood?" he asked.

"Yes," she said, pushing his hands out from under her top. "The doctor said no physical activity, remember?"

"How can I forget when you keep reminding me every five minutes?"

"You can't know how terrifying it was for me to see you lying in that hospital bed, so pale and motionless, not knowing if or when you were going to wake up."

"I don't think my life was ever hanging in the balance," he said. "But I guess I can imagine how you felt, because I know how I would feel if our situations had been reversed."

"So let me take care of you," she said, and touched her lips lightly to his. "Please."

"I'd have to be an idiot to refuse such an offer," he decided. "And since I've vowed to do my best to not be an idiot anymore, I'll let you take care of me."

"Thank you." She slid off his lap and onto the chair adjacent to him. "Now tell me how your grandmother's doing."

"My mom says she's taking some time to let it sink in. At this point, it's still a lot of speculation. Her feelings might change if the situation changes."

"That makes sense," Daphne agreed.

"I want to be there for Grandma Daisy," he said. "But if you really don't think I should go to Snowy Mountain, I won't."

"I appreciate that," she said. But she also appreciated that there was a special bond between Evan and his grandmother, and she didn't want to get in the way of him supporting her. "And while I'd prefer to have you here, I trust that your mother is up to the task of watching over you for a few hours."

"On second thought," he said.

She was smiling as she rose to her feet and held out her hand to him. "Come on—let's go up to bed."

"I thought you'd never ask."

"To sleep," Daphne clarified.

He sighed. "That doesn't sound like nearly as much fun as what I had in mind."

"I have no doubt, but you're not allowed to perform any physically demanding tasks for at least forty-eight hours after your headache goes away."

"So I'll just lie there and let you do all the work," he said with a wink.

She laughed. "I'm happy to know that you're feeling better, but we're still not having sex tonight."

"Are you sure you're up to making the trip?" Wanda asked, when Evan climbed into her minivan Saturday morning.

"I wouldn't miss it," he said, settling beside his grandmother and fastening his seat belt.

"How's your head today?" Dorothea asked, confident that he wouldn't evade a direct question so easily.

"You mean other than as hard as a rock?" Vanessa chimed in from the front passenger seat.

Dorothea's lips twitched, but she didn't shift her gaze away from her grandson.

"It's better," he said.

Which didn't tell her a whole lot, but she had to figure he was old enough to be responsible for his own decisions. And, truthfully, she was grateful he was there. She was grateful to all of them for making the trip with her.

"How's *your* head?" Evan asked, reaching for her hand.

"Spinning," she admitted.

"I'm not sure what this trip to see Josiah Abernathy is going to accomplish," Wanda spoke up from the driver's seat as they got underway. "His great-grandson said that he's lost his ability to verbally communicate and rarely shows any reaction to anything."

"I was there for the conversation," Dorothea reminded her. "You might think I'm old but my ears still work, and even if it turns out that dementia runs in my family, I've still got my faculties about me right now."

Vanessa swiveled in her seat to look at her grandmother. "It's a good sign that you can joke about this."

Dorothea shrugged. "There are so many thoughts going through my head right now—" so many feelings warring inside her heart "—if I didn't have a sense of humor, I'd probably lose my mind."

Wanda nodded. "I can understand that. It all seems so unreal, and yet, I can't imagine how I'd feel if I ever found out that you weren't my real mother."

"You've got no worries there," Dorothea assured her. "I carried you for nine months and labored for nine hours, and I've got the stretch marks to prove it."

"You were in labor for only nine hours?" Wanda was stunned.

"It still wasn't a picnic."

"I was nineteen hours with Evan and twenty-six with Vanessa, because—" Wanda glanced at her daughter "—apparently you didn't get the memo that second labors are supposed to be shorter."

"Maybe there was a mix-up with the message delivery system," Vanessa said.

"Or maybe you've always taken your sweet time to do anything," Evan suggested.

His sister responded by sticking her tongue out at him.

"Mom, Vanessa stuck her tongue out at me."

"Mom, Evan's being a tattletale."

Wanda just shook her head. "If you two don't stop bickering, I'm going to pull over and—"

"Look," Dorothea said, interrupting their playful banter. "We're here."

Snowy Mountain was a residential facility located north of Bronco Heights that offered a full range of services, from independent living to end-of-life care. Josiah Abernathy lived in Snowy Mountain West, a wing of the complex devoted to seniors with varying degrees of dementia or Alzheimer's. It was a big, open building, easy to get around in, and in which the man believed to be Dorothea's biological father got round-the-clock care.

Gabe had offered to meet them at Snowy Mountain, but Dorothea had declined. They checked in with Becky, the charge nurse on duty when they arrived, and she led them to a spacious corner room with lots of windows looking into a courtyard filled with trees and wrought-iron benches and even a gazebo. Of course, everything was covered in snow

now, but Dorothea imagined the area was scenic and peaceful in the summer.

"Josiah's just finishing up his lunch," Becky said. "I'll bring him in as soon as he's done."

"Thank you," Dorothea said.

The room was simply furnished, with a nightstand beside the hospital bed, a built-in wardrobe on the opposite wall, a tall dresser with a few knickknacks and a couple of chairs for visitors.

"There are a lot of pictures," Vanessa noted, moving closer to peruse the framed photos on the wall.

"Pictures are important to help trigger memories," Wanda said, looking at the arrangement over her daughter's shoulder. She sucked in a breath. "It's him."

Dorothea had realized the same thing, but instead of being shocked, she felt…relieved and reassured that some of the pieces were finally starting to come together.

"You mean Josiah?" Vanessa asked.

Wanda nodded.

"That's not really surprising, is it? Of course he'd be in the pictures that are hanging in his room."

Evan remained silent, looking at his grandmother while everyone else was looking at the photos.

"That's not what I meant," Wanda said. Then, to Dorothea, "Show her."

She pulled her sketchbook out of her ever-present tote bag and handed it over to her granddaughter.

Evan took a step closer, studying the sketches as Vanessa thumbed through the pages.

"Okay, that's a little…unnerving," Vanessa said.

"It's not unnerving," Wanda, always practical, denied. "It simply proves that Grandma Daisy knew Josiah Abernathy at some point in her past."

"But why was she only recently sketching pictures of him?" Evan spoke up now, asking the question that everyone was wondering about.

"Obviously something happened to stir up her memories."

Dorothea didn't think anything was obvious, but she found some comfort in looking at the array of photos on the wall.

"He lived a full life," she noted. "He got married, had a few children, then grandchildren and great-grandchildren."

"Children who might be your siblings," Evan realized.

She nodded as Becky returned, pushing a wheelchair ahead of her. Vanessa closed the sketchbook and slid it back into her grandmother's bag.

"Look, Josiah. You've got lots of company today," the nurse said, positioning the chair so the old man's back was to the window and setting the brake. To his visitors she said, "This is Josiah Abernathy. He's not much of a conversationalist these days, but I know he's happy to see you."

Then she left them alone to visit and went back to her duties.

Dorothea lowered herself into the chair closest to Josiah and searched his face.

"Do you remember him at all?" Evan asked her gently.

"My memories are little more than vague impressions… I remember his eyes were kind, and he smiled easily." But she still wasn't 100 percent certain that the man she remembered was the one sitting in front of her now. Or maybe she was afraid to believe. "And I liked when he sang…"

"What did he sing?"

"'Bicycle Built for Two.'" She leaned in closer to the old man. "Was it you who used to sing to me, Josiah? Do you remember the song?"

He continued to stare straight ahead, giving no outward indication that he heard her or even knew she was there.

And Dorothea couldn't help but feel frustrated, wondering why the man's family had reached out, wanting to find Josiah's long-lost illegitimate child when he clearly had no interest or awareness.

"Mom?" Wanda touched a hand to her arm. "Are you okay?"

She swallowed around the lump in her throat and nodded. And then she quietly began to sing:

"'Daisy, Daisy, give me your answer, do. I'm half crazy, all for the love of you.'"

Josiah's head turned then, and he looked at Dorothea. "Beatrix?"

Though his voice wavered, the name was unmistakable.

"I'm Dorothea," she said, and reached out to take Josiah's hand, surprised when he grasped hers with unexpected strength. "But most people call me Daisy." And she wondered now if the nickname had come from the song that someone—perhaps this man—used to sing to her.

He didn't say anything else, but held her gaze for a long moment, his eyes surprisingly clear.

"This was a waste of time," Evan said. "Obviously he thinks you're someone else."

"No." The response came from a petite blond-haired, blue-eyed woman standing in the doorway. "He knows exactly who she is. Beatrix is the name he intended to give his daughter, before he was forced to give her up for adoption."

"Who are you?" Evan demanded.

"Melanie Driscoll." She took a few steps into the room and addressed her next question to Dorothea. "Are you his Beatrix?"

"I'm… Dorothea," she said again. "Dorothea McGowan, formerly Hollister."

"I'm Gabe Abernathy's fiancée. He told me that you were planning to stop by to see Josiah, and I was hoping I'd have the chance to meet you. I'm the one who found the letter."

"What letter?" Evan asked.

"It's a long story," she said. "Why don't we go out to the lounge where we can all sit down and talk?"

They let Becky know where they were going and that they were taking Josiah with them, and when they were all settled with drinks and snacks from the little coffee shop, Dorothea reached into the side pocket of her tote bag for her flask.

Wanda sighed. "Really, Mother?"

"I think I'm going to need it," she said, tipping the flask over her mug to add a splash of Irish whiskey to her coffee, then she held it up. "Anyone else?"

Melanie pushed her mug forward. "Just a drop," she said.

Dorothea obliged.

As she went to put the flask back in its usual spot in her bag, Melanie spotted the sketchbook sticking out of the top. "Are you an artist?"

"I doodle," Dorothea said, never sure how to answer that question without sounding immodest. Because while she'd had some success illustrating a series of children's books, she'd never really aspired to do anything more than that. She liked to draw; it was both a pleasure and a passion, but it was never a vocation.

"Can I take a peek?" Melanie asked.

Dorothea handed her the book.

"I'd say you do more than doodle," Melanie said as she began to turn the pages. "And now I know why your name sounded so familiar—you did the Messy Marsha books."

"Only the illustrations," Dorothea said.

"I loved those books when I was a kid, although

my mom always said they should have been Messy Melanie books."

"No doubt that's why the books did so well—the themes were universal."

Melanie turned the next page, and paused on the drawing of a man that Dorothea now knew was Josiah. "When did you sketch this?"

"The date should be on the bottom."

"June," she said. "You drew this six months ago. But...how?"

"I don't know," Dorothea said. "I guess there must have been some memories of him, locked in the back of my mind. Why they were suddenly unlocked... I couldn't say."

She turned another few pages, then gasped. "This is a picture of Winona Cobbs."

"*That's* who it is," Wanda said.

"You know Winona?" Melanie asked, surprised.

"I don't *know* her, but she used to write a syndicated advice column, 'Wisdom by Winona,' and there was always a thumbnail photo of her in the corner."

"This just keeps getting stranger and stranger," Vanessa murmured, reaching into her grandmother's bag for the flask.

"And we're not done yet," Melanie warned, speaking to Dorothea. "If Josiah is your father, and all the evidence seems to support that supposition, then Winona is your mother."

While she was processing this new revelation, the young woman folded back the cover to reveal the sketch of the log home that Wanda had asked her about only a week earlier. "Have you ever seen this house, Dorothea?"

"I don't think so," she admitted.

"It's the Ambling A," Melanie said.

Evan shook his head. "That doesn't look anything like the Abernathy ranch."

"Not their house in Bronco," she agreed. "But there's another Ambling A in Rust Creek Falls."

"But… I've never been to Rust Creek Falls," Dorothea said, almost certain of it.

"I'd be happy to take you," Melanie said.

"Wait a minute," Evan said, reaching across the table for the sketchbook. He closed the cover and slid it back in Dorothea's bag. "My grandmother isn't going anywhere with you."

Dorothea rankled. "Your grandmother will go where she wants with whomever she wants."

He nodded an acknowledgment, duly chastened.

"I apologize for sounding pushy," Melanie said. "But Winona lives in Rust Creek Falls, just down the road from my parents. I've gotten to know her quite well in recent years, and I know it would mean the world to her to finally meet the baby she thought had died at birth."

"Why would she think her baby died?" Wanda wanted to know.

"Because that's what they told her when they took the baby away," Melanie explained. "When we started the search for her missing child, I wanted to tell her what we were doing, but I was worried about getting her hopes up and then disappointing her if the search was unsuccessful."

"And you still don't know if it was or wasn't," Evan said.

"We can do a DNA test—with your consent, of course," Melanie said to Dorothea. "But I think we all know what the result will be."

"Why wouldn't Josiah have told Winona that their baby was alive?" Wanda wondered aloud.

"Obviously he wanted to, because he wrote the letter," Melanie said. "But my guess is that when he went back to Rust Creek Falls to deliver it, he couldn't find her, and that's why he ended up hiding the letter in his old diary under the floorboards at the Ambling A."

"I'm still wondering...why the parents who raised me wouldn't have told me that I was adopted," Dorothea said.

"Unfortunately, the only ones who can answer that question aren't here to do so," Wanda reminded her gently.

"But it's not so surprising really," Melanie said. "Seventy-five years ago, closed adoptions were the norm rather than the exception. Which makes it even more incredible that Josiah was somehow able to locate the child he called 'Beatrix' and even enjoy occasional visits with her—sorry, with *you*—during the first few years of your life."

"Do you know when or why the visits stopped?" Vanessa asked.

Melanie shook her head. "I can only speculate, because Josiah hasn't been able to confirm or deny anything, but my guess is that maybe the adoptive parents worried that Dorothea was getting too attached to him—or vice versa.

"It's also possible that they didn't know Josiah was her biological father but as she grew, they started to see a familial resemblance, and because they wanted to keep the circumstances of her birth a secret, they asked him to stay away.

"Gabe thinks it's more likely that Josiah's wife, Cora, put a stop to the visits. He said she always seemed insecure about the relationship and oddly possessive, so it's likely that she wouldn't have been happy to discover her husband had a relationship with his daughter from a former lover."

"He wouldn't have pushed back?" Wanda wondered aloud.

"He might have," Melanie acknowledged. "But by then, Cora had given him a child, too. And if she threatened to take Alexander away…well, the thought of being cut off from another child might have been unbearable to him."

Dorothea looked at the old man in the wheelchair, and she knew Melanie was right. They could do a test, but the truth was already clear in her heart.

Josiah Abernathy was her father.

Chapter Thirteen

"So now we're going to Rust Creek Falls on Wednesday," Evan said to Daphne, as he sat on a stool by the kitchen sink, peeling potatoes for dinner—the most arduous task that she would allow him to tackle, despite his assurance that he was feeling fine.

"Why Wednesday?" she asked.

"Because it was the first day that worked for everyone's schedules," he explained. "Everyone including Gabe Abernathy and his fiancée, Melanie Driscoll, Gabe's sister Erica and her husband, Morgan Dalton...and hopefully you, too.

"I know your first responsibility is to the animals," he said, anticipating her objection. "But I'm hoping, since it's not a last-minute request this time, that you'll be able to call in some of your amazing volunteers to take over your chores for the day so that you can come with us."

"I appreciate that you want to include me, but it seems to me that what you've planned is the very definition of a family affair."

"And?"

"And I'm not family."

"But...didn't you tell the nurse at the hospital that we were engaged?"

"No," she immediately denied, her cheeks burning. "It was your grandmother who said that—or at least implied it. And how did you hear about that, anyway?"

He ignored her question to ask one of his own. "So we're not really engaged?"

"You know we're not."

"But the part where I told you I loved you, and then you said that you loved me, too—that was real, right?"

"That was real," she confirmed.

He set down the potato peeler and dried his hands on a towel before reaching for her. He drew her close and lowered his head to kiss her long and slow and deep.

"Mmm," she said, when he finally ended the kiss. "What was that for?"

"Just making sure you were real," he said lightly.

"And now it's my turn," Daphne said, linking her

arms behind his head and drawing his mouth down to hers again.

As their tongues dallied and danced together, his hands went north, under her sweater, skimming up her torso to cup her breasts. Meanwhile, she took her exploration south, sliding a hand beneath the waistband of his jeans.

"Are we starting something we can't finish?" he asked when he eased his mouth from hers.

"The evidence at hand doesn't suggest there will be a problem," she teased.

He gave a subtle shake of his head, releasing his breath on a groan when she stroked him again.

"A few days ago, you said this couldn't happen," he reminded her.

"A few days ago, you'd just been released from the hospital. Today you proved your recovery is on track by peeling all those potatoes."

He chuckled softly as he carefully removed her hand from inside his pants. "A remarkable test of my strength and endurance."

"Let's go upstairs and see if you've got any left," she suggested.

"I've got some left," he said, and proved it by effortlessly lifting her into his arms.

"What are you doing? Put me down," she demanded.

"I will," he promised, but only did so after he'd climbed the stairs and tumbled with her onto the bed.

* * *

Daphne awoke to discover Evan thrashing in the sheets. A nightmare, she guessed, and reached out to touch a hand to his shoulder. "Evan?"

He jolted awake then and sucked in a breath.

"Are you okay?" she asked worriedly.

"Yeah."

But he was still breathing hard, and his skin was clammy with perspiration.

"Were you dreaming about the fire again?"

He nodded. "It was his fault."

"Who's fault?"

"Russell's." He scrubbed his hands over his face. "He lit the candles that night."

Even in the darkness, Daphne could see the haunted look on his face.

"He didn't have much money, or much of anything really, except love for her," he continued. "And he wanted to show her, so he set the scene with candles and a bottle of wine he stole from her father's cellar.

"They drank the wine and made love, and he knew that he'd never feel about anyone else the way he felt about Alice. Afterward, as they cuddled close, they talked about their future.

"Neither of them planned to fall asleep. They knew her parents would only be gone a few hours and all hell would break loose if Henry Milton caught them together. But fall asleep they did…and one of the candles must have fallen over while they were sleeping, because Russell awoke to see flames climbing up the wall. And to hear the horses below, desperately pawing at the ground in their stalls and bumping against the walls that contained them, snorting and squealing in terror."

Daphne felt tears burn the backs of her eyes as she pictured the scene all too clearly. And her heart raced, pounding against her ribs, as she was certain Alice's must have done on that tragic night so long ago.

"He barely had a moment to realize what was happening before Alice woke up, too, coughing because of the smoke, already thick in the air around them.

"He picked up a blanket and tried to beat the flames away from the ladder. If they could get down from the hayloft, they could escape. But the fire was spreading too fast.

"They could hear sirens in the distance, but they knew the trucks wouldn't get there in time. He begged for her forgiveness as he held her in his arms, because it was his fault. He only ever wanted to love her, but instead…he killed her."

She could hear the anguish in Evan's voice, knew that whatever emotions Russell had felt that night, Evan was feeling now. She didn't quite understand what was happening, how Alice and Russell were connecting through her and Evan, why they had been chosen. But she could offer comfort to the man she loved, and share with him what she knew in her heart.

"She didn't blame him," Daphne said, sensing not just that truth in Alice's presence but the ghost's need to assure Russell—through Evan—of that truth.

"Even as she started to lose consciousness, even as she understood her life was ending, she knew that she'd lived more fully in the months that she'd shared with him than in all the years that had come before—because he'd loved her."

"He'll love her forever."

"As she will him," Daphne assured him, wiping away a tear that spilled onto her cheeks.

She sighed then, not just saddened by the tragic loss of life but frustrated by what had come after. "They should have been allowed to rest in peace, together."

Evan tightened his arms around her. "We'll make it happen," he promised. "Somehow we'll make it happen."

There were so many vehicles making the trip from Bronco to Rust Creek Falls that Dorothea felt as if she was part of a caravan. Gabe and Melanie were in the first car, followed by Gabe's sister Erica and Morgan Dalton with their newborn daughter, then came Dorothea, Wanda and Vanessa in Wanda's minivan, followed by Evan and Daphne in a blue truck with the Happy Hearts logo on the door, because Evan's SUV was still in the shop for repairs after his recent accident.

Dorothea was filled with so much anticipation, she could barely sit still throughout the long drive, and her excitement increased exponentially when they passed a freshly painted sign that welcomed visitors to Rust Creek Falls. It was a pretty town, she noted, the storefronts along Cedar Street decked out for Christmas—now only two days away—with garlands and twinkling lights.

The vehicles lined up behind one another on the street in front of Winona's small house, then the parade of visitors marched toward the front door. She hung back a little, behind Melanie and Gabe, as the group trooped inside. If Winona was at all daunted by the arrival of so many guests, she gave no sign of it as she welcomed them into her home.

Though Dorothea was eager to get the introductions done, Winona seemed less concerned, ushering them into the living room and inviting them to sit.

"It's wonderful to see you, Melanie," Winona said. "And you've brought friends to visit."

"Friends who were anxious to meet you," Melanie said.

"Well, isn't that nice? Let me just make some tea to go with the white chocolate cranberry cookies I picked up from Daisy's Donuts this morning. Eva was just setting them in the display case when I stopped in, and I bought the whole lot," she said, sounding pleased with her coup.

"Please don't go to any trouble," Melanie protested.

"It's no trouble at all," Winona said. "And it's so nice to have company."

Though Melanie had warned of the old woman's failing health, Winona seemed in pretty good shape to Dorothea. She did lean heavily on her cane when she walked and her breathing sounded a little labored, but she was mobile and living independently—a definite win for a woman of her age.

Still, Dorothea didn't like the idea of the nonagenarian—*her mother*—fussing in the kitchen on their account. Not to mention that she was eager to have an actual conversation with Winona, something she had been unable to do with Josiah.

Wanda obviously shared her concerns, because instead of sitting, as she'd been instructed, she followed Winona to the kitchen.

"Why don't you show me where everything is so I can make the tea while you visit with your guests?" she suggested.

"That would be nice," Winona said, then made her way back to the living room. She settled into what was obviously her favorite chair and, after slowly perusing the gathering of people, started to rise again.

"Where are you going?" Melanie asked.

"To get out more cups—for the tea. I didn't realize how many of you there are."

"Don't worry about the tea right now," the young woman urged. "Sit down, please, so that I can introduce you to my friends."

"That one—" Winona pointed at Gabe. "He's more than just your friend."

"Yes," Melanie agreed. "This is my fiancé, Gabe."

Dorothea wasn't surprised that Melanie didn't offer his full name. The young woman had previously expressed concern that mentioning the Abernathy name too soon might trigger a negative response, and since no one else knew Winona well enough to even hazard a guess about her reaction, they consented to Melanie taking the lead.

"I don't think I knew you were engaged," Winona said now.

"It's a fairly recent development."

"I'll get you something nice," the old woman promised. "A gift to celebrate your engagement."

"Speaking of gifts," Melanie said, determined to get the conversation back on track. "I've brought something—or rather *someone*—for you."

Winona's gaze moved around the room, finally settling on Evan. "He's definitely handsome," she said. "But a little young for me, don't you think?"

Dorothea didn't know whether to laugh or cringe at the realization that her mother was checking out her grandson—Winona's great-grandson.

"And—" Winona frowned "—he looks familiar. Have we met before?"

"I'm certain we haven't," Evan said.

"You would remember," his great-grandmother said. "I make an impression."

On one side of Evan sat Daphne, her lips pressed together to hold back a smile. On the other side was his sister, making no effort at all to disguise her amusement.

"Let's backtrack for a minute," Melanie suggested as she knelt on the floor beside Winona's chair and laid her hand over the old woman's gnarled and wrinkled one. "Do you remember Josiah?" she asked gently. "Josiah Abernathy?"

"I haven't heard that name in…a lot of years," Winona said quietly.

"But you knew him, didn't you? A long time ago?"

She nodded slowly. "A lifetime ago. But—" her gaze darted around the room, no longer assessing but fearful now "—how do you know about my relationship with Josiah? No one's supposed to know."

"It was a secret for a lot of years," Melanie assured her. "Until Maximilian Crawford bought the Ambling A Ranch and his sons found an old diary hidden beneath the floorboards when they were renovating the homestead."

"Josiah kept a diary," Winona said. "He liked to write down the things he said he couldn't tell to anyone else."

"It was Josiah's diary that they found," Melanie confirmed. "And there was a letter, hidden inside the book's lining, addressed to you."

"Josiah wrote a letter to me?" Winona's eyes brightened at the possibility. "What did it say?"

"You can see for yourself," Melanie said, and handed her the page covered with faded handwriting.

The old woman shook her head. "My eyes aren't what they used to be, and Josiah always did have horrible handwriting," she said. "Can you read it to me?"

"Of course."

Dorothea took a step forward then, interrupting

before Melanie could begin. "Actually, I think I'd like to read the letter to…Winona, if that's all right."

Melanie nodded.

As Dorothea stepped farther into the room, Gabe rose from his seat on the sofa—the spot closest to Winona, and gestured for Dorothea to take it.

She did so, then focused her gaze on the letter Melanie passed to her and began to read.

"'My dearest Winona, please forgive me. But they say you will never get better. I promise you that your baby daughter is safe. She's alive!'" Dorothea paused there for a moment, unexpectedly moved by the experience of reading her father's letter to her mother, and almost completely undone by the tears that filled the old woman's eyes.

"My baby's alive?" Winona sounded stunned.

"Your baby's alive," Melanie confirmed.

Dorothea managed to battle back the onslaught of emotion and continue reading. "'I wanted to raise her myself, but my parents forced me to have her placed for adoption. She's with good people—my parents don't know, but I have figured out who they are. Someday, I will find a way to bring her back to you.'"

Winona pressed a trembling hand to her lips. "My baby didn't die." The words were barely more than a whisper. "But he didn't… Josiah didn't bring her back to me."

"But she's here now," Melanie said.

Dorothea leaned closer, and Winona turned to face her.

"My name is Dorothea," she said. "I'm...your daughter."

Daphne hadn't been sure she should have made the trip to Rust Creek Falls with Evan. She didn't want to intrude on what she knew would be an emotional reunion for his grandmother and her biological mother. She hadn't expected it would be an emotional experience for her, too. But when Winona softly echoed her daughter's name, with tears in her eyes, Daphne could hardly see through her own.

Evan's grandmother, obviously just as moved, cleared her throat. "Most people call me Daisy."

"We were going to call you Beatrix," Winona said. "But Dorothea—and Daisy—are pretty names, too."

Grandma Daisy managed a wobbly smile.

Winona searched her daughter's face, her gaze seeming to take in every feature. "You have his eyes," she said now. "Not just the color, but the shape." Then she looked at Evan again. "That's why he looks familiar. He has Josiah's eyes, too."

"That's Evan," Dorothea said. "My grandson. Your great-grandson."

"I have a great-grandson." Winona marveled over the fact.

"And a great-granddaughter, Vanessa," Dorothea said, and Evan's sister waved. "And a few other grandchildren and great-grandchildren, too.

"And on the other side of Evan is Daphne—"

"You don't have to tell me about their relationship," Winona said. "It's obvious from their auras."

Daphne couldn't help but laugh at that observation; beside her, Evan just looked baffled.

"And this," Dorothea continued, when Wanda carried a tea tray into the living room, "is my daughter—your granddaughter—Wanda."

"I'm…overwhelmed," Winona said. "I didn't think I had any family left."

"And now you've got more than you know what to do with," Erica observed.

The old woman nodded.

"We'll figure it out," Dorothea told her, taking her mother's hand. "Together."

"Can you tell me what happened to Josiah?" Winona asked. "Is he…gone?"

Gabe was the most qualified person to answer that question, and he spoke up now to say, "He's not gone, but he's in the late stages of dementia."

Winona blinked back fresh tears as she focused on her daughter again. "Well, at least I can see him in you," she said. "Even if I can't see anything of myself."

"She might look like an Abernathy," Melanie agreed. "But she's got your gift of future sight."

"I wouldn't say that," Dorothea protested.

"You don't have to say it, you just have to show Winona your sketchbook."

So Dorothea did, and as tea and cookies were distributed all around, Winona thumbed through the pages, admiring her daughter's talent.

Daphne hadn't seen the sketches, but Evan had told her about them. If there had been a time when she might have felt unnerved to learn that his grand-mother had been able to draw the faces of the bio-logical parents she'd never really known, that time had passed when she'd started communicating with a ghost.

"Maybe there is something of me in you after all," Winona said to Dorothea. "Which is only fair, con-sidering that, only a few weeks after I told Josiah we were going to have a baby, his family packed up in the middle of the night and left town without a word.

"I was devastated," she continued. "I cried for days, maybe weeks. I could barely eat, but I forced myself to do so because I was carrying Josiah's baby and I believed—needed to believe—that after she was born, we would find a way to be together again." Her smile was wistful. "To be a family.

"When my pregnancy started to show, I was sent to a home for unwed mothers, as was the usual fate of girls who got themselves into trouble in those days."

"As if you did it all by yourself," Vanessa said, un-able to remain quiet about such an obvious injustice. "Because of course boys can't be held responsible for doing what comes naturally, but girls are expected to know better—and be the sole bearer of the con-sequences if they don't."

"I'm not saying it was right," Winona assured her great-granddaughter. "Just that it's the way it was.

"And it wasn't a bad place, really. We had chores to do around the house, and although the expectation was that most of the girls would give up their babies for adoption, we were taught how to keep a house and care for a child.

"I went into labor in the middle of the night. I didn't realize what it was at first, except that the pain was almost more than I could stand. Nothing they'd taught us about childbirth had prepared me for that— or maybe nothing really can."

"As somebody who's recently been through the experience, I'd agree that nothing really can," Erica said.

"But you were a champ," her husband said. "And most of the feeling has come back into my hand now."

Winona smiled, amused by the banter between the new parents.

"Then you know that you somehow manage to focus on breathing through the pain, because when it's all over, you'll finally be able to hold your baby in your arms."

Erica nodded, looking down at the sleeping infant snuggled against her chest. "And in that moment, you know that every minute of every hour of labor was worth it."

"It was twenty-seven hours for me," Winona said. "At the end of which I was more than exhausted, but then I heard my baby cry—I was certain I did—and suddenly I was crying, too.

"'A girl,' the doctor said. But I wasn't surprised. I'd known somehow, almost from the very beginning, that the life inside me was a girl. A daughter." She looked at Dorothea now. "My Beatrix Frances, named for Josiah's grandmother and my mother, because you were part of both of us."

"My middle name is Frances," Dorothea told her. "Because it was my mom's—my adoptive mom's—name, too."

A coincidence? Daphne wondered.

Or more proof that fate had played a big part in this family's history?

As she believed fate had brought Evan to Happy Hearts—and into her life—four weeks earlier.

Winona's smile faded as she picked up the story again. "I asked for you. I told the nurse that I wanted my baby—my Beatrix—but she shook her head and said, 'I'm sorry. She didn't make it.'

"I demanded that she give me my child. But the nurse hustled away with the baby and the doctor gave me a shot, to help calm my grief, he said.

"I lost Josiah, then I lost my baby. I had nothing left. No reason to live. They locked me up—for my own safety, they said. But I didn't feel safe. I felt empty..."

Dorothea took the tissue that Evan offered and dabbed at the tears that trembled on her eyelashes.

Daphne put a hand on his arm, a gesture of comfort and understanding. Because she knew that he was experiencing a lot of the same emotions that his grandmother was, albeit with much less intensity.

"All these years, you've been alive, living only a few hours away." Winona marveled over that fact as she brushed away her own tears.

Evan handed her a tissue, too, and she murmured her thanks before asking, "Who were your parents? Were they good to you?"

"They were very good to me," Dorothea said. "I had a good life. A happy family."

"And now you've got a beautiful family of your own."

"I've been fortunate," Dorothea agreed. "And, in addition to having been raised by one wonderful woman, I now have the opportunity to get to know the other one who gave birth to me."

"We've lost so much time," Winona said sadly.

"But we've got now," Dorothea said.

"We do, don't we?" her mother agreed.

"And the holidays are almost here," Wanda said. "Do you have any plans?"

Winona shook her head. "Not much of anything."

"Would you like to come to Bronco to spend the holidays with us?"

Fresh tears filled the old woman's eyes. "I can't imagine anything I'd enjoy more."

Daphne had always believed that Christmas was a time for making memories, and she was glad that Dorothea and Winona would have the chance to make some together this year.

She was also inspired by their ability to connect so easily after seventy-five years apart. And as she drove back to Bronco with Evan, she thought that maybe it wasn't so foolish to believe that a reconciliation with her own family was possible after all.

Chapter Fourteen

"I can't believe it's Christmas Eve and I'm only now wrapping presents." Daphne rolled her shoulders, already starting to feel tight. "I should have started this last night when we got back from Rust Creek Falls."

"We had more pressing matters to deal with last night," Evan reminded her.

"There was some pressing involved," she admitted, her lips curving at the memory. "But *that* could have waited until after Christmas. *This* can't."

"I'd offer to help," he said. "But I have a feeling that you'd want to refold every crease of paper and re-align every piece of tape—just like you moved every ornament I hung when we decorated your Christmas tree."

"*Our* Christmas tree," she said.

He nodded an acknowledgment. "Instead, I have two words to offer that will greatly simplify your task."

"What are the two words?"

"Gift bags."

"You're right," she said, then she sighed. "Except that I don't have gift bags. I've got paper and ribbon and bows and—" she glanced at her watch "—I have to be at the adoption center in half an hour because Rick Howard is coming to pick up Penny."

"Maybe I could do ribbons and bows," he suggested.

"I just might take you up on that."

"But you're not jumping at the offer right now," he noted, "so would you mind if I borrowed your truck to run a couple of errands?"

"Of course not," she said. "The keys are in the top drawer beside the stove, registration and insurance are in the glove box."

He tipped her chin up to brush a light, lingering kiss on her lips. "Do you need anything while I'm out?"

She nodded as she pulled the last piece of adhesive off the roll in her hand. "Cellophane tape."

When he returned, more than an hour and a half later, he had the requested cellophane tape, at least a dozen gift bags of various shapes and sizes and three bags of groceries. Because Daphne had realized, when she started to assemble the ingredients for her chestnut Wellington for Christmas dinner, that she didn't actually have chestnuts, so she'd texted a short list of groceries for Evan to pick up while he was out.

But maybe the list hadn't been as short as she'd thought, if he'd filled three bags with the requested items.

"You are a lifesaver," she told him.

"Because of the tape or the chestnuts?"

"Both. And the gift bags."

"Is Penny on her way to her new home?"

Daphne nodded. "And Rick promised to record Fiona's reunion with Penny and tag Happy Hearts when he posts it online."

"Hashtag-Best-Christmas-Gift-Ever?" he guessed.

"I hope so," she said, but her attention had been snagged by the courier label on the box on the counter. "What did you have delivered from Wisconsin?"

"Let's find out," he said, carrying the box into the dining room where she'd been doing her wrapping so that he could use the blade of her scissors to slice through the tape.

Curious, she peered over his shoulder as he opened the flaps, a little disappointed to see nothing more than packing peanuts.

But Evan must have had some indication of what was inside, because he didn't hesitate to reach in and pull out—

"It looks like an urn," Daphne said, studying the covered vase in his hands.

"Because it is," he said.

"It's not… Is it… Russell's ashes?"

"I sure hope so." He slid his hand into the box again, sifting through the foam pieces until he came out with an envelope. Inside was a certificate of cremation for Russell John Kincaid dated December 20, 1960.

"How did you find him?" Daphne wondered.

"Actually, Callie Sheldrick, my assistant, did a lot of the legwork. She tracked his family tree through six cities across four different states until she found a second—or maybe it was a third—cousin of Russell's."

"So you made a phone call and the cousin just put his remains in a box and shipped them by overnight courier?"

"It was a little more complicated than that," he explained. "But the bottom line is, the urn had gone into storage along with the rest of the contents of a house that was sold after the death of a great-aunt or uncle or someone, because apparently none of the surviving family members wanted the ashes of some distant relative they'd never met sitting on their fireplace mantel."

Welcome home, Russell, she thought.

But that was an emotional response, and the practical question that needed to be asked was, "What are we supposed to do with the ashes now?"

"I thought we could bury the urn under the peachleaf willow tree where Alice is laid to rest."

"Are we allowed to do that?" Daphne wondered. "From a legal perspective, I mean."

"In order to bury Alice here, Henry Milton would have gotten approval for part of the land to be designated a family cemetery. Since that's already been done, there's no prohibition against burying Alice's fiancé beside her."

"Then let's go do it," Daphne said.

"Now?"

"Yes, now," she said. "Alice and Russell have waited long enough."

So they put on their boots and coats, got a shovel from the barn and trekked across the snow-covered fields with Barkley to the marker beneath the peachleaf willow tree.

"Or maybe we should wait until the spring," Daphne said after several minutes had passed and Evan was still struggling to break the frozen ground.

"You better be joking."

Daphne smiled at the sound of Alice's voice. "I wondered when you were going to join us."

Evan paused with his foot on the step of the shovel when Daphne spoke aloud. "Alice is here?"

"I'm always here."

"I heard her." A grin split across Evan's face. "She talked to me."

Daphne couldn't help but laugh. "You realize you're getting excited about talking to a ghost, don't you?"

"But she's not only a ghost," Evan said. "She's family."

Her brows lifted. "Did your research of Russell's family tree reveal something more than what you told me?"

He shook his head. "No. But if I've learned anything over the last few weeks, it's that biology isn't the only thing that connects people. For reasons that I'm not even going to try to understand, there's a connection between Alice and you and Russell and me and all of us together. That makes us a family."

"Well said."

Evan turned toward the direction of her voice and nearly dropped the shovel. Startled by his reaction, Daphne followed the direction of his gaze and gasped.

Alice was there. The ghost was sitting on the top rail of the split rail fence, wearing a halter-style dress (pretty but totally inappropriate for the winter weather) with cowboy boots on her feet. And though Daphne had never seen any photos of Russell Kincaid, there was no doubt that the apparition standing next to Alice was the man she'd loved. He was tall and handsome, as dark as she was fair, and dressed in faded jeans with frayed hems and a Western-style shirt. Russell had an arm around her waist and his head tipped back against her shoulder.

They were both smiling, and there was such a feeling of love and contentment in the air, Daphne knew that Happy Hearts had never been so apt a name for the farm as it was in that precise moment.

She glanced at Evan and saw that he was no longer looking at the ghosts—but at her. Warmth spread through her. "I think we should stop staring and start digging, don't you?"

"Yes, ma'am." Evan grinned, and they got to work.

"Christmas at the Cruises"—as Wanda referred to the occasion—was totally chaotic and absolutely wonderful. Puttering in the kitchen beside Evan's mom, Daphne found herself reflecting on what he'd said the previous day about family, and realized it was true. Family was about more than blood—it was about shared connections. And through all those numerous and various connections ran one common thread: love. Being here with four generations of Evan's family, she felt surrounded by love and grateful that they'd welcomed her not just into their home but their hearts.

Maybe she was a little sad about the distance that had been allowed to develop between herself and her father, but she couldn't bridge the gap alone. And when Evan sat down beside her and linked their hands together, she realized that she wouldn't have to—because he was by her side.

"Why's there an extra place setting?" Vanessa asked when everyone had been seated around the table.

"That empty chair is for the Ghost of Happy Hearts," Evan teased.

His sister glared at him from across the table. "You're lucky that you're too far away for me to kick."

His teasing smile turned into a wince as he absorbed the sharp rap of her shoe with his shin.

"Or maybe you're not," Vanessa said in a deceptively sweet voice.

"Children," Wanda said. "Can we please sit down together for one family meal without the two of you bickering?"

"He started it," Vanessa said.

Before Evan could respond to that, the doorbell rang.

"That will be our last guest," Wanda said as she started to push her chair away from the table.

"I'll get it," Sean said. "I'm closer."

"Are you eager to answer the door or planning to make a mad dash out of here?" Grandma Daisy teased.

"I'm not going anywhere," Sean promised, looking at Wanda.

And proved it when he returned a minute later with Evan's admin assistant.

"We're happy you could join us, Callie," Wanda said after all the introductions had been made.

"I appreciate the invitation," Callie said shyly.

As Evan had explained to Daphne earlier, he'd found his assistant fighting back tears in the office a few days earlier. Apparently she'd just broken up with her boyfriend and her parents were going to be on a cruise over the holidays, so she was going to be alone for Christmas—a prospect that obviously made her miserable.

So Evan had impulsively asked her to join his family for the traditional holiday meal—an invitation that had probably surprised him as much as her. But he hadn't been certain, until right now, that she would accept it.

And now that all the seats around the table were filled, Wanda invited her grandmother to say grace. Winona kept her prayer brief, but there were few dry eyes around the table by the time she finished expressing her thanks for the family that had welcomed her into their fold—and the platters of food waiting to be passed around.

Topics of conversation ping-ponged across the table throughout the meal, touching upon everything from politics and current events to movies and local sports and other holiday plans. When everyone had finished eating, Daphne was pleased to note that there was nothing left of the chestnut Wellington or glazed parsnips that she'd brought—and not much of anything else, either. Callie had contributed a pumpkin pie to the feast—not homemade, she confided, but still delicious, and that had disappeared, too, along with both of the pecan pies that Grandma Daisy had made for the occasion. Of course, Evan had a generous slice of each dessert—the former with whipped cream and the latter with ice cream.

Callie spearheaded the cleanup effort after the meal, forcing Evan to acknowledge that his assistant might have more gumption than he'd given her credit for. Vanessa and Daphne were happy to help, and they dragged Evan into the kitchen, too, refusing to perpetuate the antiquated notion that cooking and cleaning were women's work.

The tidying was almost done when Vanessa approached her brother with an outstretched hand. "I want the key to your apartment."

"Why?"

"Because you're obviously not using it and I can't sleep another night on Mom's sofa. Plus, as much as I love my family, four generations of women under one roof is a little too much family."

"You're welcome to stay at Happy Hearts," Daphne said. "We've got a couple of spare bedrooms there."

"Thanks," Vanessa said. "But I'm not staying anywhere that's rumored to be haunted."

"It's not just a rumor," Callie said. "It's really haunted."

"Definitely not staying there," Vanessa said.

"But not in a scary way, like the library," Callie assured her. "I filled in on that tour after Evan had his accident, and I won't be disappointed to never go near that building again."

"You can stay at my place," Evan said, removing the key from his ring and rescuing his sister from what he knew was an uncomfortable conversation for her. "But no wild parties."

"You'd have more cause to worry about that if Grandma Daisy and Great-grandma were staying there," she said. "Or, if not parties, noise complaints from your neighbors. I swear, those two never stop talking."

"They've got a lot to catch up on," Evan pointed out.

"I just want to catch up on my sleep," his sister promised, pocketing the key.

"I don't know about you, but I'm kind of glad we don't have Christmas every day," Dorothea said, dropping down onto the sofa beside her daughter after all of their guests—and even Vanessa—had gone. "I'm exhausted."

"It was a busy day," Wanda agreed. "But a good day."

"What did you think, Winona?" she asked.

Though Dorothea didn't have any difficulty thinking about the woman as her mother, she didn't know that she'd ever be able to call her "Mom" or "Mother." Not because she worried that her use of the title might in any way detract from her memories of her adoptive mother, but because it seemed weird, at seventy-five years of age, to suddenly have a mother again.

"It was the best Christmas that I can remember," Winona said now. "And I have a very long memory."

Wanda smiled, obviously pleased by her grandmother's response. "We're so glad you could be here to celebrate with us."

"I'm so grateful to be here. So happy to have found

family again. I just wish…" Her words trailed off and her gaze drifted away.

"What do you wish?" Dorothea prompted gently.

"When Josiah left—when his family took him away," she clarified, "it was sudden and unexpected. I guess I just wish I'd had the chance to say goodbye."

"If that's something that you really want to do, we can take you to see him," Dorothea said.

"You wouldn't mind?"

"Of course not. Snowy Mountain, where he's living, isn't very far from here."

"Then yes," Winona decided. "I do want to see him."

"He probably won't remember you," Wanda cautioned, obviously not wanting her grandmother to get her hopes up about a reunion with the man she'd loved for so many years. "He doesn't take much notice of anything these days."

"It doesn't matter," Winona insisted. "Because I remember him."

And so the day after Christmas, Dorothea found herself headed back to Snowy Mountain, this time with both her daughter and her mother. Becky was on duty again and wished them "merry Christmas" as they passed the nurse's station on their way to Josiah's room.

Today his wheelchair was facing the windows, and Dorothea caught a streak of red as a cardinal swooped past before disappearing into the foliage of a poplar tree.

Winona's steps slowed as she entered the room, and Dorothea, understanding at least a little of what she must be feeling, took the arm on the side without the cane to offer some extra support. She guided her to a chair, as Wanda turned Josiah around so that he could see them. Dorothea drew the other chair a little closer to Winona's before settling into it, while her daughter remained standing by the window.

She didn't think it was her place to make introductions—obviously Josiah and Winona had known one another a long time before she was even born, but since entering the room, her mother seemed to have lost her voice and her father, by all accounts, rarely spoke anymore.

Finally, Winona reached out and touched the old man's hand.

"Hello, Josiah," she said softly.

He turned his head, an almost imperceptible movement, but there was no doubt in Dorothea's mind that he was looking at and seeing Winona.

"I wanted to see you, to let you know that I got your letter. Seventy-five years after you wrote it—" Winona managed a small smile "—but I did finally get it.

"Even more important, that letter did what you always wanted to do," she told him. "It brought our daughter, our Beatrix, back to me. And now—" Her voice broke, and she paused for a moment to regain her composure. "Now she's brought me back to you, to say the goodbye that I never got to say so many years ago."

Josiah's gaze moved from Winona to Dorothea and back again, as if he understood what she was saying, as if he knew exactly who they were.

Or maybe she was only imagining it.

"So I'm saying it now—" Winona's eyes filled with tears "—in case our paths don't cross again in this world. Goodbye, Josiah. And thank you."

He gave a slight nod then and, just before his eyes drifted shut again, his lips curved.

"This New Year's Eve party was your grand-mother's idea," Daphne said as she poured the orange juice into the punch bowl. "Why did we offer to have it here?"

"Because there's a lot more room here than at my mom's house."

"That's a good reason," she acknowledged. "And truthfully, I'm happy to have everyone here, but…"

"But you're worried about Vanessa," he guessed.

"I just hope there aren't any surprises tonight."

"Of the otherworldly kind, you mean?"

"She's your sister, and I want her to feel comfortable coming to visit us."

"For what it's worth, I don't think any shimmery apparitions or whinnying ghost horses will keep her away now that she's met Tiny Tim."

"That pig does seem to have an effect on the ladies," Daphne agreed.

"Have you spiked that punch yet?" Grandma Daisy called out hopefully.

Daphne laughed as she added 7UP to the bowl. "There's beer and wine, if you want something with a little kick, but the punch is nonalcoholic."

"Or you could doctor your own drink, like you usually do," Evan told her. "Or did Mom take away your flask?"

"It wasn't your mom, it was mine," Grandma Daisy said. "And she didn't take it, she drank it."

He chuckled at that. "I guess it's true that the apple doesn't fall too far from the tree."

"Will there at least be champagne at midnight?"

"There will be champagne at midnight," Daphne confirmed.

But apparently Evan didn't want to wait that long, because he grabbed a bottle of champagne out of the fridge, snagged two crystal flutes, then took Daphne's hand and led her out to the porch, where they could steal a few minutes alone.

Barkley darted ahead of them out the door. Daphne smiled as the Lab raced down the steps to romp playfully in the snow. Then her smile widened as she saw, through the window, Dorothea pull Winona to her feet to dance.

"Your great-grandmother is amazing," she said. "She's been going almost nonstop since she came back from Rust Creek Falls with your mom and grandma, and she isn't showing any signs of slowing down."

"I guess meeting the daughter she thought she'd lost has rejuvenated her spirit."

"It's wonderful to see them reunited after so many years apart."

"Is that what inspired you to reconcile with your dad?" he asked.

"We're still a long way from being reconciled," she told him.

"But you've taken the first steps in that direction."

Actually, her father had taken the first step when he'd adopted Boo from Happy Hearts.

But she'd taken the next one—with Evan—when they dropped by the ranch after leaving his mom's house on Christmas Day.

It had been a short visit during which she'd admittedly spent more time fussing over Button and Boo than actually talking to Cornelius, but it had been a successful visit in that no one had yelled or cried or slammed any doors.

"Which is important," he continued in a casual tone, "because I'm guessing that you'll want him to walk you down the aisle at the wedding."

She had to lean against the porch railing for support, her knees suddenly weak. "Who's getting married?"

"You and me."

"If this is an April Fools' Day prank, you're about four months early."

"It's not a prank," he assured her. "I wouldn't joke about something like this."

"You really want to get married?"

"I do." His quick grin faded and his expression turned serious. "You've changed everything for me, Daphne. You've made my life better, in so many ways. Over the past few weeks, I've not only learned to appreciate the importance of family, I've realized that I want a family of my own. With you."

Her eyes filled with tears as her heart overflowed with emotion. "I want that, too," she admitted. "But I figured it was going to take you months—maybe even years—to feel the same way."

"I don't need any more time to know that I want to spend every day of the rest of my life showing you how much I love you," he assured her. "Just don't tell me that you want Tiny Tim to be our ring bearer."

"Why not? He would totally rock a tuxedo jacket," she said, grinning.

"Not as well as Billie."

"Billie could be the flower girl."

He shook his head regretfully. "I'm not sure the flowers would survive being carried by a goat."

"I wouldn't count on rings faring any better."

"Speaking of," he said, and pulled a diamond solitaire out of his pocket.

"Ohmygod." She stared at the glittering stone, then Evan as he dropped down to one knee. "Ohmygod," she said again, unable to believe this was actually happening.

"Daphne Taylor, will you marry me?"

She nodded, her heart so full of love and happiness she thought it might burst out of her chest. "Yes, Evan Cruise, I will marry you."

He took her left hand and slid the diamond onto her third finger. Then he rose to his feet again and drew her close to kiss her, long and slow and deep.

"And now you have another reason to reach out to your dad," he said. "To share the happy news that we're getting married."

"You're right that we need to tell him," she said. "But can we maybe wait until next year?"

He chuckled. "Yeah, I guess we can wait that long—since next year is only a few hours away."

As he unwrapped the foil around the neck of the bottle, Daphne let her gaze drift to the peachleaf willow in the distance.

"You're thinking about Alice and Russell, aren't you?"

She nodded. "I haven't heard a word from Alice since we buried Russell's ashes on Christmas Eve."

"Maybe they're finally resting in peace—together," he said, echoing the words that were inscribed on the new grave marker they'd set in place earlier that day.

He popped the cork on the champagne then and poured the bubbly, handing one of the glasses to his fiancée.

"I think I'm going to miss her," Daphne said softly. "The farm feels empty somehow without her."

"It won't be empty for long," he promised. "Because we're going to fill it with lots of love and kids."

She smiled, liking the sound of that…but something about his word choice niggled at the back of her mind. "Wait a minute," she said. "When you say *kids*, do you mean children or baby goats?"

Evan laughed. "I guess time will tell."

He lifted his glass, offering a toast. "To old friends and overdue reunions."

"To the New Year and new beginnings," Daphne added, tapping her glass against his.

As they drank, a gentle breeze ruffled the evergreen garlands on the fence and rustled the bare branches on the peachleaf willow in the distance.

And happy-ever-after.

He pulled back, a strange look on his face. "Did you hear something?"

"No…" But her gaze shifted to that tree, and the marker beneath it. "I don't think so."

"I just… I could have sworn…" He shook his head now. "It doesn't matter. The only thing that matters is that we're going to spend the rest of our lives, right here, together."

She smiled. "That sounds like a promise that should be sealed with a kiss."

As Evan brushed his lips over Daphne's, Barkley signaled his approval with a happy bark and the wind blew softly.

* * * * *

MILLS & BOON

Coming next month

TEMPTED BY THE TYCOON'S PROPOSAL
Rachael Stewart

'Come with us, Sophia—come with us to Iceland.'

Her eyes shot open and she gazed down at him, hardly daring to believe the question and knowing at the same time that she couldn't. The thought, the idea of being surrounded by her fear, by the past, by the snow… She shook her head and shifted beneath him to remind him of her body, of what she wanted in that moment. What he so wanted too.

'You can't ask me that, Jack. Don't ask me that.'

He raised himself up over her, his elbows planted either side of her body to bear his weight. 'Why not?'

'Because I can't. We can't.'

He kissed her until she was breathless, panting. 'Why?'

'We don't even know they'll be available for Lily's birthday yet.'

'That doesn't matter. They will be available at some point and I want you to come.'

She shook her head, the emotions clawing at her throat and her chest, making it hard to breathe. 'We both know this has to end and that the longer we spend together with Lily, the more likely it is that she will become attached too.'

His eyes were so serious now as they blazed into

hers. The 'too' spoke volumes; it told him that fear protected her own heart, but did it protect his as well?

'That's not the whole truth, is it?' he pressed, probing for more, probing for her to admit that she feared being faced with her past. All it took was one harmless-looking snowflake, the ice forming over her windshield, and the shivers would start.

'It's enough.'

He shook his head, one hand stroking her cheek and catching a tear she hadn't known was there. 'You need to stop living in fear of your past, Sophia.'

He kissed her to soften his words and she clamped her eyes shut over the rising swell of emotion within. 'You've taught me that; you've made me realise that avoiding a base, avoiding London, is running from it. And by doing it, Lily has suffered.'

She kept her eyes closed as the tears refused to stop. He was right. She'd been a hypocrite to tell him the same and not realise it was exactly how she'd been behaving all along.

'Come with us. Not because I ask you, not because it would make Lily happy to have you there... Come because you want to. Come because you are ready to move on from it.'

Continue reading
TEMPTED BY THE TYCOON'S PROPOSAL
Rachael Stewart

Available next month
www.millsandboon.co.uk

COMING SOON!

We really hope you enjoyed reading this book.
If you're looking for more romance, be sure to
head to the shops when new books are
available on

Thursday 10ᵗʰ December

To see which titles are coming soon, please visit

millsandboon.co.uk/nextmonth

LET'S TALK
Romance

For exclusive extracts, competitions and special offers, find us online:

f facebook.com/millsandboon

🐦 @MillsandBoon

📷 @MillsandBoonUK

Get in touch on 01413 063232

For all the latest titles coming soon, visit
millsandboon.co.uk/nextmonth

LS & BOON

THE HEART OF ROMANCE

MANCE FOR EVERY KIND OF READER

ODERN

Prepare to be swept off your feet by sophisticated, sexy and seductive heroes, in some of the world's most glamourous and romantic locations, where power and passion collide.
8 stories per month.

HISTORICAL

Escape with historical heroes from time gone by. Whether your passion is for wicked Regency Rakes, muscled Vikings or rugged Highlanders, awaken the romance of the past.
6 stories per month.

MEDICAL

Set your pulse racing with dedicated, delectable doctors in the high-pressure world of medicine, where emotions run high and passion, comfort and love are the best medicine.
6 stories per month.

True Love

Celebrate true love with tender stories of heartfelt romance, fro the rush of falling in love to the joy a new baby can bring, and a focus on the emotional heart of a relationship.
8 stories per month.

Desire

Indulge in secrets and scandal, intense drama and plenty of sizz hot action with powerful and passionate heroes who have it all: wealth, status, good looks…everything but the right woman.
6 stories per month.

HEROES

Experience all the excitement of a gripping thriller, with an inte romance at its heart. Resourceful, true-to-life women and stron fearless men face danger and desire - a killer combination!
8 stories per month.

DARE

Sensual love stories featuring smart, sassy heroines you'd want a best friend, and compelling intense heroes who are worthy of t
4 stories per month.

To see which titles are coming soon, please visit

millsandboon.co.uk/nextmonth